For God, England & Ethel

Forgotten Heroes of the Royal Flying Corps

by Steve 'Buster' Johnson

Order this book online at www.trafford.com/08-1503

or email orders@trafford.com

Most Trafford titles are also available at major online book retailers.

© Copyright 2009 Steve Johnson.

"The photographs under copyright in this book have been reproduced with the kind permission of the Fleet Air Arm Museum, the Cross & Cockade International Archive and the Air Historical Branch (RAF)."

All rights reserved. No part of this publication may be reproduced, stored in a retrieval system, or transmitted, in any form or by any means, electronic, mechanical, photocopying, recording, or otherwise, without the written prior permission of the author. Note for Librarians: A cataloguing record for this book is available from Library and Archives Canada at www.collectionscanada.ca/amicus/index-e.html

ISBN: 978-1-4251-8973-0 (soft)
ISBN: 978-1-4251-9164-1 (ebook)

We at Trafford believe that it is the responsibility of us all, as both individuals and corporations, to make choices that are environmentally and socially sound. You, in turn, are supporting this responsible conduct each time you purchase a Trafford book, or make use of our publishing services. To find out how you are helping, please visit www.trafford.com/responsiblepublishing.html Our mission is to efficiently provide the world's finest, most comprehensive book publishing service, enabling every author to experience success. To find out how to publish your book, your way, and have it available worldwide, visit us online at www.trafford.com/10510

 www.trafford.com

North America & international
toll-free: 1 888 232 4444 (USA & Canada)
phone: 250 383 6864 ♦ fax: 250 383 6804 ♦ email: info@trafford.com

The United Kingdom & Europe
phone: +44 (0)1865 487 395 ♦ local rate: 0845 230 9601
facsimile: +44 (0)1865 481 507 ♦ email: info.uk@trafford.com

This book is dedicated to my wife's uncle, the late Phil Blishen, without whose encouragement I would not have embarked on such a daunting project.

Acknowledgements

The research and writing of this novel took almost six years to bring to fruition. Though it would be virtually impossible for me to recall everyone from around the world who has helped me in one way or another, it would be remiss of me not to mention at least a few. Malcolm 'Air of Authority' Barrass and Colin 'Cross & Cockade International' Huston patiently answered my early questions and pointed me in the right direction. Having established what I was trying to achieve, it was a natural progression for me to travel to Europe where I visited both the Public Records Office at Kew and the Imperial War Museum. The staff of both establishments could not have been more helpful, with archive assistant Wendy Lutterloch deserving a special mention. Whilst researching in Belgium, Liz and Jon Milward of Cherry Blossom B&B, Vlamertinge, were most hospitable and provided me with a very convenient base from which to explore the locations around Ypres. Back in Australia, the more I researched, the more 'brick walls' I hit. As luck would have it, I came across the Great War Forum whilst browsing the Web one day. With members possessing a wealth of knowledge on all aspects of WW1, I was able to obtain answers to even the most obscure of questions. For this, I would like to thank all those who helped me, particularly 'ororkep' and Carl Hoehler for specifics on howitzers as well as Fred Williams BA MA, Gareth Morgan, Mick Davies (editor of Cross & Cockade International) and more recently, Trevor Henshaw, on matters aeronautic. The forum also introduced me to Richard Price, who was generous enough to provide me with background information on his great uncle, Lieutenant Graham Price.

In researching and designing the artillery map that is reproduced at the back of this book, David O'Mara kindly allowed me access to his set of British Army trench maps, at a time when such information was not readily available. Whilst researching the vehicles used by the British Army on the Western Front, I looked at the photographs on the Crossley Motors website. Its designer and custodian, Malcolm Asquith, took the time to respond to many questions regarding the idiosyncrasies of the various Crossley trucks and cars of the period. Throughout the book I have tried to present the flying scenes as accurately as possible, based upon my own flying experiences but also vetted by my old flying instructor, Ron Berry. Though long since retired, Ron was still quite prepared to put me in my place when the situation warranted it! Thank you, Ron. To my wife Sheila I would like to apologise for my six year obsession and to my younger son Toby, I offer thanks for his proof-reading services and eagerness in offering suggestions. Finally, I would like to thank my grandfather for giving me his war diaries, albeit tantalisingly cryptic in their content. Without these diaries, the spark would never have ignited in me to find out what he and the other men of his squadron actually experienced more than ninety years ago.

Forward

In the minds of many, the men who flew in the Army Corps squadrons during the Great War were the forgotten heroes of the Royal Flying Corps, yet little has been written of their exploits. Flying two-seater aeroplanes that were no match against the fighters of the German Air Force, they became the 'Eyes of the Army' despite suffering heavy losses. In pioneering the use of airborne wireless and photography, they also changed forever the way in which wars would be waged.

For God, England & Ethel tells the story of one such squadron, based on the diaries that wireless mechanic Fred Johnstone kept during the two years he served on the Western Front with Number 6 squadron, British and Canadian official records and eye witness accounts of the period. Though it has been written in the form of a novel, most of the events actually took place and the majority of the characters are real.

No matter how factual a novel might purport to be, ninety percent of the author's research never appears in the final product. 'For God, England & Ethel' is no exception. Take, for example, the time-consuming analysis of the characteristics and performance of both aircraft and artillery shells, vital in ensuring the accuracy of the artillery registrations and flying scenes in general. For those who may wish to delve deeper into the subject matter, I have provided two maps. The first shows the road and railway systems in France and Belgium at the time of the Great War, with every location and allied aerodrome mentioned in the book. The second provides more detailed information of the two Artillery 'shoots' described in the book as well as the trench map grid system used by both the army and air crews. This system enabled observers to pinpoint allied and enemy positions to an accuracy of five yards. Finally, I have appended several pages of 'Endnotes'. These provide useful background information but are not vital to the story.

Steve Johnson
January 2009

P.S. If you wish to learn more about the research into the writing of this book and view a wider selection of photographs, please take a look at the website for the book, www.forgodenglandethel.com

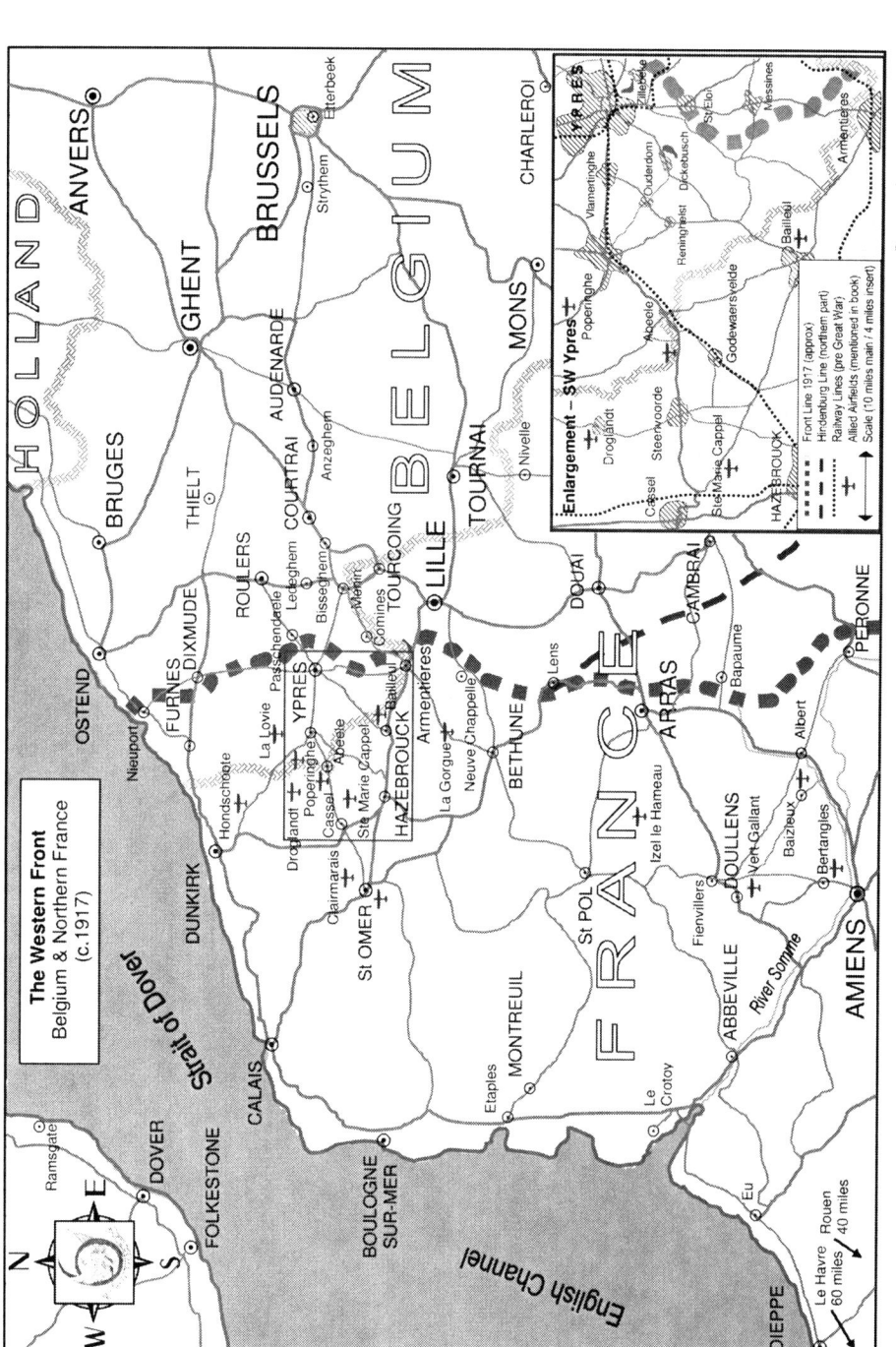

Chapter 1

Encounter at Dusk

The air was damp on a cold November evening, with ground mist drifting slowly over the cluster of huts that served as the men's living quarters. A light westerly wind played on the windsock fastened to the roof of a nearby hangar and though it was not actually raining, the surrounding land looked more like a waterlogged bog than an operational airfield of the Royal Flying Corps. After more than three months of continuous rain, very little grass remained on the surface of the main landing area and the men stationed on the aerodrome had to be mindful of the slippery conditions, especially when moving around the camp at night.

It was unusually quiet. Even the distant guns were silent. For the first time in two and a half years, since the day Number 6 squadron had arrived at the small Belgian village of Abeele, many of the hangars were deserted. A third of the squadron's aircraft had already left for their new home at Bertangles and the rest were due to follow at the end of the week. To make ready for them, a vanguard of heavy motor vehicles and tenders, each laden with men and equipment, had embarked the previous day on the seventy mile journey south. Scant information had been provided to anyone other than the three flight commanders, but it was rumoured that the reason for the move was for the squadron to take part in an allied offensive at Cambrai.

Abeele aerodrome, situated just across the French border and occupying fifteen acres of gently sloping farmland, was a mere eleven miles from the all but obliterated city of Ypres. Providing a unique challenge to the pilots who operated from the airfield, the land was bisected by a gravel road that was used to accommodate the dozens of motorised vehicles belonging to the resident squadrons. It was unusual for a Royal Flying Corps squadron to remain at an aerodrome for as long as Number 6 had been stationed at Abeele, and the order to move had caught many of the men by surprise.

The door of the sergeants' mess opened and a man appeared in the doorway, his form silhouetted by the harsh interior lights of the hut. He wore the uniform of a non-commissioned officer, the distinctive Royal Flying Corps 'maternity' jacket and flared khaki breeches with puttees wrapped tightly around his legs from his knees right down to the tops of his leather lace-up boots. At odds with the rest of his uniform, instead of a cap he wore a leather flying balaclava that all but covered his face. The man hunched his shoulders momentarily as he sensed the sudden drop in temperature before stepping out into the gathering darkness. In his hands he carried a wooden tray weighed down with full bottles of beer and an assortment of empty glasses and gripped between his lips was a lighted cigarette.

The sergeant who had opened the door followed the man outside, quickly closing the door behind him with his foot. The two men stood side by side on the front steps of the hut, looking out towards the aerodrome.

The sergeant was the first to break the silence.

"It's a cold one tonight all right," he said, slapping his arms around his chest in an attempt to keep warm. He was not wearing an overcoat.

"Don't worry, I'm well prepared," the man replied.

"You mean your lucky hat?"

"Yes. It suits me doesn't it, Jock?"

The man turned his face towards the sergeant, a glimmer of a smile visible above the chin of his balaclava.

"I'll grant you that. I can hardly see your ugly mug."

"Has anyone ever told you you're no oil painting yourself?"

"Talking of ugly mugs, did you hear that Elliott shot down a Hun this morning?"

"Well, that's one for the corporals," the man replied, ash falling from his cigarette as he spoke.

"Perhaps he'll be offered a commission. With the rate the Corps is expanding these days, the pilots fresh from Blighty are getting younger and younger. They get younger as we get older."

"Speak for yourself old man."

"I'd wager half the officers in the squadron were in short trousers when I joined up!"

"Well, don't give up Jock. You'll make a pilot yet, though you could be the oldest second lieutenant in the service."

"Always the comedian, Corporal, always the comedian. Now push off, old man. I'm getting cold standing here. If I don't see you again before we go, I hope you get a decent billet at the new place."

"Thanks Jock, same to you."

"Here's hoping."

The sergeant opened the door of the hut and returned to the warmth of the mess. Carrying the heavy tray close to his chest the man walked slowly down the wooden steps of the hut and over towards the main entrance of the aerodrome. From there he made his way across the service road to the western entrance of the airfield, taking care to avoid the many ruts and potholes that peppered the surface of the much used laneway. Almost immediately an armed soldier stepped out of the gloom and pointed a rifle at him.

"Halt, who goes there?"

"It's me Arnold, you silly bugger!"

This time the man lost grip of his cigarette and it fell out of his mouth and on to the tray, casting ash down the front of his jacket.

"Damn it!" he swore.

He attempted to tip the cigarette off the tray without upsetting the glasses.

"Stop waving that gun around would you, you might hurt someone!"

"Sorry corp, I didn't recognise you. Why are you out on such a bloody awful evening?"

"This afternoon's been a bit of a dud, so I thought I'd treat the lads in 'C' flight to a drink. They're up at the top end, patching up a machine."

"I'd join you if I wasn't on duty. Mind how you go, though. I've already been up there tonight and it's a right quagmire on the perimeter path."

"Thanks for the advice, Arnold. If you don't mind I'd better cut along, as I don't have a lamp and it's getting darker by the minute."

"Borrow mine if you want, so long as you bring it back before I go off duty."

"Thanks anyway, but I might be a while."

The guard shouldered his rifle and walked back towards his post. The man continued on his way but stopped after a few paces and turned around.

"I forgot to mention something, Arnold," he shouted.

"What's that?"

"Julia wants to put on a show for us at Margueritas. There probably won't be time before we leave, but I'll let you know the score tomorrow either way."

"Thanks corp, you're a pal."

"Keep your ears and eyes peeled. We don't want to be caught by surprise again."

"No chance of that. I can pick up a Hun machine from a mile away. Spare a thought for me when you're tucked up nice and cosy in bed."

"I'll mention you in my next despatches!"

The guard laughed and walked to the shelter of the bushes by the side of the road. The man bent down and laid the tray carefully on the gravelled surface of the driveway. Feeling in his pocket he took out a flat rectangular tin, placed it on the ground next to the tray and opened the hinged lid. Inside the tin was a box of Swan Vestas matches and several cigarettes that he had rolled earlier that day. Selecting a cigarette that was well packed with tobacco, he moistened one end and placed it between his lips. With a single strike of a match against the nearest large stone he lit the cigarette and inhaled deeply, the end of the cigarette glowing brightly in the dark. Satisfied, he returned the tin to his jacket pocket, picked up the tray and entered the western side of the airfield.

Walking along the pathway, shared by men and aircraft as it was the main thoroughfare joining the two halves of the airfield, he passed the hangars that had been vacated that morning. To his left near the southern perimeter of the airfield he could see two men setting up oil lamps along the whole length of the main landing area. One of the men bent down to light a lamp. Within seconds, a cloud of dense brown smoke billowed into the evening sky, rising from the ring of dark orange flames that encircled the top of the open tin.

"*They must be waiting for a machine to return,*" the man wondered.

Looking towards the hangars in the distance at the northern end of the airfield, he could see shafts of yellow light shining out from the cracks around the closed doors, the narrow rays spreading out like beacons in the mist. Heeding the advice of the guard, he left the well-trodden perimeter path and headed straight towards the lights, across the only part of the aerodrome that still possessed a vestige of grass cover, as it was not often used for flight operations. He strode along in the darkness, looking forward to sharing a few drinks with his friends and reminiscing over the two most eventful years of his life.

Returning to Abeele after completing their second photographic patrol of the day, Lieutenants Nigel Tuckley and Frank Harmish were well aware they were behind schedule. Their machine, a two seater reconnaissance aircraft, had been caught in enemy machine gun fire as they flew back low over the lines. With the fuselage and lower left wing peppered with bullet holes and several sections of torn fabric flapping wildly in the slipstream, the machine was travelling at well below its normal cruising speed. In addition to superficial damage, one of the four wooden longerons that formed the framework of the fuselage had been splintered by a single machine gun bullet and the weakened aircraft creaked whenever the pilot moved any of the controls.

Nigel Tuckley had recently been posted to Number 6 squadron as a replacement pilot, following the loss of an aircraft in an accident that had claimed the lives of both pilot and observer. He was anxious to get back to Abeele before nightfall as the full extent of his night flying experience amounted to a one hour training flight taken at Farnborough shortly before his departure to France. Compounding the problem of controlling a severely damaged aircraft, Nigel was concerned that he had yet to completely familiarise himself with the countryside over which the squadron patrolled. The terrain around Ypres was flat and featureless with most of the trees and buildings destroyed as a result of three years of heavy shelling, and though he had made it a habit to try and memorise even the smallest of landmarks there were still moments when he knew he was lost. He had never admitted this to anyone and hoped that he would never have to.

Flying due west at five thousand feet Nigel breathed a sigh of relief when the unmistakable shape of Dickebusch Lake came into view. He altered course to fly directly over it. From his position in the forward cockpit he could clearly see the spot at the edge of the tree-lined lake where the New Zealand born Geoffrey Cato and his observer Robert Richardson had crashed one week earlier. The engine and other salvageable parts of the aircraft had been removed and taken back to Abeele shortly after the accident but the rest of the wreckage remained embedded in the muddy shallows of the lake, with some of the wing spars protruding out of the water. The crew had been sent out on a routine contact patrol to check the positions of allied infantry, but from eye witness reports their machine had apparently broken up in a dive shortly after leaving Abeele. Though it was likely that both men had survived the initial impact, they had drowned by the time rescuers reached the scene of the crash.

Keeping a firm grip on the control stick, he twisted around in his cockpit and caught the attention of his crew, a seasoned observer five years his senior and a man who had held the rank of captain in the army before volunteering to transfer to the Royal Flying Corps as a junior officer. Nigel pointed to the crash site below but the observer merely shrugged his shoulders and turned away to resume the search for enemy scouts, in the unlikely event that a German aircraft had followed them back over the lines. Forcing his gaze from the scene below, Nigel turned around to concentrate once more on the task at hand.

The view from the rear cockpit was less obstructed by the wings. Frank Harmish stared into the east, scanning the sky for any moving object. One of his two Lewis machine guns was no longer working, having repeatedly jammed during the afternoon's sortie, and he was down to the last full drum of ammunition. Even so, he felt confident that he had enough bullets to fend off any enemy machine, especially this close to home. After a long and cold flight, he was looking forward to a mug of hot cocoa in the officers' mess and warming himself next to the stove.

Seven miles out from Abeele, the observer heard the engine misfire and felt a vibration pass down the length of the fuselage. Letting go of the guns, he turned around on his seat so that he could shout words of advice to his inexperienced pilot. He leaned forward on his stool and reached out into the slipstream so that he could touch the pilot on the shoulder. This movement made the aircraft judder and its speed reduce even further.

"The main petrol tank was probably holed on our last run, Nigel!" he shouted, his mouth close to the back of the pilot's head. "I can't see any leaks from here but I'm sure that's the problem. Switch to reserve and try to gain as much height as you can!"

The pilot nodded and reached reach forward to alter the fuel taps. Within seconds the sound of the engine returned to its normal beat.

"An extra five hundred feet should get us back to Abeele, even with a dud engine. When it starts to cut out again, lower the nose to use the last dregs in the tank. That'll give you a few more seconds."

The pilot nodded his head again and Frank sat back down on his seat, spinning around on the stool so that he could peer into the gloom behind the aircraft. With the setting sun at his back and almost on the horizon, the clouds in the east looked dark and menacing. He considered reducing weight by removing the guns and throwing them overboard but quickly realised that any extra time gained in the air would in fact lessen their gliding distance due to the strong headwind they were fighting. Despite wearing heavy leather gauntlets his hands were numb with cold and he doubted that he would be able to unfasten the guns from their mounting. And if all else failed and they were unable to reach Abeele, there were after all many fields around Poperinghe large enough to attempt a forced landing.

He looked at the large circular watch strapped to his right wrist, over the top of his leather coat. In the dim light of the cockpit he could not see the numerals clearly but he knew by the position of the luminous hands that it was a quarter to five. Darkness in less than ten minutes.

"One way or another it will all be over by then," he muttered to no-one in particular as he made ready for what he knew could be a rough landing.

Having followed his observer's instructions, Nigel Tuckley set the engine to maximum power, keeping a watchful eye on the airspeed indicator in front of him as he brought the nose of the aircraft up to the angle that would produce the best rate of climb. Illuminated by a small electric light bulb mounted inside the end of a bendable metal stalk, the gauge registered sixty eight miles per hour.

After two minutes the engine began to misfire again. Reacting quickly, he pushed the control stick forward to allow the last of the petrol to reach the carburettor, knowing that such an action would also increase their speed and lessen the chance of a stall. He was only too aware that pilots had to be cautious when flying at slow speeds in a 'Harry Tate'[1] so as not to put the aircraft into a stall, or worse still, a spin. The gyroscopic effect of the huge propeller was very pronounced at low revolutions and could quickly spell trouble for the unwary pilot. He remembered the words of his instructor.

"Never go below fifty five in level flight with power on and add another ten if you're in a turn or gliding."

He held the aircraft straight and level whilst coaxing the last few seconds of life out of the engine. When the petrol was exhausted he eased back on the control stick, holding off the stall as long as he dared as the spinning of the propeller slowed and then stopped altogether. Switching off the electrics except for the panel lights he pushed the stick forward again, watching anxiously as the airspeed slowly increased. The aneroid barometer on the instrument panel showed that they had gained four hundred feet with the last manoeuvre; not a significant increase but enough to add almost half a mile of glide to their flight.

Nigel glanced out of the cockpit as the village of Reninghelst came into view, slightly ahead of the lower starboard wing. When he was able to identify the buildings in the main street, he knew that Abeele aerodrome was exactly five miles due west of their position. Immediately he altered course and flew directly over the road that ran from Reninghelst to Abeele. Having adjusted the tail trim wheel to control the descent, he ensured that all of the loose items in the cockpit were put away or secured; his maps, pencils, cushion and notepad. With the propeller motionless and the engine turned off, the shaking of the aircraft reduced to a mild buffeting. All that he could hear was the flapping of torn fabric and the whistling of the wind as it passed through the rigging wires. He unbuckled his safety belt, fastened it behind him and then sat on it as he did not want to get trapped upside down in the cockpit in the event of a rollover. Reaching outside the cockpit he made sure that the box containing the camera and exposed photographic plates was well secured to the fuselage. Satisfied that there was nothing more he could do, he rechecked the instruments and made a quick calculation on the note pad strapped to his right leg. At their current speed they would reach the aerodrome in four minutes.

Looking straight ahead over the engine cowling and between the blades of the stationary propeller, Nigel peered into the sunset hoping that his mechanics had anticipated their plight and were already out on the airfield making preparations for a night landing. The light was fading fast and it was already difficult to distinguish the road below from the rest of the countryside. Being only a few miles from home, Nigel was not unduly concerned and after a while he recognised a double bend in the road below; the border between Belgium and France.

He looked along the line of the railway track that ran parallel with the road and in the distance saw the outline of Abeele station. Glancing again at the aneroid, he realised that the aircraft was too high and that he needed to lose height without gaining any speed. Instinctively he banked the aircraft hard to the left, compensating for the yaw by applying right rudder and easing back on the control stick to prevent the nose from dropping too much. The glide angle steepened as the aircraft descended in a sideslip, with the right wing higher than the left and the nose pointing slightly to the left of the aircraft's heading. This gave Nigel an uninterrupted view of what lay ahead. The three remaining longerons creaked as the fuselage twisted under the increased strain and there was a surge in the rush of air as the aircraft began to lose height more rapidly than before. Looking outside the cockpit, Nigel was relieved to see that the damaged area of the fuselage was now shielded from the main force of the slipstream and that the remaining fabric was holding fast.

Careful not to alter any of the controls with his arms or feet, he turned his head around and was surprised to find that Frank Harmish was already facing him. The observer was sitting low in the rear cockpit so as not to further upset the aircraft.

"You must keep it well above sixty five," Frank called out to him in a voice barely audible above the noise of the wind. "You can lose speed very quickly in a sideslip and we don't have enough height to recover from a spin. Make sure you keep the landing field in sight at all times. Fishtail if you have to but try not to make a turn as that will increase the stall speed."

"Understood Frank. Brace yourself for a rough landing. Even if we do turn over, with no fuel left, we won't have to worry about starting a fire!"

At nine hundred feet, Nigel strained his eyes to spot the trees which marked the southern perimeter of the aerodrome. Suddenly, out of the gloom, he saw the light of first one and then a second landing lamp, directly ahead at a distance of a quarter of a mile. From the position of the lights the aircraft was still too high. He was faced with two unenviable alternatives; reduce speed by raising the nose and risk putting it into a stall or aim straight towards the lights and risk landing at too high a speed.

He was about to choose the first option and pull back on the control stick when he was distracted by other lights on the ground, some distance to the right of the landing lights. Praying that they came from the hangars at the northern end of the aerodrome he quickly changed his mind, deciding instead to use the landing lights as a threshold and attempt a landing towards the hangar lights. He would just have to hope that the cross wind would not upset the touchdown. He pressed the control stick hard into his right thigh at the same time as pushing on the right rudder bar. The aircraft banked steeply, dropping like a stone as Nigel brought it around over the top of a large farm to the south of the aerodrome, whilst making sure that the distant lights always remained in his sight.

As soon as the aircraft was on a northerly heading, he centralised the controls. The wings levelled out and the wheels cleared the tops of the trees on the aerodrome perimeter by less than thirty feet. Almost immediately, the lights of a dozen landing flares flashed past under the wings, close enough for Nigel to smell their acrid smoke. Out of the corner of his eye he caught a glimpse of two men running away and realised that they were his ground crew who had been taken by surprise by his decision to land across the lighted landing strip instead of along it. Knowing that in the final approach the RE8 would drop quickly and not float in the air like other aeroplanes, Nigel gently eased the control stick back towards him. With his feet working the rudder bar he corrected for the cross wind, aiming the nose of the aircraft a fraction to the left of the hangar lights. When he sensed the ground was close he straightened out the aircraft in readiness for the landing and held his breath with his mouth closed.

A few seconds later the wheels made contact with the surface of the airfield. With a jolt the aircraft bounced back into the air, forcing Nigel down into his chair and breaking the wicker seat under the cushion. He heard a tearing noise as a second wooden longeron snapped and the frame of the fuselage twisted upwards half way between the observer's cockpit and the tail plane. Before he had time to shout out a warning, the aircraft hit the ground again, this time with the wheels and tail skid striking the grass simultaneously.

Nigel felt a bump as the propeller struck something soft. Above the noise of cracking timber he thought he heard the sound of a scream but before he had time to look around, the nose of the machine swung upwards and he could see nothing but the night sky as the aircraft lurched once more into the air. He struggled with all his strength to push the stick forward but the control wires were jammed solid inside the twisted fuselage. He tried to move the rudder bar but found that that too would not move. Realising that there was nothing more he could do, he let go of the controls and braced himself, with his hands grasping the leather-covered cockpit surround and his legs pressed against the sides of the fuselage. Holding his breath once again, he waited for the inevitable impact.

Against all reason, the stricken machine remained in the air for another fifty yards, its tail plane connected to the rest of the body by a single unbroken longeron, a collection of jammed control wires and remnants of overstretched fabric that had stubbornly remained attached to the starboard side of the fuselage. After what to Nigel seemed like an age, the aircraft hit the ground tail first and everything rear of the observer's cockpit broke away. All that he could hear from where he sat crouched on the floor of the front cockpit was the zipping sound of the bracing wires as they snapped and he realised that he had to keep his head down and trust in God he would not be struck by any of the flailing wires.

The badly damaged aeroplane had already lost most of its forward speed when it suddenly slewed around to the left, its two wheels ploughing wide furrows in the soft surface of the airfield. It finally came to rest in front of the very hangar that had proved to be their salvation.

Anxious to leave the aircraft in case it burst into flames, Nigel sat up and struggled to extricate himself from the broken seat. He looked around, fearful of the fate that had befallen his observer, but was delighted to find that Frank Harmish had already climbed out of the rear cockpit and was standing on the ground, well away from the wreckage. Standing on an unbroken fuselage cross member, Nigel grasped the shattered seat and hurled it over the side. This gave him sufficient room to pull himself out of the cockpit and on to the wing. Miraculously the camera and the exposed plates inside the camera box were undamaged and he quickly removed the whole assembly from its mounting. Grasping hold of the camera he climbed down from the wing, a task made easier as the undercarriage had been torn off during the final slide and the lower wings were now resting on the grass.

Weighed down by his heavy clothing, Nigel ran as fast as he was able to the safety of the hangar, arriving just as one of the folding doors was drawn back. Light shone from the opening on to the remains of the aircraft. Putting down the camera equipment, he took off his goggles and looked back at the jumble of wood, wires and fabric. He whistled under his breath when he realised how lucky they were to have survived and was relieved when Frank Harmish walked towards him, apparently uninjured. The observer had a broad grin on his face.

"Well done, Nigel! A sterling effort, though you had me worried with that sideslip turn. I don't think I've ever experienced one of those in a 'Harry Tate', especially one with a dead engine. Landing from the south to lose height was a good move too."

"Thanks mainly to you though, Frank. I would have made all the wrong decisions if I hadn't listened to your advice. Let's find our ground crew and get them to move what's left of the machine back inside the hangar. It'll give them something to think about tonight!"

"I'm glad you chose to put petrol in the reserve tank. Most would have left it empty or filled it with fire retardant."

"A bit of a risk but it got us home, didn't it?"

"I don't think the old bus is going to burst into flames. Let's go back and have a closer look."

As the two men inspected the damage, the members of the ground crew who had set up the landing lights ran up and saluted. They were the fitter and a rigger from 'C' flight who were normally assigned to Nigel's machine. Though mechanics occasionally worked on other aircraft in the flight, it was a matter of pride that their machine was always in peak condition and never faltered through careless maintenance.

Nigel returned their salutes.

"Good evening Davis, Gough," he called out. "I've some work for you to do and I thought I'd bring it right to your door, so to speak."

"Most kind, I'm sure, sir!" replied 1st class air mechanic Alec Davis, a man who had served with the squadron for more than two years. The rigger raised his eyebrows when he saw the remains of the tail plane that lay some distance away from the rest of the fuselage. Looking doubtful, he scratched his head.

"I can't see much in this light, sir, but I think there's too much damage for us to fix it here or at HQ. Apart from a new fuselage we'll have to take the planes off, repair them and cover them in new fabric."

The rigger ran his fingers along the length of one of the wing spars.

"Apart from the missing undercarriage and shattered longerons, it looks like some of the spars have been nicked. We should really replace the lot though I'm not sure what we have left in the stores. I don't want the wings folding in mid air like what happened to Lieutenant Cato last week, sir."

"Understood, Davis, you know best," Nigel replied. "I'm happy to leave it in your capable hands. At least by rebuilding the old girl, you'll be able to true-up everything from scratch. I'm no expert, but I don't think they set it up properly at the factory."

"We'll have a closer look at it under the lights once we've fetched the crash tender, sir. Gough can check the engine while I look at the structural damage and we should be able to let you know the score in a couple of hours."

"So long as we have something to fly tomorrow."

"We'll give it a go but if the damage is too great we'll have to send the bits back to the Repair Park. You'll have to use the spare machine if that's all right with you, sir?"

"Yes, Davis. If that's the best you can do. But first I want to find out what we hit when we came in to land. Fetch us a lamp would you?"

The rigger walked back to the hangar and pulled back the other half of the folding doors, bringing more light on to the scene outside. The smell of dope and varnish pervaded the air all around.

Nigel held his nose and turned to his observer.

"I don't know how they can carry out repairs in such a confined space, Frank. I thought we had a hard enough time breathing in petrol fumes and cordite."

"At least you've never had to fly a rotary, like the Bristol Scout we had here back in the good old days. The castor oil used to spray all over the place and the poor pilot would get caught short in the air by breathing in too much of the fumes."

"You'd never have to ask for a 'Number 9' to keep you regular though," Nigel added with a laugh.

The rigger re-appeared with a lantern and the three men walked over the airfield towards the dying light of the landing lamps. When they had covered half the distance, they came across a patch of freshly furrowed earth, standing out in relief from the flat surface of the airfield.

"This must be where we hit the ground for the second time," Nigel shouted. "Whatever it was we hit must be close by."

"It might have been a cow, you know. They seem to find their way back on to the airfield no matter how many times we move them."

"If that's the case, we could well be eating beef tonight!"

Using the gouge marks in the ground as a starting point, the men split up and began to search the surrounding area, with Nigel in the centre holding the lantern high. Suddenly, the rigger cried out and ran towards what appeared to be a pile of crumpled clothing. The other two men quickly joined him. In the soft glow of the lantern light, Nigel could see that the pile of clothing was in fact the body of a man lying prone on the grass, surrounded by pieces of splintered wood and broken glass. At first glance he thought the body was headless as nothing was visible above the top of the Royal Flying Corps jacket. Bending over the inert form, he was relieved to find that the head had merely been obscured by a dark leather flying balaclava. Thinking back to the landing, Nigel realised that the tip of the propeller must have hit the back of the man's head with a glancing blow as the aircraft bounced back into the air, slashing his helmet and knocking him to the ground. Even in the dark the man's head looked a mess, with matted hair and bloody flesh visible through a long gash in the blood-soaked balaclava.

"Be careful, Davis, he may yet be alive. No one must touch him until we can get proper help. Run over to the hospital and ask the MO to come as quickly as he can. And while you're at it you can fetch an ambulance."

"Yes, sir. Right away."

"Here, you'd better take this lamp. I see someone else is bringing another one, so we can manage all right without it."

The rigger left the two officers and ran with the lamp to the other side of the aerodrome where he alerted the medical officer who was on duty in the empty hospital hut. He then made his way back to the service road to look for the standby ambulance in the long line of parked vehicles, eventually spotting a Crossley tender with white canvas sides and a single headlight shining in his direction. As he approached the vehicle he could hear the sound of the engine ticking over, but there was no sign of the driver. Walking around to the rear of the ambulance, he heard noises coming from inside.

"Is that you Tom?" he called out.

"Who wants to know?" a muffled voice shouted in reply.

"It's me, Alec Davis. There's been an accident on the other side of the airfield and we need the ambulance right away. Some poor sod's caught a blow to the head!"

The canvas flap opened and a man's face appeared in the light cast by the lamp.

"Hello Alec, my old son. One of my lights has gone out and I'm looking for fresh carbide pellets."

"No time for that now, Tom. You'll have to make do with one."

"Right you are."

Realising the gravity of the situation, the driver threw the small waterproof bag he was holding back inside the ambulance before jumping down and securing the rear flap.

"Just let me put the other light back together and we'll be on our way."

"Make it quick, would you?"

The rigger ran around to the front of the ambulance and climbed up into to the passenger's seat, waiting impatiently whilst the driver reassembled the discharged headlamp. Two minutes later the ambulance was bouncing at full speed across the airfield towards what was now a large group of onlookers.

By the time they reached the scene of the accident, the medical officer and two orderlies were already attending to the injured airman under the feeble light of a battery lamp. The driver stopped the ambulance, with the single acetylene headlamp projecting an unflickering broad beam of white light on to the body of the fallen airman. For the men watching from the distant hangars it would have presented an eerie scene; a little piece of daylight in the middle of absolute darkness, as it was the night of a new moon with no stars visible from the ground.

With great care the medical officer cut the flying helmet from the man's head. As he did so, he pointed out the injuries to the orderlies.

"His neck doesn't appear to be broken but as yet I can't detect a pulse. He's lost a lot of blood and most likely has a scull fracture but I won't know for certain until we can get him to the hospital." He gestured to the ambulance driver. "Bring a stretcher over here would you."

The driver ran to the ambulance and removed a canvas stretcher from the rear compartment. Placing it on the ground next to the injured man he waited for the medical officer's next orders.

"You two help me roll him on to his side, but be careful not to twist his neck. I'll have another look at his wound before we place him on the stretcher."

In less than a minute the injured man lay on his side with his head supported by an army blanket. The medical officer knelt on the ground with his back to the ambulance so that he could see what he was doing without being blinded by the brilliant headlight.

"Let's have a closer look shall we?"

He opened his bag and took a small mirror, placing it directly under the nose of the patient. After a few moments a patch of condensation appeared on the mirror and he placed two fingers on the man's neck. There was a faint pulse.

"He's still breathing so there's a chance."

Using a piece of sheet to clean the wound of blood, the doctor continued his examination.

"It's a nasty head wound, three inches long I'd say. See, the skull's exposed here. The cut is straight and clean so the leather helmet has obviously protected him somewhat."

"Is there any dirt in the wound, sir?" asked one of the orderlies.

"I don't think so. Falling flat on his face was a godsend. Even though he's suffered facial cuts and a broken nose, the scalp wound looks quite clean."

The flow of blood from the man's head had slowed to a trickle. Carefully pressing the edges of the wound together the doctor applied a thick field dressing and secured it with a length of bandage. Then, upon his command, the two orderlies once again took hold of the man, lifted him up and placed him on the stretcher.

The medical officer looked at the rough surface of the airfield, the bumps exaggerated in the light cast by the ambulance's headlight. He frowned.

"I think we'd better carry him to the hospital rather than risk compounding his injuries by taking him there in the ambulance."

He pointed to one of the orderlies.

"Here, pass me that blanket."

Taking the blanket, he rolled it up into a cylinder before wrapping it around the man's head.

"This will stop his head from moving from side to side."

The medical officer stood up. Unable to see with the intense white light shining directly into his face, he shouted in the direction of the ambulance, hoping that the driver was sitting in the open front cabin and would hear his orders.

"Follow close behind! Your headlamp will show us the way. When we've reached the hospital, wait outside with the engine running. We may yet need to send this man to the nearest clearing station."[2]

"Very good, sir. I'm ready when you are!" the driver shouted back.

The two orderlies picked up the stretcher and with the medical officer supporting the head of the injured man, the procession moved slowly across the airfield, past the empty hangars and on to the hospital. The rest of the onlookers dispersed and returned to their duties whilst several men from Number 4 squadron, who had witnessed the unfolding drama from the shelter of their hangars, watched with interest as the ambulance drove by.

The hospital hut was empty. With only a small number of sorties being flown in recent days, few injuries had required hospital treatment and the majority of cases had resulted from accidents and not from operational flying.

The injured airman was placed on the operating table under the glare of half a dozen naked electric light bulbs. The medical officer removed the temporary dressing and closely examined the wound, quickly determining that the man had sustained a linear fracture to the base of the skull. The fracture measured one tenth of an inch at its widest point and he was relieved to find no evidence that it was depressed. He was however concerned that as the man had been hit from behind and fallen to the ground without making any attempt to soften his fall, he would most certainly have suffered trauma to both the rear and the frontal regions of his brain.

The medical officer made a note on the patient's chart that a close watch be maintained as the next few hours would be a critical period in the man's recovery. Suturing the wound he cleaned the facial cuts before setting the man's broken nose. Only then did he give the order for the airman to be dressed in pyjamas, wrapped in blankets and placed in a bed close to the only stove in the hospital hut. The man had been lying on the cold airfield grass for almost an hour and there was always the risk of hypothermia.

With nothing more to do but wait, the medical officer telephoned the commanding officer of Number 6 squadron and informed him of the accident. Then, having repeated the instruction to the orderly that a watch be kept on the patient throughout the night, he packed his bag and returned to his quarters.

Morning came and a heavy mist clung to the surface of the aerodrome. It had rained steadily throughout the night and the pilots who were scheduled to leave at first light received the order that there would be no flying until the weather improved. In the hospital, the patient had yet to regain consciousness. He was breathing steadily and had no fever, but the pallor of those parts of his face that were not covered in bandages was a matter for concern to the orderly who had spent the night sitting in a chair next to the patient's bed. The injured man had moved occasionally during the night and once had groaned, but he had not opened his eyes.

Billy Strickland, the orderly who had kept watch over the patient since his admittance, was about to get up and go in search of the medical officer when he became aware that the patient's eyes were open and that he was trying to say something. He leaned forward and looked into the man's eyes.

"Did you say you were thirsty?" the orderly asked in a gentle voice.

The patient blinked his eyes and once again tried to talk, but no words came out of his mouth. The orderly picked up the water bottle from the bedside table and attempted to pour some of the liquid into the man's open mouth. Most of the water ran down the man's face and on to the pillow. The patient blinked his eyes again and gave a deep sigh before lapsing back into unconsciousness.

At that moment the relieving orderly, Corporal James Boyd, entered the room and approached the bed.

"Anything happening, Billy?"

"Perfect timing, Jim. You take over whilst I'll go and tell the MO that the patient has regained consciousness, albeit briefly. He'll need to come and have another look and decide what to do next. It looks like a Blighty wound to me."

"You might be right, but that'll be up to the MO. Not much we can do about it. Anyway, there's food left for you in the mess if you want it."

The relieved orderly stood up, said goodbye to his colleague and left the ward.

Later that morning, the man stirred again. James Boyd, who was sitting on a wooden chair reading a newspaper, jumped up and bent over the injured airman.

"Starlight, I need Starlight," the patient moaned.

"What's that you're saying? Is the light in here too bright for you?"

"Starlight," insisted the man. "You must find Starlight".

"Hold on son, I'll go and fetch the doctor. He can sort out who or what Starlight is."

Chapter 2

A Time to Decide

THE CONGREGATION FILED out of the Church of the Most Holy Trinity, with many of the parishioners stopping to chat on the forecourt before going home. The weather was unseasonably warm for late October and the Reverend Arthur Hanwood stood at the entrance, shaking hands with everyone as they left. He had just delivered a sermon on the dichotomy presented to Christians in times of war; to fight and kill for one's country or to stand by one's beliefs and reject the call to arms. At the start of the service he had noticed the absence of many of the regulars and he had taken the unprecedented step of asking the congregation to fill in the gaps by leaving their customary pews and moving closer to the pulpit. A few people had begrudgingly obliged but the majority had ignored his plea and remained where they were.

Inside the church, far away from the noise of the busy main road, the young organist was playing the Toccata from Widor's Fifth Symphony. He particularly loved this piece of music as it was loud and joyful but required a high level of concentration. His fingers moved effortlessly over the three keyboards, interrupted only when he had to change a stop setting. At the same time his feet danced over the wooden keys, giving rise to the rich bass notes that blasted from the longest pipes above the organ console. To his left an attractive and well-dressed woman in her mid thirties read the sheet music over his shoulder, turning the pages of the score for him whenever he nodded his head.

The church was almost empty by the time the organist stopped playing. When the echoes of the last notes had faded away, he turned around on his seat and looked up at the woman, a hopeful expression on his face.

"Ethel, we've been seeing each other for five years and you must know how I feel about you. My parents like you and I'm certain they'd welcome you into the family, especially now that I've finished my apprenticeship and can offer you a secure future. Would you please do me the honour of marrying me?"

Ethel touched him gently on the shoulder.

"Dearest Fred, the last thing I want to do is to hurt you but you must realise the position I'm in."

"I don't understand. What position?"

"I'm considerably older than you and it has taken me years of hard work to be able to live independent of my family. If I give this up, how do I know that you won't tire of me and fall in love with someone closer to your age?"

"I'd never do that," Fred insisted, reaching forward and grasping her hands in his. "I knew you were the one for me when we first met. Besides, you can continue to work at Burberry's if that would make you happy."

Ethel pulled her hands away from his and sat down next to him on the organist's bench. Though no-one else was nearby, she was well aware that even a whisper could be heard anywhere in the nave and there were still a few people in the church who had stayed behind to listen to the music.

"Part of me would love to say yes, but I really cannot consider marriage at the moment with all that's going on. And the thought of starting a family scares me."

Fred looked away for a moment as he tried to hide his disappointment.

"If that's the case then, I think I'll volunteer for war service. The sermon this morning made me realise I've been sitting on the fence far too long."

"We've talked about this before and you said that you didn't want to fight. Tell me what has changed?"

"I've been reading about the new army service called the Royal Flying Corps. It uses flying machines to scout on the enemy side of the lines and bring back information to the army commanders."

"But you know nothing about flying, dearest. How would that help you?"

"I've already made a few enquiries and they told me that my watchmaking skills would put me in good stead to qualify as a wireless or instrument mechanic. I'd serve at the front but not be directly fighting the enemy."

Ethel was silent for a moment before taking Fred's hands and looking him straight in the eye.

"To be honest Fred, though I'd die if anything happened to you, I wouldn't feel comfortable if we married and set up home whilst everyone else around us is doing what they can for the war effort. Have you talked to your parents about this?"

"Not as such, but I don't think they'd be surprised."

"It will be a shock to them, especially as you're their eldest."

"There's another reason why I should do it now, Ethel."

"What is that, dearest?"

"If I volunteer I can choose the service, but if I wait and they bring in conscription I won't have a choice and could end up in the Infantry."

Fred put his hand inside his waistcoat pocket and took out an old silver pocket watch. He opened the case and looked at the time before quickly returning the watch to his pocket. Rising from the bench he faced Ethel, a forced smile on his face.

"We'd better get a move on or you'll miss your train and will have to borrow my old bicycle! Come, we can talk along the way."

They walked arm in arm down the aisle and out of the main door, just as the minister was getting ready to close the church door. The Reverend Hanwood was a huge man and towered over Fred as they shook hands in the vestibule.

"Thank you for playing the organ today, Fred. As always it was a joy to hear the old pipes sing. I'm sure most people came to listen to your music and not to me."

"I'm sure that's not true, Reverend. I for one took notice of your sermon, but I'm afraid it may have an impact on the church."

"And why is that, young sir?"

"I've decided to enlist, so you'll have to find another part-time organist."

The minister laughed loudly and patted Fred on the back.

"At least my words weren't lost on everyone today. It's funny that in times of war, we tend to either turn towards God or away from Him. I trust you won't be one of the latter."

"No, Reverend. I think I've found a way that will allow me to keep my faith yet still serve my country."

"I'm glad to hear that. Don't worry about leaving us short an organist. I'm sure old Ben will come out of retirement if I ask him nicely."

"Thank you, Reverend. That's a relief."

"Don't mention it, Fred. If I don't see you again before you leave, may God protect you and yours in these troubled times."

Turning towards Ethel, Reverend Hanwood took hold of her gloved hand.

"I realise you don't live in Reading, Miss Pocock and are unlikely to attend our church services, but if ever you're in need of someone to talk to whilst Frederick is away, you will always be made most welcome at the Manse. Besides, Mrs Hanwood and I would love to hear news of what's happening at the front. I can always post it on the church notice board. Not that we get to hear much these days, with the way our boys' letters are censored."

"Thank you, Reverend," Ethel replied. "If I can't come in person, I'll make sure that I write to you from time to time with news."

"That would be much appreciated. Now if you will excuse me I must go and shut up shop before lunch."

Fumbling under his vestments, the Reverend Hanwood extracted a long iron key from an unseen pocket and with a wave turned and walked back inside the church, leaving Fred and Ethel alone in the vestibule. Anxious that Ethel might miss her train, Fred handed her his music case and ran down the steps of the church to a clump of bushes where he had earlier hidden his bicycle. When he returned with the bicycle he joined her on the footpath and with one hand around her waist and the other balancing the bicycle by its saddle, they set out on the short walk to the railway station.

Matters progressed far quicker than Fred had anticipated. In the evening he broke the news to his parents by telephone and asked their permission for his belongings to be moved from his rented accommodation back to his old room at the family home in Basingstoke. He also promised that he would visit them before he enlisted so that they could say their proper goodbyes.

The following day Fred went to work as usual but left early and cycled into town, stopping at the enlistment office. It wasn't long before he found out that in order to enlist as a 'special trades' recruit he would have to make his application at the London office. Not only that, he would first have to take a trades test at Farnborough to see if his skills were appropriate for one of the new technical trades. In spite of these unexpected setbacks, Fred left the office armed with a test appointment and a list of instructions as to where to go and what to take.

Tuesday should have been like any other working day but Fred found it impossible to concentrate. He was seeing everything through different eyes, his world turned upside down even though nothing had actually changed. In the afternoon, just before finishing work for the day, he was given leave by his manager to telephone Ethel at the store where she worked. As a buyer in the haberdashery department Ethel was allowed to take personal telephone calls provided that they were brief. Fred wasted no time in telling her his news. Since Ethel had already planned to spend the rest of the week in Tunbridge Wells for the purpose of visiting glove suppliers, she agreed to take the Thursday afternoon off and travel up to London so that they could meet for afternoon tea.

Early the next morning Fred walked to the station and caught a train to Farnborough. Once there, he followed the directions he had been given and made his way to the Royal Aircraft Factory[3] establishment at South Farnborough. Entering the depot at North Camp he presented his letter of introduction and was directed to a large room where many other would-be recruits were already waiting.

The test was not as difficult as Fred had expected. He was led to a table where he was ordered to disassemble a pocket watch and put it back together again. This he accomplished with ease. He was then questioned on his knowledge of basic electricity and magnetism, as the science of aircraft wireless[4] was still in its infancy and tests had yet to be devised on the subject. After waiting for a short time, Fred was informed by the instructor that he had passed and was presented with a certificate. Before he was allowed to leave, Fred was asked if he wanted to sign on for 'four years plus four years on reserve' or for 'hostilities only'. Without any hesitation he chose the latter.

Fred left the training camp late in the afternoon and caught a train to Basingstoke. He walked to his parents' house, less than a mile from the station, and was soon sitting down to high tea in front of a roaring fire. After talking about what lay ahead, he turned to his father.

"Now that I've told you all that I know, may I ask you a favour, father?"

"How can I help you, Frederick?"

Fred's father was a kindly middle-aged man, small of stature but impeccably dressed and sporting a well groomed beard, much like that worn by the King of England.

"I have to enlist in London tomorrow but I'd like to stay here tonight and catch the train to town in the morning, if that's all right with you. Would you telephone Mr Lewis tomorrow and tell him that I won't be at work until later in the afternoon?"

"Certainly, my boy. With all that's going on that's the very least I can do. If you give me your spare key, I'll organise the removal of your belongings and have them brought back here. Would you like me to contact your Ethel as well?"

"She's in Tunbridge at the moment. I spoke to her yesterday on the telephone and we plan to meet in London tomorrow afternoon. It may well be our last chance to see each other before I'm marched off to training camp."

"Mind that you buy her some flowers," Fred's mother interrupted. "You may find that Ethel won't write to you if you don't."

"Leave him be, mother. I'm sure the lad knows his own mind."

Fred's mother got up from her chair and walked over to the mantelpiece. She picked up a framed family portrait that showed Fred as a young boy. After looking at the photograph for a moment she sighed, put it back in its place and bent down to place another log on the fire.

"You two carry on talking while I go and find a hot water bottle. When I come back down I'll make us all a nightcap."

Fred and his parents talked late into the night, each reluctant for the moment to pass. Finally, having said goodnight, Fred climbed the stairs to his bedroom. Tired as he was, he only managed to sleep fitfully.

The next morning after a simple breakfast, he sorted out the documents[5] he would need to take to London and placed them in his music case, an old leather satchel that had been given to him when he left school. As an afterthought he decided to include the 'perfect attendance' medal he had been presented with as a student. Hugging his parents one last time he left to catch the train to London and ninety minutes later alighted at Waterloo station. Fred stopped to eat a sandwich at the station café before buying a single tube ticket for Oxford Circus and joining the early morning workers on the short escalator ride down to the Underground. Taking the next electric train going north on the Bakerloo line, within minutes he was back in the fresh air, walking along Regent Street.

Even before he reached the address that he had been given by the sergeant at the enlistment office, Fred recognised the Polytechnic[6] building. He had seen a newspaper photograph of it three years earlier when the six storey building had been extensively modified to incorporate a theatre and gymnasium as well as a swimming pool. Entering the imposing building, Fred followed the signs and climbed the stairs to the floor that had been set up as an enlistment office. He gave his name to the clerk behind the desk and was told to sit in the waiting area with the other attestants. When it was his turn to be examined, he was ushered into a large room where he was greeted by a white-coated doctor.

"Ah, Frederick Johnstone I see. Undress down to your drawers behind that screen over there and then come back and lie on the table. You can keep your socks on if you like."

Fred did as he was ordered and walked over to the screened area of the room. After he had finished undressing, he placed his clothes in a neat pile on the chair provided, with his shoes and music case pushed underneath. Feeling self conscious in his socks and suspenders he removed them also, laying them carefully on top of his shoes before stepping out from the privacy of the screen. The doctor, who was standing in the centre of the room next to a portable operating table that had been set up directly beneath the only electric light in the room, beckoned him to approach. Avoiding eye contact, Fred scrambled up on to the table and lay down on his back, staring up at the ornate ceiling to take his mind off what was about to take place.

For the next thirty minutes Fred was poked and prodded and made to carry out all manner of physical exercises. The doctor hardly spoke a word, merely noting the results of each test on a sheet of paper. For one of the tests Fred was asked to stand on one leg, close his eyes and raise himself on the tips of his toes whilst keeping his balance. Within a matter of seconds he started to wobble and had to open his eyes to stop himself from falling over. Feeling slightly ridiculous, he stifled a laugh.

"I suppose I've failed that one."

The doctor made no comment, wrote a number on his clipboard and continued with the next test.

At the end of the examination Fred was ordered to dress. With relief he sought the privacy of the screen and quickly put his clothes back on, but struggled when he attempted to tie his shoe laces. He looked down to find that his hands were shaking uncontrollably. When he finally emerged from behind the screen, the doctor handed him an envelope that contained the results of the tests.

"Give this to the clerk at the front desk and then take a seat in the waiting room until your name is called."

Relieved that the examination was over, Fred handed in the test results and sat down on the only vacant chair, right at the back of the waiting room. After a few minutes a sergeant came out of the room opposite the examination room and called out his name. Following the sergeant into the interview room, Fred was directed to sit on a plain wooden chair that had been positioned in front of a large desk. The sergeant took the documents around to the other side of the desk and sat down to read them whilst Fred waited in silence.

"So you'd like to join the Royal Flying Corps?"

"Yes, sir."

"Well, you're not as fit as most men your age but I suppose that won't matter with the job we have in mind for you."

Fred tried not to look nervous.

"Does that mean I'm accepted, sir?"

"I could ask you a lot more questions but from the results of your interview in Farnborough you seem to fit the bill. So the answer is yes. And it's 'Sergeant', not 'sir'. You only call officers 'sir'."

"Well, that's one for the record books, Sergeant. I thought you'd give me the third degree."

"At the moment we need as many qualified men as we can get, so I probably would have passed you if you only had one leg!"

"And I was beginning to feel pleased with myself."

"Only kidding, son. I think you'll be well suited for the job. Do you have any questions before you sign your life away?"

"Yes, Sergeant. Can you tell me what rank I'll have and when I'll be sent overseas?"

"Well, young sir, we're in the middle of some big changes in the way we're recruiting for the Royal Flying Corps but I can tell you that at the moment we're very short of wireless mechanics. I'd say that you'll be posted to an operational squadron within a month."

Fred raised his eyebrows but said nothing.

"With regards to your rank, you'll be signed on as an acting 1st class air mechanic. You already have plenty of experience in watchmaking so that qualifies you to be a first class tradesman."

"But I know nothing about wireless, Sergeant."

"I wouldn't worry too much about that. You'll pick it up quickly once you're in a squadron. In no time at all you'll find that your rank will be confirmed. Promotion after that will be up to you and how well you do your job."

Fred was rather startled at the speed at which everything was happening and it dawned on him that the afternoon tea with Ethel might well be the last time they would have a chance to be together before he was sent abroad.

"What happens next, Sergeant?"

"If you're ready now, you can sign on the dotted line and wait with the other new recruits in the hall. We'll then march you all down to Waterloo station some time this afternoon and you'll be in Farnborough by nightfall."

"That's all a bit too soon for me, Sergeant. I've not even sorted out things with my employer. Would it be all right if I start tomorrow?"

The sergeant thought for a moment before replying.

"It's a bit irregular, but I'll mark on the form that you'll present yourself at Farnborough tomorrow afternoon. I'll give you a travel warrant and the necessary papers that'll show you where to go. Mind you be there though, or we'll have to send a search party out to find you!"

The sergeant laughed when he saw the look of dismay on Fred's face.

"Don't worry son, I'm sure that won't be necessary. You'll be kitted out at Farnborough and they'll teach you all you need to know about the army and the Royal Flying Corps. After that, you'll be sent out to France, though I can't tell you which squadron you'll be posted to."

"But I don't even have a passport, Sergeant."

"Don't you worry about that either. You're in the army now. We look after all those sorts of details. Anything else I can help you with?"

"That's all I can think of at the moment, Sergeant."

The sergeant leant across the desk and pushed a document towards Fred.

"All right then, you need to sign this Short Service Attestation form that I've already filled out and then come with me to the front counter. They'll fix you up with the necessary travel documents."

Fred signed the document and followed the sergeant to the reception desk where they waited whilst the travel warrant was prepared. He then shook hands with the sergeant and left the building in a daze. He had joined the British armed forces and would soon be going overseas. Up to this point in his life, the farthest he had ever travelled had been the island of Jersey in the English Channel.

Fred opened his coat and took out his watch, realising when he looked at the time that he was not due to meet Ethel for another half an hour. As it was a warm day for late October, he decided to take a stroll before catching a bus to Piccadilly Circus. Crossing the road through a gap in the traffic, he walked though the park in Cavendish Square, intending to go as far as Regents Park. He stopped for a moment in Harley Street, impressed by the grandeur of the four storey terraced Georgian buildings and the beautiful trees that lined the road. The few leaves that still clung to the branches had already turned to various shades of yellow and brown. Looking at the people walking in the street, Fred was surprised at the high percentage of army officers. That is, until he realised that as many of the men bore evidence of recent injury, they were most likely visiting physicians who rented rooms in the fashionable district. Deciding to cut short his walk, he changed direction and headed east towards Portland Place where he hoped he would be able to catch a bus that would take him to the West End.

In spite of heavy traffic in Portland Place, Fred could not see a single bus[7] going his way. As it was getting close to the time he was due to meet Ethel, he walked briskly back towards Regent Street whilst keeping a watchful eye for any southbound bus. He need not have worried, for within a matter of minutes he heard the rattling sound of a motor bus. He turned around to read where the bus was going. Though he could not clearly see the number displayed above the driver's compartment, he could make out the words 'Piccadilly Circus' as one of the destinations listed on the sign fastened to the front of the upper deck.

As the red 'General'[8] drew alongside, Fred jumped on to the rear boarding platform and seized the grab rail to steady his balance.

"You shouldn't oughta do that," a gruff voice called out. Fred looked around but at first could not see who had spoken to him.

"Mind your backs. Let me through." It was the same voice. The people standing in the aisle on the lower deck were forced to one side of the bus by a man who was attempting to reach the stairway. After much pushing and shoving, he appeared at the entrance to the lower deck; a tiny man dressed in a smart uniform with a ticket machine strapped to his chest and a leather change bag hanging from his shoulder. Clasping a ticket rack in one hand he held on to the grab rail with the other as the bus hit a rough patch of road.

"Don't you know it's dangerous to jump on to a moving bus?"

"I'm sorry. I wasn't sure which bus to catch for Piccadilly Circus and when I saw yours I didn't want to miss it. How much is a single fare?"

Realising that Fred was not attempting to get a free ride, the conductor's demeanour softened.

"A halfpenny to you, guv. Mind how you go if you want to sit upstairs, though. Them steps are very slippy."

Fred took out a handful of coins from his coat pocket and gave the conductor two farthings.

"Keep the change," he said with a smile.

Immediately the conductor reverted to his earlier mood. Removing a halfpenny ticket from the ticket holder, he punched a hole through the ticket before thrusting it into Fred's hand.

"It's all right for some. Others have important work to do."

Fred thought it prudent to mollify the conductor.

"You sound a bit glum. What's up?"

"This war is changing everything, it is. I heard at the depot only this morning that our opposition Tillings is going to put women on as conductors. Women! Whatever is the world coming to?"

"I'm afraid we'll all have to put up with worse changes than that. We'll just have to make the best of it and hope everything returns to normal in a few months. I'm off to the war myself soon and I'm certainly not looking forward to it."

"Well, you can tell the Kaiser what I think of him when you see him. If I didn't have a gammy leg, I'd be over there meself."

Clutching the ticket in one hand and his case in the other, Fred climbed the shiny metal steps up to the open deck on top of the bus. As the conductor had warned, the steps to the upper deck were very slippery and Fred realised that it must have rained earlier along the route. With no-one else sitting outside, Fred chose one of the seats at the rear of the bus, close to the top of the stairs. Removing the waterproof seat cover from its holder he sat down and placed it across his knees, anticipating that there could be more rain on the short journey to Piccadilly Circus. He knew the cover would also keep his legs warm and protect him from the draughts. Pulling his bowler hat further down on his head just in case the wind strengthened he laughed out loud when he read the words on the sign fastened next to the seat, warning passengers of the dangers of leaning over the side whilst the bus was moving!

Travelling not much faster than a bicycle, the bus juddered every time it hit a rut in the road, its solid rubber tyres unable to absorb anything but the smallest bump. With only a few stops before he had to get off, Fred had no time to settle back and relax. As the bus approached the junction at Piccadilly, he looked out at the busy intersection and understood immediately why it was called a 'circus', though he knew that his interpretation of the word would certainly not have been shared by the designer Sir John Nash,[9] almost one hundred years earlier.

All manner of vehicles, horse-drawn as well as motorised, were converging at the confluence of the six streets that ran into Piccadilly Circus. The fountain monument erected in honour of the late Earl of Shaftesbury stood roughly in the centre, the crowning winged cherub poised on one leg thirty feet above the ground, for all intents and purposes in the act of shooting an arrow at the heads of passing bus passengers. With motor buses vying with private automobiles, horse drawn carriages and commercial vehicles for right of way across the intersection, the scene would have convinced any stranger to London that it was only by sheer good fortune that accidents were not commonplace. As a guide to the drivers, though also no doubt creating a safe haven for any pedestrian who happened to become stranded whilst crossing the busy intersection, several small islands had been constructed at strategic locations. Each of them bore a street lamp and several small bollards, the latter to be used by drivers should the need arise to temporarily secure their horse-drawn conveyances.

Fred was unsure as to the route the motor bus would take after it reached Piccadilly Circus, so he quickly folded the knee apron and stowed it back in the receptacle at the end of the seat. He stood at the top of the stairwell, ready to alight at short notice, just as the bus joined a long line of vehicles waiting to negotiate the busy intersection. Looking up he noticed with surprise that the façade of Piccadilly House, next door to the old Café Monico building, was covered with permanent advertisements. Each sign was illuminated by dozens of round electric light bulbs and even from a distance he was able to read the words. The largest sign, for Bovril, was made up of letters eight feet high.

The bus started to move but after only a few yards it stopped yet again, this time right at the foot of the Shaftesbury monument.[10] Fred seized the opportunity and ran down the steps to the platform below.

"Cheerio," he shouted to the conductor as he jumped from the bus on to the pavement at the base of the monument. He heard a muffled response from deep inside the lower deck and waved as the bus moved off in the direction of Shaftsbury Avenue.

Fred had arranged to meet Ethel on the steps in front of the fountain, but from where he was standing she was nowhere to be seen. He decided to walk around to the other side just in case she was early. As he moved around the base of the monument, his attention was drawn to an old flower lady who was sitting on the steps of the water trough. In front of her on one of the lower steps was a large wicker basket crammed with cut flowers of various varieties, colours and lengths. Remembering what his mother had told him the previous evening, he stooped down to look inside the basket. Unable to find what he was looking for, he decided to ask for advice. Looking into the rheumy eyes of the old lady he could not help but notice that though her skin was heavily weathered she was probably a lot younger than she looked. Dressed in a dingy ankle-length light brown coat with the collar turned up at her neck, she wore on her head what appeared to be an old boater.

The flower lady peered up at Fred, an imploring look on her lined face.

"Like to buy some flowers for your lady friend, luv?"

"That depends on what you have."

"Well, I've got some nice chrysanthemums. They always go down well with the ladies. Or if you want something pretty, you can't go wrong with these. They're late season, a bit unusual for this time of year."

The flower lady fumbled through the flowers at the back of the basket, eventually holding up a bunch of white cornflowers. Fred leant forward to see if the blooms were fresh.

"Exactly what I was looking for. Cornflowers are my Ethel's favourite. If you have any blue ones I'll take two bunches."

The flower lady sniffed loudly and put back the flowers, searching once more through the contents of her basket until she eventually found what she was looking for.

"There you are dearie, I thought I'd have some somewhere. That'll be sixpence for the two. I'll wrap them nicely for no extra charge."

The amount asked was far more than the flowers were worth but Fred said nothing and handed over a sixpenny piece. He waited impatiently whilst the flower lady wrapped the cornflowers into a single bouquet and then helped her to lay it carefully at the bottom of his music case. Closing the flap loosely so that it wouldn't squash the blooms, he touched the brim of his hat briefly and bade her good-day.

"Thank you dearie, God bless you," the old lady called after him.

Several people were sitting on the steps at the foot of the fountain but many more were walking around the base of the monument. At any time of the day it was a popular meeting place as it was common knowledge that Piccadilly Circus was the true centre of London. Reaching the side of the monument that faced the 'new' road,[11] Shaftesbury Avenue, Fred saw a woman standing on the top step next to the fountain trough. He recognised Ethel's hat before he could discern her features. Holding the case behind his back, he quietly walked up to her, raised his hat and addressed her in a deep voice.

"Good afternoon Miss Pocock."

Startled, Ethel turned around and then smiled when she recognised Fred.

"Well, good afternoon sir," she responded with a half curtsey. "What is that you're hiding behind your back?"

"You've never been one for pleasantries have you, Ethel!"

Fred laughed, replacing his hat as he brought the bulging case out from behind his back.

"I thought I'd try and surprise you."

Raising the flap of his bag he removed the bouquet and presented the flowers to Ethel.

"Blue cornflowers, my favourites. Fred, you're such a dear."

"Something to brighten your room in Tunbridge."

Fred took Ethel by the arm and guided her down the steps to the road.

"Now to the matter at hand. I thought we might go and sample the delights of a certain Joe Lyons establishment that I've been known to frequent."

"Oh, the Troc, the best restaurant in town! Fred, you really shouldn't!"

"I didn't mean that Joe Lyons establishment!" Fred spluttered, caught off guard. "I don't think the exchequer is quite up to that at the moment, though I'd certainly take you there if I could afford it. I had in mind the Lyons tea house on the corner of Coventry Street. It's always nice there and the tea is 'the best available' as they say in the brochure."

Ethel laughed out loud and poked Fred in the ribs.

"I didn't imagine for one moment that you were serious. But the Trocadero is rather a grand place isn't it?"

From where they stood they could just see the entrance to the famous restaurant, one hundred yards into Shaftesbury Avenue, though most of the building was blocked from view by the wall of the nearby London Pavilion. Fred's gaze was distracted by a poster fastened to the facade of the London Pavilion. It was his turn to give Ethel a nudge.

"See the sign right up there on the corner? It must have been put there especially for me!"

Ethel turned around and looked up, shielding her eyes with a gloved hand. Erected below the 'RESTAURANT' sign for the Piccadilly Restaurant was a huge white placard, twenty feet high and fifteen feet wide.

"I wonder how many have taken heed today?" she said. "With all the talk of conscription in the newspapers, there may soon be no choice."

"What's the latest? I've not read a newspaper today."

"Apparently the Derby Scheme is not proving successful in getting single men to attest. I hear Mr Asquith's government is now debating a Military Services Bill."

"Really? Looks like I volunteered just in time doesn't it?"

"Perhaps you know people in high places."

"Not me, my love. I'm just a humble worker. Anyway, enough of politics. Let's forget about the war for a moment and go up the road for a nice pot of tea."

Taking her by the arm Fred guided Ethel across the road, through the bustling traffic and on to the opposite pavement. From there they walked past the main entrance of the London Pavilion, across Great

Windmill Street and down to the corner of Rupert Street where they stopped outside an imposing four storey building. The ground floor façade was faced with white glazed terra cotta tiles and bore the familiar sign of 'J Lyons & Co Ltd', the letters written in gold writing on a white background right across the top of the shop front window.

Fred opened the door and bowed with a theatrical flourish.

"After you, my lady."

"Why thank you, kind sir."

It was a quarter past four and most of the tables were empty, so they made their way to a window table well away from the entrance. After helping Ethel with her coat, Fred left her to take their outdoor clothes to the cloakroom where he left them in the care of an attendant. On the way back to the table Fred raised his hand to catch the eye of a waitress who had just walked out of the kitchen.

Fred sat down next to Ethel just as the waitress approached their table, notepad at the ready. To Fred, she looked no older than seventeen and she was wearing the standard Lyons uniform for a Gladys,[12] a long sleeved black dress almost completely covered by a full-length white cotton apron that was pinned to her chest. To complete the uniform she wore smart wristbands, a high collar and a cap; all made from stiffly starched white cotton.

"Good afternoon, sir, madam," the waitress greeted them respectfully. "May I offer you afternoon tea or would you prefer something more substantial?"

Fred picked up the Lyons Tariff card upon which the menu was printed in black and red.

"I think we might have a pot of tea for two and a bun or something similar."

Fred turned to Ethel and handed her the menu.

"What would you like to eat, dearest?"

"I'll have a toasted bun with butter, thank you."

"Make that two toasted buns with butter."

Fred's eyes were drawn to several endorsements that were printed on the bottom of the menu.

"And make sure that 'the tea is the most perfect the world produces' or I'll be forced to send it back!"

The waitress laughed and wrote down their order. When she left them to return to the kitchen, Ethel leaned towards Fred and whispered in his ear.

"Why do you have to make light of everything, especially at a time like this?"

Fred took her hands in his and looked into her eyes.

"Dearest, I know that this must be as difficult for you as it is for me. I'd like to say the war will be over by Christmas, but someone told me that last year and look what happened."

Fred let go of her hands and cleared his throat quietly as he tried to recall the short speech he had prepared that morning on the train ride to London.

"Listen Ethel, I want to be serious for a moment."

Ethel picked up the bouquet of cornflowers from the table and made a pretence of sniffing the blooms.

"All right Fred, I'm listening."

Fred looked around and made sure that no-one was within hearing distance before continuing.

"Dearest Ethel, I have a duty to conduct myself in a Christian manner at all times and I also have a duty to serve England in this war to the best of my ability. But as well as these, my love, I've made it my duty to ensure that I come back from this madness and make you my wife."

Ethel smiled as tears welled up in her eyes.

"I haven't finished yet," Fred continued, in an attempt to lighten the mood. "It will also be my pleasant duty when the war is over to take you for a slap up meal at the Troc. We'll get all dressed up and go to the Theatre as well. There's a new farce[13] on at the Criterion that's been getting good reviews. You like Ruby Miller don't you? I'll take you to that if it's still on."

Ethel took out a lace handkerchief and dabbed her eyes with it. With a look of resignation she returned the handkerchief to her bag and sat upright.

"Enough of your fanciful promises, young Frederick. Tell me exactly what happened today."

"I hate it when you call me that. You sound just like my mother."

"I'm sorry, I didn't mean it to come out like that."

Fred realised how close Ethel was to breaking into tears again and he quickly told her his news.

"Well, I went to enlist just up the road at Marylebone and to cut a long story short, they've accepted me into the Royal Flying Corps as a wireless mechanic. I know it's very short notice but I have to go to Farnborough tomorrow and start my training."

"Oh my!"

"I don't know how long that will take but as soon as they think I'm ready I'll be shipped off to France and posted to an aeroplane squadron. There, you have it in one minute!"

Ethel reached a hand across the table.

"This is happening quicker than I had imagined," she said quietly, touching his arm. "I thought we would have more time together to get used to the idea of being apart, if you know what I mean. Might this be our last time together until you come home on leave?"

"I'm afraid so, my love. I didn't think it would be this quick, either. Perhaps I'll be able to telephone you as I can't imagine the Corps will cut us off from the whole world whilst we're in training."

The tea arrived and the waitress placed their order on the white tablecloth. Fred glanced at her to indicate that he did not want to be disturbed and without a word she left them to serve their own tea.

Ethel poured tea into the two cups, added milk from the silver milk jug and passed one of the cups on a saucer to Fred. In silence they drank their tea and ate hot buttered buns as there was little to be said and no plans that could be made.

When they had finished eating, Fred once again caught the attention of the waitress and asked for the bill, which she brought over to their table. He gave her a shilling piece and told her to keep the change. Thanking him she politely wished them both a good evening before leaving to serve another a group of people who had just entered the shop.

"If you'll excuse me, I'd better go and collect our things."

"All right, Fred. I need to leave soon if I'm to make it back to my lodgings in time for dinner."

Fred left the table to retrieve their coats and hats from the cloakroom. When he came back, Ethel was already standing at the door.

"What would you like to do? I'm going back to Reading as I have to go to work first thing and pack up my tools. I could travel with you to Waterloo but the train home from there would take twice as long as one from Paddington."

"Don't worry about me Fred. I know my way around London well enough. Waterloo station is only three stops from here."

"If you're sure then. I'll walk with you as far as Piccadilly Circus as I'll be travelling on the Bakerloo line as well."

Leaving the tea house they set off towards the 'Circus'. The sky had begun to darken and the moon was just visible above the skyline of London. All around them, office workers were heading home after a long day's work. Most would be catching a motor bus or taking an electric train but the more affluent would hail one of the many taxi cabs that plied the streets of the city.

Ethel looked up into the twilit sky as they strolled along the pavement

"Looks like there's a full moon tonight, Fred. Its light should help us when we cross over the road."

"That's just as well. The street lamps are too far apart to be of any use and not many carriages will have their lights on yet."

Upon impulse Fred pulled Ethel into one of the doorways and they stood still, taking in the beauty of the city's skyline and counting the stars as one by one they came out in the night sky. After a few minutes standing together in silence, Fred leaned forward and whispered something in Ethel's ear. She laughed and took hold of his hand, leading him out of the doorway and back on to the street. As they reached the end of Coventry Street, the billboard lights on Glasshouse Street came on, the bright electric bulbs suddenly illuminating the winged statue in front of them.

"Look over there. Fred. It must be an omen."

"They're only electric lights, Ethel. Nothing more."

Fred placed his arm around Ethel's waist as they stepped off the pavement.

"Let's make straight for the Criterion."

"Whatever you say, Fred. I'm in your capable hands."

Waiting for the right moment, Fred deftly guided Ethel between two horse-drawn carriages and across to the safety of the pavement on the other side of the road. From there they walked to the entrance of the Piccadilly Circus Tube station where they joined the queue of people waiting at the ticket office. When it was Fred's turn at the counter he asked the clerk for two singles, one for Waterloo and the other for Paddington. Paying for them with loose change from his pocket, he handed Ethel her ticket.

"I'm afraid we won't be able to say our goodbyes in private."

"It's probably just as well, Fred. I don't like saying goodbye at the best of times and this isn't one of those."

"All right, my dearest. Let's make this quick. I'll talk to you on the telephone as soon as I can. Who knows, I might even get a few days of leave before I'm sent to France."

The two lovers paused for a moment before making their way to the top of the escalator. As they descended to the platforms, Fred stood behind Ethel with his hands on her shoulders. Reaching the bottom of the escalator they sought the privacy of an archway and stood facing one another, holding hands.

"Chin up, old dear. It'll all be over before you know it."

"Promise you'll take care of yourself, Fred. Promise."

"Of course I promise."

Fred let go of Ethel's hand and she turned away without looking him in the eye. Waiting until she had disappeared from view around a bend in the tunnel, he walked off in the opposite direction towards the southbound platform.

A train was waiting at the platform with its doors open. Most of the passengers had already taken their seats. Running to the rear carriage Fred managed to find a vacant seat and he travelled deep in thought on the short journey to Paddington. He only had to wait a few minutes at the main railway station for the next train to Reading. Within two hours of saying goodbye to Ethel, he was back in his rooms, feeling very miserable and unsure as to whether or not he had made the right decision.

He spent the evening tidying up his rooms and packing his belongings into cardboard boxes. He then wheeled his bicycle in from the hallway and oiled the chain and pedals, not knowing how long it would be before he would ride again. When this was done, he packed a single suitcase with everything he would need for Farnborough and went to bed early, uneasy at what the future might hold.

The next morning, after eating a hurried breakfast, Fred caught a motor bus to the town centre and walked to the jewellers shop with his suitcase under his arm. It was early and the manager had to let him in by the back door.

"Good morning, Frederick. I wasn't sure you would be here at all today."

"Good morning, Mr Lewis. I thought I'd come to work early so that I could finish off what I had on my desk and leave at lunchtime. Now that they've accepted my application I have to go to Farnborough straight away. I trust this isn't too inconvenient?"

"I must say I'm not surprised. Remember what happened when young Jenkins enlisted in the army? He didn't even come back to collect his things."

"Is there anything particular you would like me to do, sir?"

"Just finish off what you can. I will arrange for one of the lads to take over whatever is left. Come and see me when you're ready to leave and I'll give you your final pay packet."

"Thank you, Mr Lewis. That is most considerate of you."

Fred walked through the hallway and into the empty workshop. He unrolled his watchmaker's tools and by the time the other employees arrived he was already hard at work, replacing the mainspring of an old fob watch. By mid morning he had cleared all of the jobs that had been allocated to him at the start of the week. With time to spare, he was reflecting on how quickly he had gone from leading an orderly life with a secure job, to enlisting in the Royal Flying Corps, when the door leading to the shop burst open. Fred's manager stepped down into the workshop and, with an air of importance, strode up to the workbench. With everyone in the room watching, he placed an envelope on the table right in front of Fred.

"I have a telegram for you, Frederick. Might it be something to do with the Army, do you think?"

Fred removed the watchmaker's eye glass and put it down on the green baize work cloth. Reaching forward he picked up the envelope.

"Thank you Mr Lewis, I expect it is."

Fred opened the envelope and took out the telegram. As soon as he saw that the Office of Origin was stamped as Tunbridge Wells he knew it was not from the Army. The message, roughly scrawled in pencil by the local Post Office clerk, was short and to the point and he smiled when he read the name of the sender.

Heartiest congratulations. I am proud of you. Starlight.

Chapter 3
A New Perspective

Acting 1ˢᵀ class air mechanic Frederick Johnstone reported for duty at Farnborough aerodrome and was provided with his uniform and kit, including a greatcoat, a jacket, two pairs of breeches with braces, puttees, a size 14 tunic, two pairs of boots size 6 ½, one cap size 7, a Webley service revolver and what he considered a rather fancy swagger stick. He was also given a knife, fork and spoon set that packed away neatly inside a wooden case and a kit bag that was to hold everything he was not wearing.

For the next eight days, Fred and the other new recruits undertook their initial army training and were taught the basic drills on the Queens Parade ground, dressed in full Royal Flying Corps uniform and carrying their swagger sticks. It was constantly drummed into them that the Corps placed great store in individual smartness and they were required to attend lectures on personal cleanliness and hygiene. During off-duty hours they were on occasion permitted to use the telephone for personal calls but they were not allowed to leave the camp.

At the completion of his basic training, Fred was ordered to report to the Aircraft Park on the other side of the airfield, where he was taught the principles of flight, basic aeroplane mechanics and the operation of magnetos and various cockpit instruments. He also received training inside a fully equipped workshop lorry which had been set up to contain exactly the same tools and equipment that would be found at any front-line squadron. Each lorry was a self-contained workshop with power for the machines and lighting provided by a petrol-driven generator. The equipment on board included lathes, drills, a tool grinder and even a small forge with an anvil. With canvas sides that could be rolled up to provide more elbow room, a single lorry[14] could enable six men to work at the same time, albeit in cramped conditions.

After a further twelve days of intensive training, Fred was ordered to pack his kit bag and board a train bound for Southampton. Upon arrival at the docks, he and hundreds of other servicemen were crammed on to a troop ship which left the quay several hours later after nightfall. The passage across the English Channel was slow and rough and it wasn't until two o'clock the next morning that the ship finally berthed at le Havre. With many of the men afflicted by sea sickness during the voyage, Fred was looking forward to setting foot on dry land and breathing fresh air. His relief was short-lived however, as everyone was ordered to remain on board until dawn. Finally, when the first rays of sunlight burst over the roofs of the town buildings, Fred and a number of other new recruits were transferred to a smaller vessel which was to take them on a journey up the river Seine.

By evening the ship reached the town of Rouen, where the troops were disembarked on to the quay before being marched under the orders of an army officer to a nearby rest camp. The next morning they were marched from the rest camp to the railway station and packed on to a troop train that was to take them to St Omer. Upon their arrival at St Omer they were ordered off the train and marched once more, this time in pouring rain, to the nearby aerodrome[15] that had been constructed on the site of the town's racecourse. Here they set up camp, erecting tents for their sleeping quarters.

St Omer was to be Fred's home for the next week, during which time he and the other men received further training and were used as a source of manual labour in various jobs around the aerodrome. The weather was cold and wet and most of the men experienced for the first time the discomfort of sleeping in a tent and waking up to find frost on the ground outside.

On the morning of the ninth day after leaving the relative peace and comfort of England, Fred was informed by the officer in command of new recruits that he was being posted to Number 6 squadron at Abeele, thirty miles east of St Omer and just across the Belgian border. As he was to travel alone rather than with a group of other recruits, Fred was given leave to choose the method of transport; a five hour train journey, a ride on a motorised tender that was taking petrol and spares to Abeele or to fly as passenger in a new aircraft being delivered to Number 5 squadron, also based at Abeele. With trepidation, he opted to take his first ever flight in an aeroplane.

Following directions given to him by the captain, Fred made his way to a nearby Bessoneau hangar where he had been told that he would find the commanding officer of the Pilots' Pool. As he approached the side of the hangar he heard the loud noise of an aircraft engine. He stood still for a moment, unsure what to do. The canvas walls of the hangar flapped violently against the metal supports as if caught in the grips of a hurricane. Shielding his face with his hands he edged his way around the corner of the building. Directly ahead, thirty feet away, was a single-engine biplane, its propeller pulsing in time with the rise and fall of the sound of the engine. Clouds of dense grey smoke emitted from the two vertical exhaust stacks and sitting in the rear cockpit was the hunched figure of a heavily clad man.

Fred had never seen a military aircraft. In fact he had never even been close to any flying machine, though on one occasion he had caught a fleeting glimpse of one as it passed over his parents' house at Basingstoke. He stood motionless, admiring the delicate lines of the aeroplane, its beauty marred only by an ungainly engine cowling and the exhaust pipes that stuck out of the top of the engine as if a design afterthought. He was about to move closer when, without warning, the sound of the engine rose to a crescendo and he was caught in a blast of mud and grass, thrown up by the spinning propeller. Stepping quickly to one side he watched two servicemen, who moments earlier had placed wooden chocks in front of the aircraft's wheels, take up position on either side of the fuselage, each man grasping hold of one of the interplane struts. Whilst they were doing this, a third man ran to the rear of the machine where he used the weight of his body to keep the tail skid from lifting off the ground.

The aircraft strained against the chocks and the combined strength of the three men until the engine was brought back to an idle and then stopped altogether. It was eerily quiet compared to the earlier crescendo of noise, the silence broken only when the man in the cockpit stood up, stepped out on to the wing and began to shout commands to the men on the ground. Transfixed, Fred watched the man turn around and place the toe of his left boot in a metal stirrup that protruded from the underside of the fuselage, before jumping to the ground in a single leap. This ungainly manoeuvre looked all the more incongruous as the man wore a long leather coat on top of his officer's uniform as well as soft leather boots that reached up to his thighs. The officer's face was almost completely hidden by a brown leather flying balaclava and covering his hands and wrists were heavy leather gauntlets. Realising how exposed the open cockpits were to the elements, Fred began to wonder if he had made the right decision in choosing to fly to Abeele.

After the officer had dismissed the ground crew, Fred waved to attract his attention. Acknowledging his wave, the man started to walk towards Fred, removing his goggles and flying helmet as he came closer. To Fred's surprise he looked no more than seventeen, though his confident demeanour belied his youthful appearance.

"You look lost, airman," the officer shouted in a lilting Irish accent. "Can I help you?"

Fred put down his kit bag and saluted.

"Yes please, if you wouldn't mind, sir."

Fred felt uncomfortable at having to address a mere youth in such a manner, but was determined to be appropriately courteous.

"Sir, I was ordered to report to the OC Pilots' Pool regarding a ride to Abeele, as I've just been posted to Number 6 squadron, sir."

"You can lighten up a bit on the 'sirs' for a start. My name is Lieutenant William John Charles Kennedy Cochran-Patrick[16] and I am the Officer Commanding the Pilots' Pool. What's your name soldier?"

"Acting 1st class air mechanic Frederick William Johnstone of the Royal Flying Corps, sir," Fred replied, unable to resist a smile.

"That's a bit of a mouthful. Tell you what, I'll call you Johnstone and you can just call me Lieutenant. That simple enough for you?"

"Yes, that would be fine, sir. Lieutenant, I mean."

Fred was beginning to wonder how long it would take for him to get used to his new life, when only weeks ago he had been a civilian and knew exactly where he stood in the social order. Now that he was in the military, the familiar class system had been supplanted by a ranking structure that he found rather bewildering. He had already noticed that many seasoned observers, who had held senior positions in the Army before being attached to the Royal Flying Corps, were now outranked by younger men; newly commissioned pilots straight out of pilot training.

"Well, now that we've cleared the air on that matter, we can plan what to do next. The first thing I'll do Johnstone is to show you around this machine, as you've probably never seen one like this before."

"I have to admit that I haven't, sir."

"Well, you'll need to get to know it like the back of your hand."

"Does Number 6 use this type of aeroplane, Lieutenant?"

"Yes it does, but mostly older versions. The newer machines they have will be mechanically identical to this one and will look very similar too."

The lieutenant paused to unbutton his leather coat, giving Fred time to look at the aeroplane more closely.

"You'll soon get to know your own aeroplane numbers, which you can see are painted on the vertical stabilizer at the tail. The only visual difference between the machines of the two squadrons currently stationed at Abeele is that yours will have an extra vertical white stripe."

"Where exactly, sir?"

The lieutenant walked to the rear of the aircraft and pointed to a blank area in front of the tail.

"Right here. Anyway, let's take a closer look at the business end."

The lieutenant led Fred around the wings to the front of the aircraft, stopping a safe distance from the propeller. At close range the machine was larger than Fred had expected and the top wing towered above him. The colour of the fuselage was a greenish brown khaki with the underside of both wings a light shade of ivory.

"This, Johnstone, is a Royal Aircraft Factory Be2c. It's the very latest of its type and can fly faster and farther than the old version. It can also carry more. With the big ninety horsepower RAF engine it has a top speed of seventy two miles per hour[17] and can stay in the air for three and a half hours."

"That sounds impressive, sir."

"If you look at it side-on you'll notice that the planes are staggered, with the lower wing positioned slightly behind the upper wing. This makes the machine very stable in the air but does obscure the pilot's downward vision."

Fred looked along the fuselage towards the rear cockpit, where the lieutenant had sat only minutes earlier, and was surprised at how restricted the view would be for the pilot, especially when the aircraft was on the ground with its nose pointing up into the sky. His thoughts were interrupted when the lieutenant tapped him on the shoulder.

"Come. I'll show you how it all works."

The lieutenant led Fred around to the rear of the wing and pointed to a hinged section in both the upper and lower planes.

"These hinged flaps are called ailerons and they're used for lateral control. Rolling if you like. This system is far better than the wing warping you'll find on older machines. If you went over to the other side of the fuselage you'd see two more in a similar position on the starboard planes. When the ailerons on one side move upwards, those on the other side automatically move downwards and vice versa, if you know what I mean. A cable runs from each aileron to a control stick mounted in the centre of the pilot's cockpit."

Fred tried to remember some of the aeronautical terms he had been taught at Farnborough.

"Aren't there also cables that connect the tail wing to the control stick to make the machine go up and down?"

"That's true, Johnstone, but the proper term is 'tail plane'. You can move the control stick forwards or backwards and to the left or right, with any combination in between. All your feet have to do is to work the rudder bar that's connected by wires to the vertical fin on the tail."

"It all sounds very complicated, Lieutenant."

"Not really. The skill in flying is being able to move your hands and feet smoothly at the same time. No sudden movements. They say that horse riders make the best pilots."

Fred ran his fingers along the surface of the wing.

"I don't think I'll ever get the chance to do either, more's the pity."

"You never can tell. You might surprise yourself one day."

"There's just so much to learn, sir."

"Don't worry, Johnstone, you'll pick it up in no time at all."

Fred looked up at the aircraft as he tried to think of a sensible question.

"Sir, what's the purpose of that wooden rack just below the rim of the observer's cockpit?"

The lieutenant walked to the aircraft and with the aid of the mounting stirrup he climbed up on to the wing. Kneeling down, he put his hand inside the wooden rack, pointing out to Fred the three semicircular holes that had been cut out of the upper outside edge at equal intervals.

"These slots are for holding spare pans of ammunition for the Lewis gun. There's a rack for three more on the other side of the fuselage."

"How many bullets can they take?"

"Forty seven rounds, the same calibre as used in the 'three oh three' rifle."

"That's not much, sir. Doesn't the Vickers hold more than that?"

"True, but it's twice as heavy as the Lewis. They're currently developing a double drum which will hold ninety seven rounds."

Still kneeling, the lieutenant reached over into the front cockpit and grabbed hold of the back of the seat. Unable to see from where he was standing, Fred scrambled up on to the wing to get a closer look.

"If you look here at the rear of the observer's cockpit, just behind the seat, you'll see a rather odd-looking metal pole arrangement. This is what we call a 'Strange'[18] mount. It's adjustable and a Lewis gun can be fastened to it and fired in almost any direction."

The lieutenant laughed and grabbed hold of the top of the mount, rotating the coupling to demonstrate its capabilities to Fred.

"That looks very close to the pilot's head, Lieutenant."

"Yes it can be a trifle painful on the ears. This particular machine isn't armed yet, so it might be difficult for you to see what I mean. Tell you what, stay where you are and I'll get a Lewis from the gun room. I'll be back in a half a mo."

The lieutenant squeezed past Fred, jumped down to the ground and walked off at a brisk pace, his unbuttoned leather coat flapping around the tops of his boots. He returned a few minutes later cradling a Lewis machine gun in his arms with a drum of ammunition bulging out of one of his coat pockets. Fred had seen pictures of Lewis guns being fired on the range but this one looked a lot smaller and was obviously lighter than those used on the ground.

"Here, take this while I climb into the cockpit."

Fred reached forward to take the gun and was relieved to find it was not as heavy as he had expected. Once again the lieutenant climbed up on to the wing and squeezed past him, this time stepping right inside the front cockpit before kneeling on the seat. Using all of his strength, Fred lifted the gun clear of the fuselage and handed it to the officer.

"See what I mean? The Lewis attaches to this arm."

"Yes I can, sir. It looks quite stable too."

The lieutenant pulled the drum of ammunition out of his coat pocket and snapped it on to the top of the gun.

"And this clips on like so."

Crouching low in the cockpit and facing the rear of the aircraft, the lieutenant knelt on the wicker seat and grasped hold of the gun handle with his right hand and the pistol grip with his left, as if firing at an imaginary foe.

"The old BE2b had no fixed guns and was easy prey to Hun scouts. These new machines can have more than one machine gun and they can be moved from one mount to another, depending upon where the observer needs to aim his fire."

Fred peered into the observer's cockpit and then out towards the front of the aircraft, a puzzled expression on his face.

"Could you fire this gun in a forward direction, Lieutenant?"

"Not unless you're really careful. The bullets would destroy the propeller. Six months ago the Huns developed an interrupter firing mechanism that enables a machine gun to fire through the propeller without hitting it. It's caused us many aircraft losses. You've may have heard of the term 'The Fokker Scourge'."

"Yes I have," Fred replied. "I've also heard of a synchronised gun, but I wasn't sure exactly what it meant."

"We're working on our own method of synchronisation, but at the moment unless you're flying a pusher machine the best way to fire directly ahead is to mount a gun on the top plane, above the arc of the propeller. Trouble is that you then have the problem of pulling the gun down in flight to reload it or to clear any jams."

The lieutenant removed the Lewis gun from the mount and handed it back to Fred, who was caught off guard by the added weight of the ammunition. The lieutenant reached over to help him.

"Wait, Johnstone, I'll get down and you can hand it back to me. You look a trifle awkward with that thing in your arms."

"Thank you, sir. Dropping it through the wing wouldn't be an auspicious start to my army career."

"That's all right. It would be difficult for anyone to dismount from an aircraft carrying a loaded Lewis."

The lieutenant squeezed past Fred and jumped to the ground without using the metal stirrup. Fred inched his way across the width of the wing as close to the fuselage as he could until he was standing right on the edge. Holding the weapon out in front of him he passed it down to the lieutenant, relieved to be rid of the responsibility. He too then jumped the short distance to the ground.

"I think that will do us for now, Johnstone. We'd better get a move on and deliver this machine to Abeele or else I'll have two majors after me."

"Rightio, sir. I appreciate the time you've given me."

"You're very welcome. Come with me and I'll find you a helmet to wear on the journey. We'll only be in the air for half an hour but you'd be surprised at how cold one can get in such a short time."

On the way back to the gun room Fred asked for news of his new squadron. The lieutenant thought for a minute before replying.

"I did hear that one of your observers put up a splendid show last week."

"Why's that, Lieutenant?"

"They were attacked by two Huns and he managed to shoot one of them down."

"That is good news, sir."

"But that's not all. Just as they were chasing off the second Hun, a shell burst nearby and put his machine into a spin."

The lieutenant paused for breath before continuing.

"You may not know it, but the FE2b[19] has an open nacelle in front of the engine that holds two cockpits. The observer sits right in the nose with no protection from the elements. He has to stand up in the slipstream if he wants to fire to the rear."

"That sounds dangerous, sir."

"It most certainly is. Well, having looked behind he could tell his pilot was dead, hit in the head by a piece of the shell. So he stood up and climbed up over the rear gun, sat on the dead pilot's lap and brought the machine safely back to earth."

"How did news of this get back to the squadron?"

"Being behind enemy lines he was captured of course, but the German he'd forced down came up to shake his hand and later arranged for his pilot to be given a decent burial. One of our agents in Hunland reported in yesterday and gave us the full account."

"Well, it's nice to know that the enemy can be honourable, sir. In England the newspapers always report at how barbaric the Germans are."

"You should see what they write about us in the German newspapers!"

Having returned the machine gun to the armoury, they walked across to the stores where the lieutenant signed an authority for Fred to be issued with a flying helmet. The clerk disappeared down one of the aisles and returned a few minutes later carrying a large flat cardboard box. Placing it on the counter he removed the lid.

"These are what the observers generally choose sir. They're a bit longer around the neck. Better for the draughts."

The lieutenant selected a brown leather helmet from the box and passed it to Fred.

"Try this one on for size. You'll find it will feel strange at first but the leather is soft. It will eventually be as comfortable as wearing a pair of kid gloves."

Fred removed his cap and pushed it inside one of his coat pockets. He pulled the balaclava over his head, noticing at once that it was longer at the front and that it fitted loosely around his neck. Despite being brand new the helmet felt soft, as it was lined with chamois leather.

"How can I make this tighter, sir? It won't fit under my collar."

"Here, let me fasten it for you. First you have to tighten the small strap above each eye. That better? Next you adjust the main strap to make the whole thing snug, really important when your head's sticking out in the slipstream."

"Is that the only strap?"

"Yes. When you take it off you'll see that the cord running across your forehead on the inside of the helmet is part of the same cord that wraps around the front of your neck. It goes through these leather loops and around to the back of your head. There, I've fixed the leather buckle. Is that too tight for you?"

"It does feel a bit strange, sir, but I'm sure I'll get used to it."

"Don't worry, the leather will stretch and I promise you'll soon be thankful you're wearing it. Keep it with you wherever you go as you never know when it might come in handy."

"Thanks, Lieutenant. I'll make sure I don't lose it."

Having thanked the clerk they left the stores and walked back to the aircraft.

"We're about ready to go, I think. Put your gloves back on and climb up into the front cockpit. There should be enough room for your kit bag down by your feet as we're not carrying any wireless equipment or guns on this flight."

Once again, Fred climbed up on to the wing. The lieutenant handed him his kit bag and he stowed it beneath the instrument panel in the observer's cockpit. He then stepped over the side into the cockpit, lowering himself on to the woven wicker chair whilst taking great care not to touch anything he did not recognise. Having made himself comfortable on the cushioned chair he looked ahead of the aircraft through the semicircular windscreen. He was amazed at how little he could see. The engine cowling, exhaust pipes and propeller blades obstructed his forward vision and on both sides most of the view was taken up by the wings, inter-plane struts and bracing wires. Intrigued, he looked all around and realised that the best view from the cockpit was straight ahead in front of the lower wing, as the overhead view was almost completely obstructed by the upper wing.

"And this is where the observer sits!"

Fred turned around in his seat and knelt down, positioning himself as if he was firing at an enemy attacking from behind and below. Apart from the raised screen in front of the pilot's cockpit and the tail section of the aircraft which partially obstructed his view, Fred could see that there was still an effective arc of fire around the rear of the aircraft. With small rectangular sections cut out of the trailing edges of both the upper and lower wings close to the fuselage, he realised that a gunner would also be able to fire at a target directly above or below the aircraft, provided he was careful.

The lieutenant brought Fred out of his reverie.

"All right, Johnstone, make yourself at home and we'll be on our way."

Fred looked up and saw that the lieutenant had already taken up his position in the rear cockpit and was in the act of putting on his goggles and gloves.

"I'm as ready as I'll ever be, sir. I just have to fasten my belt."

"As this will be your first time in the air, I'll make a bit of a detour and show you the front. There's not a lot happening on the ground at the moment so we shouldn't get into any trouble. To be on the safe side though, I'll stay on our side of the lines."

Fred nodded, turned around in the cockpit and sat back down on the chair. He reached behind him, grabbed hold of both ends of the safety belt and fastened the buckle tightly around his hips.

The lieutenant stood up in the rear cockpit and shouted to attract the attention of the ground crew who were working on another biplane just inside the doors of the hangar. Upon hearing his command they stopped what they were doing and ran outside. One man moved to the leading tip of the starboard wing whilst the other approached the front of the aircraft and stood immediately in front of the four-bladed propeller. Leaning out of the cockpit, the lieutenant waited for the mechanic in charge to raise his arm and give the order.

"Switch off!" the mechanic shouted.

The lieutenant checked that the controlling switch on the instrument panel was down in the 'off' position.

"Switch off!" he shouted back.

The mechanic standing in front of the propeller reached forward with both hands raised above his head and grasped the upper surface of the rightmost blade. Slowly he pulled the propeller down before letting go of it and stepping back. He repeated this motion until he felt the resistance of the compression stroke. Standing clear of the propeller, he stood motionless with his arm raised high in the air before shouting out the next instruction to the pilot.

"Contact!"

The lieutenant flicked the master switch to the 'on' position.

"Contact!" he shouted back.

The mechanic stepped forward and once again grabbed hold of the propeller blade. This time he pulled it down smartly, stepping back quickly as the propeller started to spin and the warm engine burst into life. The aeroplane flexed from the torque generated by the spinning propeller and the whole of the fuselage began to vibrate.

The lieutenant reduced the throttle control until the engine was idling smoothly and the mechanic who had spun the propeller walked around to the leading tip of the port wing. Simultaneously the two mechanics bent down and picked up the ropes that were attached to the wheel chocks. When the lieutenant raised his right arm above his head and swung it from side to side, they pulled back on the ropes and dragged the chocks away from the wheels. With the engine idling, the lieutenant waited whilst the mechanic in charge looked all around to see if there were any other machines operating in the area. After a few moments the mechanic turned to face him and saluted, indicating that the way ahead was clear. The lieutenant waved his right arm above his head as a signal that both men should stand clear of the aircraft. After they had retreated with the chocks to the safety of the hangar, he opened up the throttle.

Once again the blast from the huge propeller sent a spray of debris out past the aircraft and down the side of the hangar. As the machine inched forward through the mud, the lieutenant gave his men a final wave before steering towards firmer ground. With no other aircraft in the landing area he wasted no time in taxiing across to the eastern edge of the airfield, adjacent to the main road and opposite the Aircraft Park. With a quick burst of power and full right rudder, he spun the machine around on the muddy gravel so that it was pointing due west. Keeping a constant lookout for other aircraft, he throttled back and checked the instruments on the panel in front of him. When he was satisfied that all was in order he raised his head above the level of the Triplex windscreen and shouted to Fred who was crouched low in the seat in front of him.

"Off we go, Johnstone. Hold on tight!"

The lieutenant opened the throttle half way and the aircraft started to move, slowly gathering momentum as the narrow tyres rolled through the soft surface of the edge of the aerodrome on to the firmer grass of the main airfield. Steering the machine gently from side to side to make sure that the way ahead was clear, he looked back at the aerodrome buildings to confirm that the windsock was still registering a light westerly wind. Satisfied, he opened the throttle fully and the aircraft accelerated swiftly, reaching flying speed in a matter of seconds. The tail lifted immediately without him having to push forward on the controls, enabling him to see ahead through the blur of the propeller blades. With only the wheels in contact with the ground he eased back on the control stick at the same time as applying left rudder. With a single gentle bounce, the aeroplane became airborne and rose effortlessly into the sky.

Sitting in the front cockpit, Fred felt exhilarated by what had just taken place. Many times he had imagined what it would be like to fly in an aeroplane, but what he was now experiencing was beyond his wildest dreams. The noise of the engine was deafening and the ground dropped away quickly as he peered out over the side of the leather-rimmed cockpit, tears welling up in his eyes from the force of the cold slipstream. Immediately below he could see a curved section of the old St Omer racecourse, though most of the track had long since been obliterated by the wheel marks of countless aircraft. To his right, on a hill that stood out from the surrounding countryside, he watched as the buildings of the ancient town of St Omer came into view. He turned around in his seat and waved enthusiastically to the pilot, but as he could not see the lieutenant's face beneath the goggles and helmet he turned around to face the front again.

When they had reached a height of about four hundred feet, the right wing dropped as the aircraft made a gentle turn to the right, flying over the roofs of the town buildings before passing to one side of the aerodrome. Fred was amazed at the number of aircraft parked around the airfield. Without goggles, the rushing air made it difficult for him to see clearly, but he was nevertheless able to count more than twenty. And this number didn't include those that had been put away inside the storage sheds. Several more aircraft were in the process of taking off or landing. The crowdedness of the scene below reminded him of his visit to London, when he had looked down at Piccadilly Circus from the top of a motor bus.

Fred watched the instruments in front of him with interest, though he was not familiar with all of them. When the compass indicated that they were heading due east, the wings of the aeroplane became level, but he could sense by the position of the horizon that they were still climbing. Crossing over the river Aa and the outlying buildings of St Omer, the aircraft passed through scattered cloud at two thousand feet. It was a strange experience to fly through the middle of a cloud, though he had often dreamt of doing so as a child. There was a sudden drop in temperature and the air became damp until the machine emerged from the clouds, back into clear air. The sky above was grey but Fred was unable to gauge the height of the clouds.

Ten minutes after leaving the aerodrome they had reached an altitude of four thousand feet and had already penetrated deep into the heart of the French countryside. Looking to his left Fred could see the line of the English Channel far away in the distance and he tried to guess where the ports of Calais and Dunkirk might be. He turned his gaze to the fields below, a patchwork all shades of green and brown. Directly ahead in the distance was a large forest, in the middle of which were two lakes and he noticed with interest that the shape of the wood bore a distinct resemblance to the outline of England and Wales.

Fred gradually became accustomed to the sensation of flying and, cold though he was, he was enjoying the experience. He had found that the most comfortable position was to sit leaning forward with his head below the level of the windscreen. With the engine and main petrol tank directly in front of him, he guessed that he was probably benefiting from the heat generated by the engine as well as the warm air radiated by the exhaust pipes.

After a while the aircraft stopped climbing and its speed over the ground increased for a few moments until the revolutions of the engine dropped back. Fred looked up at the instrument panel and noticed that the gauge indicating the air speed was registering a little over seventy miles per hour, the same cruising speed that the lieutenant had mentioned when he was shown around the aircraft.

With nothing else to do, Fred continued to study the surrounding countryside and for almost ten minutes the aircraft flew over land as flat as it was featureless. Certainly there were a few small villages with roads and railways linking them, but to Fred they all looked very similar and merged quickly into the background as the aircraft sped across the sky.

He was beginning to get bored with the scenery when he happened to look directly ahead through the blur of the spinning propeller. They were approaching a long and irregular shaped hill that was covered with trees, with a narrow winding road cutting a path through the trees along the ridge of the hill. The road widened at the crest of the hill with closely packed buildings lining both sides of what was obviously a busy village thoroughfare. At the foot of the hill, Fred could see another road, wider and straighter than the first. Straddling the village on either side, some miles apart, were two railway lines, both of them swinging in a southerly direction towards a large township.

"Now this is more interesting," Fred said out loud.

Upon impulse he searched around the inside of the cockpit. If the aeroplane had been flown out from England with an observer on board, it was just possible that a route map might have been left behind. At first he could not find anything as the map pocket was empty, but when he slid his hand beneath the seat cushion he touched something that felt like stiff cloth. Leaning forward so that he could pull the object out from beneath him, he discovered that it was indeed a map. He unfolded it carefully inside the cockpit, making sure that he kept it well out of the slipstream lest it be torn from his grasp. Examining the map, he saw that it covered an area from the south of England to the north coast of Belgium. Two straight lines had been drawn across the map in pencil, one between the towns of Farnborough and Dover and the other crossing the Channel from Dover to St Omer.

Fred placed his forefinger over St Omer aerodrome and moved it slowly across the map in the direction in which they had been flying, east north east towards Ypres. Looking carefully at the contour lines on the map, he managed to identify the nearby hill. On the map, the large town to the south of the hill, clearly visible on the right hand side of the aircraft, bore the name of Hazebrouck. He also noticed that the village at the crossroads on top of the hill was marked as Cassel and that the road leading east from Cassel passed through a town called Steenvoorde.

With the hill slowly disappearing into the distance, the aircraft flew on without changing course. As the minutes passed, Fred became more adept at interpreting the land features displayed on the map. He tried to pinpoint Abeele, even though he knew it was but a small village. Tracing a line with his forefinger, using a midpoint between the villages of Steenvoorde and Godewaersvelde, he eventually found the word Abeele printed in small letters. The township was eight miles east of the hill, according to the map. He looked out of the aircraft, endeavouring to see what lay ahead. Though he could see no evidence of the village itself, he was able to detect the shape of a larger town slightly beyond where he had first looked and quickly realised that this must be the railhead town of Poperinghe.

By the time the aircraft was abeam of Steenvoorde, Fred was able to identify the village of Abeele as well as the buildings of Poperinghe. With the city of Ypres only eleven miles further to the east it suddenly dawned on him how close his new home would be to the main battle front. He remembered being told at St Omer that the aerodrome at Abeele had been bombed in recent weeks and at the time he had found it hard to imagine the enemy reaching this far into allied territory. Now that he had experienced the speed at which an aeroplane could fly, he realised that a distance a troop of infantry would take a whole day to march, or a steam train hours to travel, could be flown in just a matter of minutes.

Deep in thought, he felt the wings of the aircraft dip, first to the left and then to the right. The rolling motion made him queasy. He turned around in his seat and saw the lieutenant gesticulating towards the ground. Looking down over the left hand side of the aircraft Fred assumed that they were flying directly over the aerodrome, one mile west of the village of Abeele. From what he could tell at first glance, the airfield appeared to occupy an area of land between a small farm to the north and a main road to the south, the land bisected by a smaller road that ran past the farm and joined the main road at a T junction. With no clearly defined perimeter fences to mark the airfield's boundaries, Fred realised that if the lieutenant had not attracted his attention, he probably would not have spotted the aerodrome at all.

The small farm was clearly visible, as was a larger farm to the south of the aerodrome on the other side of the main road. To Fred, from the height at which they were flying, each building looked the size of a Tate's sugar cube. Mid way between the farm and the main road were two ponds, one on each side of the access road. The larger of the ponds was at the centre of a field on the eastern side of the airfield. The second pond was much smaller than the first and bordered the western side of the access road.

Now that he knew where to look, Fred was able to count ten smoothly shaped objects. Each was the size of a farm building but greyish green in colour, making them hard to distinguish from the surrounding fields. Upon closer examination he noticed that some were shaped like darning mushrooms whilst others resembled domes. It was only when he spotted several smaller objects nearby, each one the shape of a cross, that he realised he was looking at aeroplane storage sheds and aircraft that had been left out in the open. Shifting his gaze back to the eastern side of the airfield, he counted more than a dozen white circular dots as well as many small rectangular shapes. They were all in a small area bounded by the large pond and a stone wall, the only wall on the entire airfield.

"*Those round dots must be bell tents. I wonder if I'll be sleeping in one of those tonight.*"

Fred turned around and waved excitedly to the lieutenant, who waved back and pointed east towards Ypres. As the aircraft had not lost any height, Fred hoped that the flight was not yet over and that he was in for a closer look at the infamous Western Front. Though he could not be certain, he felt fairly confident that they were high enough to be beyond the range of machine gun fire, just in case the soldiers on the ground mistook them for an enemy aircraft. To Fred in his inexperience, one biplane looked very much like any other.

Still looking at the scene below, he became aware of movement and saw what he thought to be a long writhing shadow on the road between the aerodrome and the village. He stared for a few moments before realising that the shadow was a line of marching soldiers and he wondered if the men would be continuing on to Ypres or would be stopping off at Poperinghe for refreshment.

As the aircraft approached Ypres, Fred was able to get a good view of the besieged city. The photographs he had seen in the British newspapers had not prepared him for the scene of total devastation that was presented below. Almost the whole of the city centre had been obliterated by shelling, the roads were non existent and the drainage system completely destroyed.

The aeroplane banked to the left as they flew over the city. Fred recognised the horseshoe shaped moat around the ancient ramparts, the road that ran over the low brick bridge and the famous Lille Gate, the southern entrance to Ypres. Most of the buildings immediately beyond the gate had been reduced to rubble. Within seconds they were flying directly over the main square and the almost unrecognizable ruins of the best known building in Ypres, Cloth Hall.[20]

The aircraft banked again, swinging around to the east and recrossing the moat over the top of what remained of the Menin Gate. Looking down at the acres of destruction, Fred marvelled at how the allied forces had managed to retain hold of the city and he at once understood the desperation of the situation.

There was something at the back of his mind that eluded him. Something to do with the landscape and its colours. Or was it the lack of colour? Looking back over his shoulder to where they had flown only moments before, the realisation of what it was struck him like a blow to the head. The land that was multi coloured, contoured and covered with trees and dwellings to the west of Ypres changed totally on the other side of the city. To the east, the countryside had been churned to a monotonously lumpy plain, the land was a consistent dark brown in colour and all that remained of the forests and buildings was the occasional clump of tree stumps and a few seemingly indiscriminate piles of bricks. Fred also noticed that from the west, right up to the allied trenches, there was a constant movement of troops and that all of the roads were packed solid with carts and lorries. As soon as he looked over towards No-Mans-Land and into enemy territory he could see no evidence of the German military, nor any sign of its vehicles. From a height of four thousand feet the wasteland stretched ahead into the distance as far as the eye could see.

Looking back once more at the British lines, Fred began to notice other things. Marks on the ground that looked like animal tracks he realised were in fact trenches, the hundreds of brown ant-like creatures swarming around the trenches or clustered around large objects were in reality soldiers and the larger objects were army vehicles or gun emplacements.

Fred was suddenly pressed against the side of the fuselage as the aeroplane banked again, this time moving in repeated wide circles half a mile to the south of what appeared to be an allied artillery position.

His gaze was drawn to the scene below with the same fascination as an unwitting witness to an accident, watching as a group of men milled around one of the four large guns. A puff of smoke billowed from the gun's barrel but Fred waited for the sound to reach him before turning in his seat to look in the direction the gun was aimed. With difficulty, his view altering from second to second as the aircraft changed in its heading, he tried to keep the target area in sight. After half a minute, an explosion erupted on the ground several miles away. Fred caught a glimpse of a tiny aircraft, flying towards the battery from the area of the explosion. Keeping the aircraft in sight, he watched as it approached, eventually passing immediately beneath him, before turning around and flying back towards the target.

Fred recognised the aircraft as the same type as the one he was riding in. He guessed that it was on a Registration sortie, communicating by wireless with the battery and directing the aim and range of the guns each time a shell was fired. When the receding aeroplane had passed over into enemy territory, Fred continued to watch as puffs of brown smoke suddenly appeared in the sky, enveloping the aircraft like a swarm of bees as it tried desperately to evade them. Some of the anti-aircraft shells exploded so close to the aircraft that Fred was amazed that it was not damaged. The machine held its course, continuing in a straight line until a second large explosion occurred on the ground, a little to the left of the first one. Witnessing this act of army cooperation from a distance, Fred began to appreciate the meaning of the motto for Number 6 squadron, 'Oculi Exercitus', or 'The Eyes of the Army', and he was filled with a sense of pride at the prospect of joining the squadron.

The aeroplane he had been watching must have successfully ranged the gun on to the enemy target as the three other guns of the battery below opened fire simultaneously. Fred counted out the seconds and watched the shells explode on the ground. Before he could tell if they had been successful, he fell back into the centre of the cockpit as the wings levelled out and he lost sight of the target area altogether.

Leaving the battery behind, the aircraft flew back over the southern outskirts of Ypres before heading west towards Abeele. After a few minutes they were over a large lake, with the town of Poperinghe plainly in view in the distance. Fred guessed that the lieutenant had reduced power when the aircraft slowed suddenly as if invisible brakes had been applied. The whistling of the wind through the bracing wires decreased for a moment until the nose of the machine was lowered and the airspeed increased once more. Looking through the spinning propeller, Fred guessed that they were heading straight for Abeele and that it would only be a matter of minutes before they would be landing at the aerodrome.

Now that they were getting closer to the ground, Fred was able to see the countryside in greater detail and could identify the types of vehicles that were being driven on the roads. What had appeared to be a quiet scene from four thousand feet presented a totally different picture at half that height. Lorries were travelling in both directions on the road that linked Abeele with Poperinghe and he could see lines of soldiers marching along by the side of the road.

As the aeroplane commenced its final approach to the aerodrome it passed to the left of the village of Abeele. Fred could see dozens of vehicles parked nose to tail in the small road that separated one side of the airfield from the other. He could also easily distinguish between the different types of aircraft shelters, tents and huts. Directly ahead, there were several aircraft manoeuvring on the ground and he wondered how they all came and went without mishap.

The engine roared briefly as they flew over the main road, the machine barely clearing the trees that lined the avenue. From the flattened shape of the top branches, Fred guessed that the trees had been lopped to give the pilots more of a safety margin when coming in to land. With the engine throttled back to an idle, the aeroplane descended in a steep glide. Just when Fred thought that they would hit the ground at speed, he felt the nose rise as the aeroplane continued in its glide, losing speed and dropping slowly as it went.

"*Just like a duck landing on a pond.*"

With the nose of the aircraft pointing above the skyline and blocking his view, Fred could no longer see anything straight ahead. He held his breath with his eyes closed, possessed with an inexplicable desire to hold his hands over his ears. Instead of the sound of splitting timber and tearing fabric, he felt only a soft pressure on his seat as the aircraft landed gently, the wheels and tail skid touching the ground simultaneously.

As soon as the aircraft had slowed to little more than walking speed, he heard the engine roar back into life. The machine spun around in a tight circle before bouncing over the grassy airfield towards one of the larger of the canvas aircraft sheds. As they got closer, Fred could see that fastened over the doors of the hangar was a roughly painted sign upon which was written 'ALL VISITING PILOTS REPORT TO THE OFFICE UPON ARRIVAL'.

The aircraft's engine stopped and all was quiet. Fred sat back in the observer's chair, collecting his thoughts.

"So how was your first flight?"

The lieutenant had already taken off his helmet and goggles and was standing on the wing, unbuttoning his leather coat.

"Absolutely topping!" Fred exclaimed, immediately annoyed with himself at his choice of words. "It's hard to believe that we're only a few minutes from the front and yet we're perfectly safe here."

"I wouldn't be too sure about that. This aerodrome was bombed a few days ago. If you look over there by the hedge, you'll see what's left of the craters."

"Was anyone killed?"

"Only a couple of cows that had wandered on to the aerodrome, but I did hear that a farm labourer was slightly injured."

Fred stood up in the cockpit and looked to where the lieutenant was pointing. Just in front of the perimeter hedge he could see three holes in the ground, roughly circular in shape and ten yards apart. Earth was scattered all around. Close to a hole that had already been partly filled, three men dressed in Royal Flying Corps uniform were shovelling gravel out of the back of an open tender.

Pulling his kit bag out from under the instrument panel, Fred passed it over the side to the lieutenant, who threw it to the ground before jumping down. Fred climbed down after him and took off the balaclava helmet, replacing it with the RFC cap that he had earlier put in his coat pocket.

"Welcome to Abeele, Johnstone! I'll say goodbye now as I have to report to the office and you need to report to your major."

"Do you know where I'd find him, sir?"

"The major's hut is easy to find. Just walk back along the direction in which we landed, cross the road and go past the aircraft shelters towards the bell tents. Follow the wall and you'll see the officers' huts. The CO's mansion is the hut closest to the tents and the big pond. You can't miss it. And if you stumble into the latrines early on, you've gone the wrong way!"

"Thanks for everything, Lieutenant. I hope you get back to St Omer safely."

With a final salute, Fred slung the heavy kit bag over his shoulder, turned around and walked away from the aircraft towards the encampment.

Chapter 4

Settling In

THE LIVING QUARTERS resembled a tent city, with bell tents[21] and thatched huts erected by the side of an old wall that ran from the aircraft shelters to the hedge that represented the eastern perimeter of the airfield. Remembering the directions he had been given, Fred walked along the well-trodden gravel path that ran past the officers' huts until he reached a wooden hut. It was the largest cabin in the compound and one that was close to the pond. He stepped up on to the verandah, took a deep breath and knocked on the door.

"Come," he heard a man call out.

Fred opened the door and stepped inside what appeared to be a small anteroom. Directly ahead of him was a closed door that led to what he assumed would be the major's office and behind the desk to the left of the door sat an officer. By the three pips on the man's jacket, Fred knew that he was a captain. Assuming that he was in the presence of the squadron adjutant, he put down his kit bag, stood to attention and saluted.

"Air mechanic Frederick Johnstone reporting for duty, sir."

"At ease, Johnstone," the adjutant replied. "We weren't expecting you until the petrol delivery later this afternoon. I take it you came by aeroplane?"

"Yes, sir. Lieutenant Cochran-Patrick kindly let me take the observer's seat in a machine he was bringing here."

"You did well to get your introduction to flying from that young officer. He's one of the finest we have in the Corps."

The adjutant took out a manila folder from the top drawer of his desk, opened it and removed a handwritten report.

"It says here in your references that you're an accomplished piano player and a dab hand at repairing watches. Is that correct?"

"It's not for me to say, sir, but I completed my watchmaker's apprenticeship last year and I've been playing the piano since I was six years old. I can play most music by ear and can sight read any sheet music."

"That's good enough for me, Johnstone. We have church services every Sunday morning and the major would like you to volunteer to play the piano for us. The standard of singing has been pretty woeful over the past few weeks since we lost our only decent piano player."

"That would make it difficult, sir."

"We don't have a piano ourselves, but we use Number 5's whenever we have a combined 'C of E' service."

Fred thought what a strange beginning this was to his life in the Corps.

"I'd be delighted to help out, sir."

"Splendid, that's a good chap. Before we go any further, I'd better get you organised with a bed. We're a bit tight on space at the moment with two squadrons on the aerodrome, so you'll be billeted out in the village with some of the other men. We're planning to build additional quarters but I'm afraid it'll be some time before they're finished."

"I don't mind that, sir."

The adjutant reached over towards a brown Bakelite telephone that was mounted on a wooden shelf under the window sill. He picked up the receiver, indicating to Fred that he should remain where he was.

"Put me through to the orderly room, would you?"

Fred gazed out of the window towards the nearby pond, surprised that he could hear the croaking of frogs through the open doorway.

"Hello, Sergeant. The new wireless mechanic has arrived. He's with me in the major's office. Would you show him around the aerodrome and then take him to his billet in the village? I have all the details you need right here."

The adjutant replaced the receiver and took out a pad of billet requisition forms from one of the drawers. In pencil he scribbled Fred's details on the top form before adding his signature and tearing the original from the book.

"The major's out at the moment but he'll send for you tomorrow once you've settled in. In the meantime I'll have the sergeant introduce you to the other wireless boys."

"Thank you, sir."

"You'll find our workshop lorries are exactly like those you trained in back at Farnborough, so things won't be too different for you. Your first priority is to get to know our wireless sets and how we use them in the air. Have you learnt Morse?

"We didn't spend long on it, sir. I can send messages all right but I still find it difficult to decipher them. They tell me it's only a matter of practice though."

"Quite so, quite so. Wireless is a whole new world for us and there aren't many experts, so we'll have you working with one of our most experienced mechanics. Apart from Sergeant Trotter, who will supervise you on a day to day basis, you'll report to the equipment officer, Lieutenant Mason."

"What is the lieutenant's role, sir?"

"He's in charge of the broader issues like the ordering of spare parts and liaising with the batteries. Do you have any other questions?"

"Who should I see about being issued with a pay book, sir?"

Before the adjutant could reply, they were interrupted by the sound of heavy footsteps on the verandah. Fred turned around just as a burly man in sergeant's uniform appeared in the doorway. The sergeant stood stiffly to attention and saluted.

"You wanted to see me, sir?"

"At ease, Sergeant," the adjutant replied, getting up from the desk and gesturing towards Fred. "This is acting 1st class air mechanic Johnstone. He's straight out of training so won't know anything about the way we operate here. Show him around would you and introduce him to the other wireless chaps."

The adjutant handed the sergeant the signed requisition form.

"This is the address where Johnstone is to be billeted. There's no more room in the farm up the road, so he'll have to sleep in the village for now. Take him there after you've finished showing him around."

"Yes, sir."

"You don't need to introduce him to everyone right now as he'll be playing at the church service tomorrow. They'll all get a chance to meet him then."

"Yes, sir."

The adjutant turned to Fred.

"I hope for your sake you really can play the piano or you may be in for a rough time of it. We've a good bunch of lads here but they don't suffer fools gladly."

"I'm sure I'll manage, sir," Fred replied, sounding more confident than he felt.

"All right, you can go. Johnstone, I trust you'll work hard and become an asset to the squadron. Number 6 has a lot to be proud of. We're one of the original squadrons and one of only a few to be awarded a Victoria Cross."

Dismissed by the adjutant, the two men left the office. Once outside, Fred waited for the sergeant to speak.

"My name's Sergeant Trotter and it's my job to look after you and the other wireless boys."

"Yes, Sergeant. The adjutant told me that."

"Don't worry about bringing your kit bag with you. It'll be safe enough where it is. You can pick it up later when we go into Abeele."

"That's a relief, Sergeant," Fred replied. "I've been carrying it around with me for ten days. I'll be glad when I can unpack my stuff and settle in properly."

"Well it's no hotel if that's what you're expecting. You already saw the officers' huts on your way in. They only have two to a cabin so they're all right. Each flight has its own officers' mess as well."

"What about the likes of us, sarg?"

"The NCOs and the rest of the men have to make do with a dormitory up the road at the farm or one of the bell tents on the airfield. With eighteen men to a tent it's an acquired taste I can tell you."

The smile on Sergeant Trotter's face made Fred feel uneasy, but he said nothing as the sergeant led the way back along the path towards the first of the aeroplane shelters.

"It's all a bit higgledy-piggledy at the moment. We only have canvas shelters and not enough of them to store all of the machines. Next year if we're still here we should be getting some proper hangars with corrugated iron roofs."

"How big will they be?

"Big. Each one will hold four aircraft. We'll be able to keep our machines under cover and work on them in comfort. Being out in all weathers makes the machines a lot less reliable, you know."

They passed close to a biplane that was parked next to one of the shelters. With chocks wedged in front of the wheels and a two-wheeled trolley positioned under its tail so that the wings were parallel to the ground, the machine was held fast by a multitude of ropes and pegs.

"Reminds me of bit of Gulliver's Travels," Fred joked. "Is that because you get strong winds here, sarg?"

"That's right. If we don't keep the machines tied down when we're not using them, a sudden gust could easily turn one over on its back."

"I can see why you want more sheds."

"Come over here and have a look," Sergeant Trotter interrupted, leaving the path and walking up to the aircraft. "This is a Bristol Scout. We call it the Bullet. You can see it has a rotary engine and room for only a pilot."

"How many scouts does the squadron have?"

"Three at the moment, but this one's going back to St Omer. We already have its replacement. The other one's an old Martinsyde S1."

"What are they used for?"

"To chase the Huns away from our reconnaissance machines. Mind you, the Bullet's a lot faster than the S1. It can reach one hundred miles an hour in level flight."

"That's thirty miles an hour faster than the machine I flew in this morning!" Fred exclaimed. "And I thought that was fast."

"That's why scouts are so useful. Come over here and see what the old girl's made of."

Fred walked up to the aircraft and felt the fabric that covered the surface of the lower wing.

"It doesn't look very strong, sarg."

"This is one of the problems we're up against. Doping shrinks the fabric and makes it nice and taut over the wooden framework. It also makes it more or less waterproof. But when a machine's left out in the rain for a long time the fabric loses its strength and lets in the water."

"Couldn't you cover them up with tarpaulins when they're on the ground?"

"Too hard. Besides, it would make them even more likely to get blown over. In the early days we had a shed for every machine but nowadays half of the aircraft have to stay out in the open. Look here at the difference between the original fabric and the repaired sections."

Fred examined the fuselage and noticed that the older fabric looked frail and porous when compared with the patches of new material.

"What happens if the rain gets in?"

"We inspect the wings daily. If they're waterlogged we have to open them up, drain out the water and patch them up again before the machine can be flown. You can imagine how long that takes."

Sergeant Trotter reached up and patted the side of the cockpit with obvious affection.

"This was Captain Hawker's old machine. He won the Victoria Cross in it a few months ago. See the Lewis gun fastened to the side, sticking out at a funny angle? That was his idea. We're going to take it off and mount it in the same position on the new scout."

"So he was the pilot who won the VC. Is Captain Hawker[22] still with the squadron, sarg?"

"Not any more. He was posted back to Blighty two months ago. Rumour has it he'll be back in the New Year with his own squadron."

"Is there a lot of competition between the squadrons?"

"I suppose so, me lad, but it's only a bit of friendly rivalry. You any good at football?"

"I'm afraid not, sarg. Not one of my stronger points."

"That's a pity. We're always looking for good players. The major's set his heart on winning the championship this year."

Fred tried to change the subject.

"Has the squadron lost many men?"

"We've been fortunate since we came here last April. Only lost four flyers. Having the scouts has helped and we've also got four of the new

FE2b fighters. Not quite as fast as the Bullet 'cos they're two seaters, but still very effective nonetheless."

"Why's that?"

"Listen son, I can't stand around nattering all day. We'd better try and find some of the wireless boys. They can answer all of your questions."

Sergeant Trotter led Fred to a nearby aircraft shed and pulled back the canvas awning. At the rear of the hangar Fred could see a two seater BE2c biplane, similar to the one in which he had flown to Abeele. By the number of spare parts strewn about on the ground, it was evident that repairs were being carried out, though no-one was in sight. Outside on the grass to one side of the hangar, a Crossley motor lorry was parked. Its rear compartment was enclosed in tarpaulin but the front cabin was open to the elements. Fred could hear the sound of a spinning grindstone and though he could see nothing as the canvas flap at the back had been rolled down and fastened, a ladder had been placed against the rear of the platform.

Sergeant Trotter walked up to the driver's compartment and squeezed the bulb of the horn twice. The noise echoed across the airfield.

"Are you there, Jock you old bastard?"

The noise of the grinding stopped immediately. A few moments later, the canvas flap at the back of the truck was drawn aside, revealing the face and upper torso of a slightly overweight man in his mid twenties. Squeezing through the gap, the man jumped to the ground, gasping in pain as he landed awkwardly. He struggled to regain his balance.

"Hello, sarg. Is this the new bloke?"

The man was short in stature and his uniform looked as if it had been slept in.

"Yes, Jock, this is acting 1st class mechanic Frederick Johnstone and he'll be working with you until he finds his feet. If you know what I mean."

"Very funny, sarg."

Fred reached out and shook Jock's hand.

"Nice to meet you, Frederick. I'm Allan Cardno, but everyone calls me Jock."

Recognising the two-bladed propeller badge on Jock's shoulder, Fred knew that Jock's rank was also that of 1st class air mechanic.

"Call me Fred, would you? Only my parents call me Frederick."

"Right you are, Fred, Fred it is," Jock replied with a grin.

"Why are you called Jock when you don't have a Scottish accent?"

"Long story. I'll tell you about it one day when we're swinging the lead."

Sergeant Trotter placed a hand on Jock's shoulder.

"Listen, Jock, I've got things to do and I'm supposed to be taking Johnstone to his billet in Abeele. Clear a space for him this afternoon would you?"

"Will do, sarg."

"I've not heard anything yet about any 'ops for tomorrow so you should be able to start teaching him the mysteries of wireless. Take him to meet the men of the other trades too as he probably knows very little about what they do?"

"Rightio. Lieutenant Mason's up at the battery checking the new radio frequencies but he'll be back by nightfall. I'll tell him Fred will be here in the morning."

Fred was keen to find out more about his future duties.

"What should I expect tomorrow, Jock?" he asked.

"I'll probably start by showing you the different wireless sets we've been using. You'll find the biggest problem is keeping up with technology. Only a year ago the aircraft transmitters weighed more than one hundred pounds and took the whole of the observer's cockpit. Nowadays they're a lot lighter, small enough to mount next to either the pilot or observer."

"Who transmits the messages now?"

"Could be either. All our new observers have been trained in the use of Morse code and wireless, so you'll be working with both pilots and observers."

"That's fine by me."

"Anyway, I can tell you all about it tomorrow. Listen, Fred, I know you've only just arrived but a few of us are going into Pops tonight to see a show called The Fancies. Would you like to come along?"

"I think I've had enough for one day thanks, Jock. But I'd certainly like to join you another time."

"What about you, sarg? Can I interest you in two French girls called 'Lanoline and Vaseline'? I've heard it's a really funny show. The girls don't look bad either, even though they can't speak the King's English."

"They'd have to be better than the men of 6th Division," Sergeant Trotter replied with a grimace. "I could only stand ten minutes of their last performance."

"I know what you mean. We're leaving here at six thirty if you want to join us."

"Don't wait for me, but I'll make it if I can. I should be off duty by then, once I've sorted out young Johnstone, that is."

Fred could tell that Sergeant Trotter was anxious to leave.

"We'd better get going Jock as I left my kit back at the major's hut. I'll see you tomorrow after the service."

"All right, Fred. Your billet should be a pleasant surprise after this place."

Fred turned around to find that Sergeant Trotter had already left and was striding towards the western side of the aerodrome.

"Wait for me, sarg."

"Don't get lost," Jock called out after him.

Fred caught up with the sergeant at the main entrance where he had stopped to talk to one of the soldiers on guard duty. Fred waited by the side of the road as four tenders approached from the north, each one laden with servicemen. As the last vehicle came abreast of the entrance, the soldier who was sitting on the end seat leaned out of the back of the tender and shouted at the top of his voice. Fred could not understand what the man was saying and cupped his ear with his free hand.

"Don't think much of your bloody maternity jacket, mate," the soldier repeated. "Why don't you join a proper Service and get a decent uniform? Even your greatcoat looks sissy. It barely covers your arse!"

Sergeant Trotter stopped talking to the guard and leaned over towards Fred.

"Don't worry about him. With that accent I'd say he was Australian. I'm told they're great soldiers, but you have to watch their sense of humour."

"He's a long way from home, sarg. Aren't all the Australians out at Gallipoli[23] fighting the Turks?"

"Yes they are, along with the New Zealanders. This man must have come over under his own steam to join the British army."

"And I was beginning to feel sorry for myself! Do the Australians have a Flying Corps?"

"Only a small one as yet. They've got five machines out in Mesopotamia.[24] Who knows, if they can rustle up some more aeroplanes, they might even send a squadron over here!"

"That would be one for the Australians."

The road clear of traffic, Fred and the sergeant crossed over to the western side of the aerodrome, through the entrance and on to the airfield itself. On their left were two canvas covered aircraft shelters. Built in the shape of a 'T', each shelter could only accommodate a single aircraft. Directly opposite, right next to a small pond, stood two square single-bay sheds.

"When the machines are put away, there's not much room for anything else. On a busy night though, you'll often find the mechanics taking a nap under the wings."

Sergeant Trotter pointed to a large wooden hut, just visible beyond the pond.

"The most important thing you need to know is where to go for a crap, if you'll pardon my French. The open-air latrines are over there behind that hut and are used by everyone except the officers."

"How do they work, sarg?"

"There's a horizontal pole mounted just above the ground that you use to keep your balance. It stops you falling into the hole on to some other bastard's shit."

"It all sounds a bit archaic to me."

"I suppose it is, but how else would you do it for so many men when we could all be ordered out of here at a moments notice?"

"What about the flies?"

"Well, when you've finished powdering your nose, use one of the shovels and cover it up with earth. There's a pile of dirt next to each hole. When a row of holes gets full, we move along and use the next set of holes. It's a bit basic but you'll soon get used to it. At least you won't have to put up with other people's bad smells as it's all in the open air."

The thought of using an outside toilet filled Fred with dread.

"What about the mud, sarg?"

"It works better in the summer, I must admit. Anyway, you won't have to worry as you'll have your very own lavatory for the next few weeks."

"That'll only be when I'm in my billet. Aren't there any urinals on the aerodrome?"

"If you look over there by the corner of the nearest tent, you'll see a petrol tin with no top to it. We have them dotted around the place so that if you want to go for a piddle, you only have to go as far as the next corner. Clever, eh? Just don't try using the contents to refuel an aeroplane!"

The sergeant laughed and pointed behind him.

"Over there are the hangars of Number 5 squadron. Even though they have their own major and HQ, you'll find that the squadrons work together quite a bit. We even have combined entertainment and film nights as they have the only piano on the aerodrome."

"Do you think they'll let me use their piano?"

"Can't say, I'm no musician. You'll have to sort that out yourself."

"I'll ask the major tomorrow, sarg."

"And now for the last part of the tour. All of the open grass on both sides of the service road, even the field over on the left behind the hangars we just visited, is used for taking off and landing. It's really up to the pilots what they do but they normally operate into the wind."

"Does the wind direction change much?"

"In these parts it's almost always a westerly. Landing into the wind reduces the ground run of an aeroplane."

"I know that, Sergeant. They taught us the principles of flight at Farnborough."

"To make things even easier, we mark the best spot for landing. If you look over there in the corner of the field you should be able to see a white 'T' shape laid out on the ground. It's about half the size of an aeroplane and points in the direction of the wind."

"That makes a lot of sense."

Sergeant Trotter took out his pocket watch.

"Listen son, I've got to get going 'Toot Sweet' as I'm duty sergeant and I've got other things to do before I can sign off. Now that you know your way around, you should be able to find your billet if I give you directions."

Fred took the requisition form from the sergeant and tried to read what the adjutant had written.

"Heh, don't look so worried. All you have to do is hand it in at your billet. They'll do the rest."

"How do I get there, Sergeant?"

"It's easy really. Once you've picked up your kit bag, keep going along the path by the side of the huts until you come to a line of trees. Go through the trees and follow the path around by the side of the hedge, right down to the main road. Rue de Steenvoorde I think it's called, but you probably won't see a sign anywhere."

"I think we flew over it as we came in to land, sarg. Is it a very busy road?"

"Yes, that's the one. When you reach it, turn left and walk towards the village. You'll pass a road on the left and a graveyard on the right before you get to a dead-end lane. That's the one you want, the road before the one that leads down to the railway station."

"What's the name of the road, sarg?"

"It's written on the piece of paper I gave you but I can't pronounce it. Your billet is in the house that's all by itself at the end of the footpath. Is that clear enough for you?"

"I think so, Sergeant. If I get lost I can always ask someone in the village. Do they speak English?"

"Some do and some don't and some don't when they could. You just have to find the right person. Being right on the border, the locals speak a mixture of French and Flemish, I've been told. I can't speak neither."

"I know a little Cyrillic but I don't suppose that would help, would it?"

"You're asking the wrong person, son. Listen, you get settled in and then have a look around the village for the rest of the day. You can get some grub at the canteen just past the major's hut or you can buy eggs and chips at one of the cafés in Abeele."

"How much would that cost?"

"About the same as in Blighty. To give you an idea, a Belgian franc is worth about ninepence halfpenny in real money."

"I think I'll eat later, thank you, Sergeant."

"All right then. Make the most of the afternoon off as this could be your last chance for a while. Now if you'll excuse me, I have to attend to an urgent call of nature."

Without waiting for Fred to reply, Sergeant Trotter walked off in the direction of the latrines. Fred stood still, wondering how he would cope in a foreign country where he was unable to speak the language, had little money in his pocket and knew no-one. Taking out his watch he was surprised to find that it was only two thirty. He strolled back to the main entrance and waited to cross the roadway. Once again, there was heavy traffic on the road. An ambulance was approaching from the left, closely followed by an open-top staff car. The ambulance passed by slowly, the driver navigating around the deep potholes. As the staff car drew alongside, Fred jumped involuntarily at the sound of somebody shouting at him.

"Hello, acting 1st class air mechanic Johnstone. How's your first day at Number 6 turning out?"

Fred looked up, amazed to be hailed by someone who knew him. Immediately he recognised the face of Lieutenant Cochran-Patrick.

"Hello, Lieutenant. Returning to St Omer in style, I see."

"The major came back early and needed his driver to pick up a package from St Omer. I heard of it in the mess and asked if I could go along for the ride."

The driver slowed the car so that Fred could finish his conversation with the lieutenant.

"Thank you again for showing me around, sir. It certainly gave me a better appreciation of what this war's all about."

"Something you'll never forget, I'm sure. Look me up if you're ever in St Omer and I'll take you for another flip. I should be there for a while unless I get posted. Cheerio."

"Goodbye, sir."

As the car accelerated down the road, the lieutenant waved his arm in the air without turning around. Fred crossed the road and for the second time in the day took the path that led to the major's hut. When he reached the steps he found his kit bag exactly where he had left it. Picking it up he slung it over his shoulder, but just as he was about to leave, the door opened and the major appeared in the doorway. Fred put down his bag, stood to attention and saluted.

"At ease, Johnstone. Just the man I wanted to see."

Without waiting for Fred to answer, the major cleared his throat and continued.

"I've been speaking with your flight commander, Captain Moore. He'll talk to you tomorrow and tell you what the form is."

"Thank you, sir."

"I wanted to thank you personally for volunteering to play for us. Drop by my office first thing and my adjutant will give you a list of the hymns. Did you bring any music with you?"

"Yes, sir. But not for any hymns. As long as I know the tune I'll be able to play the music. For those I don't know, perhaps one of the officers would be kind enough to sing the melody for me."

"That we can do. Till tomorrow morning then?"

"Yes, sir. I'll be there."

Dismissed by the major, Fred picked up his kit bag and set off for Abeele. He had no difficulty in finding the track that ran through the encampment along the base of an old stone wall. Reaching the line of trees that marked the eastern limit of the aerodrome, he turned on to a narrow footpath that ran down to the road, making his way tentatively along its edge to prevent his boots from getting muddy. His legs ached from wearing puttees all day and he was looking forward to taking a long hot bath. In the distance he caught a glimpse of several motor vehicles as they travelled slowly past the aerodrome in the direction of Abeele.

When Fred reached the road it was wider than it had appeared from the air. Not only was there sufficient space for motor vehicles to travel in either direction, there was enough room at the edges for troops to march along in relative safety. Looking towards the village, he saw the trucks disappear around a bend and was surprised to find that they were being driven on the right hand side of the road. In his naivety he had assumed that the English rules of the road would have been adopted on the Western Front, at least for the duration of the war.

Fred was relieved to find that the surface of the road was firm underfoot. At some time in the past it had been raised above the level of the surrounding countryside, with large ditches excavated on either side to drain away any excess water. Apart from a few farm labourers who were working in the fields nearby, no-one was in sight. As Fred walked towards Abeele, a troop of soldiers came into view, marching towards him on the opposite side of the road. In the sombre grey afternoon light, all that Fred could see was a blur of khaki against a dark brown background, though he could distinctly hear the heavy rhythmic crunching of the soldiers' boots on the gravelled road. The scene changed when the sun emerged briefly from behind a large black cloud, projecting beams of light through the branches of the naked trees that lined the avenue and dazzling Fred with the reflections off the shiny road surface and the soldiers' weapons. Almost as quickly as it had appeared, the sun slipped behind another cloud and the scene returned to its former drab colours.

From the cut of their uniforms, Fred could tell that the soldiers were British. He waved to the leading men as they passed by and they waved back. One of soldiers shouted that they were all looking forward to a few days rest and Fred wished them luck. As the sound of the marching soldiers faded into the background, Fred heard the sound of approaching horses. Looking around, he counted twenty soldiers on horseback, each rider wearing a tin hat and leading a heavily laden packhorse. There was a gap of two hundred yards between the first rider and the rest of the group. From the insistent shouts of the trailing riders, it was evident that they were endeavouring to catch up with the leader.

As the first horseman drew near, Fred waved his hand to catch the man's attention. The rider slowed from a canter to a trot so that Fred could keep up with him.

"Where are you heading?" Fred shouted.

"The trenches!" the soldier shouted back. "There was a problem with the ammunition train this afternoon and we had to pick up from Godewaersvelde instead of Poperinghe. That's an extra hour of riding for us to get this ammunition to the front by nightfall."

"What's in your bags?"

"Light ammunition. Each saddlebag holds a man's weight in 'three oh three'."

Fred tried to imagine how many bullets would weigh the same as twenty men but quickly gave up.

"That should keep them going for a while!" he shouted.

"You'd better watch out for the limbers behind us. They're pretty big and they're carrying shells."

"I'll try and keep out of their way."

"Are you going far? I'd offer you a ride if I had the room."

Fred was out of breath trying to keep up with the rider. "I've just come from the aerodrome," he panted. "Don't worry about me, I'm only going as far as the village."

"That's all right then. I'll press on."

"Cheerio. I hope you make it there in time."

"Cheerio to you, too. Drop one on the Huns with the name Stan painted on it, would you?"

The soldier waved goodbye and spurred his horse into a gallop. The other riders in the group soon passed Fred, close enough for him to see the determined look on their faces as they rode by. The noise of the horses' hooves on the gravelled road was deafening, but when the riders rounded the bend in the distance, all was again quiet. Fred continued on his way and soon reached the outskirts of the village. Single and two storey cottages lined the avenue, making the road appear narrower than it actually was. Many of the houses lay well back from the road, their gardens neatly fenced and well-tended, but of the inhabitants there was no sign. Looking to the south through a gap between the buildings, Fred could see the outline of hundreds of gravestones, partially blocking the view to the hills in the distance. Realising that he was nearing his destination he increased the length of his stride, continuing up the slight incline towards the centre of the village.

Two heavy trucks appeared from around the bend and came towards him on the opposite side of the road. At the same time he became aware of a metallic rumbling sound that grew louder by the second. He turned around to see what was making the noise. A large number of horses were approaching at speed and though he could not tell what they were pulling, he could see that only half of the horses bore riders. As the convoy drew closer he could see that there were four sets of horses, each set harnessed two abreast and three deep, pulling what appeared to be gun carriages. Each pair of horses was under the control of a single rider and positioned over the centre of every axle was a large bundle wrapped in tarpaulin and fastened down with ropes.

As the limbers thundered towards him, Fred stepped off the road and into the entrance of the cemetery so that he would not get caught between the ammunition limbers and the two trucks when they crossed paths. The rumbling grew to a crescendo as the carriages sped past, the lead rider waving to Fred in acknowledgement. Fred knew he had made the right decision in getting out of their way when a huge spray of muddy water rose from the rear wheels of the last limber, its driver forced to take it off the road in order to avoid a collision with the first truck. The danger soon passed and in less than a minute, both the trucks and the convoy had disappeared from view.

Fred picked up his bag and continued on his way. Rounding the bend he noticed that the buildings on either side of the road no longer had gaps between them. Almost all of dwellings were two storey cottages built of brick and stone but they varied in height. With no front gardens, their front doors opened out directly on to the cobbled pavement.

To Fred, the village looked drab and uninviting and he was surprised at the absence of civilians in the street. Some of the few villagers he did see nodded to him or touched their caps, but the rest ignored him completely. He walked past a laneway that led to a large church and was beginning to wonder if he had misunderstood the sergeant's directions when he caught sight of the entrance to a narrow road on the opposite side of the road. Crossing over, he noticed a faded sign that was fastened high on the brick wall of the corner building.

"Hanekampweg," he read out loud.

Taking the requisition form from his pocket, he read the address that had been roughly handwritten in pencil by the adjutant. Fairly confident that he was in the right street, he looked past the row of closely packed terraced buildings. Sure enough, the road ended abruptly after a hundred yards.

Moving the heavy kit bag from one shoulder to the other, Fred walked to the end of the lane and took the winding footpath that meandered along the banks of a small stream. He could see a cottage in the distance. It was set well back from the other buildings in the village and partly hidden by the trees and bushes of a large and overgrown garden. Reaching an old wooden gate, he opened it and walked through the garden towards the front entrance of the building, passing along the way a row of wooden tables with benches stacked upside down on top of them. From the condition of the timber and the long grass growing through the planks of the tables, it was evident that no-one had sat in the garden for a long time.

Reaching the front door, Fred stood for a moment in the porch, looking up at the sign that bore the words 'Café Evalina'. He searched for the doorknocker and eventually found it, almost completely hidden by ivy that had spread across from one side of the porch. The brass doorknocker was cast in the shape of a sheaf of barley and Fred recalled being told at St Omer that before the War, the area around Poperinghe had been famous for producing beer.

Not expecting anyone to be at home, he raised the knocker as high as it would go and then let it drop. A loud metallic clang echoed through the house. Putting his bag down on the ground he took the form from his coat pocket and strolled back into the garden, imagining what it would be like to sit there on a summer's afternoon. He felt sad when he realised that Ethel would never be a part of his life in Belgium and he made a resolution that he would write to her every day so that she could at least share his experiences.

Fred's thoughts were interrupted by the sound of a low flying aircraft. Looking up, he saw the Bristol scout the sergeant had earlier shown him on the aerodrome. Its shape was unmistakable and the constant noise of the engine sounded almost comforting. The machine looked a lot smaller in the air than it had on the ground and with no other aircraft accompanying it, Fred wondered if the pilot was on a mission. The aeroplane passed through a patch of low cloud before turning towards the west and Fred remembered that it was being returned to St Omer.

"Hallo, monsieur. Can I help you?" a voice called out.

Fred turned around and saw the face of an attractive woman peering out of one of the side windows.

"*Er, bonjour, madame,*" he stuttered, not sure whether she would understand his schoolboy French. "*Je suis un aviateur anglais et je voudrais avoir un lit depuis quelques nuits.*"

For a moment the woman looked puzzled, but then she smiled and laughed out loud.

"You must be the one I hear about this morning. Not to worry about talk to me in Frans, I can speak Engels. Wait there, I open the door."

The woman closed the window and Fred waited patiently in the porch as the sound of her footsteps moved from the window to the front door. The door opened with a creak and she re-appeared, wiping her hands on an old apron that partly covered a floral-patterned frock. She ushered Fred into the house.

"Come in, come in. Make you at home."

Once inside, Fred put his bag down and looked at his new landlady. At five feet five inches tall, with short dark curly hair and a pale complexion, she was of slim build and stood erect. In spite of her smile, her demeanour suggested pain and long suffering. Smiling briefly, Fred handed her the requisition form, crumpled from being squashed inside his coat pocket.

Whilst the woman read the document, Fred looked around him. They were standing in a hallway in front of a flight of wide stairs. To the left of the stairs was a large dining room in which were squeezed three wooden trestle tables arranged in the shape of a horse shoe. Each table had two matching wooden bench seats. At the rear of the dining room Fred could see a doorway that led to what he guessed would be a scullery and under the stairs to his right were two closed doors. As he turned around he noticed an old upright piano on the far side of the dining room. He walked towards it to get a closer look.

"You like to play?"

"Yes, I do. Is the piano in tune?"

"My husband he play it every day, but now he is dead and there is no one else. If you like you can play it when you want. There is music in the seat."

"Thank you, I'd like that, but I don't want to disturb anyone. Are you sure that would be all right?""

"*Bien sur, monsieur.*"

Fred suddenly realised that he had not introduced himself.

"Forgive me for being rude, madame. My name is Frederick Johnstone."

The woman smiled and held her hand out for Fred to take.

"My name is Evalina Segher but you can call me Evelyn. Like the other soldiers who stay here. I am pleased to meet with you, Fredrik Johnstone."

Evalina turned around and pointed to the top of the stairs.

"There are nine soldiers here and they sleep above. I not normally fit more but there is small room next to where I sleep. My sister use it when she stays with me. Is that good with you?"

"I'm sure it will be," Fred replied, relieved that he would not be sleeping in a dormitory like the other men of the squadron.

Evalina led him to the first door beyond the stairs, opening it to reveal a small room measuring nine feet square. Fred followed her inside. In the corner nearest the door, only inches from the edge of a narrow iron bedstead, stood a small wooden table upon which had been placed a white enamel basin and water jug. Resting against the wall behind the basin was a large but tarnished mirror. An old wooden chair with padded armrests filled the space between the single bed and the far wall, and a wooden clothes cupboard rested crookedly against the wall opposite the foot of the bed, leaving a gap just wide enough for Fred to squeeze through. On the far side of the room, to the right of a small window, was a fireplace with a tall mantelpiece, its flue blocked with rolled-up newspapers. Between the doorway and the bed a threadbare rug covered a small section of unpolished floorboards, barely large enough for a person to stand on when getting out of bed. Knowing what the other men of the squadron had to put up with on the aerodrome, to Fred, the room bordered on the luxurious.

"This will be fine, thank you."

He rested his kit bag next to the fireplace and lay on the bed to test the springs. The bed sagged in the middle under the extra weight of his heavy uniform but held firm, with no broken springs poking into his back. With difficulty, he swung his legs up over the side of the bed and stood up.

"If you'll pardon me, Evelyn, would you please tell me where the lavatory is?"

"Up the stairs. It's the room above the kitchen."

"Thank you, I can find it."

"You look tired monsieur. Would you like for me to make you a hot bath? I get the mattress and blankets while you bathe."

"That would be most kind of you, madame. It's been a long day and I've not had a decent wash for more than a week."

Within an hour of arriving at the cottage, Fred had unpacked his kit bag, enjoyed a long hot bath and was sitting in the dining room eating fresh bread covered with jam and taking sips from a mug of hot chocolate. The other men had not yet returned from the aerodrome, so for the time being he had the whole room to himself. When he had finished eating he walked across to the piano, pulled the seat out from under the keyboard and sat down. Raising the cover, he began to practice his scales and straight away discovered that several of the middle and upper notes sounded flat. He stood up, opened the top of the piano and felt around inside, eventually finding a tuning hammer clipped to the inside of the casing. Removing the front panel he located the pins for the notes that were out of tune and one by one he corrected them by tightening the strings with the hammer.

When he was satisfied that the piano was roughly in tune, Fred walked back to his bedroom and took out from the bottom of the wardrobe the roll of green baize that held his watchmaking tools. Pleased that he had decided to include his piano tuning equipment when he had packed his belongings in England, he unrolled the cloth and extracted a tuning fork and two felt-covered wooden wedges. By the time he returned to the dining room, Evalina had already cleared the table and was waiting for him by the opened piano.

"I see you come here with instrument. The piano it has not played for more than a year, since my husband die."

Fred noticed the look of concern on Evalina's face.

"Don't worry. I do this often. I noticed a few of the notes were out of key and I've tuned them already."

"You are most kind, monsieur."

"I may need to raise the overall pitch to make it play as it should. Listen, I'll show you what I mean."

Fred reached forward and tapped the end of the tuning fork on the side of the piano. He rested the peg of the fork on top of the piano, at the same time striking Middle C on the keyboard.

"Can you hear that pulsing sound?"

"Oui."

"That shows the pitch of the piano needs correcting, even though all the notes are in tune."

"Will this be hard?"

"Not really. It'll take me a couple of hours, but I'll have to do it when no-one else is around as I need it to be quiet."

"For this I would be most grateful, monsieur. There are many pianos in Abeele that are like so. Perhaps if I speak with your major, you would mend these too?"

"I'm not sure if I'll be allowed to work outside the camp. When I know what's what, I'll ask my captain if you like. This is all foreign to me and I don't yet know what I can and cannot do in my spare time."

"Thank you, Fredrik. You tell me what is good. I go now and prepare food for tonight."

"Thanks for the bread and jam, Evelyn. Just one more adjustment and I'll be off to my room if you don't mind. It's been a long day and I need to collect my thoughts."

Evalina smiled and returned to the kitchen. Fred reached forward and located the pins for the last note that needed re-tuning before blocking two of the strings with the wedges he had brought from his bedroom. He struck the note hard on the keyboard with his forefinger before playing the same note one octave lower. With the hammer pressed into place on top of the pin, he adjusted the tension. Striking the same notes again, he listened carefully to the sounds. Satisfied with the result he removed the two wedges and played the high note again, cocking his head to one side as he listened for any variation in the sounds of the three strings. He replaced the front panel of the piano and snapped the tuning hammer back into place inside the casing. With a flourish, he played one more arpeggio before closing the lid.

Returning to his bedroom, Fred sat down in the old armchair and reached out for his overcoat, searching through its pockets until he eventually found the small leather notebook that he carried with him at all times. He pulled out a small pencil from the spine of the book and started to write.

By the time Fred had written a summary of the day's events in his diary and was about to write a letter to Ethel, it was well after sunset and the scene outside his window was bathed in cold moonlight. Uncertain as to how to begin his first letter from Belgium, he got up from the bed and walked to the window. Ice patterns had already started to form around the edges of each pane of glass. Looking out on the skyline of Abeele, he watched as the moon passed slowly behind the church spire half a mile away. He shivered and closed the curtains, a wistful expression on his face. Sitting down on the bed, he placed a sheet of paper on top of an old magazine and started to write.

My dearest Ethel,

Tonight I watched the full moon rise over the roofs of the village and it made me feel sad, remembering the last time we were together watching the moon rise over Piccadilly Circus. I pray it won't be too long before I get my first leave and we can be together again. In the meantime we will have to make do with letters I'm afraid.

Today was a most eventful day . . . . .

Chapter 5
A Reversal of Fortune

THE START OF the New Year brought with it technological advances that would have a significant impact on the two squadrons based at Abeele. Six months earlier, the German Air Force had introduced a single seater scout that was capable of firing a machine gun through the arc of the spinning propeller without the bullets striking the blades. Though not particularly fast or manoeuvrable the Fokker E-I monoplane, or 'Eindecker', quickly achieved an alarming success rate in aerial combat as the only allied aircraft capable of firing straight ahead were the ageing pusher-engine Vickers FB5 fighter (or 'Gunbus'[25]) and a few tractor-engine biplanes with machine guns fastened to the top wings. As a short term solution to the 'Fokker Scourge', until such time a reliable method of gun synchronisation could be developed, the Royal Flying Corps called for the design of a new fighting scout. In response to this call, two aeroplanes were developed according to the stated specifications; single seater, pusher-engine and a forward firing machine gun. They were the de Havilland designed DH2 (built by the Aircraft Manufacturing Company[26]) and the Farman Experimental FE8 (built by the Royal Aircraft Factory). Though both used the same engine and looked somewhat similar from a distance, in detail their fuselage and wing designs were quite different. For various reasons[27] it was not until January 1916 that examples of both aircraft were available *for evaluation and what better place to carry out the trials but Abeele, where the original prototype of the DH2 had been tested six months earlier.*

To the men standing around in front of the hangar, the approaching aeroplane sounded no different to any of their Gunbuses. Few even bothered to look up from their afternoon break. They had all been ordered outside the hangar, away from air thick with the smell of highly combustible dope vapour, as the senior rigger was concerned that the glowing end of a cigarette might accidentally destroy in a few moments what had taken several hours of hard work to achieve.

Ted Murphy, the youngest of the mechanics, dropped his cigarette butt and ground it into the gravel. Looking into the sunset with his hands cupped over his eyes, he watched as a solitary biplane approached from the west. Suddenly the noise of the engine changed from an insistent buzz to a hesitant 'BZZSST   BZZSST   BZZSST'[28] and the aircraft started to drop. Only when it had passed over the perimeter hedge did Ted realise that it was not a Gunbus, as there was only one cockpit in front of the engine.

"What do you make of this, chaps? Looks a bit like our new RAF machine, but I know that's been put away for the night."

The other men looked up as the biplane flew overhead in the direction of Abeele, the setting sun reflecting off the tubular framework of the fuselage and the raised egg-shaped vertical fin. The noise of the engine stopped altogether as the aircraft banked and swung around, descending rapidly on its final approach to the runway. Twice the engine surged for a few moments and then the machine touched down smoothly on the grass, stopping fifty yards from the perimeter hedge. With the engine brought back to life, the aircraft taxied over the grass towards the sheds, its pilot spinning it around at the last moment and bringing it to a halt immediately in front of the hangar where the men were congregated.

Ted was about to run over and offer assistance to the pilot when he was joined by Sergeant Bill Hopkins, the senior rigger for Number 5 squadron. He had to shout to make his voice heard over the noise of the aircraft's engine.

"What do you think it is, sarg?"

"It's not an FE8, that's for sure! The tail booms are fastened to a sternpost and the tail is bigger."

"More like the 'Fees' of Number 6."

"It's probably one of the new de Havillands. The captain told me we're being lent one to compare it with his new scout."

"Nobody tells me anything, sarg. Do you think Captain Powell will be flying both machines?"

"My guess is he'll ask his old flight commander to join him. For the trials at any rate. Age versus beauty it'll be."

"Which machine would you say is better?"

"Couldn't say, young Ted. Let me get a closer look and then I'll give you my opinion."

"Tell you what. How about we have a bit of fun and run a book on the trials?"

"What you do with the other men is up to you, but I don't want no part of it. There wouldn't be much in it anyway, what with both of them having the same engine."

Their conversation was brought to an abrupt halt when the other men pushed past to get a closer look at the new machine. By the time one of the mechanics had brought a ladder out from the back of the hangar, the crowd was too dense for him to reach the aircraft.

Denied an easy exit, the pilot stood up in the open cockpit and stepped over the side, feeling for the foot hole in the nacelle with the toe of his right boot. With many eager hands to guide him, he slid all the way to the ground, a manoeuvre made all the more difficult as he was wearing a heavy leather coat and long sheepskin boots.

Bill Hopkins elbowed his way through the throng of men.

"Let me through, would you!" he shouted. "And someone fetch a trolley so we can move this machine out of the way. We're fighting a war you know!"

The crowd parted, opening up a narrow pathway between Bill and the aircraft. He walked up to the pilot and saluted.

"Can I help you, sir?"

The pilot pulled off his helmet.

"Yes, Sergeant. I'm Lieutenant Cochran-Patrick and I've brought this de Havilland scout for you to try."

"Captain Powell told me to expect you sir."

"That's good. Whilst I go and see to the paperwork, would you put the machine somewhere safe. Even if it means moving one of yours out into the open. This is one of the first off the production line and I don't want anything to happen to it."

"Very good, sir."

"It has to go back to the depot next week, you know."

"Yes, sir."

"And there's to be no combat flying.[29] Understood?"

Bill found it hard not to smile but eyed the lieutenant with respect. He had heard much about the flying prowess of the young commander.

"Rightio, sir. We'll move the BE out of this shed and park it next to the Martynside. With the other new scout in the shed next door, we can easily keep an eye on both of them."

"Thank you, Sergeant. I'll be in the operations hut if you need me."

The lieutenant walked away and Bill turned to shout at the men who had already placed a trolley beneath the tail skid and were about to move the aircraft away from the front of the hangar.

"Hey there, leave that machine where it is and bring out the old 'Quirk'. You can put her to one side of the shed, out of the wind."

"But what about the new repairs, sarg?" asked one of the carpenters.

"Cover the fuselage with a tarp and pray it doesn't rain tonight."

"I don't think a tarp will make any difference."

"I'm sorry, Sid, but it can't be helped. We need the de Havilland under the lights to check it out properly. We'll just have to make do with less space for the other machines."

The carpenter shrugged his shoulders.

"All right, Sergeant, you're the boss. But don't blame me if it all comes apart at the seams."

As soon as the new scout had been pushed back into the shed, Bill took a closer look at it under the hangar lights. The aircraft was spotless, with no streaks of castor oil on the nacelle or wings. Even the bracing wires sparkled. The fabric was doped in a neutral colour and other than the number '5920' painted on its tail fin, there were no identifying markings. Bill was about to start checking the alignment of the rigging when he felt a tap on the shoulder.

Lieutenant Adrian Breaker had been entrusted to oversee the trials and, though proficient in his job as equipment officer, knew little about the mechanicals of the squadron's aircraft.

"Sergeant, check the whole of the rigging as I don't want there to be any hiccups tomorrow."

"Yes, sir," Bill replied.

The lieutenant turned towards Ted Murphy, who was standing inside the framework of the fuselage inspecting the engine and propeller.

"Murphy, I want you to go over the engine with a fine tooth comb. It's a Gnome Monosoupape, the same as in the Vickers."

"Thank you, Lieutenant. I had already noticed that."

Bill detected the obvious sarcasm in Ted's reply and thought it prudent to intervene.

"Sir, I see they've mounted a two-bladed prop on the new de Havilland, not like the four-bladed jobbie on the RAF machine. Do you think that's a good idea?"

Lieutenant Breaker looked at Bill with a blank expression on his face. Instead of answering straight away he cleared his throat and turned as if to examine the nacelle of the new aircraft. Bill ran his finger along one of the shiny control wires.

"Sir, have you had a chance to talk to Lieutenant Cochran-Patrick?"

"Not yet, but before he goes back to St Omer I intend to ask him if he's happy with the way the rigging's been tuned. You can never trust the bods at the factory."

Bill looked over the lieutenant's shoulder and caught sight of Ted rolling his eyes. With difficulty he managed to keep a straight face.

"Right you are, sir. I won't do anything until I hear from you, then."

"I'll also talk with the adjutant and confirm who'll be flying tomorrow. No doubt the major will want Captain Powell to fly the FE8 as he's our 'gun' pilot, but I also know he's scheduled for a morning patrol."

"That could be a problem, sir."

"True, but I'll be able to tell you what's happening before you knock off tonight."

"Thank you, sir."

"Very well, Sergeant. Carry on."

As soon as Lieutenant Breaker had left the building, Bill breathed a sigh of relief, happy that he and his men would be left in peace for at least a few hours.

The following day was cold and sunny, with a layer of high cloud streaked across the sky to the west of the aerodrome. Due to low overnight cloud there was no frost on the ground and the condition of the landing area was soft but firm as it had not rained for two days. A busy flying schedule had already been set for the two squadrons, but at eight o'clock, just after the sun had risen, a small crowd of officers and men gathered around the aircraft sheds of Number 5 squadron. They were all looking forward to what promised to be an interesting flying display.

The two new aircraft were standing in front of the hangars belonging to 'B' flight, having already been fuelled and their engines warmed up. Lieutenant Breaker kept the men well back before giving the order for a row of chairs to be set up across the entrance to one of the hangars. The seats were for the convenience of those officers who wished to watch the display in relative comfort. Bill Hopkins and George Townsend, Bill's counterpart from Number 6 squadron and the man with the most experience on the two-seater FE2 fighter-bomber, were standing on the ground by the cockpit of the FE8 scout, deep in conversation.

"Listen, Bill," George spoke in a raised voice. "I hear what you're saying, but I know how the 'Factory' designs its wings. See how they're longer and narrower than those on the de Havilland."

"So what?"

"They have a high aspect ratio, more efficient than stubby wings. That'll mean the FE8 should be faster, fly higher and be more stable coming in to land. I've done the sums and the ratio is exactly the same as our Fees."

"I still think the de Havilland will win the day, George my old son," replied his old friend and verbal sparring partner. "I'm not that technically minded but the shape of the wings is similar to our Gunbuses and I've no complaints with them. The tail fin is much bigger too. That should make it more directionally stable."

"But what about the propeller?" George countered. "Give me a smaller four-bladed propeller any day. Easier to reach the optimum engine speed and less torque effect besides."

"You're biased just because it's a RAF machine."

"Well, we'll just have to wait and see, won't we? My money's still on the FE8, especially if your Captain Powell's flying it."

"If you're really talking money, George, Ted's running a book on the outcome. I can't join in but I'll make a side wager of twenty cigarettes that the de Havilland will win the day."

"I'll take you on, Bill. I could do with the extra gaspers."

The two old rivals were interrupted by the arrival of the pilots. As expected, one was Captain 'Freddie' Powell[30] who, despite being only twenty years of age, already had extensive experience in aerial combat and had recently been promoted to captain and flight commander. He had also used the FE8 as his personal machine since it had arrived at Abeele three weeks earlier. To the surprise of the onlookers, but exactly as Bill Hopkins had foretold, the pilot chosen to fly the de Havilland DH2 was forty year old Captain Robert Loraine,[31] one of the most experienced pilots in Number 5 squadron and the senior flight commander. With one of the youngest and best pilots in the squadron pitted against his former mentor and commander, everyone was looking forward to an interesting diversion from the daily squadron routine.

The two pilots donned their heavy outer clothing before pulling on their goggles and thick leather flying gloves. With the aid of ladders, they climbed up into their allotted machines and waited whilst their mechanics scrambled inside the tubular framework to turn the propellers. When all was ready, the fuel tanks were pressurised and the engines started. With the tips of the propellers spinning only inches from the ground, the two mechanics shielded their eyes from the blast and carefully climbed out through the tail booms. Other ground crew members joined them in removing the wheel chocks and moving the aeroplanes out on to the grass. The pilots had already decided to take off towards the north, using the greenest part of the airfield, as the aerodrome windsock was hanging limply on its pole.

The two scouts accelerated side by side as they sped across the grass, the onlookers straining their necks to see which one would leave the ground first. After only a few seconds the de Havilland took to the air, closely followed by the FE8. By the time they cleared the perimeter hedge, the de Havilland was slightly ahead but the FE8 was much higher off the ground. Once clear of the airfield, the two pilots steered their steeds in wide climbing circles over the aerodrome, levelling out ten minutes later at six thousand feet.

What followed was a delight to the audience below. The pilots took turns in carrying out mock attacks on one another. They weaved and zoomed, first one taking the advantage and then the other, losing height the more they duelled. After thirty minutes of aerobatics, by which time the machines had dropped to below two thousand feet, the pilots cut their engines and descended in a wide circle, landing one behind the other on the east-west landing area of the airfield. Once on the ground, the two captains brought their machines back to the hangars where the ground crews rushed forward to grab hold of the wings and turn the aircraft around.

All was quiet until the pilots climbed down from their cockpits, whereupon a crowd of onlookers rushed forward, eager to get the opinions of the experts. Even from a distance it was easy to tell the pilots apart, the figure of Robert Loraine towering over the diminutive form of Freddie Powell. Leading the charge were Bill Hopkins and Ted Murphy.

Bill was the first to reach the pilots who by now had removed their helmets and were talking excitedly to one another. At first Bill could not hear what they were saying, so he moved closer on the pretext that he was inspecting the rigging on one of the aircraft.

"The de Havilland needed full left rudder on take off, Freddie."

"Mine only took a little to keep her straight and she lifted with hardly any pressure on the controls. You got off the ground a bit quicker but I out-climbed you as usual, Robert. You always were a bit of a ground hugger."

"Mind you, the DH2 is slightly heavier than the FE8."

"I noticed when we came in that your machine dropped quicker than mine. I almost had to abort my landing so as not to hit you!"

"That wouldn't have gone down well with the powers that be, Freddie. They already think I've had too many accidents and don't care enough about their precious machines."

"Having already flown the FE8, I'd be the first to admit that I didn't want you to get your grubby hands on it."

"You're beginning to sound like the others. I would have looked after it!"

"I'm sure you would, Loraine. It's just that I'm getting rather attached to the little bus and I don't like sharing with anyone. I just hope I can keep it for a while longer."

"It's only a machine, old boy. I suppose there's no point asking you which one you'd rather have?"

"I can be as dispassionate as the other man. In many ways they're very similar but I think I'd still choose the RAF machine. It seems to be a fraction faster and with those long wings it should have the height over the de Havilland. And in my opinion the quality of the finish is better."

"You could be right, Powello, my boy. Mine was very nimble in high speed manoeuvres but you have to be careful in steep turns as she's quite keen on going into a spin, especially to starboard."

Freddie Powell laughed.

"I did notice."

"Sounds like the de Havilland would be the aeroplane for the experienced flier and the RAF machine would be better for the average pilot fresh out from Blighty."

"I wouldn't say no to either of them in a scrap against an Eindekker."

"Amen to that, Freddie, my boy. Anyway, we'd better go over to Breaker and make our report before he sends out the guards."

Bill had overheard enough to confirm his views and he walked over to where Ted was standing.

"That's good enough for me. I'll take the word of Captain Powell any day. The FE8 has it in my book, so you can settle up with the men when we get back to our quarters."

"Hold your horses, sarg," Ted replied indignantly. "If you don't mind, I'll wait until we get the official word on the matter."

Fred climbed out of the wireless lorry, closely followed by Jock. It had taken them three hours to check the wireless installations on two of the aircraft that had just left on a combined mission. Fred looked up as the machines roared overhead on their second circuit of the aerodrome, gaining altitude at what seemed an agonisingly slow rate.

"It doesn't seem that long ago the whole of the front cockpit was taken up with the wireless set, does it Jock?"

"But look at how slowly they're climbing."

"We'll have to commission a special breed of lightweight observers!"

Jock laughed.

"That I'd like to see, but more powerful engines would be a better bet."

As the noise of the aircraft gradually faded to a distant drone, the sound of four rotary engines echoed around the aircraft sheds. Fred looked around and watched as a flight of FE2b fighter-bombers lined up on the airfield, making ready to join the aircraft that had already departed from the aerodrome. Within seconds, the machines reached flying speed and they took off in pairs, climbing rapidly into the sky.

"I bet you the Fees catch them up well before four thousand feet, Fred."

"And so they should. They're only carrying fuel and ammunition."

In the two months since his arrival at Abeele, Fred had settled into his new way of life as a wireless mechanic. He had learned all about the theoretical and practical aspects of wireless telegraphy and the fitting of wireless equipment in aircraft. Working for most of the time in the mobile workshop he had noticed many similarities between his new role and working in the jeweller's workshop back home in England. However, with the novelty of airborne wireless, the demands made upon him were inconsistent and left him with several hours of free time each day.

"What are we going to do now?" Jock asked. "There's nothing much we can do until they all come back."

"Well, I might as well go and mend the major's watch. It'll be my fourth repair job this week."

"You'll soon be making more out of watchmaking than what the Flying Corps is paying you."

They were interrupted yet again by the sound of more aircraft.

"Look over there, Fred. That's Captain Powell, lining up in front of his flight."

"That little scout seems to be all he flies these days."

"I don't blame him. It looked pretty impressive in that exhibition he gave us the other day."

"Yes, that was well worth watching. I hope he's learned how to use a machine gun now there's no longer an observer to look out for him."

"A bit like you playing the piano and mending a watch at the same time."

"At least I have outside interests. Not like some people I know."

Jock grinned and slapped Fred on the back.

"Doesn't drinking count as one?"

After the four aircraft had taken off, Fred and Jock returned to the relative peace of the workshop lorry. All of the squadron's aircraft not already out on operations were being worked on in the canvas hangars and the off-duty pilots were either in the officers' mess or relaxing in their quarters. Whilst Fred busied himself repairing the major's watch, Jock walked over to one of the hangars of Number 5 squadron and sought out his old friend, Bill Hopkins.

"Hi, Bill. Do you want a hand? Everything's up in the air at the moment and I always enjoy a bit of rigging when I get the chance."

"Only if you make a decent job of it. I'll be for the chop if something goes wrong with one of my machines."

"You can trust me, Bill. I always do a good job."

"All right, you can give me a hand with the Bristol scout. Lieutenant Sanderson reckons she's pulling to the left."

"What have you done so far?"

"I've had the wings off and trued up the fuselage and centre section. We've already reattached the left lower plane and I've got the upper plane slung from the roof, ready for lowering."

"Isn't that a bit risky?"

"Don't worry. I know what I'm doing. Mind you, I could bring the shed down on our heads if anything goes wrong."

"Mum's the word," Jock replied, well aware that the procedure Bill was following was frowned upon by the authorities. "What do you want me to do?"

"I'll get on with bringing these two planes together and then I'll do the same for the other side. Adams and young Jenkins can give me a hand as I need to keep and eye on them."

"Not much point all four of us working on it. Anything else I can do?"

"Why not have a go at truing up the tailplane. I'll shout if I need your help. You'll find a straight edge and spirit level over in the corner, next to the dihedral boards. Just yell out if you need anything."

"Thanks Bill, I should be all right by myself."

For the next two and a half hours the four men worked on the aircraft, totally absorbed in what they were doing and barely exchanging a word. Jock was rummaging around inside a toolbox in search of an adjustable spanner when he heard a commotion outside the hangar. Stopping what he was doing he walked to the open doorway and looked out on to the airfield. The FE8 scout had returned from patrol and the ground crew were trying to move it from the landing area. As they grasped hold of the wings, the pilot blipped the engine to help them spin the machine around. Jock could see that the men were shouting excitedly to one another as they deftly manoeuvred the diminutive aircraft to one side of the hangar.

"What's all the kerfuffle about?" Jock shouted, but his words were drowned by the noise of the engine.

He stepped outside the hangar, squinting in the bright sunlight. As quickly as it had started, the noise ceased and all was quiet. The propeller of the tiny scout had stopped spinning and the pilot was sitting motionless in the cockpit. As Jock waited to see what would happen next, one of the mechanics who had been working with him inside the hangar, rushed past carrying a wooden stepladder. Reaching the aircraft, the mechanic placed the ladder against the side of the nacelle, positioning it immediately in front of the cockpit. The pilot stood up and turned around in the cockpit before stepping out backwards and climbing down the ladder. As soon as he reached the ground he was surrounded by half a dozen excited men.

"Well done, sir," one of the mechanics shouted. "That's the first Hun we've downed in a long time, and you got it with the new machine."

Freddie Powell removed his goggles and helmet and smacked his gloved hands together.

"Thanks, Sperry. It all went pretty well, though it took three drums to finish him off. I followed him down from eight thousand but had to break off, so I won't be able to claim it as a victory."

"Perhaps one of the batteries saw what happened sir," 1st class air mechanic Walter Sperry replied. "What type was it?"

"A two seater Aviatik. Give me a hand to get these off would you?"

"Certainly, sir."

Grasping the captain's gloves by the finger tips, the mechanic roughly pulled them off before handing them back. Freddie Powell rubbed his hands together, at the same time jumping up and down on the spot.

"You know, Sperry, thawing out is worse than being cold. I couldn't feel the trigger because my fingers were numb and I dropped an empty drum overboard when I was reloading. If it had hit the propeller or one of the tail booms that would have spelt the end of my war."

"Glad it turned out all right then, sir," the mechanic replied, a look of relief on his face. "Before you go, sir, are you happy with the fixed gun position? It's very different to the mounting on your Gunbus."

"Not really. With the barrel sticking straight out of the nose, I have to fly directly at the Hun to have any chance of hitting him. If you think you can safely cut a hole in the nacelle just in front of the cockpit and install a pole mount, I'll be able to fire in any direction."

"I'll have a chat with the other lads, sir and we'll see what we can come up with. Anyway, you can ask Lieutenant James if he can confirm your claim sir, as his Gunbus has just landed."

Freddie Powell stood shivering by the side of his aircraft as the two-seater Vickers FB5 taxied towards him, coming to a halt twenty feet from the entrance to the shed. The mechanics left him to take the ladder across to the newly arrived aircraft. Once the ladder was in position, the observer stepped out of the front cockpit and climbed down, his legs apparently frozen stiff by the way he moved. He was soon joined by the pilot, who climbed out of the rear cockpit and on to the wing before jumping down to the ground. The two men exchanged words with the ground crew before walking to the hangar.

"Hello, Archie," Freddie Powell called out to the pilot, when he was within earshot. "Did you by any chance see an Aviatik go down in a spin over Becelaere? It would have crashed near Zonnebeke."

2nd Lieutenant Archibald James[32] was four years older than his commander and, like Freddie Powell, had served in the British army before transferring to the Royal Flying Corps. The two officers were of similar build, being trim and short in stature. Both sported a clipped moustache.

"I'm sorry, sir, I can't help you. We were attacked from behind and it took all my attention to escape from the Huns. I simply didn't have the speed."

"I'm afraid the old Vickers Fighter is no longer up to the task, Archie."

"I did see the machines of Number 6 having a go at a couple of Aviatiks over Polygon Wood on the way back, though. Could it have been one of those?"

"I don't think so, Archie. Mine was all by itself. Never mind, I'll put it down as an 'Unconfirmed' for the moment. Come, I'll walk with you to the office."

"How I hate filling out combat reports."

"Me too, Archie, but someone's got to do it."

Chapter 6

A Town Like Piccadilly

ONE BY ONE the aircraft landed from the morning's sorties and were returned to the shelter of their canvas hangars. Several machines had suffered superficial damage but nothing that could not be fixed at the aerodrome. By midday, the two scouts of Number 6 squadron had yet to return and the batteries in the area were contacted to see if anyone had seen the missing aircraft. When word was received that both machines had been damaged and the pilots forced to land at a forward landing area, the major ordered two crash tenders to be sent out in the hope that they could be repaired and flown back to Abeele. If the damage proved to be too severe,[33] the machines would be towed back to the aerodrome with their wings removed and lashed to the back of the tender. Before the tenders left the aerodrome, a sudden deterioration in the weather forced the major to call off all operational flying for the rest of the day.

"Let's go into Pops," suggested Jock. "I've not been there since before Christmas and I'd like to look for a new pocket watch."

"What happened to your old one?" Fred replied.

"I lost it somewhere on the airfield."

"If it fell in the mud it won't be found for a hundred years. If you like, I'll help you choose a good one. Most you'll find in the shops these days will be cheap and nasty."

"Thanks, Fred, you're a pal."

"Why don't we visit Talbot House[34] while we're in town?"

"The new place that opened a month ago?"

"That's the one. Lieutenant Mason went there last night."

"Isn't it 'officers only'?"

"Not a bit of it. Anyone's allowed in. They'll even give us a bed if we need to stay overnight."

"Count me in then."

"How'll we get there? We'd be lucky to find a tender going there this time of the day."

"We can always walk there and get a lift back on the water cart."

"But it's five miles."

"You worry too much, Fred. It's only an hour by Shank's pony and if we're lucky we can cadge a lift. There's always traffic on that road."

"Oh, all right. Let me first take this watch back to the major. If you close up the lorry, I'll meet you at the main entrance."

"Don't be long."

Fred arrived at the aerodrome entrance just as a crash tender was leaving to pick up one of the stranded pilots. Running out into the road he waved the driver down.

"Can you squeeze in two more and drop us off at Poperinghe?"

"You'll have to ride on the back as there's no room up front!" the driver shouted back. "Just be careful what you sit on as there's a whole new tailplane under the tarp!"

"Sounds like you've got your work cut out," Fred added.

"You're not wrong. The two hopefuls up here with me think they can fix the Martynside right where it landed!"

The driver laughed and clapped his hand on the shoulder of man sitting next to him.

"Isn't that right, Walter?" The mechanic grimaced but said nothing.

"Thanks, that would be dandy," Fred replied. "After all, beggars can't be choosers and it'll save us a long walk."

Fred made his way to the rear of the truck and pulled himself up on to the tray. Balancing on the edge of the platform, he worked his way around the mound of covered spares to the back of the driver's cabin, the only place that offered protection from the wind. He was about to lift up the edge of the tarpaulin when Jock arrived, out of breath.

"Over here, Jock!" he shouted, moving quickly to the side of the truck. "Quick, grab my hand!"

Jock had already clambered up on to the running board of the tender and was reaching towards Fred with both hands. Leaning over as far as he dared, Fred grabbed an arm and pulled his friend up on to the back of the lorry.

"I'm getting too old for this," Jock panted.

"And you wanted to walk. Come over here, I've found a good place to sit."

Jock followed Fred and they sat down with their backs against the driver's compartment, their collars turned up and the tarpaulin pulled over their legs

Fred banged on the wooden dividing panel to alert the driver and the tender moved off with a jerk. At the first intersection Fred lost his balance and he had to grab hold of Jock to stop himself from falling over the side. After twenty minutes of discomfort, they reached the market square, the heart of the bustling railhead town of Poperinghe. Shouting their thanks to the driver, they jumped down on to the cobbled surface and waited as the tender continued across the square towards the Town Hall, finally disappearing from view as it turned into the Rue d'Ypres.

Fred brushed the dust from his uniform and stepped on to the narrow cobbled pavement.

"Where to now, Jock? I've only been here at night and I've already lost my bearings."

"I'm not sure. Perhaps we should just head west and see where it takes us."

Fred looked up at the large building directly in front of them. It was constructed out of large stone blocks and there was a sign over the top of the ground floor windows that read 'Poperinghe Ville Estaminet'. Looking through one of the downstairs windows, he noticed that the room was packed with servicemen and he could hear the sounds of their laughter even though the window was closed.

"Did you know they call this the Piccadilly Circus of Belgium?"

"No. Why's that?"

"Because the square and the roads leading into it look similar and it's a good place to go for entertainment."

"More likely to make the soldiers feel at home, I'd say. They've even got a Piccadilly Circus in the Ploegsteert forest, south of Messines."[35]

"That would be right. The names over here are impossible to read. Some are in French and others are in Flemish, but they're all 'Double Dutch' to me."

Fred's gaze shifted further down the street.

"Now there's a place I've heard a lot about."

"Where?"

Fred pointed to a small two storey building, fifty yards down from the estaminet. With an unprepossessing façade, it looked like any other shop in the town, rather than a place an off-duty soldier might want to visit.

"It's a club called La Poupée,[36] and it's run by a shoemaker and his wife. They've even got a pianola for the dancing, but only officers are allowed in."

"No chance of us 'tripping the light fantastic' there unless we go there in disguise, eh Fred? We could go to 'Little Paris',[37] but I hear the girls there aren't that pretty."

"Not a place you'd ever find me in," Fred replied with disdain. "Enough of this, Jock, we should really get a move on."

Half a dozen empty staff cars were parked in the centre of the square, the drivers huddled nearby around a glowing brazier as they waited for their passengers to return. Acknowledging the drivers as they walked past, Fred and Jock made their way to the opposite pavement. Forced to wait for a column of trucks as they drove past, Fred looked around the market square at the other shops and cafés. The buildings were constructed of brick and stone, plain in design with flat facades and no balconies or bay windows to give them any sense of individuality. Differing only in minor detail and in the number of storeys, they had been erected with no gaps between the buildings. The majority had steeply sloping tiled roofs and those with eaves that faced outwards had stepped edges made of stone blocks rather than the customary straight line gutters. Only the roads that led on to the square provided a welcome visual break to the sombre architecture.

Fred was about to walk out from behind the last truck in the convoy when he heard a rushing sound. He looked up into the evening sky to see what was making the noise, but before he realised what was happening a loud explosion rocked the nearby truck, tearing its canvas covering to shreds and spinning it around on all four wheels. Fred was thrown violently to the ground, struck by a blast of hot air and pieces of flying masonry. With his ears ringing, he struggled to his feet and looked around. Jock had suffered a similar fate and was sprawled on his back, a few yards away.

"Bloody shell, I tell you!" Jock yelled out to him, rubbing his left shoulder vigorously. "Lucky we stopped for the lorries."

"I didn't think the shells reached this far into town!" Fred shouted back. Spitting pieces of gravel from his mouth, he ran over to where his friend lay. "Can I do anything for you?"

Jock looked up at Fred, a broad smile on his face.

"Everything seems to be working all right thanks, though I could do with a drink if you're offering."

"I was being serious, you idiot. Quick, we'd better get out of here. We might not be so lucky next time."

Fred reached down and pulled Jock to his feet, dragging him to the other side of the square in case another shell struck. Behind them, men were running in all directions. The drivers of the parked cars had left the comfort of the brazier to return to their vehicles. Some had already driven out of the square in search of a safer place to wait. Reaching the pavement, Fred pointed to the roof of a building that had received a direct hit.

"Just look what the shell did to that house!"

"It looks worse than it is," Jock replied. "There might be a big hole in the roof but the building's still intact. A few new rafters and a handful of tiles, it'll be as right as ninepence."

"Don't you mean as right as a franc?"

"I don't even know a Frank."

"We should go on the stage, you and me. We could make a fortune."

"I wouldn't give up your day job just yet, Fred."

"Come on, it looks like nobody's hurt so we might as well get going. Probably just a stray one."

"I hope so, but I wouldn't bet on it," Jock replied, turning his coat pockets inside out to shake out the last of the debris.

Keeping to the pavement they skirted the square, walking along the Rue de l'Hopital[38] in the opposite direction to the German guns. In spite of Jock's concern, there were no more explosions and within a few minutes everything was back to normal. The roads leading into the square once more became crammed with soldiers as well as all manner of horse-drawn and motorised vehicles. A company of soldiers formed a line in the centre of the square under the directions of a sergeant major. Realising that these men would soon be marching to the front along the only road that led to Ypres, Fred noticed how quiet they were compared to the soldiers he had earlier seen enjoying themselves at the estaminet. Further away to his left, other soldiers were queuing at an army canteen that had been set up at one side of the square, in the shelter of the town hall.

Leaving the square, Fred and Jock continued to walk in the direction of the setting sun. Dozens of small shops lined both sides of the road. Many of them were boarded up, their owners having left for the safety of villages beyond the range of the enemy's artillery. Though it was late in the afternoon a few of the shops were still open, their front windows displaying wares behind glass or rabbit wire, where the glass was missing or damaged.

Having looked in a few of the windows without finding what he was looking for, Fred noticed a small souvenir shop on the opposite side of the road, next to a large hotel. Trays of watches and jewellery were displayed in the shop front window on one side of the door with a selection of what was marked as 'Genuine Ypres Lace' in the window on the other side.

"Come on, Jock, there might be something over there in the shop next to Skindles. If it's open that is."

Fred led the way across the narrow road. He pushed at the door of the shop and it opened easily, the bell over the door making a light tinkling sound as he entered the dimly lit front room. Jock followed, joining Fred at the counter. After a few moments an old lady emerged from a curtained off area at the rear of the shop. She looked closely at their uniforms before greeting them in English.

"Good afternoon, messieurs. Can I interest you in some fancy lace for your young ladies?"

"No thanks," Jock replied. "But I'd like to see some pocket watches."

"Would you show us some second hand watches as well as new

ones?" Fred interrupted, touching Jock on the arm as he spoke and moving closer so that he could whisper in Jock's ear.

"It would be worth your while considering a good old watch. That's of course if you don't mind who owned it last and how it got into this shop."

Jock nodded and raised his eyebrows, but said nothing.

The old lady walked to the front window and returned a few minutes later, carrying a velvet-covered wooden tray upon which were more than a dozen pocket and wrist watches. Some looked new whilst others were obviously second or third hand. Fred leaned forward and looked closely at each watch on the tray before selecting two silver pocket watches. He picked them up and placed them on the counter next to the tray.

"What do you think of these two, Jock? They both have Swiss movements."

Jock looked down at the watches. Both had white faces with painted numerals and one had a large sweep second hand.

"They look all right, Fred, but I think the one with the Roman numerals is in better condition."

"That's an Omega, a good strong watch and about five years old I'd say. The movement's exactly the same as the Air Military[39] though the face is different. Have a look at this one though, before you make up your mind."

Fred picked up the second watch and held it up to the light. Jock peered over his shoulder to get a better view.

"Look closely and you'll see that the hinges are much finer and the attention to detail is better. This watch is a Vacheron and Constantin, a Geneva firm that makes some of the best watches you can buy, but a name not familiar to many. And if I'm not mistaken, the movement has twenty jewels."

"So what?"

"Roughly speaking, the more effective jewels there are in a watch, the more accurate it will be."

Fred walked back to the counter to talk to the old lady.

"Excuse me madam, would you mind if I took the covers off?"

With an air of reluctance, the old lady picked up a piece of green baize cloth and laid it out on the counter.

"Certainly, monsieur."

She moved the oil lamp from the end of the counter to where Fred was standing. A wisp of black smoke escaped from the top of the lamp glass and spiralled up towards the ceiling. Fred put his hand in his pocket and took out a small ivory clad pocket knife.

"My twenty third birthday present from Ethel," he said, showing the knife to Jock as he opened the smaller blade. "See my initials engraved on the side? She wanted to give me something that would remind me of her every single day."

"Nice thought, Fred."

Reaching deep into another pocket, Fred extracted the watchmaker's eyeglass he carried wherever he went. He picked up the Omega and gently prised off the rear case, placing it on the cloth before opening the inner hinged dust cover. Fixing the eyeglass in his right eye, he bent down to inspect the watch under the flickering yellow lamp light. He counted the number of jewels that could be seen without removing the watch from its casing and guessed that the movement contained fifteen or at most seventeen jewels.[40] With the aid of his eyeglass he also detected minute scratch marks on the bottom plate. The watch had evidently been repaired at some stage. Nonetheless, it was in excellent condition.

"Take a look at this," he said, handing the opened watch to Jock.

"I've not seen the insides of a watch before. It's less intricate than I imagined. Not fancy like a grandfather clock."

"This one wasn't designed to be an ornate watch. You'll notice the difference though when you look at the other one."

Fred closed the case and put the Omega down before picking up the second watch. He opened the outer case to reveal the cuvette, with the engraving 'VACHERON & CONSTANTIN' clearly visible around its circumference. Opening the hinged cuvette, Fred admired the intricate gold and silver mechanism of the timepiece. The bottom plate was finished in frosted mercuris gilt and bore the words '20 JEWELS'.

"Look at this for fine quality, Jock. You could use it for the rest of your life and then leave it to your grandchildren."

Jock examined the delicate mechanism and whistled under his breath.

"A bit too grand for me, Fred. It might be the only thing in my will and everyone would have to fight over it!"

Fred snapped the watch shut and placed it on the cloth next to the Omega. He thought for a moment before addressing the old lady.

"How much for each of these?" he asked, leaning forward over the counter so that his face was close to hers.

"Monsieur, I can sell you the Omega for seventy francs and the Vacheron for one hundred and eighty francs. The Vacheron is worth at least twice what I'm asking, don't you think?"

"What do you say, Jock?" Fred asked, looking around at his friend.

"Easy decision. I'll have the Omega."

Fred thought for a moment and then stood up straight with both hands on the counter.

"Would you accept two hundred and ten francs for the two?"

The old lady frowned and stepped back, touching her forehead nervously. She looked first at Fred and then at Jock as if gauging how serious they were.

"I'm not sure, monsieur," she replied. "I will have to go and ask my husband."

She placed the tray out of reach under the counter, picked up the two watches and disappeared behind the curtain into the back room of the shop.

Fred turned to Jock.

"Even though it's more than a month's pay I'd really like to buy the Vacheron for myself. It's worth far more than she's asking and as I mentioned earlier, it would last forever."

"Seventy francs is still a bit more than I wanted to pay."

"Tell you what, Jock. If she agrees to my offer, I'll split the difference with you. That means yours will cost you about two guineas, half the cost of a new greatcoat!"

"It still sounds a lot to me, but I agree it's better to buy a decent second hand watch than a cheap new one. I might have to give up the fags for a bit, though."

"I don't think you'd get a better buy anywhere else."

"All right then, Fred. See what you can do."

"If you ever get tired of the white face, I can always replace it with a standard black one and paint luminous figures on it for you."

"The white face doesn't bother me. I don't mind being a little different."

The old lady returned from the back room, placed the two watches on the counter and stood back with her arms folded.

"My husband say he agree if you buy chains also."

Fred scratched his chin and picked up the Vacheron. The old lady unfolded her arms and thrust her hands deep inside her apron pocket, all the while looking intently at him. Fred waited a few moments before replying.

"My offer still stands, but we really don't need new chains. It's already more than I can afford and I have other chains."

He smiled as he spoke so as not to offend the old lady but put the watch back on the counter in the pretence that he was losing interest.

"All right, monsieur." The old lady moved quickly out from behind the counter. "You drive a hard bargain, but I accept."

For the first time since they had entered the shop, the expression on the old lady's face softened and she even smiled when Fred shook her hand to seal the deal. Humming to herself, she wrapped each of the watches in tissue paper and then in brown paper, before tying the two small packages with string. The two men emptied their pockets and counted out the correct number of francs, then waited patiently while she recounted the notes under the light of the lamp.

"It is all there, monsieur."

The old lady rolled the notes into a tight bundle and fastened them with a rubber band. Reaching beneath her apron, she stuffed the roll of notes into her frock pocket before guiding the two men to the front door.

"Good night, gentlemen. May good fortune go with you."

"And the same to you, madame," Fred replied politely.

"Thank you," Jock added as the old lady opened the door for them.

The two men left the warmth of the shop and ventured out into the cool evening air.

"I thought that went well."

"Yes, it did. Thanks Fred, I couldn't have done it without you."

"Don't mention it. I think everyone was happy in the end." Fred looked up and down the street in indecision. "Which way is Talbot House?"

"It's further down this way, just around the bend on the other side. You can't see the sign from here but you can just see the semicircular window at the top of the building. Come on, it's not far."

"Lay on McDuff. I'm famished."

They strolled along in silence, occasionally forced off the pavement by soldiers who were marching in the opposite direction towards the town square. After a few minutes, they reached an imposing three storey building. A sign bearing the words 'Everyman's Club' jutted out above the doorway and though the massive filigree iron outer doors were wide open, the entrance was blocked with soldiers.

Taking the initiative, Fred squeezed his way through the throng, finding himself inside a long hallway that bisected the building. Eight feet wide with a floor of diagonally-laid off-white tiles, the hall reached to the rear of the building where French doors opened out on to a large garden. Both walls were covered with signs of various shapes and sizes. One of the signs in particular caught Fred's eye. It was the picture of a hand pointing back to the front door, with the words 'TO PESSIMISTS WAY OUT' painted next to it.

"This could be a very interesting place, Jock. If you can find the canteen I'll treat you to supper."

"How could I refuse such an offer."

As they moved down the hallway a voice boomed out from behind them, clearly audible over the noise of the soldiers who crowded the hallway.

"Welcome, welcome. I think there's enough room for two more unfortunates."

Turning around, Fred was confronted by a bespectacled man of about thirty years of age. Short in stature and wearing an open shirt with riding breeches, in one hand he held an unlit pipe as he extended the other in greeting.

"I'm the Reverend Clayton, though some people around here have given me the rather dubious nickname of 'Tubby'." The reverend patted his stomach. "I can't imagine why, I'm sure! Anyway, welcome to Talbot House."

"Thank you, Reverend," Fred responded, shaking the minister by the hand. "I'm Fred Johnstone and this is my friend Allan Cardno."

Jock lent across and shook hands with the founder of 'Toc H'.

"Feel free to look around," the reverend continued. "On the ground floor you'll find the canteen and a dining room as well as a large meeting room and a small parlour for want of a better word. On the first floor there's a library of sorts, but as yet we don't have many books. Just leave your cap as a token if you want to take a book somewhere else to read."

"That's a good idea," said Fred.

"When the spring comes, the garden will be a perfect place for reading and we're going to place benches along the walls if anyone wants a bit of peace and quiet."

A meeting had just concluded in a nearby room and the hallway became even more crowded than when they came in.

"I think we should get out of the way."

Fred and Jock followed the reverend past the low wooden barrier that served as a vestibule and walked along the hallway until they reached an ornate chaise longue. Having gestured for them to sit down, the reverend continued his welcoming address.

"On the same level as the library there's also a quiet room and two bedrooms, with more sleeping accommodation on the next floor up. You'll also find the Chaplain's Room on the first floor. That's where I officially work and sleep but more often than not it's full of people."

"That confirms what our equipment officer told us!" Fred shouted, in an effort to make his voice heard above the noise of the soldiers. "He's been here a few times and has already made several friends."

"Quite so, quite so, but I've left out the most important part of the introduction. In the Upper Room[41] we've made a chapel where we hold several services each week."

"C of E?" asked Fred.

"Strictly speaking we're Anglican but effectively it's a non denominational service. We even have a portable harmonium that one of our regulars brought back from leave, but as yet I've not found anyone who can play it properly."

"I've tickled the ivories of a harmonium on occasion."

"You don't say. Is it difficult to play?"

"Not really, but there are fewer notes than on a piano and you need to work the bellows to keep the sound going."

"Would you like me to show it to you, Fred?"

"Could we make it in about half an hour? Jock and I haven't eaten since breakfast and that was before dawn."

"Certainly, my son," the reverend replied, rising from the settee. "I'll be in the small front room. If you're wanting the canteen, you'll find it down the hall on the left."

"Thanks, Tubby. I'll come and find you when we've finished."

The canteen was easy to find and they joined the queue of men waiting to be served. In one corner of the room a small group of soldiers had just finished singing a song. The pianist, a major in the artillery, stood up and bowed when the other men in the canteen applauded, before walking over to rejoin his friends who were sitting at one of the trestle tables.

When it was his turn, Fred ordered poached eggs on toast and a mug of tea for both himself and Jock. With just enough money to pay for the meal he was given a numbered ticket and told to find a seat. Looking around the room he noticed space on the table occupied by the singers.

"Over there, Jock. Quick, before someone else sits there."

Fred walked briskly across the room and sat down on the bench seat. He made room for Jock.

"Say, pal, what's your name? Mine's Vernon Jones."

Fred turned at the sound of the unusual accent and looked into the piercing blue eyes of the man sitting next to him. The officer was in his late twenties, tall and muscular and exuding an air of confidence.

"Frederick Johnstone, sir," he replied deferentially.

"Haven't you read the sign over the chaplain's door, son?" the soldier said in an admonishing tone, though smiling as he spoke. "We don't use rank here. Where are you from, Fred?"

"A town called Basingstoke in England. Are you American, Vernon?"

"Hell no, I'm no Doughboy. I'm from Vancouver. Came out last September with the twenty ninth battalion. See the badge on my shoulder? We've come to give you Brits a hand, especially since your old buddies have chosen to remain neutral in this war."

"Hi Vernon, my name's Jock," Jock interrupted, leaning across Fred to shake hands with the captain. "There seem to be a lot of Canadians over here?"

"There sure are, Jock. Say, are you a for real Scotsman? You'd like our pipers. They wear kilts of the Hunting McKinnon tartan and march to 'Scotland the Brave'."

"Sorry to disappoint you, Vernon, but I come from a place called Newcastle in the middle of England."

"So why are you called Jock?"

"I was given the nickname when I moved south to London as a child. What with my middle name being Scott, everyone thought that I came from Scotland because they couldn't understand my 'Kings English'. If you know what I mean."

"I've been having the same problem over here. Everyone thinks I'm from the 'US of A'."

"Have you been here long, Vernon?"

"About two hours, I suppose, but it's easy to lose track of time. We had a good old sing song earlier on. Are you musically inclined, Fred?"

"I play the piano and bassoon."

"That's swell. Let's meet up sometime and you can accompany me. The piano here is a little out of tune, but that's never stopped us from belting out a few good songs."

"Was that you singing when we came in?"

"Yes, that was me and the boys. Tell you what, Fred. I'll write my name on the board in the Friendship's Corner whenever I aim to be here. If you do the same, we can keep in touch."

"That's a good idea. I noticed the board on the way in and wondered what it was for."

The three men spent the next half hour chatting about their lives before the war. By the time their meal arrived, it was dark outside and the lights had been turned on in the canteen. Vernon made his apologies and left, as he had earlier arranged to go with a group of fellow Canadian soldiers to one of the cinemas in Poperinghe. The canteen was almost empty as Fred and Jock ate in silence, both men glad to sit down and relax after a long day on their feet. The room was warm and cosy even though no fire had been lit and with no-one playing the piano, the only men left inside were those who were eating or writing letters.

"I've not felt this relaxed in ages," said Jock, scraping the last morsel of poached egg from his plate with a piece of bread and cramming it into his mouth. "I could easily lie down and take a nap. What's the time Fred? I haven't unwrapped my watch yet."

Fred took out his old watch and looked at the faded dial.

"A quarter past six."

"So what's wrong with your old watch? I could have bought it off you and saved myself some money."

Fred looked embarrassed and quickly put the watch back in his pocket.

"Sorry, Jock. In the excitement of the moment I didn't think of that. It's seen better days though and would have let you down eventually."

"That's all right, Fred. I know you'd never dud me."

"Are you coming to see the chapel?"

"No thanks. You know what I'm like with churches. I'll find someone here who'll take me on at draughts."

"That suits me. I should be back before you've finished your game."

Fred got up from the table and carried the dirty dishes back to the counter. Making his way to the front of the building, he found that the door to the parlour was wide open with no-one inside. He walked back along the hall and climbed the stairs to the first floor. Leading off the landing on three sides were doors, with windows on the outside wall that overlooked the gardens. The door to the Chaplains's Room was open and the Reverend Clayton was sitting at a large desk in front of the window, his back towards Fred. Fred knocked quietly on the door.

"Come in, come in," the reverend called out without looking up. "There's no need to knock in this house. Nobody else does."

Fred was about to introduce himself when the reverend turned around in his chair.

"Hello again. Fred the organist isn't it?"

"Yes Reverend. You said you'd show me the chapel."

"That I did. Come with me and I'll show you what we've done. It's early days yet, but we're getting there."

The reverend stood up and led Fred up the stairs, pausing for a moment when he reached the next landing.

"We've plenty of room if ever you want to stay the night. Most of the beds are in dormitories but every floor has a bathroom. We serve a good breakfast as well!"

"I'll remember that."

"We have to go up another two floors to get to the loft. Be careful when you climb up into the chapel as the floor's not very strong."

The final flight of stairs was narrow and steep, with handrails mounted on either side. As he climbed into the centre of the loft, Fred caught sight of an altar at the far end, with pews facing inwards on either side of the room.

"As you can see, Fred, it's quite rustic. We found a carpenter's table in the garden shed and I thought it would be fitting to use it as our altar. The benches we've either had made or acquired from other churches in the area."

Fred walked to the end of the loft where a small portable harmonium had been set up to one side of the altar. He took off his cap and coat and removed the lid, placing it carefully on the floor. Sitting down on the low wooden seat in front of the keyboard, he pumped the bellows to build up the pressure.

"How about playing something for me, Fred?"

"All right. I'll try and choose a piece of music that will sound good on such a small keyboard."

"God Save the King would do."

"I can do better than that. Something especially written for the harmonium. You may have heard of it. Romanze A-Moll".

"That will make a pleasant change from the hymns."

For the next few minutes Fred played the harmonium. As he played, he gazed out of the small semi-circular window at the end of the loft, watching the lights of the vehicles in the street below flicker through the thick panes of glass.

"Well, what do you think?"

"The old Groan Box has never been worked so hard. If you can make hymns sound like that, we'd always have a full house!"

"That would be one for the organists, but I only chose this piece to show you what a harmonium can do."

"I realise that, but I'd love you to play for us whenever you are able."

"I'd be delighted, but I couldn't give you much notice."

"Thanks, Fred, I can't ask for more than that."

Distracted by the sudden creaking of the floorboards, Fred looked up. Jock had entered the loft and was walking towards him with his hands over his ears.

"I thought it might be you, Fred. I could hear the sound of the harmonium as I came up the stairs. It sounds a lot different to the piano in the sergeants' mess."

Jock touched the reverend on the shoulder.

"I'm sorry, Tubby, but we really have to go. The water cart leaves the main square at seven and if we don't want to walk back to Abeele, we'd better get a move on."

Fred jumped up from the stool, shook hands with the reverend and picked up his coat and cap.

"Goodbye, Reverend. I will come again soon, I promise. I've already made friends with a Canadian officer and we plan to meet up here whenever we can."

"You'll always be made welcome at Talbot House, Fred. That goes for you too, Jock. And don't forget that you can come up here at any time for a quiet prayer or just to sit and think."

Fred and Jock took their leave and made their way back to the ground floor. The hallway was almost empty as they walked out of the building and into the cold night air.

"I think we'd better start walking in the direction of Abeele, just in case the water cart has already passed by."

"I really hope we don't have to walk back tonight, Jock. It's been a long day."

They walked briskly for a few minutes before stopping at the Rue de la Dunkirk.

"What's the time now, Jock?"

"A little after seven."

"I don't think we've missed it. Let's wait here." Fred rested against a roadside bollard and looked up at the buildings that lined the intersection. "I know it's dark but haven't we been to a little café just up the road from here?"

"The one run by two sisters?"

"Yes, that's it. I didn't realise it was so close to the market square."

"How about we go there for a decent meal next time we're in town?"

Before Fred could answer, the sound of horses' hooves clattering on the cobblestone road behind them broke the silence. He jumped up and stepped off the pavement, just as the water cart was turning into the road that led to Abeele. Waving his arms frantically in the air he tried to catch the attention of the driver. The street was dark and he doubted he would be seen in the dim light cast by the cart's oil lamps. The driver reined in the horses and brought the cart to a sliding halt, only inches from where Fred was standing.

"Have you lost the will to live?" the driver called out.

"Sorry to scare you, but we'd like a lift to Abeele if you're going that way."

"I'm taking this load to the aerodrome. You can squeeze up here next to me if you don't mind the mess."

"Is there anyone else coming along behind you?" asked Fred.

"I'm not sure. I saw a couple of Crossleys parked in the square but I've no idea when they'll be leaving."

"This will suit us fine then. Jock here is going to the aerodrome but would you mind dropping me off in the village?"

"Sure. It's on my way anyway. I'd put your collars up if I were you, as it's a bit nippy tonight. I've got an old cape you can wrap around your legs, if that would help."

Fred and Jock walked around to the other side of the cart and climbed on board, squeezing next to one another on the exposed wooden bench seat.

"Just push that mess out of the way. I didn't think I'd be carrying anyone tonight."

The driver clicked his teeth and slapped the flanks of the nearest horse with his whip. The water cart moved away from the kerb with a jerk and he pulled hard on the reins to steer it into Abeelseweg, the main highway leading south from Poperinghe. With almost no traffic on the road, it wasn't long before they reached the outskirts of Abeele. Even so, both Fred and Jock were shivering by the time the water cart approached the main village crossroads. Fred touched the driver on the arm.

"Would you drop me off at the next laneway on the right? It's just before the big church."

"Right you are, squire. I won't be able to see it in the dark, but I know roughly where you mean."

A hundred yards further down the road, the driver slowed the two horses to a walk before pulling up at the curb. Fred scrambled past Jock and climbed down from the seat on to the cobbled surface of the road. In the pitch dark he stood clear from the wheels of the water cart.

"Thanks for the lift."

"You're welcome. Just don't jump out at me next time."

"I won't. Cheerio Jock. I'll see you in the morning, bright and early."

"Goodnight, Fred. Thanks again for your help with the watch."

Fred smacked his hand on the side of the water cart and it moved off in the direction of the aerodrome. As he waited in the middle of the road for his eyes to become accustomed to the darkness, the full moon emerged from behind a large cloud and he was able to see sufficiently to make his way into the cul-de-sac that led to Café Evalina. The last part of his journey was easier than he had expected. Lights shone from some of the buildings that lined the laneway and he could see the lighted porch of the estaminet away in the distance.

Feeling his way along the gravel footpath, Fred stumbled across the gate to the cottage and walked through the overgrown garden to the front door. He took off his gloves and felt along the top surface of the lintel for the large iron key that was kept there in case of emergencies. Taking the key down, he inserted it carefully into the keyhole and twisted it with both hands. The lock opened with a heavy metallic clunk.

Fred raised the latch and opened the door before returning the key to its hiding place. The dining room was full of soldiers, some eating their evening meal whilst others were sitting around a gramophone, listening to music. Through the open doorway to the kitchen Fred saw Evalina standing at the sink with her back towards him. As he walked across to greet her, a woman came out of the kitchen, carrying a mug of hot cocoa. Fred smiled when he recognised who she was.

"Hello, Caroline. A pleasure to see you again. Are you here for a while?"

"Allo, Fredrik, you are late at home tonight, no? Oui, I am here for one week."

"Do you want me to move out of your room?"

"You not to worry, I sleep with my sister. She has a spare mattress."

Caroline Maes, though born in Belgium, had for many years lived in France in a small village near the city of Lille. Moving there shortly after qualifying as a secondary school music teacher, she had developed the habit of speaking in French except when in conversation with her sister, who was eight years her senior. Strikingly pretty with dark brown hair and a vivacious personality, it surprised Fred that Caroline had few friends. On the occasion of their first meeting several weeks previously, Caroline had told Fred that she had once been engaged to a Frenchman. Her fiancé had enlisted in the army at the outbreak of the War and had been killed a year later during the French offensive at the Battle of Neuve Chapelle. Outwardly, Caroline appeared philosophical about the tragedies of war, but she had recently confided in Fred of her reluctance in starting another relationship.

"I won't be allowed to stay here much longer, anyway" Fred added. "We're building more huts on the aerodrome and I'll have to move back when they're finished. You can move back into your old room then."

"We shall be sad when you have to leave. You are the only soldier here who talks to us as friends. I enjoy too singing to your music."

"I enjoy playing for you, Caroline. Whatever happens, I promise I'll come back whenever I can to make sure that the piano is in tune. And your voice too!"

Evalina, who happened to be walking past carrying a tray of dirty dishes, tapped Fred gently on the shoulder.

"Fredrik, I would like to ask of you a favour."

"By all means, Evelyn. What is it?"

"A friend of mine ask if you would tune her piano also. It is what you say a Grand. Would you do this? She will pay you and she say that you can practice on it whenever you want."

"I'd be happy to, Evelyn. Though to be honest, the only reason I'm agreeing is so I can play her grand piano."

"Thank you, Fredrik. Her name is Mademoiselle Julia Denecker. I tell her that you will visit when you are able. Her café is called

Margueritas and it's on the Rue de Steenvoorde, quite close to the cross roads. You cannot mistake the sign outside."

"I'll try and visit her later this week, though I can't promise."

Fred picked up his coat and cap, smiled and bowed slightly.

"Now it you will excuse me mesdames, I must retire to my room and catch up with my letter writing. Goodnight to you both."

"*Bonne nuit, Fredrik*," the sisters replied in unison.

Chapter 7

One Patrol too Many

THE FIRST TWO months of 1916 brought significant changes to the way in which the Royal Flying Corps operated. Until that time, each squadron operated several different types of aircraft in order to fulfil their many varied duties. With the acceleration in the formation of new squadrons, the decision was made to split these duties into two main areas and allocate squadrons to either a Corps Wing or an Army Wing. Wings would be allocated to a Royal Flying Corps Brigade, with each Brigade supporting a single British Army. As part of this plan, both squadrons at Abeele became part of the 2nd Corps Wing in II Brigade, to be used solely for artillery support, aerial photography and close reconnaissance for the 2nd Army. This left the roles of strategic reconnaissance, distant bombing and air fighting in II Brigade predominantly to those squadrons allocated to the 11th Army Wing. The impact of this directive was immediate. The popular FE2 fighter bombers ('Fees') of Number 6 were reassigned, as were the ageing Vickers FB5 fighter biplanes ('Gunbuses') of Number 5 squadron. With the exception of a few single seater scouts that the two squadrons were permitted to retain for a few more months, the only type of aircraft operating from Abeele would be the largely unpopular BE2c reconnaissance aircraft, a type not originally intended to carry weapons. The final reorganisation at Abeele came into effect in early March when it was decided that Number 5 squadron would be replaced by a new Army Wing squadron, equipped with the DH2 scout.

"Where do you want this 'ere piano?"

The driver of the Leyland crash tender had just arrived from the other side of the aerodrome where, with the help of several volunteers, he had removed the piano from one of the messes. Several men gathered around the back of the lorry, waiting with interest to see what would happen. Hearing the commotion, the adjutant came out of the major's hut and walked over to talk to the driver.

"It needs to be taken to the sergeants' mess, Corporal."

"Yes, sir, but I'll be needing some help, begging your pardon."

The adjutant looked anxiously towards the aerodrome entrance. Seeing nothing out of the ordinary, he shouted at the bystanders.

"You men there! Give this man a hand in getting the piano off the lorry and into the sergeants' mess. And be quick about it!"

The soldiers did as they were ordered and as soon as the driver had untied the ropes, the piano was manhandled off the lorry and on to the snow-covered ground. The driver threw down two lengths of narrow timber and the soldiers lifted the piano on top of them so that an equal length of wood stuck out at either end, to be used as handles. With a man positioned at each corner, the piano was lifted off the ground and carried to the mess. In a matter of minutes it stood in pride of place, just inside the door of the main room.

2nd Lieutenant Charles Hickie, recently posted to Number 6 as technical equipment officer, walked up to the driver who had already packed up the ropes and was about to throw the pieces of timber back on to the truck. The driver saluted and approached him with diffidence.

"Don't tell anyone that it was me who did this, will you, sir? The major will have my guts for garters if he ever finds out."

"I think you'll find that our major has already cleared it with him," Charles Hickie reassured him. "Anyway, I hear that there's already a piano waiting for you at Droglandt."

"That's all right then, sir. I'd better get this lorry back before they miss it."

"That's fine, Corporal. Just watch out for our new huts when you reverse out."

Fred had watched what was going on from the front cockpit of a new BE2c, where he had been carrying out final tests on the wireless equipment.[42] The aircraft was shortly due to leave on an operation, with twenty five year old 2nd Lieutenant George Fincham as pilot and twenty nine year old 2nd Lieutenant Graham Price acting as his observer. Fred stood up in the cockpit and waved when he saw the equipment officer approaching.

"How are you going with the new machine, Johnstone?"

"Fine thanks, Mr Hickie. Isaac's just finished filling the tanks and has run up the engine to make sure it's firing smoothly."

"What about the oil?"

"He overfilled it by two pints. That should keep it running if they're out for longer than expected."

"And your work?"

"I've already checked the wireless set and have sent a test message to HQ. I managed to get some pretty healthy sparks too, so the accumulators are in good fettle."

"Excellent. You've obviously got things covered. Anything else I should know about?"

Fred stood up and moved to one side of the cockpit to make room for the lieutenant, who had climbed up on to the wing to get a better view.

"All I have to do, sir, is to check the aerial's winding mechanism. We had some trouble with it yesterday."

"Has anyone test flown the machine to see if it's still in balance?"

"Last night, sir. They had to alter the stagger because the added weight made the machine nose heavy."

"Good man. The crew will be along shortly as they're scheduled to fly out in half an hour."

"It will be ready by then, sir."

"By the way, I thought you'd like to know that we now have a piano. Number 5 graciously donated it to us as a leaving present."

"That's very decent of them, sir. It'll make life a lot easier for us."

"Just one thing. You'll have to keep mum because their CO knows nothing about it. I told a white lie to keep the driver happy."

At that moment, an observer strolled into the hangar and climbed up on to the wing next to Charles Hickie.

"I hear that congratulations are in order, Graham. Flying officer now eh?"

"Thanks, Charles, but it'll be a few weeks before I can return to Blighty for pilot training."

"You're obviously too valuable an observer for the squadron."

Graham Price laughed as he peered into the cockpit.

"Are you ready to give me the rundown, Johnstone?"

Fred, who had been working behind the observer's seat, stood up in the cockpit, spanner in hand.

"Yes sir, I am," he said, passing the spanner to Charles Hickie.

"I've spoken to the battery commander and have confirmed the target coordinates, but this is a new machine and there may be differences."

"If you change places with me, sir, I'll show you where things are. I've also got the latest signal codes[43] and transmitting wavelengths."

"Do I need to remember all of that?"

"Probably not, but it pays to be prepared. Mind how you get in, sir. You'll find it a bit cramped, especially when you have to fire the Lewis. Not like your old machine."

Fred climbed out of the cockpit and stood on the wing next to Charles Hickie, making sure that he stayed close to the fuselage where the wooden frame would safely support their combined weight. Graham Price climbed over the side and took Fred's place, kneeling on the chair so that he could listen to what Fred had to say.

"This is very similar to what we have in the other BEs, sir. The wireless set and accumulators are located behind the seat between the two cockpits and the telegraph key is mounted on that small shelf to your left. Don't forget to connect the safety plug before you use the wireless though."

"Yes I know all that. What about the aerial?"

"The reel's mounted within easy reach on the outside of the fuselage. There's a one pound lead weight on the end so if you forget to wind it in you could cause a nasty accident. Don't laugh sir, it's happened before."

"Your equipment officer told me that you were having trouble with the winding mechanism. Has that been fixed?"

"Yes, sir. It was sticking when we installed it yesterday but it's working all right now."

Graham Price turned around on his chair and tested the feel of the

Morse key. Satisfied, he reached outside the cockpit to where the aerial reel was mounted. He grasped hold of the handle.

"Have you marked the aerial at the correct extension?"

"I did, sir. If for some reason you miss the mark, a rough guide is to unwind as many feet as there are metres in the wavelength and then add fifteen percent. At the moment we're using a wavelength of one hundred and eighty metres[44] on this short wave set. That works out at one hundred and eighty plus twenty seven, which gives you a total of two hundred and seven feet of aerial."

"That's a handy trick."

"You won't need to change anything unless you have to use a different wavelength," Fred continued. "And in most cases we'll fix that here on the ground."

"Good show. What about the codes you mentioned?"

Fred held out a piece of paper.

"These are what we use at the moment, Lieutenant, but they're always adding new ones. We're hoping to standardise them for every squadron before too long."

Graham Price examined the sheet before replying.

"Well, this is different to the roneo'd copy the captain gave me the other day."

"The observer's lot is an ever changing one, Graham," said Charles Hickie, joining in on the conversation.

"Between you and me, Charles, I'd rather be in my old machine where my main job is to be on the lookout for trouble. I'm really not sure about all this wireless tomfoolery."

"I wouldn't worry, sir," Fred volunteered. "I knew absolutely nothing about wireless four months ago and I'm now in charge of the section."

They were interrupted by the sound of footsteps on the gravel. Charles Hickie jumped down from the wing and walked to meet the pilot who had arrived dressed in heavy leather flying gear and thigh-length boots.

"Hello, George. Ready for a game of hide and seek?"

"Not funny, Charles." The pilot removed his heavy leather gauntlets so that he could button up his leather coat. "I'd much rather be up there chasing the Hun than have him taking pot shots at me. The Quirk's too stable to be an effective fighter and I'm always worried that Graham might accidentally shoot our tail off."

"Thanks for the vote of confidence," Graham Price shouted from the cockpit.

"But if this is what they want us to fly, who am I to complain," George Fincham added, ignoring the comment. "Just so long as they send up a few scouts to watch over us."

"Listen, I won't hold you up, George," said Charles Hickie. "Johnstone has already finished giving your observer the rundown. I'll get the men to clear everything and move your machine out into the open."

"Thanks, Charles. Do that would you. If you'll excuse me, I want a brief chat with Graham before we leave."

Charles Hickie waved to the ground crew who started to move the pile of empty petrol tins from the front of the aircraft to the side of the hangar. George Fincham, seeing that his observer had already climbed down from the cockpit and was getting ready to don his balaclava, called out to him.

"I've got something to tell you, Graham. Would you come over here?"

"What's up, George?"

"The major told the commanders this morning that we're no longer to operate from the eastern side of the aerodrome."

"Why's that?"

"He thinks it's no longer safe with all the buildings we now have over here."

George pointed towards the team of soldiers who were fixing curved sections of corrugated iron sheeting to the wooden framework of the new Nissen huts, only yards away from the well-worn track used by aircraft in taxying from one side of the airfield to the other.

"When the new hangars are finished up near the top farm, these canvas sheds behind us will go."

"What will happen to our machines?"

"Our flight's been promised the two hangars closest to the small pond, so we'll be the quickest off the ground."

"It will make life a lot easier for everybody," Charles Hickie added.

"People like Johnstone here will be able to sleep on the aerodrome instead of being billeted out in the village.

The pilot turned to his observer.

"How many targets do we have this morning, Graham?"

"Only four. I confirmed them with the battery commander a few minutes ago. The first three are gun emplacements and the last one's a supply dump. I've already drawn the positions on my map."

"Good. Let me mark the coordinates on mine and then we can get going."

"Right you are."

Having compared notes, the two airmen left the others and walked across to their aircraft, which had already been moved out into the open. Pulling on their helmets and goggles, they climbed up into their cockpits. After a few minutes spent in final preparations, George signalled to the ground crew that he was ready to leave. Upon his command the four-bladed propeller was swung by one of the ground crew. The engine burst into life, with smoke billowing high into the air from the vertical exhaust pipes. Having given the engine time to warm up, he waved to the mechanics for the chocks to be removed and then slowly increased the throttle.

The force of the back draft shook the sides of the canvas hangar and the onlookers had to shield their eyes from the blast. After a few seconds, the wheels overcame the grip of the muddy surface and the machine moved up on to the gravelled track.

George taxied the aircraft past the huts and across the road to the western side of the airfield, the perimeter guards holding back the traffic at a safe distance until the way was clear. Turning the aircraft from side to side to see what lay ahead, he lined up facing the landing 'T', two hundred yards away. With most of the airfield covered in a light dusting of snow, he found it difficult to see the white sign. At the same time he looked all around and made a mental note of the other machines that were also preparing to take off.

When all was clear, he opened the throttle fully. With the control stick pressed into his stomach and applying a small degree of left rudder to maintain a straight course, he waited for the machine to pick up speed. Seconds later, he relaxed his grip on the stick as the tail skid lifted off the ground and the aircraft climbed slowly into the air.

Clearing the roofs of the hangars by only a matter of feet, George continued to hold the aircraft in a climb as he made a gentle turn to the right, gradually bringing it on to an easterly heading. Leaning forward in his seat he smacked hard on the fuselage. Graham Price turned around and gave him the 'thumbs up' before reaching over the side of the cockpit to let out the aerial. Looking over the side of the cockpit as they climbed over the aerodrome in wide circles, George saw three other aircraft take to the air. The first was another BE2c of the wireless flight but the machines that followed were the DH2 and FE8 scouts of Number 5 squadron. Knowing that the two fighters would be patrolling in the same area was reassuring to him.

Twelve minutes into the flight, he levelled the machine out at four thousand feet. He set a course for Ypres, all the while keeping a lookout for the aircraft they were to replace. After a further ten minutes, just as they were nearing the outskirts of the city, he spotted an aircraft approaching at about the same height. Though not expecting to see a German aircraft over allied territory, he was nonetheless relieved when he recognised the familiar shape of a BE2c. It was evident that his observer had also seen the machine, for he was gesticulating towards it with his left arm. As the returning aircraft sped past in the opposite direction, its crew waved their arms in the air to indicate that their mission had been successful. Feeling more at ease, George began to hum a tune, pleased that the squadron's record of no losses since the beginning of the year remained intact. Then, having rechecked his position on the map clipped to the instrument panel, he changed course for the assigned battery, located near the village of Voormezeele.

Flying over Dickebusch Lake with the buildings of Ypres clearly visible in the distance, George looked down at the ground and saw numerous plumes of grey smoke billow briefly into the air, evidence that the allied guns were in action along the whole length of the front. To the south of the city, just inside enemy-held territory, he also noticed dozens of puffs of brown smoke. Each the size of a small haystack, the shell-bursts appeared in the sky like magic as German anti-aircraft gunners tried to anticipate the track of a slowly moving British aircraft. As the older puffs of smoke faded away, they were replaced by fresh explosions closer to the aircraft. Filled with a detached sense of security, he watched as the tiny aircraft continued to evade its foe. His feeling of complacency evaporated when the machine suddenly disappeared in a single large explosion. All that remained of it was a brown stain in the sky. Brought back to reality, George grimly realised that within a matter of minutes he and his observer would be facing a similar danger, flying on a repetitive and predictable course at a constant height, over the top of several German anti-aircraft gun positions.

He checked the position of the British six inch howitzer battery, marked on his map with a pencilled cross. Its exact location was a farm one mile east of Dickebusch Lake, close to the hamlet of Elzenwalle. Looking over the side of the cockpit, George eventually succeeded in locating the four guns on the pockmarked surface of the ground, half a mile ahead of the aircraft. Though little remained of the actual farm buildings, he could see that the battery's position on the side of a small hill gave it a certain degree of protection from the German guns. He glanced again at the map and started to estimate the heading for the first of the targets, a gun emplacement six miles east of their current position.

George was distracted from his calculations when Graham Price turned around in the front cockpit and pointed down towards the battery. Over the noise of the engine he could barely make out what his friend was saying.

"I've just sent down a signal. Fly over the top of the battery so we can see if they've picked it up."

"Will do, Graham!" he shouted back.

Aiming towards the battery, George lowered the port wing in a sideslip to get a better view of what the gun crews were doing. Looking over the side, he saw one of the soldiers place a white sheet on the ground next to the end howitzer, signifying that the battery had received their call signal and that the guns were standing by, awaiting further instructions. With no time to lose, he changed course, steering the aircraft in the direction, but slightly to starboard, of the first target. Crossing over the lines into enemy territory, he knew that his observer would continue to transmit their call sign as a precautionary measure in case the wireless operator on the ground needed to make minor corrections to the wavelength[45] of his receiver.

In less than four minutes they were within sight of the enemy gun emplacement and the sky all around was filled with bursting anti-aircraft shells. The shells were exploding well below the aircraft as the German gunners had yet to determine the correct altitude for the setting of the fuzes. Slapping on the fuselage, George waited again for the 'thumbs up' signal from his observer, indication that he had also spotted the target and was ready to go back. With the signal received, George put the aircraft into a gentle turn to starboard, pointing it directly towards the allied battery. This completed the first part of the shoot. It was now the responsibility of his observer to range the battery on to their first target.

In the front cockpit, Graham Price looked at the map strapped to his knee and estimated that the distance between the battery and the target was a little over ten thousand yards. He knew that a one hundred pound shell would take about forty seconds to reach the target, compared to the five minutes it would take for them to fly the same distance.

Removing his gauntlets, Graham reached into his coat pocket and took out a small transparent celluloid disc. At the centre of the disc was a small hole that acted as a bullseye and radiating from the hole were eight concentric circles of increasing diameter. In addition to the circles, whose purpose was to register the distance an exploding shell was from the intended target, the hours of the clock were painted around the circumference of the disc. These would be used in conjunction with the circles to accurately report the aiming correction to the gunners on the ground.

He pulled out a spare pin from the leather surround of the instrument panel and pinned the disc to the map, with the bullseye directly over the target and the twelve o'clock position pointing due north. Reaching for the Morse key, he transmitted the 'KQ' code to the battery, requesting confirmation that the guns were standing by. He then sat back and waited until the aircraft was close enough for him to be able to read the gunnery officer's reply. When he was able to see the white strips of cloth laid out on the ground in a pattern that indicated the battery was ready to fire, he raised his right hand with his thumb pointing upwards to indicate to the pilot that all was well. Almost immediately, the starboard wing dropped as the aircraft went into a tight turn before heading towards the target on the first observation run.

Graham turned around in his chair and shouted over the windscreen to the pilot.

"George, you'll need to fly closer this time so that I can see exactly where the shell hits! I'll raise my right arm again when I am ready for you to turn back!"

"Make it sooner than later, would you old chap?" the pilot shouted back to him. "I think Archie must have worked out our elevation by now."

Three quarters of the way to the target and once more in the thick of enemy anti-aircraft fire, Graham had a clear view of the enemy gun emplacement. He raised his right arm as a signal to the pilot who once again turned the aircraft around. As soon as they were on their way back to the battery, he took hold of the Morse key and transmitted the 'G' firing code, repeating it several times. Looking down at the end howitzer he waited for the muzzle flash of the first round. Sooner than he expected, a puff of smoke billowed from the gun's barrel. Turning around in his seat he tried to estimate the direction of the target, four thousand yards to the east. At his signal, the pilot executed a turn to port, steering the aircraft across the path of the shell and towards the target.[46] As he waited for the shell to hit, Graham counted off the seconds with the aid of the pocket watch strapped to his arm.

He had reached a count of thirty two when the machine was pushed violently downwards as if hit by a huge invisible force. It rocked from side to side as the pilot struggled to bring it back on to an even keel. Eight seconds later an explosion erupted on the ground, two miles ahead, at precisely the correct range but slightly to the left of the intended target. A huge plume of earth rose into the sky, creating a ripple in the ground mist that spread out from the explosion like a stone dropped in still water.

"We cut that a bit fine!" he called out. "That must have been the shell coming down over our heads. Next time we'd better go closer to the target and a little more off the line of fire."

"Keep your eyes on the explosion, Graham!" his pilot shouted back. "I'll fly towards the target a little longer next time, so you can get an accurate correction."

The shock wave of the near miss had dislodged the disc from his map and Graham had to reposition it in order to work out the appropriate correction. After studying the map, he wrote 'B12' on the notepad strapped to his other leg, signifying that the shell had burst between fifty and one hundred yards to the north, or left, of the target. [47]

Graham was about to instruct the pilot to turn the machine around, when he was knocked sideways by the force of a nearby anti-aircraft explosion. Looking over the side, he noticed several large holes in the fabric of the lower port plane, each hole ragged and with burnt edges. Almost immediately, the aircraft was rocked by a second explosion, though this time the shell burst fifty yards behind them.

He heard a slap on the side of the cockpit and turned around to face the pilot.

"I think we're through the worst of it! Have you worked out the correction?"

"Yes I have, George. You can turn back now!"

The aircraft lurched again as yet another anti-aircraft shell exploded nearby. Before he could brace himself, Graham was pushed down in his seat, experiencing three times the force of gravity as the pilot pulled the aircraft into a tight climbing turn to starboard.

When the German anti aircraft guns stopped firing, Graham realised they were safe until the next run. Peering over the side, he tried to gauge the severity of the wing damage. Though a significant portion of fabric was missing from the lower wing, as far as he could tell no bracing or control wires had been broken. He turned to shout to the pilot.

"It looks worse than it is, George! I can't see any broken wires though she could be pulling to port from the holes in the wing."

"All right, Graham, let's press on. I'll keep heading towards the battery whilst you send them the correction. Let me know when you've sent the message so I can be ready to make the turn as soon as the gun fires again. That will save us some time."

"I've just sent the signal so it won't be long now."

The aircraft was at about the same position where it had almost been struck by the first shell when the howitzer fired again.

"I can see the smoke, George. Let's go back into Hunland!"

This time the pilot made a hard turn to starboard with the wings of the BE2c almost vertical. Counting out the seconds, Graham was forced back in his seat, the wooden shelf holding the telegraph key pressing painfully into his right arm as he twisted around to keep the target area in sight. Having reached a count of forty one, he spotted another explosion on the ground. This time more than just a column of earth erupted into the air. The initial blast was followed by several more explosions, each one larger than the first and a huge cloud of black smoke rose hundreds of feet into the air.

"By jove, we've scored a direct hit in two!" he shouted excitedly. "Just look at those fireworks!"

Coming again within range of the German anti-aircraft guns, the aircraft was buffeted by a series of blasts. Pieces of fragmented shell whizzed through the air all around, some of them penetrating the left side of the fuselage and burning holes in the fabric.

"Don't wait around any longer, George. Head back towards the battery and I'll transmit the 'OK' signal on the way. They won't need to fire again on these coordinates."

"Rightio, Graham. Hold on to your horses while I get us out of here!"

It took another hour to successfully range the batteries on to the next two targets, though both targets were destroyed without further mishap. The third objective proved the most difficult. Marked as a supply dump and positioned next to a crossroads it should have been an easy target, but the intensity of the anti-aircraft gunfire made George unwilling to risk taking the aircraft as close as his observer would have liked. It took five aiming corrections before the four howitzers obliterated the supply dump as well as a large section of the cross roads.

With one remaining target, George was anxious to complete the mission and return to Abeele. They had been in the air for two and a half hours and were running low on fuel. He decreased the throttle in order to reduce the speed and wind noise, so that he could more easily communicate with his observer.

"We must press on, Graham, as we're low on petrol and I don't want to risk having to land on the wrong side of the lines. The holes in the wing aren't helping us either."

"I've not seen our escorts for a while, George. Climb higher on the way back to the battery would you, so I can get a better look at what's around?"

"I'll see what I can do, but I can't promise anything. I'm not sure how badly we're damaged and I don't want to chance my arm."

"You're the pilot. I'm about to transmit to say that we're ready for the final target. Tell me if you want to call it a day and I'll send them the CI[48] instead."

"Let's try at least one run. We're right over Zillebeke now, so it won't take us long to get back to the battery. The observer on the ground can probably see us already if he's using his binoculars."

"Our time's almost up, so we might even overlap with the machine that's next up. Let me test the Lewis before I send the message."

"Right you are, Graham."

With the aircraft in a steady climb on a direct heading towards the battery, Graham stowed his maps and unbuckled his waist belt. He turned around in the cockpit and knelt on his seat so that he could make ready the machine gun. Having checked the magazine, he swung the gun through the safe arc of fire and fired off six practice rounds. He smiled at his friend, though he doubted the pilot could see his expression behind the large goggles and close-fitting balaclavas that they were both wearing.

Sitting in the rear cockpit, George Fincham instinctively flinched at the sound of the machine gun, the muzzle only inches from his face. He waited until the firing had ceased before he tried to say anything.

"I'll keep an eye out while you send your message, Graham. I can see a small speck in the distance, about two miles away. It's a lot higher than we are and it's coming towards us from the west, so I'd put my money on it as being our relief."

"I hope they'll be as lucky as we've been today."

"We're not home yet!" George replied, but his words were lost in the wind.

The speck grew closer, decreasing in height as it approached. Within a few seconds what had at first appeared as a small black dot quickly grew into the shape of an aircraft. George looked intently at the oncoming machine, its image blurred by the spinning propeller. Lowering the nose momentarily to get a clearer view, he sensed that there was something odd about the silhouette. It only took him a few moments to identify the aircraft as a monoplane. Knowing of no such allied aircraft operating in the area, he quickly realised that it had to be a Fokker scout. They were directly in its path, unable to return fire as their only weapon was pointing in the opposite direction.

At a range of five hundred yards he could tell that the enemy aircraft was attacking in a steep dive. As it came closer, he could see flashes of light erupt from the muzzle of the centrally mounted machine gun as the German pilot fired straight at them.

"Eindekkker!" he screamed as he pushed the throttle wide open. Forcing the aircraft into a violent turn to port, he tried to manoeuvre into a position where his observer would be able to fire upon their attacker. Without warning, the steep turn developed into a spiral dive as the damaged fabric tore away from the wing ribs. He struggled to regain control and gradually brought the aircraft out of the dive. Looking around to check their position, George discovered that they were flying in an easterly direction, back towards the German lines. With the aircraft back under control he gradually increased the throttle so that he could gain height yet minimise the strain on the damaged wing surface.

"I think he overshot us!" he shouted into the slipstream, hoping that his observer would hear. "See if you can spot him as I turn back towards our lines. With God's help we can still make it home, Graham!"

This time he banked the machine in the opposite direction. He briefly looked over the side of the cockpit to get his bearings and saw the outline of Zillebeke Lake come into view immediately below. Knowing that they were only minutes away from Abeele, he quickly reassured himself that there should be sufficient fuel to make it home, provided the wing held out. His thoughts were interrupted by the deafening sound of the Lewis gun. He quickly glanced behind but could not see anything. Between bursts of gunfire his observer was trying to tell him something, but the only words he could hear were, 'Immelman turn'.

These two words were enough for George to realise that they were in grave danger. The enemy pilot must have zoomed up into a loop, rolled his machine over at the top of the loop and positioned himself for making another attack, this time from behind. But, as they had already crossed over the British lines, there was still a chance that the enemy might break off and leave them in peace.

The firing stopped and he watched as his observer removed the spent drum of ammunition and let it drop to the floor the cockpit.

Just as Graham Price reached out over the side to take a new drum of ammunition from the storage rack, George felt a searing pain in his back and left arm. At exactly the same moment, three blood-encircled bullet holes appeared in the Triplex windscreen directly in front of him. The observer's body jerked backwards as if he had been tackled by an invisible rugby opponent, his hands simultaneously letting go of the Lewis gun and the new drum of ammunition. Caught in the slipstream, the heavy drum scraped along the side of the fuselage, before striking the tailplane and punching a neat hole through the vertical fin. Unable to reach into the front cockpit, George watched as Graham Price slid to the floor with arms outstretched, the back of his head striking the instrument panel as he fell. The aircraft slowed as if it had encountered a sudden head wind and with no-one manning it, the Lewis gun spun around in random circular movements as the aeroplane faltered in the sky. Smoke began to pour out of the engine and the whole machine vibrated violently as pieces of wood flew off the propeller, striking the fuselage in a hailstorm of splinters.

"I'm shutting it down, Graham!" George shouted, praying that his friend was still alive. Switching off the aircraft's electrics, he looked over the side for a suitable place to land. "The engine's been hit and the propeller's shattered, so there's no chance of reaching the airfield, I'm afraid. Hold on old chap, I'll do my best for you!"

George grappled with the controls using his right hand and both feet, his left arm hanging useless by his side. The control stick felt warm and sticky in his grasp. With all the strength he could muster, he tried to hold the aircraft on an even descent in order to give them at least a chance of making a successful landing. As he did so, he fought to remain conscious, but all he wanted to do was close his eyes. He had no idea where the enemy scout was and did not even care, knowing that he had no strength to turn around in his seat even if he wanted to. Waves of pain and nausea swept over him and every time he relaxed his grip on the controls, his peripheral vision closed in so that it seemed like he was looking through the wrong end of a telescope.

Somehow the shattered machine held together, testimony to the designers at the Royal Aircraft Factory, and George aimed for a large field where cows were grazing. As the aircraft fell from the sky, it left behind it a trail of dense grey smoke the shape of a giant corkscrew, visible all around to hundreds of allied and enemy soldiers alike, who had watched the conflict from the relative safety of their trenches with a detached sense of interest and sympathy.

Using the last of his strength, George pulled back on the control stick as the ground rushed towards him.

"Almost there, Graham. Almost there," he murmured.

The stricken machine slowly came out of the dive, stalled momentarily in mid air before rolling over on to its back and plunging vertically into the ground, bringing to a swift conclusion its first and only mission.

Chapter 8
Eine Kleine Nachtmusik

Fred sat down at the table and took out a tiny red notebook from his jacket pocket. He removed the elastic retaining band, opened the book and searched for the entry he had made the previous day. Removing the small from the spine of the notebook, he wrote the date followed by the words:

Install and test new wireless. Concert at Julia's in the evening.

"What are you doing, Fredrik?"

Julia Denecker was a strikingly attractive woman 'of a certain age', a term commonly used to describe a mature woman who was not young enough to be addressed as mademoiselle but had yet to reach middle age. Julia enjoyed the company of men but had never married, and since the war had removed so many of the eligible men from the Belgian population it was unlikely that she ever would.

"I'm just writing in my diary, Julia. If I miss even one day I find it hard to catch up. There's only enough room for a few words, but it's small enough to carry around."

"Why bother? You could keep a proper diary in your room."

"Because I keep other details in it. Like watch repairs and Flying Corps matters that I'm not at liberty to show you."

Julia reached over and tried to grab the notebook, but Fred held it from her at arm's length.

"It looks more like an autograph book to me." Then, after a pause, she added slyly, "Would you permit me to write something in it so you won't forget me also?"

"I suppose so. If you really must."

Reluctantly, Fred handed her the notebook.

"Choose an empty page, though. I wouldn't want you to make a mess of anything important."

"I wouldn't dream of it, Fredrik."

"Here, use this pencil. It's only small but it is sharp."

Julia sat down opposite Fred. Opening the notebook at the centre page, she wrote her name elaborately on one side with the words 'Abeele, Belgium' printed underneath. She paused for a few moments and then started to draw a picture, her face contorted as she concentrated on what she was doing. Fred leaned over the table to get a better view.

"Don't look, I want to surprise you," she scolded.

Fred sat back on his chair and pretended to look out of the window.

After a few minutes, Julia put down the pencil and pushed the diary towards him.

"Do you like? I tried to make it as real as I could."

Fred looked at the carefully drawn sketches of a flying machine, one viewed from the front and the other in profile. From the shape of the fuselage it was evident that the aircraft was meant to be a BE2c.

"This is really good, Julia. It does look like one of our machines. The only part that's wrong is the tail. It doesn't droop quite like that. May I correct it for you?"

Julia nodded and handed him the pencil. He carefully redrew the shape of the tail with stronger pencil lines, adding the extra vertical fin that was fitted as standard to all of the squadron's newer machines.

"There you are. That's perfect now. It will be a permanent reminder of my dearest Belgian friend."

Julia got up from the table, walked around to where Fred was sitting and stood behind him. Leaning forward, she kissed him on the cheek.

"You are most kind, monsieur," she whispered.

The noise of the kitchen door slamming shut made them look up.

"What's going on here? I thought you had a girl pining for you back home in Blighty!"

"Hello, Arnold. I was beginning to wonder when you'd turn up. Was your crew late back?"

Arnold Makepiece was also a mechanic with Number 6 squadron. Like Fred, he was a keen musician and played the violin whenever the opportunity arose. Earlier in the day he had promised Fred he would meet him at Julia's so that they could practice for the evening's concert.

Arnold put down his violin and sat down.

"They didn't make it back at all, Fred. One of the batteries saw a machine fall near Voormezeele, just the other side of Dickebusch Lake. They raised the alarm and when the medics reached the scene of the crash, it turned out to be one of ours."

"Was anyone hurt?"

"Lieutenant Price was already dead and Lieutenant Fincham so badly wounded that he died on the way to the field hospital. The whole squadron's cut up especially as we've not lost anyone in four months. What with that and the accident last week."

Fred looked up, shocked at the news. He had been talking with the crew only hours earlier and now both men were dead and their aircraft destroyed.

"I'm so sorry, Arnold. Do you know what happened?"

"It appears they were attacked by a Fokker. None of our scouts were in the area at the time so they had no protection."

"What about Archie?"

"That was pretty heavy today. The other machines came back with dozens of holes in them."

"It's strange how some machines go on forever and yet others get struck off charge[49] soon after they arrive. I wonder if the lieutenants would still be alive if they'd been flying their old 'Fee'."

"Either way, it doesn't help them now, does it?"

"Should I cancel tonight's show?" Julia interrupted, a frown crossing her face.

"No fear. The captain came to see me just before I left. He thinks it's important for morale that the officers spend a bit of time away from the aerodrome."

"Well, if that's the case, we've only got half an hour before they start turning up," said Fred, putting away his notebook and rising from the table. "Do you need us for anything, Julia?"

"No, Fred. I have to organise the food for tonight and you can't help me with that. Go through to the dining room if you like. There's nobody there to disturb you."

Julia touched Fred on the arm and walked off in the direction of the kitchen.

"Let's run through what we're going to play," Fred suggested. "Julia told me there's no-one to sing for us tonight, so we'll have to be careful what music we pick."

"I wouldn't worry about that, Fred. If the officers drink as much as they normally do, we'd be hard put to stop them joining in, whatever we play."

"Let's do it anyway, even if we don't have time for a run-through."

"All right, Fred. Ready when you are."

Arnold picked up his violin and the two men, dressed in their Royal Flying Corps uniforms, walked down the wide hall side by side. When they reached the main dining room they passed through the open doors and walked across to the large wooden dais on the far side of the room. Standing in the middle of the dais was a large piano. Unusual for a grand, it was cased in a walnut veneer with delicately crafted diamond shaped inlays.

Fred stepped up on to the platform, sat down at the piano and played a two octave arpeggio.

"This Pleyel always delights me. The craftsmanship is superb and the sound's as clear as a bell. Did you know that Chopin never played on anything else?"

Arnold removed his violin from its case and fingered the many scratches on its body.

"It's certainly better than my trusty instrument. This has seen more pubs than concert halls, that's for sure. I don't even know who made it." Grasping the violin by its neck, Arnold plucked the strings roughly with his fingers. "It still does the job though."

"A bit like you, would you say?"

Fred avoided Arnold's steely glare and reached down to pick up the pile of sheet music that he had earlier placed on the floor next to the lyre shaped pedestal. Sliding one of the candelabra trays out from the piano, he laid the music on top of it.

"We can't all be choir boys, Fred."

"Sorry, Arnold, I wasn't being serious. I think most people we play to would rather listen to you than me any day."

"Apology accepted. So what shall it be, then?"

"Let's do what we normally do. A little bit of classical mixed with popular music, followed by a few songs if it looks like anyone wants to join in."

Fred turned to the back of his diary where he kept a list of his musical repertoire.

"Let's start with some Dixie to put them in a relaxed mood. How about 'All Aboard for Dixie Land' or 'Rag Picker'? You've played those before haven't you?"

"Yes I have. Let's do both."

Fred ran his finger down the list of tunes.

"And if they're slow in arriving, we can add 'Dixie Bazaar' to the list. We can move to something a bit more serious once they've all settled down."

"That's all well and fine for you Fred, but my strings are getting old."

"All right, just the first two then. What about following them with a waltz? 'Merry Widow' is always a favourite."

"That's good. Can we also play some of the music from 'Girl on the Film'? I like that show."

"Will your fingers be able to cope?"

"As long as I can take a break after that and have a few ales with the chaps. You could play some Rachmaninoff whilst I'm away."

"Yes, I could certainly do that," replied Fred, searching through the pile of sheet music and removing several pages. Sorting the sheets into the correct order, he placed them on the piano's music rack. "That should do us, I think."

"Listen, Fred, I'm famished. Let's ask Julia if she'll give us a bite to eat before the guests arrive."

"Good idea. We can leave our things here. No-one's going to steal them."

By seven o'clock the tables were almost full. Most had been reserved for the squadron's officers and their guests, but a few tables at the back of the room had been kept for the regular customers. Fred and Arnold were about to start the evening's entertainment when a young Royal Flying Corps lieutenant walked up to the stage.

"Good evening men, we're all looking forward to a good show tonight. Johnstone, can I have a word with you in private?"

"Yes, sir."

Fred recognised the lieutenant from a brief encounter at the aerodrome when he had thought the officer looked hardly old enough to have left school.

"We can pop into the adjoining room," he added. "It's not being used tonight."

Fred got up from the piano and led the lieutenant through to the small lounge room, closing the door behind him.

"How can I help you, Lieutenant Worstenholm?"

"I understand you're billeted at Café Evalina and that you're on good terms with its owner."

The lieutenant paused for a moment, nervously fingering his moustache.

"Would you do me a favour and ask her to give this letter to her sister?"

"Certainly, sir. I'll probably have supper with Caroline later tonight, so I can give it to her personally."

The lieutenant blushed as he handed Fred a small envelope.

"Be a good chap and don't mention this to anyone, eh?"

"Mum's the word, Lieutenant."

Fred placed the envelope in his jacket pocket and the two men returned to the main dining room, by now almost full to capacity.

The evening went according to plan and by nine thirty Fred and Arnold had completed the music schedule. When Fred started to play tunes at the request of the audience, Arnold seized the opportunity and left the stage to walk to the bar at the rear of the dining room. His friends had been drinking there since the start of the entertainment. After playing a few songs by himself, Fred became concerned that Arnold might not return, and he waved to attract his friend's attention. With a reluctant look on his face, Arnold rose unsteadily to his feet and left the bar, squeezing his way through the crowded tables and up on to the dais. Relieved, Fred was about to ask the audience for another request when he became aware that someone had walked up behind him. Turning around, he saw that Julia had placed a glass of brandy on top of the piano and was waiting patiently to talk to him.

"What's the matter, Julia?"

"Can you make this the last song please, Fredrik? I have a long day tomorrow and there are only two girls to help me clear up tonight."

"All right, we'll make it a good one to finish up."

Fred drank the brandy in one gulp and handed the glass back to Julia.

"Thanks for the nightcap."

"What do you mean 'night cap'? I give you no night cap."

"Sorry, Julia, I was thanking you for the brandy."

"You are very strange, Englishman. Just when I think I understand you, you confuse me again."

"It's the English language that's strange, not me."

"Fredrik, I must go and open the cloakroom. Come and see me before you leave, would you?"

Julia kissed Fred on the cheek and turned to walk away, narrowly avoiding a collision with Arnold who had walked up behind her.

"What have you got that I don't have?" Arnold muttered, steadying himself against the side of the piano as he tried to place the violin under his chin.

"You wouldn't understand if I told you."

Fred turned to the audience.

"Ladies and gentlemen, I'm afraid we have to conclude the evening's entertainment. There's time for one more song and I thought we'd finish off with a lively one. It's called 'Alabama Jubilee'. You would all know the melody but may not know the words, so I'm asking for a volunteer to come up and lead the song for us."

Looking around the room Fred counted five raised hands, but his attention was drawn to a Canadian officer who was sitting with a group of civilians at one of the rear tables.

"Thank you, Captain," he said, pointing to the soldier. "If you would be so kind as to join us on the stage, we will show the audience a good example of Anglo-Canadian cooperation."

The captain walked up to the piano as Fred and Arnold played the first few bars of the song. When he joined them on to the dais, Fred continued to play but leaned forward so that he could speak without anyone else hearing.

"Hello Vernon. I never expected to see you here."

"Hi Fred. Long time no see. Listen, this may be our last chance to share the stage together for a while. I've heard a rumour the battalion's on the move again."

"Do you know when?"

"They're planning a counter attack at St Eloi and we've been ordered to join in. It'll be our first real battle, so we need to make a good impression."

"Can we talk later?"

"Sorry, Fred. I'm with a few people tonight so I can't hang around, but I'll keep you posted as usual via the notice board."

"All right, let's make the most of it." Fred turned to Arnold. "Are you ready?"

"Yes, Fred. Let's get it over with. I'm bursting for another piss."

Fred played the first four bars of the song again to give Vernon the key. Arnold joined in with the honky tonk melody on his violin but towards the end of the third bar he faltered.

"Bugger and damnation," he cried out, well within earshot of the diners sitting at the front row of tables. "I've broken my 'A' string."

The audience laughed and applauded the unfortunate violinist. Fred stopped playing and Arnold took a bow, nearly falling over when he tried to stand up again. Fred leant over towards Arnold and spoke quietly.

"That could be one of the reasons why I have more success with the ladies than you do. One never knows what you're going to say next!"

Fred stood to face the audience.

"Sorry about that, ladies and gentlemen. We will now play for you a three stringed version of 'Alabama Jubilee'."

Once again they played the opening bars and this time all went well. Vernon came in on cue and sang the words to the first verse. By the time the trio had reached the last chorus of the song, almost everyone in the room had joined in, and when the final echoes of *'Oh honey, hail! hail! the gang's all here, for an Alabama Jubilee'* had faded away, the audience broke into applause.

Vernon took a bow and turned to Fred.

"I've not had as much fun since 'Yeoman of the Guard' back home last year. We must do this again, Fred."

"Yes, we must. I really enjoyed it too. Perhaps next time we should find a sober violinist with a complete set of strings!"

"Now you've really hurt my feelings," Arnold called out in a slurred voice from the other side of the piano.

"Sorry, Arnold, but I wasn't sure you'd last the evening. Do you want me to walk you back to the aerodrome?"

"You don't have to worry about me, Fred, the night's only just started. I can make my own way back, thank you very much."

"If you're sure, then."

"Course I'm sure. There's nothing wrong with me."

Vernon left the stage to return to his table and received another ovation from the audience. Arnold packed his violin and walked off quickly in the direction of the bathroom whilst Fred remained behind to put away the music and close the piano. With the entertainment at an end the diners finished their drinks, settled their accounts and moved into the hall where they collected their outdoor clothes from the cloakroom. Julia farewelled everyone individually at the front door before letting them out into the cold night air.

Fred sat at the piano, sorting through the sheet music as he waited for the room to clear. He happened to look up just as Vernon was leaving the dining room with several fellow Canadian officers. Vernon caught his eye and waved. Then he was gone.

Fred closed the lid of the piano and slowly walked through the hall to the front door. The last of the guests had already left and Julia was waiting for him.

"That went well, didn't it?"

"Yes, it did. Thanks to you and Arnold."

Fred winked at her.

"Well, that's one for the mechanics."

"Who is the man who sang for you? What a lovely voice he had for an army captain."

"Don't judge a man by his uniform, Julia. You can never tell what talents lie beneath. Take Arnold for example. You'd never know he was a brain surgeon, would you?"

Julia laughed and handed Fred his overcoat.

"Here are ten francs for you to share with your inebriated friend. You deserve more, but it's all I can afford at the moment."

"Thank you Julia, but you know I don't do it for the money."

He leaned forward and kissed her on both cheeks.

"Goodnight then. Thank you for signing my autograph book."

"Promise me you won't tear the page out."

"Of course I won't. It will be there for all time."

Julia smiled and waited until Fred had buttoned up his coat, before opening the door for him.

"Until the next time, Fredrik."

"I'm not sure when that will be, Julia. There's a rumour of a big push and I may not be allowed out for a while. Anyway, I'll let Evelyn know what I'm doing and she'll get a message to you."

"I'm sure we can come to some arrangement, as you say. Bon nuit, Fredrik, thank you again."

Fred walked out of the front door, through the porch and on to the road. It was quiet and no-one else was in sight. With a lull in the fighting since the end of the Battle of Loos and the loss of the Bluff a few weeks earlier, there was very little night-time traffic on the road from Abeele to Poperinghe. He knew it would be a different story on the road from Poperinghe to Ypres, which was always jammed with vehicles and soldiers.

With no moonlight to light the way, it took a few minutes for Fred's eyes to become accustomed to the darkness. Stepping out on to the road he cautiously made his way in the direction of the estaminet, only a ten minute walk from Margueritas. Upon reaching the Café Evalina and letting himself in using the spare key, he found to his surprise that everyone had gone to bed. Everyone, that is, except Evalina and Caroline, whom he could hear talking in the kitchen. Taking off his coat, he walked through to the kitchen.

"Bonsoir mesdames, how are we tonight?"

The two women stopped talking and looked up from where they were sitting. Evalina was the first to speak.

"Bonsoir, Fredrik. Did you have a good night at Margueritas?"

"Yes I did, thank you," Fred replied, sitting down on a chair on the opposite side of the table. "I played for a soldier who I met a few weeks ago at Talbot House. He's over here with the Canadian Expeditionary Force."

Caroline got up from the table and walked over to the stove. Picking up a saucepan, she poured some steaming hot liquid into a clean mug before passing the mug to Fred.

"Thank you. Hot chocolate is just what I need." Fred warmed his hands on the mug before taking a sip. Then, remembering the envelope, he reached into his pocket and took it out, pushing it across the table towards Caroline. "Here. This is for you, Caroline. It's a letter from one of our officers, Lieutenant Worstenholm. He was at Margueritas tonight."

Caroline blushed deeply and picked up her mug to disguise her embarrassment.

"Oh really, Fredrik?" she replied with feigned innocence. "I'm sure I don't know why he would be writing to me. Perhaps it's a mistake."

"I don't know either but he made me promise not to mention the matter to anyone!"

The blush spread across Caroline's face as she picked up the envelope. She pushed it into the pocket of her frock without even glancing at the writing.

"Thank you, Fredrik. Now, please excuse. I must go to my sleep. It has been a long day. Bonne nuit."

"Bonne nuit, Caroline," said Fred, exchanging glances with Evalina as Caroline squeezed past him and walked out of the kitchen.

"What do you make of that?"

"I know my sister is seeing someone but I did not know he was a British officer. I hope she is not serious with this man as he will either die or go home to his woman."

"I'm inclined to agree with you, Evelyn, but she's been so happy recently. It is good that she's started to enjoy herself again." Fred reached out and picked up his mug. Looking thoughtful he drained the last of the hot chocolate. "You know, Evelyn, there's a lot I'm going to miss if this war ever ends. For one thing, hot chocolate never tasted this good in England."

"It's funny how things change Fredrik. You were so sad when you first come here and now look at you."

"I used to have a simplistic view on life and it took me a long time to adjust."

Fred carried the empty mug to the sink and dropped it in the dirty water. He turned around to Evalina.

"Now I too must go to bed. It will be a busy day tomorrow as we'll have to train two new officers. Bonne nuit, Evelyn, I will see you at breakfast."

"Good night, Fredrik."

Chapter 9
A Visit to the Trenches

Two days after the deaths of the airmen, Number 5 squadron packed up its equipment and left for Droglandt. Though the new aerodrome was only ten miles north west of Abeele, the 'other ranks' of the two squadrons would no longer share off-duty time in the villages of Abeele, Godewaersvelde and Poperinghe. Nor would they engage in the friendly rivalry that had been an essential part of their lives for the past eleven months.

Life continued much the same for Number 6 squadron, with daily artillery cooperation patrols keeping everyone fully occupied. High winds, low cloud, rain and even the occasional snowstorm reduced flying to a minimum for most of March but towards the end of the month the squadron took part in what was to be four weeks of bombing around the St Eloi[50] craters, five miles south of Ypres. During this action the crews were called to fly as early as three thirty in the morning, two hours before dawn. The pilots had to quickly acclimatise themselves to flying in the dark, with no cockpit illumination and only flares and explosions to guide them to the targets. The task of keeping the aircraft in the air for extended periods meant that the ground crews had to work around the clock, taking whatever rest they could beneath the wings of their machines.

"Thank God it's Saturday."

Fred was sitting opposite Jock on the workbench inside the wireless lorry.

"I know it won't last, but I like being the only squadron here. For one thing, you can always pick a time of day when the latrines are quiet."

"I've never understood what you have against our delightful toilet arrangements, Fred," Jock replied with a laugh. "I think they're bloody efficient."

Jock yawned and put down the screwdriver he had been using so that he could light a cigarette.

"I feel like you look, Jock. I'll be glad when they ease up on all this bombing."

"Especially as our boys have lost most of what they gained in the first week."

"We're still managing to hold on to a couple of the craters, though. Thanks to our Canadian chums."

"Talking of Canadians chums, have you heard from Vernon?"

"Not recently. Last time I saw him he told me his battalion was being sent to St Eloi."

"He wouldn't be getting much rest then, either. Do you want a ciggy?"

Jock reached across the table with an opened pack of Woodbines, flicking the back of the pack with his forefinger so that a single cigarette protruded.

"Thanks, Jock," Fred replied, taking the cigarette and licking one end before placing it between his lips.

Jock struck a match against a table leg and held it out towards Fred, who leant forward and lit the cigarette without removing it from his mouth. Sitting back, Fred inhaled deeply and was caught unawares by an unexpected yawn. The cigarette dropped out of his mouth and on to the floor.

"I'm really missing my sleep, you know."

"At least you've got a cosy billet to go back to most nights. Not like Jock and I."

The mechanic who was working on the lathe had stopped what he was doing to join in on the conversation. At almost twenty five, Ernest Walter Dexter was the oldest of the squadron's wireless mechanics to hold the lowly rank of 2nd class air mechanic. Like Fred, he had grown up in Hampshire, but had moved to London to work for the Marconi Wireless Telegraph Company. By the time he enlisted in the Royal Flying Corps in July 1915, he already had extensive experience in wireless telegraphy. In his spare time, he played the violin and often accompanied Fred at squadron concerts.

"You're going to miss your digs when you move back to the airfield," he added. "Any news when that will be, Fred?"

"A couple of week's I'd say, Dexter. The huts have been completed but we're still waiting for the furniture. Mr Hickie might know more, but I'm not asking as I'm happy where I am."

Their conversation was interrupted by a commotion outside the lorry. Fred got up from the work bench, rolled up the rear curtain and peered outside. Several men were running in the rain towards the other side of the aerodrome. Leaning out of the lorry he shouted out to one of the passing airmen.

"What's all the fuss about, Stan?"

"The new squadron's[51] arrived and their machines are coming in to land right now," the mechanic replied. "With this low cloud I can only see three but I expect the others aren't too far behind."

Fred craned his neck to see if he could catch a glimpse of the aircraft.

"What type of machines do they have?"

"The new de Havilland scout. You know, the one that Number 5 trialled here two months ago. Come and have a look for yourself."

"I will."

Fred jumped down from the lorry and ran to join the men who had congregated inside one of the empty hangars, where they were protected from the driving rain but still had a good view of the landing area. With limited visibility over the whole of the aerodrome, Fred knew that the low cloud and strong winds would provide an additional challenge to pilots unfamiliar with the aerodrome.

One by one the aircraft came into land, the first three in plain view to the men on the ground as they came in on their final approach. Seven more machines appeared out of the mist at irregular intervals over the next ten minutes, evidence that the strong winds had caused the pilots to separate on the short flight from St Omer. Some of the men watched for a few minutes longer before realising that no more aircraft would be coming.

Jock joined Fred inside the hangar just as the last two aircraft were taxiing in, both pilots having carried out perfect three-point landings.

"These new machines will give our boys something to smile about."

"Why's that, Jock?"

"No more waiting for escorts. All the machines can leave here at the same time. The top brass have made a good decision this time, don't you think?"

"Yes I do, except we'll have fewer wireless sets on the aerodrome."

"You can't have everything, Fred. With your skills, you should be able to mend almost anything."

"Talking of skills, did you know that I've just been appointed the squadron's optical expert?"

"News to me. What does that mean?"

"The major's asked me to go to Poperinghe hospital next week to fit out some of the nurses with spectacles."

"Lucky you. Can I come too?"

"No fear. You'd be trying it on whilst they were trying them on!"

"You always want to ruin my chances, Fred."

"Air mechanic Johnstone, I've been looking for you everywhere!"

Fred turned around at hearing the voice of Charles Hickie. The lieutenant was accompanied by an airmen Fred had not seen before. Fred stood to attention and saluted.

"What can I do for you, sir?"

Normally when they were alone, Fred and Jock were less formal than the regulations demanded, but when in the presence of newcomers or other officers they treated the lieutenant as they would any other officer.

"This is air mechanic Brown. He's fresh out from Blighty where he trained as a wireless operator. Though he's officially with us, he's been seconded to the artillery chaps in 43rd Brigade, so you won't be seeing much of him at the aerodrome."

Fred shook hands with the latest addition to the squadron.

"I'm Fred and this is Jock. What do you prefer to be called?"

"Horace will do. Pleased to meet you both."

"The 43rd covers a big area, Horace. Which battery are you working with?"

"The 154th I think it is, but so far I've only spent a day with them."

"Brown's correct. It is the 154th Howitzer Regiment," Charles Hickie interrupted. "They're currently moving their guns to a new position east of Dickebusch."

"Quite a few batteries in that area now, aren't there, sir?"

"Enough to make it even harder for our pilots. Anyway Johnstone, before Brown goes back out to the battery, I'd like you to give him a bit of a run down on what we do. That way he won't feel so much of an outcast when he's out there working by himself."

"He'll be talking to us on the telephone every day and the observers often visit the batteries, so he won't have much time to get lonely."

"Be that as it may, would you spend the next couple of hours with him? Show him how we send messages and how they're interpreted and acknowledged."

Fred nodded in reply as Charles Hickie continued.

"I'll arrange the necessary transport and the three of us will take a drive out when you're ready. We won't be in the way as it will take them a day or so to finish setting up the guns. I can have a talk with the battery commander whilst you help Brown in setting up his various procedures."

"Very good, sir," Fred replied, relieved that the guns would not be firing. He had often experienced the noise that the big howitzers made on previous visits to the batteries.

"If you don't need me, sir, I might as well get back to my work."

"Before you do that, Cardno, I'd like to have a word with you in private. Come with me to the major's office would you?"

"Certainly, sir," Jock replied, a doubtful look on his face.

After Jock and the lieutenant had left, Fred took Horace to the workshop lorry. Stopping at the foot of the ladder, Fred pulled back the canvas and climbed up into the back of the truck. He rolled up the canvas and fastened it with a strap so that Horace could more easily climb on board.

"Having the flap up will give us more light."

"Don't worry about me, Fred. I'm used to working in dark, confined spaces."

At the front of the lorry, Dexter was busy at work on the lathe, but he stopped what he was doing at the sound of a strange voice.

"Who do we have here, Fred?" he asked, eyeing the young stranger dressed in Royal Flying Corps uniform.

"Dexter, meet air mechanic Horace Brown. He's going to be our ears on the ground at the 154th howitzers. The lieutenant asked me to show him the wireless side of things on our machines."

"Hello, Horace, welcome to Number 6. My name's Ernest but you can call me Dexter. Everybody else does. Tell me, what made you volunteer as a wireless operator instead of one of us?"

"Good question, Dexter. I suppose being a sailmaker by trade, I really should have signed on as a rigger, but I didn't like the idea of working in a closed shed breathing in acetone fumes. Not good for the health you know."

"Well, you'll damned soon get sick of the smell of dirt and cordite where you're going! And the best you can expect is a sandbagged hole in the ground, covered by a sheet of tin."

"At least I'll have my own place."

"Rather you than me, old son. Your chances of being killed are much greater than if you were a rigger."

"Hold on, Dexter, you'll put the man off before he's even started."

"Sorry about that, Fred, I didn't mean anything by it. I've got a few things on my plate at the moment. Listen, I'll leave you in peace so you can show Horace what we have here."

"Thanks Dexter, we won't be long."

"I'll be in the hangar next door if anyone wants me."

Dexter switched off the lathe and put away his tools before brushing himself down. Instead of climbing down the ladder he jumped over the side of the lorry and walked away, whistling loudly.

Fred waited a few moments before speaking.

"Don't mind him. He's probably the most experienced wireless mechanic we have in the Corps, yet he's the same rank as you. Mind you, he keeps telling us that one day he'll get his commission."

"It's good to have an aim, even over here," Horace replied. "My plan is to do my job and keep myself to myself. If I make it through the war in one piece I want to start my own boat building firm."

"Talking of making it through, did you see the new scouts?"

"I saw the last two as I walked over here with the lieutenant. They certainly look impressive but I expected more to arrive. Could be the days of the Fokker Scourge I keep hearing about are well and truly numbered."

"Same goes for our BE2s. Or perhaps I'm being a trifle hopeful!"

Fred spent the next two hours showing Horace the workings of an aircraft wireless set as well as the various wavelengths and codes used by the squadron. All the while, the rain beat down on the canvas roof of the lorry, making conversation difficult. Eventually the rain eased and Fred took Horace into a nearby hangar to show him a typical wireless installation. Fred climbed up on to the lower wing of one of the aircraft and pulled Horace up behind him. At his direction, Horace stepped into the front cockpit and sat down on the observer's chair.

"So this is where the 'Piccadilly Johnnies' sit. All very different to the crystal sets I've been using."

"What do you mean by Piccadilly Johnnies?" Fred asked, surprised at the look of disdain on Horace's face.

"Well, your observers are given warm clothing and sit up here all nice and cosy. When they come back down to earth they can relax in the mess, not like the men in the trenches. I've heard that some can't even transmit Morse code properly. They wouldn't let me qualify until I could send twenty words a minute."

"I think you've been given the wrong end of the stick, Horace. An observer has a lot more on his plate than simply sending Morse messages. He has to defend the aircraft and generally observe for the pilot. And if something goes wrong and the machine crashes, he's the one at the front, right behind the engine and petrol tank. And another thing . . ."

Horace realised he had overstepped the mark.

"No offence intended, Fred. I'm new here and I'm only saying what the other wireless operators have told me. It can be pretty dangerous sitting right next to a battery that could be shelled at any moment. I think some of them feel that their work is not recognised."

"Why do you say that?"

"Even though they might wear the Royal Flying Corps uniform, they don't really have much to do with their squadron."

"I think you'll find that Number 6 is better than most. Lieutenant

Hickie is keen that we keep in touch with all of our wireless operators, either by us making trips out to the batteries or by bringing the operators back to the aerodrome from time to time. We're only on the end of a telephone wire, so you can talk to us whenever you want."

"I'm sorry. Next time I'll keep my big mouth shut until I know what I'm talking about."

"That's all right. Is there anything else I can help you with?"

"I'm not sure. I'm having trouble at the moment differentiating between the signals. Is there a special knack to it?"

"One of the biggest problems we have is interference and false signals. These can be from other aircraft in the area using the same wavelength or from the enemy trying to jam our transmissions. It can happen even though your receiver may be properly netted with the aircraft's transmitter."

"You don't have to tell me that. I've only been practicing so far and I find it hard to keep track of any one signal."

"Well, there's a new technical advance we call the 'Clapper Break' that changes the note of the signal. We can adjust a set so that it transmits a medium note or a low note instead of the normal high note. The range of a signal improves as you lower the frequency, so we use unaltered sets for close work like artillery cooperation and the adjusted sets for long range reconnaissance."

"Does that mean I can ignore all but the high notes for ranging?"

"In principle, yes, but I can show you more when we get to the battery. Listen, the rain has almost stopped. Why don't we take a break and go for an early lunch."

Half an hour later, having eaten a meal of egg and chips, they left the canteen to return to the workshop lorry and almost immediately bumped into Charles Hickie.

"I had a feeling I'd find you two here. Come with me, I've got a tender waiting for us at the entrance. The driver's going to Poperinghe on an errand for the major, so he can drop us off first and come back to pick us up later in the afternoon."

"Do you mind if I get out at Pop on the way back, sir?" asked Fred. "If you remember, I have a half day off and I'd planned to meet up with my Canadian chum. I can make my own way back to my billet."

"That's fine, Johnstone. It's on our way."

The lieutenant led the way along the sodden pathway to the eastern entrance of the aerodrome. The squadrons' vehicles were parked nose to tail along one side of the road as far as the eye could see. Looking up the road, he caught the attention of a driver who was standing next to a Crossley tender, one hundred yards away. The lorry was parked in the driveway that led to one of the farms bordering the airfield. The driver saluted in acknowledgement, climbed up into the cabin and brought the lorry out of the line of vehicles, down towards the waiting men. With nowhere to park he stopped in the middle of the road, effectively blocking both entrances to the aerodrome. Before he had time to jump down from the truck, a guard ran out into the road, waving his rifle in the air.

"You can't park there. We've got machines taxying across here all of the time."

"At ease, Corporal. The driver's only stopping to pick us up," Charles Hickie interrupted. "We'll only be a few seconds."

"Sorry, sir, I didn't realise it was for you. I'll get back to my post then."

"Right you are, Corporal."

Charles Hickie pointed a finger at Fred and Horace.

"All right you two, be quick. Hop in the back whilst I climb up next to the driver."

Fred and Horace did what they were told and ran to the back of the truck. Wasting no time, they scrambled inside without first pulling the tailboard down and sat down, facing one another. Two fixed wooden benches ran along the full length of the tender and could accommodate eight men, but on this occasion they were the only occupants. Fred leaned across and pulled down the canvas flap.

"Prepare yourself for a bumpy ride, Horace."

"You don't have to tell me, Fred. I made the same trip yesterday and I've bruises to prove it."

In the front cabin, Charles Hickie sat with his coat collar fastened tightly at the neck. At his request the driver had pulled the canvas hood over the top of the front cabin, but with no side protection he belatedly wished that he had chosen to ride in the back of the lorry with the other two men.

"Where exactly do you want to go, sir?" the driver asked.

"It's a gun battery that's on a farm to the east of Dickebusch. I suggest you take the Reninghelst road out of Poperinghe. It's further, but the road is wider and less muddy than the more direct route."

"I know what you mean, sir. The Ouderdom road is a bit tight if you happen to meet anyone coming in the other direction."

"Once you've driven through Dickebusch, take the road to Voormezeele and keep your eye out for a small track on the right after a quarter of a mile. It's easy to miss but I'll give you plenty of warning."

"Right you are, sir," the driver replied.

Though only a twelve mile drive from Abeele, it took almost an hour for the truck to reach the village of Dickebusch, as the recent prolonged period of wet weather had made even the lesser-used roads dangerous. Dickebusch was only three miles from the front line, and though most of the buildings in the village had suffered the effects of enemy shell fire, many of its inhabitants had refused to leave and carried on with their daily lives as if nothing had changed.

Without stopping, the driver continued through the centre of the village and on past Dickebusch Lake, its barren foreshores lined with ragged tree stumps. Having taken the turning for Voormezeele, he slowed down when Charles Hickie pointed to a rough cart track, the entrance to the farm where the howitzers were located. Keeping to the centre of the narrow track, the driver proceeded slowly down the slight incline towards what appeared to be a derelict farm. As they approached the first of the outbuildings he was forced to make a detour through a gap in the stone wall and across a field in order to avoid several weathered craters, evidence that the site had previously been a target for the German artillery. When he brought the tender back on to the gravel track, he drove on until he reached the main farm buildings which were nestled in the lee of a small hill, out of the direct line of sight of the German lines.

"Thanks for the lift, Corporal."

Charles Hickie stepped out of the lorry and on to the driveway, returning the salute of the driver as he closed the passenger door.

"Come back for us in about two hours, would you?"

"Yes sir. I only have to pick up a package for the major so I'll be back in plenty of time."

Charles Hickie walked to the back of the lorry.

"Out you come, you two."

Fred and Horace climbed out of the tender and the three men walked towards the main buildings. As they approached the farmhouse, an army officer came out of the front door and walked to greet them.

"We've been expecting you, Lieutenant. I'm the commander of 'A' battery. What do you think of our new position?"

"Good morning, sir," Charles Hickie replied, saluting the captain. "Even from here I can see it's well protected. Where are your guns?"

"We're in the process of setting them up in between these two buildings behind me. The guns of 'B' battery are a little farther down the track. Being nine point two's, the howitzers take some time to move and set up."

"Is everything going according to plan sir?"

"More or less, though we managed to break one of the steering wheels on our Caterpillar tractor this morning. We've had to borrow half a dozen Clydesdales so that we can finish the job today."

"That would be a very different experience for your men, sir."

"Yes, my gunners are rediscovering the ancient art of horse handling!"

"If I may, sir, I'd like to have a word with you about our squadron's role, whilst Johnstone helps Brown get his wireless tent shipshape."

"Certainly, Lieutenant. Now's as good a time as any."

"We've recently brought in a number of changes in the way we work with artillery. Perhaps you'd care to invite the commander of 'B' battery to join us."

"Very well," the captain replied. "Let's go and find him. We can convene a meeting in my office. It used to be the kitchen, but it's the only dry room left on the farm."

Charles Hickie turned to Horace.

"You know where you're going, don't you, Brown?"

"Yes, sir. They've set up my wireless tent right next to 'B' battery."

"That's good. I'll come and find you when I've finished."

Horace led Fred past the farmhouse towards a large mound of earth, reinforced on one side with sandbags. Beyond the mound, they stopped and watched as four gunners attempted to direct a team of horses that were harnessed to one of the main sections of a fifteen ton howitzer.

Horace called out to one of the gunners.

"How's it going, Alan?"

"Don't be fooled by all the shouting, Horace. We may look disorganised but we know what we're doing. Mark my words, both guns will be ready this time tomorrow."

Horace turned to Fred.

"At least that will give us time to practice in peace and quiet."

They walked on past the battery, keeping a respectable distance between themselves and the horses, and eventually reached a camouflaged tent that had been erected a few yards beyond the furthermost gun. In front of the tent was a vertical aerial mast, thirty feet high. Horace opened the front flap of the tent and peered inside. With nothing disturbed since he had left the battery that morning, he invited Fred to enter.

"Welcome to my very own bivvy. After you, Fred."

Fred stooped down and squeezed inside the tent. Opposite the entrance was a table upon which had been placed a crystal detector receiver with spark key and headset. There was also a standard line telephone that Fred knew would be used for passing on messages to the battery commanders. The block of accumulators for the wireless set had been positioned out of the way, on the floor beneath the table. Even so, there was very little room inside the tent for anyone other than the wireless operator. Horace followed Fred inside and sat down at the table, gesturing towards a folding chair that was resting against the wall of the tent. Fred opened up the chair and placed it next to Horace's.

"Is that a Mark III, Horace?"

"Yes. Pretty standard these days but then we don't have to worry about weight like you do."

"All right," said Fred. "Switch it on and let's see what we can pick up. I've worked a cat's whisker before, so this should be simple enough. Some of our machines will be within range as I know we had some artillery ops planned for this afternoon in the Zillebeke area."

Horace switched on the apparatus and placed the earphones on his head whilst he waited for the valves to warm up. Handing a second headset to Fred, he adjusted the dials to search for signals on the wavelength that Fred had mentioned earlier, back at the aerodrome. After a few minutes, he raised his hand excitedly.

"I've picked up a signal, Fred, but is it a medium note or a low note?" he shouted, forgetting for a moment that he was wearing earphones.

Removing his headset, Horace looked at Fred for confirmation. Fred twisted one of the earpieces around and held it close to his ear.

"This is a low note signal from one of our longer range reconnaissance machines. I can recognise its calling signal. Wait for a moment and you should hear a closer signal. There, I've got one."

Horace put the headset back over his ears and listened in silence as he tried to interpret the code. He wrote down the message on a note pad.

"Yes, I've got it now. It's from one of our machines. It's sending a signal to a battery a little to the north of us. I'll write down all of the messages the observer sends down."

"And I can check it to see if it makes sense."

The two men spent the next hour listening to signals and practicing the synchronisation of the wireless receiver to the transmissions of the nearest observation aeroplane. They also discussed the various ground procedures that Horace would need to learn for sending confirmation signals to the observers in the air.

"Have you finished in here, Fred?"

Charles Hickie had entered the tent whilst they were working and was standing at the entrance, holding the flap back with one hand.

"Yes, sir, I think we can call it a day. There's not much more we can do until the battery is operational. Brown is a lot quicker at Morse than I will ever be. When we get back to the aerodrome, I'll have to chivvy our observers to improve their sending rate."

"Let's move along then. I want to get back to Abeele before dark and avoid the evening traffic blocks."

"Do you know where our driver is, sir?"

"He's already waiting for us down by the farmhouse. He didn't want to risk bringing the tender any closer in case a Hun shell came over."

"He must be the nervous type, sir. With the battery not even set up, I wouldn't think there'd be much chance of an attack."

"I'm inclined to agree with you. Brown, you know where to find us should you have any problems."

"Thank you, sir. Today has been very useful."

On the way back to the tender, the two men discussed the events of the afternoon.

"Mr Hickie, Horace asked me a question I couldn't answer. Why do we send up a machine for each battery, especially when several batteries could be within range of a single target? Isn't there a way we could direct more than one battery with a single machine?"

"He's not the first to ask this question, Fred. HQ wants us to come up with a plan to do just that. It won't change what the observers have to do, but every squadron will be forced to use the same codes." [52]

"Won't it put more pressure on the ground wireless operators?"

"Not if they know what zone they're in. The rest of it will be the same and the sky will be less congested."

"When will this start, sir?"

"I'm not sure, but you'll be the first to know, Fred."

They reached the tender to find the driver sitting at the wheel, staring anxiously towards the east. Charles Hickie tapped his stick on the windscreen and the driver jerked his head around. Recognising the lieutenant, he saluted and jumped down from the driver's compartment so that he could open the passenger's door.

"As you were, driver. I think I'll travel in the back with Johnstone. It looks like rain again and I don't want to get wet twice in one day."

"Very good, sir. Will we be driving straight to Abeele?"

"No. You need to stop off at Poperinghe, as Johnstone will be leaving us there."

"Talbot House, just down from the main square," added Fred.

"Yes, I know where that is."

The driver walked around to the front and bent down to grab the starting handle. The engine burst into life at the first swing and he climbed back into the front seat, the whole lorry throbbing with the engine idling at a slow tickover.

The journey to Poperinghe took almost half an hour as they came across several ammunition convoys travelling in the opposite direction and had to pull off the road to let them pass. With the flap rolled down at the back of the truck, the two men could hardly see one another's faces. To pass the time, they chatted for a while about life in Belgium, before Charles Hickie broached the subject of England.

"And how are things back home, Fred?"

"As well as can be expected, sir, thank you."

"And your intended?"

"My Ethel secured a job as a buyer with another firm and went back to live with her parents. She thought she'd be safe in Rochester but she had a bit of a scare the other week."

"Why? What happened?"

"She was out on a walk when a Zeppelin came over and started to drop bombs. One of them was so close the blast knocked her right through a shop window. She woke up covered in haberdashery and a loud ringing noise in her ears. My, was she lucky, sir."

"I trust she wasn't hurt."

"Not at all, I'm glad to say. It's funny, I never imagined any trouble at home, what with us all fighting over here. Thank goodness the Hun bombers can't reach Blighty."

"With the way their machines are improving, that could all change. All the more reason for us to put a stop to this nonsense, eh?"

"There was a debate at 'Toch H' a couple of months ago and the consensus was that the war would be over before Christmas."

"And which year would that be, Fred?"

Their conversation was brought to an abrupt end when the tender screeched to a halt, causing them to slide along the bench seats. Fred made his way back to the rear of the truck, opened the flap and peered outside. Even though it was late afternoon, the fading sunlight was bright enough to make him squint. Looking up he saw the familiar sign.

```
┌─────────────────┐
│    TALBOT       │
│    HOUSE        │
│    1915 - ?     │
│   Every-Man's   │
│     CLUB        │
└─────────────────┘
```

"Looks like it's my stop, sir."

"All right, Fred, enjoy what's left of the afternoon and I'll see you at the morning service. I know all of the hymns, so you can rest assured I'll be in the front row. That should please the major."

"I'll be there bright and early, sir."

Fred picked up his coat and jumped down on to the pavement. He banged on the tailgate and the tender pulled away, continuing on down the Rue de l'Hopital towards Abeele.

Entering the open doorway of Talbot House, Fred noticed that it was quieter than the last time he was there. A group of soldiers had just come out of the dining room and were walking up the hall towards him. From the sound of their accents it was evident that they were Canadian, giving him renewed hope that Vernon might be somewhere inside the building. He stopped at the Friendship's Corner and scanned the bulletin board, looking for Vernon's name. Eventually he found the most recent entry made by Vernon. No change had been made to the date originally entered. Pleased that his visit was not in vain, Fred walked into the main meeting room on the ground floor. The room was full of soldiers of different nationalities though, as on his last visit, the majority were Canadians. With the Canadian Infantry given a significant role in the recent fighting around St Eloi, Fred assumed that the men standing around him were taking respite from that action.

Several soldiers were standing around the piano singing 'Rag Picker'[53] to an energetic piano accompaniment at the hands of a red-faced Infantry major. Fred waited in the doorway as the last lines of the song were sung.

Most any time of the day
You'll find him picking away
He's a rag picker, a rag picker
A ragtime picking man

Squeezing his way through the singers, he managed to get close to the pianist. He shouted in the major's ear so that he could be heard above the noise of the cheering audience. The officer nodded his head, stood up from the piano and held his hands in the air to call for silence.

"Quiet, you rowdy lot! This man is looking for Vernon Jones. Does anyone know if there's a Vernon here today?"

The room was quiet for a moment and then a soldier on the far side of the room raised his arm. He climbed out from the bench table where he had been sitting with a group of other soldiers.

"Did you say Vernon Jones? Is he a big fella, a captain with Tobin's Tigers?"

The question confused Fred and it took him a few moments to remember what Vernon had told him the first time they had met.

"Yes, he's a captain but he's serving in the 29th Infantry Battalion," he shouted back.

"That's them all right," replied the soldier. "I'm with the 27th and his men relieved us a week or so ago."

"Do you know if he's here today?" Fred asked anxiously.

"Listen, I'm real sorry to tell you this son, but Captain Jones was killed yesterday. They survived the debacle at the craters and were due to come off the line for a break but he and his men were ordered back to help the other battalions. Was he a friend of yours?"

Fred was not really listening as he was overwhelmed by the unexpected news. He had lost his first wartime friend outside the squadron. During the times they had met, neither of them had ever talked about the war and they had planned to meet up at the end of the hostilities. Fred left the room in a daze and walked out of the building.

Hoping to find somewhere where he could collect his thoughts, he walked towards the town square and bought a ticket at the first cinema he came across. Once inside the auditorium, he sat down in the dark and watched a film of the latest war news. Ironically, the first scenes projected on to the screen were of St Eloi and from the graphic images shown, it was patently clear that the Canadian infantry had been presented with a daunting task of trying to hold on to the craters.

When the newsreel came to an end, the woman who was playing the piano paused whilst the first reel of the main feature was loaded on to the projector. According to the poster in the foyer that Fred had glanced at on his way in, the film was 'Uncle Tom's Cabin', starring veteran actor Sam Lucas. Looking around, Fred noticed that the audience was comprised mostly of soldiers. They were talking in huddles and few of the men were alone. After a few minutes the pianist resumed her seat, indication that the film was about to start.

Fred watched the opening scene where Arthur Shelby, a character in the story, was about to lose his farm as a result of gambling debts. Knowing the story from reading the novel at school, he quickly lost concentration. His eyes strayed to the piano player and he immediately thought of Vernon's parents and how they would react to the news of their son's death, fighting in a far-off land in a bid to save the British Empire. Realising he had made a mistake in coming to the cinema, Fred got up from his seat and made his way back to the foyer in the dark. At the box office he had to squeeze past a group of weary looking Canadian soldiers who had just bought tickets and were waiting to be shown to their seats. Once outside, he buttoned up his coat, as the evening was cold and the cobbled surface of the pavement wet from a recent fall of rain. He crossed over to the centre of the square where several lorries were parked. The drivers were standing around a lighted brazier, smoking cigarettes.

Fred pushed his way to the centre of the group.

"Is anyone driving back to Abeele tonight?"

A soldier wearing a hat and heavy waterproof cape caught his eye.

"I'm about to head back to the aerodrome. You can have a ride in my sidecar if you don't mind carrying a box on your lap. It'll be a bit draughty but I don't think it'll rain again in the next half an hour."

"Thanks, I'd appreciate that. Would you drop me off at Margueritas in the village on the way through? I've just lost a close friend and I need to talk it through with someone."

"Sure thing, guv," replied the rider. "Let me just finish this fag and we can be on our way."

Vickers FB5 - 'Gunbus' :Air Historical Branch (RAF)

Royal Aircraft Factory FE2b – 'Fee' :Air Historical Branch (RAF)

Royal Aircraft Factory BE2c – 'Quirk' :CCI Archive

BE2c observer taking aim :Photograph courtesy of the Fleet Air Arm Museum

Aircraft Manufacturing Company (Airco) DH2 :*Air Historical Branch (RAF)*

Royal Aircraft Factory FE8 (7457) :*Photograph courtesy of the Fleet Air Arm Museum*
Flown by Captain F Powell

Royal Aircraft Factory RE8 – 'Harry Tate'   *:CCI Archive*

RE8 crew about to leave on a mission   *:Photograph courtesy of the Fleet Air Arm Museum*

RE8 crew ready for action   *:Photograph courtesy of the Fleet Air Arm Museum*

RE8 crew in final preparations   *:CCI Archive*

DH2 scouts of Number 29 Squadron, Abeele

My grandfather's wedding ring, with 'GEE' inscription :Steve Johnson

My grandfather (on right), manager of Botley & Lewis – c1957 :Steve Johnson

Chapter 10
Jock's Career Takes Off

THE OUTSTANDING PERFORMANCE of Number 6 squadron during the Battle for the St Eloi Craters was mentioned in the first despatch sent to England by Sir Douglas Haig, Commander-in-Chief of the British Forces in France. This distinction was shared only by one other squadron in the same despatch and not repeated during the war for any other squadron serving on the Western Front. Sharing the aerodrome at Abeele with Number 6 squadron, Number 29 squadron suffered mixed fortunes over the next few weeks, with a young pilot killed in a flying accident, the squadron's first aerial victory[54] as well as the first death in combat of one of its pilots.

In the lead-up to the next major allied offensive, planned to take place in the Somme Valley, the size of every squadron in the Royal Flying Corps was increased from two to three flights, a total of eighteen aircraft per squadron. Number 29 squadron received four DH2 scouts as well as two of the new FE8 scouts, making it the first operational squadron to fly this type of aircraft. For its third flight, Number 6 squadron was promised six of the latest BE2d two seaters. The plan to concentrate forces along the Somme front received a setback, however, when on the 2nd June the Germans launched an attack at Mount Sorrel[55] near Zillebeke. After eleven days of fierce fighting, the Allies regained the ridge though heavy casualties were incurred on both sides. Throughout the battle, the aircraft of Number 6 squadron were constantly in the air supporting the Canadian artillery, with the scouts of Number 29 squadron providing escort. Though there were constant rumours that Number 6 would move south to take part in the Somme offensive, Major Reginald Mills[56] was eventually informed that his squadron would remain for the meantime at Abeele.

Jock wheezed as he bent over in the front cockpit of a brand new BE2d, a long screwdriver gripped tightly in one hand.

"It's a tight fit in here."

Fred, who had been watching Jock's antics from the relative comfort of the pilot's seat, could not stop himself from laughing.

"You must have put on weight, Jock. There should be more room now they've made the sides of the cockpit lower."

"It's not me. It's these ruddy extra controls. Don't they know we have to put wireless sets in here?"

"They must think it's more important for the observer to be able to fly, than send messages in these new machines."

"Pass me down the quarter inch spanner would you, Fred? If I move from this position I'll not be able to get back down again."

Fred leant as far as he could over the windscreen to bring the tool within reach of Jock's raised hand.

"Here you are, try this."

"Thanks, Fred." Jock dropped out of sight for a few seconds before bobbing up again, a look of satisfaction on his face. "That's fixed it. All we have to do now is to connect the set to the accumulators and see if it works."

"It should. The way they prepared the machine at the depot looks almost the same as our older BEs."

"Have you heard how the big push went this morning down south?"[57]

"No, but it's early days yet. We've not started an attack on a Saturday before. Do you think we'll still get the afternoon off?"

"Only if we can finish the installation on the other new machine[58], Fred."

"We'd better get to it, then."

For the next hour the two men worked together in silence. When they had finished, they climbed down from the aircraft and started to walk back to the workshop lorry

"What difference will the extra stripe make, Jock?" Fred asked.

"Well, for one thing, it'll be nice to go into the sergeants' mess without having to be invited."

"Is that such a big thing?"

"It's all right for you. You're either there already, playing the piano, or in your nice new Nissen hut."

"I must admit I've been very lucky."

"Make the most of it, Fred. Things can change very quickly around here."

"Talking of change, what's this I hear about you having a go at observing?"

"Blimey, can't anyone keep a secret!"

"I heard it in the sergeants' mess," said Fred, trying hard not to laugh.

"Well, I might as well tell you the whole story as you'll probably hear a different version from anyone else. Dexter keeps telling us that he's going to be an officer one day and I didn't want everyone laughing at me as well."

"So why are you interested in observing?"

"You know that I really want to be a pilot. Always have. When the captain told me I'd been recommended for sergeant's stripes, I asked him if I could apply for pilot training."

"Did he fob you off?"

"Not a bit of it. He told me you needed more experience in looking after the wireless lads before he'd agree to let me go, and that the best way for me to impress the major would be to first get my observer's wing."

"Sounds a funny way to get to be a pilot."

"Not really. If I do it now, I'll be able to train here as an observer. If I wait much longer I'll have to go back to Blighty.[59] Once I've left Abeele I'll probably get transferred to a different squadron, so why would the major agree to that?"

"That makes sense, Jock. Can I take it from what you're saying that I'm to be given your job, or is that just a rumour?"

"Not for me to say, old chap. Perhaps you could ask around in the sergeants' mess, next time you're there!"

They reached the workshop lorry and Fred held the flap open whilst Jock clambered up into the back of the truck. Following Jock up the ladder, Fred went to the far corner of the workshop where a new wireless set had already been unpacked from its crate.

"Let's get this up on to the table and see if anything was damaged in transit."

"All right, Fred, we can test it here if nothing's been broken."

The two men worked together in silence as they removed the casing and examined the set. Pausing to look for a spanner, Fred returned to the subject of Jock's future.

"How long would it be before you could apply for pilot training, Jock?"

"I'm not sure. All the captain would tell me was that when I've earned my 'Feathered O' he'll ask the major to put my name on the list of potentials."

"Couldn't you train here as a pilot? Then Number 6 wouldn't lose your invaluable skills!"

"It doesn't work that way, old son," Jock replied, pausing in his work to wave to Dexter who was walking past the open side of the lorry. "All pilot training is carried out in England and when you get your wings you join the bods in the Pilots Pool like any other new pilot. You then get posted to whichever squadron has a vacancy. If I'm recommended for pilot training, the squadron will lose me altogether, but if they train me here as an observer they won't have to find a replacement."

"That doesn't sound very fair on you."

"It isn't supposed to be fair. It's just the way the system works. But it also saves me time as I already know Morse, can shoot reasonably well and know my way around. All I have to do is complete two successful observation shoots."

"You could do that standing on your head. When do you start?"

"First thing tomorrow morning, weather permitting. With the big push down south, I hear it was fairly quiet around Ypres today. Now that we know we're staying put for the moment, we're going to work with some of the new batteries."

"Like the one I visited a couple of months ago?"

"The very same, Fred. Lieutenant Robinson ranged for a Canadian battery around Hollebeke this morning and it went really well. Almost no Archie and not one Hun machine to bother him."

"That would be a good way for you to start."

"The plan is for me to have a go at registering a target for the same battery. They've only just arrived at the front, so we can all learn and get a bit of practice while there's a lull in the fighting."

"I hope it all goes well for you, Jock."

"Thanks. So do I. Now pass me that cable and we'll see if this set's in working order."

Fred passed Jock the end of a length of electrical cable that was connected to a bank of accumulators. Making sure that the master switch was in the 'Off' position, Jock wrapped the exposed end of the cable around the terminal on the back of the wireless set, securing it with a knurled nut.

"Anyway, enough of me," Jock continued. "I hear that congratulations are in order, air mechanic first class."

"Thank you, Jock. See my shoulder badge. Not as fancy as yours, though."

"If I'm lucky, in a few weeks I could get my observers badge as well. Now, that would be something, wouldn't it?"

"Definitely one for the sergeants. You'd better watch that promotion doesn't go to your head. You'll be applying for a commission next!"

"Not me, Fred, I know my place," Jock said, laughing as he spoke. "But I'd dearly love to become a pilot before this war is over."

"Don't laugh. More and more sergeants are getting their wings these days. Do you remember the sergeant who was a pilot with Number 5 when they were based here? He's back here with Number 29 as a scout pilot."

"I'm not sure Noaksie's a good example, Fred. I saw him land yesterday after making a vertical turn near the ground. He had everyone running for cover."

"All I mean, Jock, is that if you want something badly enough, it will happen. Tell you what. If you can find a map, I'll test you on what you'll have to do. We can even practice with the same target coordinates that were used today."

"Thanks Fred, I'll take you up on that. First though, I need to go and see if they know anything about Lieutenant Coxe. His machine was one of those that bombed Cambrai[60] train station early this morning, but there's been no news of him since he left."

"A bit tough being sent on a mission with no observer to look after you."

"And he was only eighteen, poor chap."

"If the squadron takes part in many more long range bombing missions, you could be out of a job before you even get it."

Jock scratched his head before answering.

"You could be right, Fred. Anyway, whatever decision is made, the wireless flight will be just as busy as we now have two extra machines to look after."

The chateau presented an imposing sight, rising like a ghostly apparition from the low lying mist that covered all of the surrounding land. From a distance, a casual observer would have been unaware that the magnificent four storey mansion stood in the centre of a battlefield, less than half a mile inside German held territory and within range of dozens of allied guns. It was early morning and the only sound that echoed around the building was the lonely call of a solitary bird. With the concentration of forces shifted south to France, the battle front around Ypres was quieter than in recent weeks and the day's shelling had yet to commence.

Closer examination of the chateau would reveal a different picture however, with gaping glassless windows and countless holes in the masonry where gun aimers had scored direct hits. Sections of the roof were missing or partly consumed by fire and the very feature that had given the mansion its unique beauty had also been its nemesis. It was not called the 'White Chateau' by accident. On a clear day, the white-faced stonework could be seen for miles to the west and the building provided a perfect target for artillery ranging, standing as it did against a backdrop of brown countryside churned flat by the impact of countless shells.

The silence was broken by the sound of a falling shell. The noise of the explosion ripped through the air, echoing off the walls of the deserted mansion. The unseen gunner's aim was long and a shower of brown earth and bricks burst up through the ground mist fifty yards beyond the main building, where once had stood a pair of imposing iron gates. A huge ripple of white mist spread out in an ever increasing circle, flowing up the walls of the chateau like an ocean wave hitting the face of a cliff.

The 3rd Canadian Siege Battery had set up the four breach-loading howitzers five days earlier at a farm three quarters of a mile to the north of Dickebusch Lake. For the men of the Battery, it was their first active posting since completing their training in England and being ordered out to France. In spite of continuous heavy rains, it had only taken the crews two days to assemble and place the four brand new 26 cwt guns[61] into position. To avoid detection by the enemy, most of the initial work had been carried out under cover of darkness. When the guns were finally in position and firmly secured, it had taken the gunners a further three days to successfully register them on to a distant target. For this, they had used the right hand spire of the church in the nearby village of Vlamertinghe as their aiming point to ensure the consistency of the gun sights. After much deliberation, the major in charge of the Battery decided to use the landmark of the White Chateau at Hollebeke as the registered standard line for all of their shoots.

The second day of July started out fine but misty and the commanding officer, thirty eight year old Major Edmund Cape,[62] decided to check the guns' registration one more time from a newly established observation point one mile east of the battery. He wanted to ensure that the guns were functioning correctly before the aircraft of Number 6 squadron arrived for the next artillery shoot. A successful registration had already taken place the previous morning, the first time ever that the battery's guns had been guided on to their target by an aircraft of the Royal Flying Corps and it was important that his men continued to perform well in spite of their inexperience in battle.

Major Cape put down his field glasses and shouted to the wireless operator, who was standing nearby.

"The shot was long, but the line was perfect. Signal the gunnery officer to drop sixty yards and confirm that the range is six thousand two hundred. By my reckoning he should lower the elevation by fifteen minutes. Ask him to fire another round when he's ready."

"Yes, sir. Right away."

The wireless operator ran back to the wireless tent, erected on the lee of the hill and camouflaged to avoid being spotted by enemy observers. Richard Killick, though trained in England as a wireless operator and attached to the Canadian battery, was officially part of Number 6 squadron and held the rank of 1st class air mechanic. It was his first action since arriving at the front and he, like many of his fellow wireless operators, felt isolated. The Canadian soldiers with whom he worked treated him well but regarded him as an outsider and he had so far had little contact with the men of the squadron. Spending most of his waking hours cooped up in a small dugout adjacent to one of the guns, he had readily accepted the invitation to visit the forward observation point with his commanding officer.

Major Cape glanced back at the battery as he once again checked his calculations. He had already had a meeting with the gunnery officer and knew that the shells for this particular shoot were filled with a Number Two charge[63] and that the elevation of the guns had been set at twenty one degrees. Satisfied that he had passed the right correction to the gun aimer he sat down on the ground and waited. After a few seconds he saw the flash of the second shell being fired.

He stood up and once again looked through his field glasses at the distant target. With a keen interest in European architecture since studying Architecture at the University of Montreal before the war, he felt uncomfortable that he was participating in the destruction of such a beautiful old building. As he looked at the crumbling remains through his binoculars, he made a promise to himself that should he survive the war, he would concentrate on creating buildings rather than destroying them.

Thrusting all such thoughts aside, he continued to count out the seconds. When he reached a count of twenty he saw an explosion rip through the right hand side of the chateau, combining the cavities of what had once been two first floor windows into a single gaping hole. He was surprised that the heavy shell had not caused more damage and he marvelled at the strength of the old chateau. Twelve seconds after the impact of the shell he heard the sound of the explosion.

Richard Killick returned from the tent and stood next to him.

"How was that, sir?"

"Spot on this time, Killick. Pass down the order to commence firing with the other guns."

The two men remained at the observation point whilst the three other guns were successfully ranged on to the target. As the noise of the last of the shells died away, they heard the sound of an aircraft approaching from the west. Training his field glasses on to the aircraft, Major Cape studied its shape to make sure that it was not a German bomber. Looking doubtful, he passed the glasses to the wireless operator.

"Here, you take a look, Killick. You'd have a better idea as to what sort of machine that is. Is it one from your squadron?"

Pleased to be asked his opinion, Richard Killick looked closely at the oncoming aircraft. Even at a distance of four hundred yards, he could tell from its outline that it was a BE2d biplane. The lower wings were of a shorter span than the upper wings, unlike those of the older BE2c. As with all of the men who served in the Royal Flying Corps, he had learned from looking at silhouette drawings how to differentiate between the different types of allied and German aeroplanes.

"It's a BE2d, sir and it's not carrying any bombs as far as I can see," he said, handing the glasses back to the major.

"Then it's probably Number 6's machine. We might as well stay where we are as I didn't get the chance to watch yesterday. Let's see if Captain Leggat can manage without us."

The aircraft passed overhead at two thousand feet, the pilot waving as he drew abreast of their observation position. Major Cape sat down on the ground and unfolded a trench map. Taking a pencil and ruler out of his pocket, he drew a line between the observation position and the White Chateau,[64] the latter located at grid coordinates O4d.10.80. He then drew another line from the observation point to the new target, a suspected ammunition supply dump at a cross roads two hundred yards south of the chateau.

"Look," he said, pointing his finger to the end of the new line as Richard Killick looked over his shoulder. "The target's right here at O4d.20.10. Stand up and train my glasses on the chateau, then swing fifteen degrees to the south, mid way between the Bluff and the hills to the north of St Eloi. That's where the crossroads should be."

Richard Killick picked up the field glasses and followed Major Cape's orders.

"I've done that, sir, but I can't see anything."

"Look again. Even though you can't see the actual target from here you should still be able to spot the exploding shells."

The major made a few quick calculations on the bottom of the map.

"Increasing the elevation by half a degree should do it and it'll take an extra second for the shell to reach the target. Let's see if I'm right."

Standing next to Richard Killick, the major watched as the aircraft flew directly towards the chateau, gradually disappearing from sight as it became enveloped in the heat haze. A minute later he knew the machine had crossed over into enemy territory when tiny puffs of smoke appeared in the sky, evidence that the German anti-aircraft gunners had the aircraft in their sights. Taking the field glasses from Richard Killick, he watched as the aeroplane turned around and flew back towards the Battery. The anti-aircraft guns stopped firing as soon as it was out of their range and in less than two minutes the aircraft once again passed directly overhead. Instead of continuing on towards the battery, as it had on the first run, the machine turned again and headed back towards the target.

Major Cape handed the glasses back to the wireless operator.

"Your turn, Killick. Wait until you see a flash from our guns, then turn around to face the target and start the count. When you reach twenty three with any luck you'll see an explosion."

Before either of them had time to glance back at the battery, they heard the loud report of a howitzer. Richard Killick dropped to the ground, with his elbows supporting the field glasses, and watched the target area as he counted out the seconds. Twenty two seconds later, almost exactly as the major had predicted, he saw the blast of the shell as it exploded four and a half thousand yards south east of their position.

"I don't think it hit anything, sir. All I could see was a fountain of earth to the right of the chateau, just next to the rise at St Eloi."

"Let's wait and see what happens on the next run, Killick," Major Cape replied. "The observer up there is as new to this as we are. It'll be interesting to see how many corrections he has to send before we hit the target."

Once again the aircraft turned back towards the Battery, but before it reached the observation point it veered away suddenly to the east.

"Has something gone wrong, sir? He's turned around too soon."

"From what I learned yesterday, the quicker the observer passes the correction the sooner his pilot can turn back. That way they can be closer to the target when the shell hits and be able to give a more accurate correction. Don't forget the shell's travelling seven times faster than the aeroplane. Pass me the field glasses again, would you, Killick?"

Major Cape trained the glasses on to the receding aircraft.

"They're getting a lot more Archie this time, as they're further over the Hun lines."

The second shell exploded with no more apparent success than the first. The two men watched as the aeroplane quickly turned around, flying back towards them through another barrage of anti-aircraft gunfire.

"I wonder how close we were with that one, sir."

Before Major Cape could reply, the air was filled with the sound of four howitzers firing in quick succession.

"He must have wirelessed the go-ahead for all four guns. This is better than I'd expected. I suggest you go to the tent and fetch another pair of glasses, Killick. This could be worth watching."

Richard Killick ran to the tent and when he returned the two men lay on the ground with their field glasses pointing towards the target. The first shell of the salvo exploded with little to be seen from their position. A few seconds later the second shell burst, closely followed by two more, the last two explosions causing a huge plume of earth to rise into the sky. Suddenly there was a brilliant flash of light above the target and a billowing cloud of dense black smoke rose into the air. This was followed almost immediately by several smaller explosions which continued after the sound of the first explosion had reached them.

"I would say that was a definite 'OK'. Not bad for a beginner eh, Killick?"

"They've certainly made our job easier, sir."

Major Cape stood up and brushed the grass off his uniform with his free hand.

"I'm going back to the battery to send a message of congratulations to Major Mills. That was a sterling effort on the part of his new observer."

One hour later, an elated Jock walked into the sergeants' mess. Being a Sunday afternoon and with no wireless work outstanding, he was not surprised to see that Fred was already inside the inner room, playing the piano.

"Thought I'd try looking for you here first!"

Fred stopped playing and closed the lid of the piano.

"How did it go, Jock? Tell me the whole story."

Jock drew up a chair and sat down next to Fred.

"I was nervous at first, especially when we were archied. The puffs didn't look real from a distance but some of the shells were so close they rocked the machine from side to side."

"Did you manage to range the target?"

"Hold your horses. I'm the one telling the story."

"Sorry, Jock, I won't interrupt you again."

"Well, I telegraphed my identification code on the way out and they laid out the signal to say that they were ready. Luckily they fired a practice shell as we were approaching the lines and that helped me locate the target on my map. It was a supply dump at Hollebeke, close to the ruins of a large white chateau."

"I've heard of the White Chateau. It's quite famous, you know."

"Well, the weirdest part about the whole shoot was that the ground was covered in a heavy mist. I couldn't see the trenches or any of the soldiers. Just as if they'd disappeared. It was only when Archie started that I realised nothing had changed and I could see the flashes from the Hun guns that were above the level of the mist."

"So how did you go with the shoot?" It was Fred's turn to be impatient.

"With only the second shell they were within twenty five yards, so I took a chance and signalled all four guns to fire. The next shell missed but the following three hit the dump, setting off the ammunition. I'm not sure what was stored there, but it made a jolly good fireworks display."

"Did you try for any other targets?"

"We weren't able to, Fred. After I'd sent the 'OK' and we were back over the battery, they laid out the signal for us to go home. The mist had got worse by that time, so I doubt we could have spotted any of the other targets from the air anyway."

"Could you see well enough to navigate home?"

"I had a go, but if it wasn't for Lieutenant Handley, who I'm sure can fly blindfolded, I might have taken us all the way to Boulogne!"

"This calls for a celebration. How about we go to dinner at the Mill? I'm supposed to be on perimeter guard tonight, but I'm sure I can quietly swap my duty with someone."

"Well, was it all worth it, Fred?" Jock asked, as four weeks later the two friends walked along the road to Abeele on a balmy Saturday evening. It was the first time they had spent any time together since celebrating Jock's success.

"How was I to know that the MPs would come and check up on me. Anyway, being confined to camp for fourteen days did have its benefits."

Jock smiled as he remembered the three extra guard duties that had also been imposed on Fred, for leaving the camp without permission.

"And what might they have been? Wearing full uniform in this weather couldn't have been much fun."

"Well, I caught up with my repairs and my exchequer is replete as I spent almost nothing for that fortnight."

Traffic on the road leading into Abeele was light. With the recent lull in the fighting around Ypres, the emphasis on the squadron's operations had changed from that of artillery observation to day and night bombing, the purpose being to hinder the enemy in its attempts to reinforce the armies down in the Somme valley.

Fred looked up into the clear night sky.

"What's the target for this evening, Jock? I've never seen so many machines take to the air. There can't be a full tin of petrol left anywhere on the aerodrome."

"We were talking about it in the mess this morning. Apparently it's the railway yards at Courtrai. The major's called for every serviceable aircraft."

"How many machines altogether?"

"After some last minute repairs, we managed to put fourteen into the air."

"That's near enough the whole squadron," Fred said, raising his eyebrows.

"Yes, the first time we've sent them all out on a single mission."[65]

"Well, that's one for the squadron."

"It had better go well or we could both be out of a job! Number 29 put up twelve of their scouts, so the aerodrome's almost deserted."

"So why aren't you up there, Jock?"

"Not possible with the weight of the big bombs. The observers have all got the night off."

Fred took out his pocket watch and looked at the time.

"It's all right for some. How long have I got before I have to get back to the aerodrome?"

"Well, Courtai's twenty five miles east of here, so allowing for them to get into formation they'll be there in just under an hour. Add half an hour for the bombing and half an hour to fly home and they should be back here by half past seven. It'll take a while to get all of the machines down and put away, so you should be all right until at least eight o'clock, Fred."

"I hope they don't run into trouble. We need all the machines we can get at the moment and I don't have any spare wireless sets."

"Well, they'll have the sun behind them on the way out and it'll be low in the sky by the time they come home."

"With a dozen Hun aerodromes in easy reach, they'll need all the help they can get."

"Especially without observers."

"If the squadron keeps up with this long range bombing, you may have to come back to the wireless section."

"Nice try, Fred. I'm happy where I am thanks."

The two airmen reached Lea's, a small estaminet on the Rue de Steenvoorde, mid-way between the cemetery and the centre of Abeele. Over the past few months, Fred had come into the habit of visiting Lea's on evenings when Margueritas was full or when he felt disinclined to engage in conversation with Evalina or Caroline. Lea Vandermartierd, the owner and manager, was a quiet and capable person who allowed

Fred and the other squadron musicians to use one of her rooms for music practice, as she possessed a fine old upright piano.

Jock knocked at the door. It was immediately opened by a young girl.

"Hello, Mr Frederick, Mr Cardno."

Curtsying, she led them into the hallway.

"My mother is in the kitchen cooking. Will you be eating with us this evening or can I get you a drink?"

"Hello, Maisie," Fred replied. "It's a pleasure to see you again. I must say your English is almost as good as mine. I shall have to mind my Ps and Qs in future."

"I don't know what you mean, monsieur."

"It means we'll have to be careful what we say in front of you," Jock interrupted, laughing at the puzzled look on the girl's face.

"Don't listen to him, Maisie. I only meant it as a compliment."

Jock pushed Fred to one side impatiently.

"In answer to your question, Maisie, we're here for supper. Would you ask your mother if we could each have a plate of egg and chips and a glass of ale? We don't have very long as Fred has to get back to the aerodrome."

"Certainly, messieurs. Please take a seat and I will arrange this for you."

"What a girl," said Jock. "She'll make someone an excellent wife one day."

With no-one else in the dining room, they sat down at a table next to the front window and chatted whilst they waited for the food to arrive. Maisie returned a few minutes later with a bottle of Bass beer and two glasses, placing them on the table so that the men could help themselves. Making apologies for the delay, she left them and returned to the kitchen.

"How's your new job going, Jock?"

"Very well thanks, apart from missing out on tonight that is. I only need one more successful shoot and then I qualify for my observer's wing."

"When will you go up again?"

"I'm not sure with these new bombing raids. At the moment, I'm a stand-in for anyone who gets injured or sick, but hopefully I'll soon have my own pilot. What about you, though? How's the new boy coming along in the Wireless section?"

"Derek's a natural though I wish he were tidier. The lorry always gets in a mess when I leave him alone for more than a few minutes."

"You'd never accuse him of being smart, would you? Anyway Fred, talking of promotions, don't be surprised if you make corporal in the not too distant future."

"What makes you say that?"

"Just from a conversation I overheard in the mess last night. And if you play your cards right, you could even get your sergeant's stripes before this war's over."

"I'd say there'd be more chance of Dexter becoming an officer than of that ever happening."

"Don't you be so sure, Fred."

Maisie arrived with the food and set the plates down on the table.

"Is there anything else I can get you two gentlemen?" she asked, smiling shyly at them.

"No, this will do quite nicely thanks," replied Jock. "Don't worry about looking after us. We'll leave the money under a plate when we go. Same price as usual?"

"My mother says that you only pay for the food. The beer is 'on the house' as you say in England."

"Please inform your mother that she is most kind," Fred added.

Maisie left them and they ate their meal in silence. Fred was the first to finish and wiped his mouth with a napkin. He was about to speak when there was a loud noise outside. He leaned back on his chair and peered out of the old bay window. At first he could see nothing, but then, just as two of the window panes began to vibrate in the window frame, a low flying aeroplane roared past less than fifty feet away. He twisted his head around to try and catch sight of the identification number on the tailplane.

"What on earth was that?" Jock shouted.

"It was too quick for me to read but it's probably one of Number 29's."

"The way the engine was popping means it has to be a DH2. Only a rotary could sound like that."

They heard the sound of more aeroplanes, this time further away over the fields behind the village.

"If the escorts are returning now, our machines can't be far behind. We'd better push off and get back to the aerodrome."

"My treat," said Fred.

Reaching into his pocket, he took out a small bundle of foreign notes and placed five Belgian francs under one of the plates.

"Thanks Fred, you're a pal."

"Goodnight, Lea," Fred shouted.

There was no reply from the kitchen as they left the table and walked to the front door. Outside on the front doorstep were several army officers who had just arrived for dinner. The two men stood back to let them enter, saluting each officer as they passed by.

By the time they had walked half a mile towards the aerodrome, four more scouts had passed overhead, as well as a BE2d with a badly misfiring engine.

"We'd better get a move on or you might have work waiting for you, Fred."

"Especially if Archie was accurate tonight. It only takes one bullet to smash a wireless set and we've only got bits and pieces left in the stores."

"You'd better check with Lieutenant Hickie as soon as you can, to see what the score is. Maybe he can pull some strings at HQ."

"I'll talk to him tomorrow morning after the church service."

"I'll be in the mess all evening if you want me, Fred. Let me know if you need a hand."

"Thanks Jock, I will."

Chapter 11
A Little Friendly Rivalry

*I*T TURNED OUT to be a busy night for the squadron, with the ground crews forced to work into the early hours of the next morning. Only one machine did not make it back to the aerodrome, the pilot being forced to land in the relative safety of a forward landing area. The others returned in loose formation with varying degrees of damage. Eleven of the squadron's aircraft succeeded in reaching Courtrai, dropping twenty one bombs on the railway yards and causing major damage. Aircraft from the other squadrons dropped a further eight bombs on to the target. Number 29 squadron fared better than most but only because many of its scouts had to abort the mission when the bombers they were escorting became lost in the haze and were forced to turn back. Nevertheless, the mission was deemed a success and heralded what was to become a pattern of large scale bombing missions in the northern region.

One month after the start of the Somme offensive, an ambitious bombing mission was planned. The aim was to attack the Zeppelin sheds at Brussels, deep inside enemy territory and further than a BE2 loaded with bombs had ever flown. Having twelve of the latest BE2d aircraft, with improvements that included a greater maximum speed and an increased fuel capacity of nineteen gallons, Number 6 squadron was for the first time capable of sending a fully laden aircraft out on a flight lasting more than four hours. However, the extra weight of the bombs and petrol halved the *aircraft's rate of climb*[66] *and obliged the pilots to fly without observers. In conjunction with the attack on Brussels it was planned that a second group of aircraft would attack a closer target, the railway sheds at Courtrai, at exactly the same time that the first group would be dropping their bombs over Brussels.*

On the morning of the 2nd August 1916, on what would turn out to be the hottest day of the year, six BE2d machines assembled at Abeele. Joining the two aircraft from Number 6 squadron were two from Number 5 squadron and two from Number 16 squadron, flown in from their respective aerodromes at Droglandt and La Gorgue. Each aircraft was loaded with two 112 lb bombs and its fuel tanks filled to capacity. Three Morane LA biplane scouts of Number 1 squadron arrived from their base at Bailleul and were topped up with petrol. At 11:30 am, the nine aircraft left Abeele, climbing towards the lines in wide circles. One of the pilots was unable to gain sufficient height by the allotted time and returned to Abeele whilst the remaining eight climbed eastwards, crossing over into enemy territory whilst still within the range of ground fire, before setting a course for Brussels. Forty five minutes later they encountered heavy anti-aircraft fire over Ledeghem and one of the aircraft of Number 5 squadron was hit and forced to land.

Just after noon, at about the same time that eighteen year old Captain Charles Snook was forced down twenty miles to the east, the second group of bombers prepared to leave Abeele. Larger than the first, the group comprised a total of thirteen BE2s; six from Number 6 squadron, five from Number 5 squadron and two from Number 16 squadron. Their escorts for the mission were five FE2d fighter bombers from Number 20 squadron, based at Clairmarais, and six DH2 scouts from Number 29 squadron, which was still operating from Abeele. The aircraft took off and headed east, reaching the railway sheds at Courtrai without incident and commencing bombing a little after 1:30 pm.

At exactly the same time, the aircraft of the first group arrived at the outskirts of Brussels and split up to seek out their individual targets. The two machines from Number 6 squadron, accompanied by a single escort, successfully bombed a Zeppelin shed at Etterbeek before rejoining the other aircraft nine miles west of Brussels at the Strythem crossroads. From there, the seven aeroplanes began the journey home, one hundred and sixteen miles to the west, and into a light headwind. Their route was to take them past Courtrai, within range of a dozen enemy aerodromes.

To offer them added protection during this, the most dangerous phase of the flight, the FE2d fighter bombers from the second group had orders to fly east to meet the first group of bombers, once the aircraft they had been escorting had finished their mission and were on their way back to Abeele. The pilots of the aircraft returning from Brussels saw no sign of their escorts at the allotted time whilst flying over Audenarde, but within five minutes they spotted the five aircraft flying towards them from the west, though at a greater height. The twelve aircraft then formed over Anzeghem and with the escort scouts flying overhead for protection, they flew west and safely crossed the lines. From there, the aircraft split up and returned to their home aerodromes. Flying higher than the other aircraft in the group, the FE2d fighter bombers were able to glide most of the way back to their aerodrome at Clairmarais. The last aircraft to return were the two BE2d machines from Number 6 squadron that had taken part in the bombing of Brussels. They landed with empty tanks a little before 4:00 pm, four and a half hours after they had departed from Abeele.

At sunrise on the morning after the raid, it was evident that it would be another hot day. By noon, the temperature had soared to eighty four degrees Fahrenheit.

"Attention. It's the new sergeant," said Fred, who had stopped what he was doing at the sound of approaching footsteps.

Dexter, who was sitting next to him in the workshop lorry, chuckled beneath his breath but said nothing.

"All right, all right, give it up," replied Jock. "It's been a couple of months so you both should be over it by now. Haven't heard about your commission yet, have you Dexter, or has your recent promotion to 1st class air mechanic satisfied your career ambitions?"

It was Fred's turn to laugh as Dexter squirmed on his seat.

"It's in the pipeline, Sergeant."

"I'll be a sergeant's aunt before you ever make lieutenant," said Fred, slapping him on the back.

"Enough!" ordered Jock. "I've come to escort you two to the range for the firearms test I told you about yesterday. Have you got your revolvers with you?"

"Yes, we put them under the bench for safe keeping," replied Fred.

"Hand them over then. We don't want you shooting anyone by mistake."

Jock held out an empty canvas bag and the two men placed their weapons inside it.

"Don't worry about wearing jackets. No-one's going to be strict on dress standards today. It's far too hot for that."

Fred pushed his chair away from the table and stood up.

"Let's get it over with then."

The three men left the shade of the lorry and walked over the airfield towards the hangars belonging to Number 29 squadron. The canvas curtains of the first hangar they reached were drawn back and two DH2 scouts were just visible in the gloom, parked against the back wall. A solitary DH2 was pegged to the grass on the forecourt of the second hangar. When they got closer, the mechanic sitting in the exposed cockpit stood up and waved to attract their attention.

"Hey sarg, we've got another sergeant pilot joining us today!" the mechanic shouted.

"Do we know him?" Jock yelled back.

"His name's McCudden. [67] He was one of the 'Fee' pilots who escorted your chaps yesterday."

"They did well, escorting one group out and the other coming back."

"Well, the powers that be have decided to take him off two-seaters and send him over to us. They must reckon he's scout material."

"Perhaps he'll bring you good luck."

"Here's hoping. I've been asked to get this old bus ready for him, so you'll know which machine to look out for."

Jock left Fred and Dexter and walked over to the front of the aircraft. He patted the aluminium nacelle and looked up at the mechanic.

"Do you think if I transferred to your squadron I might get to be a pilot too one day?" he asked, a hint of bitterness in his voice.

"Don't worry, Jock, it'll happen. This war's got plenty fighting left in it, you'll see."

"I have my doubts, Stan. When does the new chap arrive?"

"Some time today apparently."

"Sergeant Noakes will be glad to have another pilot with him in the sergeants' mess."

"That's true. He's got nothing in common with any of the other sergeants."

"I hope this McCudden fellow doesn't do stunts like Noaksy."

"So do I, but I'm pretty safe working in this end hangar."

"Well away from where the sergeant normally operates!" Jock added with a laugh.

The mechanic smiled and wiped the sweat from his brow with a dirty rag, before climbing down from the cockpit.

"It's a hot one today all right. I'll carry on with this when it gets a bit cooler. See you later, sarg."

"Cheerio Stan," Jock shouted back. "I'll keep an eye out for the new chap."

With a parting wave, the mechanic turned and retreated to the shade of the hangar. Jock rejoined Fred and Dexter and they all made their way along the side wall, through the row of lopped trees that marked the western perimeter of the airfield and on into the neighbouring field where a firing range had been set up. Fifteen yards from a white line that had been roughly painted on the grass were three targets, set at five yard intervals. Made from palliasses stuffed with straw, the targets were held in a vertical position by wooden stakes driven into the ground. A circular cardboard target was pinned to the front of each mattress. To the left of the white line a small wooden table had been set up, covered with a sheet. Jock walked up to the table and carefully emptied the contents of his canvas rucksack on to the clean surface.

"All right you two. Come over here and take your weapons."

Fred and Dexter did as they were ordered and went to pick up their side arms. Fred removed the Webley Mk V1 revolver from its holster, turning it over in his hands to see if it had collected any rust since he had last used it.

"I haven't fired this in months," he said.

"Me neither," added Dexter. "And I'd be surprised if I could hit the mattress from here, much less the target."

Jock took eight .455 calibre bullets from a small cardboard ammunition box and stood them up on the table in two separate piles.

"You two are right handed with a pistol, aren't you?"

Both men nodded in reply.

"All right then. Once you've loaded the bullets, select a target and take up position with your right foot on the line and your weapon held at your side. Then wait for me to give the order to fire."

Fred broke open his revolver by releasing the latch with his right thumb and taking hold of the barrel with his left hand. One by one he carefully picked up the bullets from the table and loaded them into four of the six empty chambers. Snapping the pistol shut he rotated the cylinder until there was a bullet in the first chamber to the right of the barrel. Dexter followed suit and the two men went to take up their positions.

"I'll take the one furthest away from Jock, if you don't mind," Fred said with a smile. "I'm less likely to hit him from there."

"That's fine by me," Dexter replied. "I'll use the middle target."

As instructed, they each stood on the white line, facing side-on to their chosen target. Fred looked across at the table before realising that Jock had already moved behind him to the shade of one of the large trees. Keeping his revolver at his side, Fred looked over his shoulder and shouted at Jock.

"Do you mind if I fire my gun with the hammer already cocked? It will give me a better chance of hitting the target!"

"I suppose so, Fred. But don't tell anyone I said you could. The same goes for you, Dexter, but you're a better shot than Fred."

"It's all right, sarg," Dexter replied. "I'll fire the normal way if you don't mind. You're always telling me I go off half cocked anyway."

"Right you two, enough of this nonsense."

Jock left the shelter of the trees and approached the firing line.

"When I give the order, I want you to fire four shots in your own time. Try and get them as close as you can to the centre of the target. When you've finished, break your weapons and wait until I tell you to stand back."

Jock paused, waiting for the two men to get into position.

"Fire when ready," he commanded, stepping away from the firing line and walking back to the table.

Standing straight with his free arm down by his side, Fred slowly raised the cocked pistol until the sights were slightly below the centre of the target. Though he tried hard not to be distracted by the sound of Dexter's shots, he was nevertheless aware that his friend had already fired twice. Squeezing the trigger gently, as he had been taught at Farnborough, he was caught by surprise when the gun suddenly discharged, its barrel kicking upwards and back towards him.

Not knowing what to expect, Fred peered at the target in the distance. He could see no evidence that the bullet had penetrated it. Looking to his left, he noticed that Dexter had already stopped firing and was standing still, with his revolver pointing down to the ground. For the second shot, Fred once again cocked the revolver before taking aim, this time focussing on a point at the bottom of the circle and with a tighter hold on the weapon. He squeezed the trigger more gently than before and was better prepared for the sudden recoil when the gun went off. Looking again at the target, he noticed a small hole through the rim of the outer circle. Encouraged by the result of his second attempt, he fired two more shots before breaking open the revolver and ejecting the spent cartridges on to the ground.

"Stand back from the line," Jock ordered. "And come back to the table for a reload."

Fred glanced at Dexter, who raised his eyebrows and laughed.

"I thought your gun must have jammed."

"I never was fast at this," Fred replied. "Let's hope I'm never called upon to fire in anger."

"I watched your last two shots, Fred, and they weren't that bad."

Jock met them at the table and handed them each four more bullets.

"Now for the fun part," he said. "Same as before except that I want you to fire left handed." He laughed. "This time to be on the safe side I might retreat to the other side of the airfield!"

Once they had reloaded their revolvers, Fred and Dexter lined up again in front of their targets and waiting for Jock's command.

"Fire when ready!" Jock shouted again, this time from the safety of the trees.

Facing in the opposite direction, Fred could not see what Dexter was doing. Though he was no longer afraid of the recoil, he found it difficult to hold the gun steady in his left hand. Before he had finished taking aim, his arm began to shake uncontrollably. Frustrated with his lack of success, he lowered the revolver and took another deep breath before once more taking aim. This time he reached out quickly, firing the shot before his arm had time to shake. Looking at the target, Fred could see another small hole, though well outside the marked circle. When he had fired the fourth shot with his left hand, Fred broke open the revolver and ejected the spent cartridges. Looking across at Dexter, he shrugged his shoulders.

"I'm glad that's over!"

"You'll never make sergeant on that performance!" Dexter shouted back. "Let's go and see how many hits we had between us."

While the two men were talking, Jock had walked back to the table. Seeing that they were about to leave their positions, he shouted at them.

"Before you two do anything, bring your weapons over to me for safe keeping. We don't want any accidents do we?"

"Bit of an old woman, isn't he, Fred?"

"Yes, but orders is orders. We'd better keep him happy."

They handed their empty revolvers to Jock, who placed them on the table before joining them at Fred's target.

"I can see seven holes, Fred, but only two inside the circle. What happened to the eighth?"

"Probably in a tree somewhere, Dexter" replied Fred. "How did you go with yours?"

"Six inside the circle and two just outside."

Jock walked up behind Dexter and slapped him on the back.

"Definitely officer material, I'd say."

"Don't start that again. Here, you might as well take our targets for all the good they'll be."

Fred and Dexter unpinned the targets and handed them to Jock, who wrote their names on the back in pencil before placing the targets in the canvas bag.

"That's it for now. Take your revolvers and put them back in your cabins whilst I go and give your scores in at the office. Fred, you might as well take the rest of the day off so that you can get ready for the concert tonight."

"Are you sure?"

"Quite sure. There's not much happening at the moment and the next bombing raid isn't scheduled for a couple of days."

"Thanks, Jock."

"Are you playing with Fred tonight, Dexter?"

"Yes, sarg. And at all of the others as well. We've got six concerts over the next ten days, so any time we can have off for practicing would be greatly appreciated."

"All right, you might as well take the afternoon off as well. I'll clear it with the captain after I've given in these results. If he's in a good mood he won't hold your poor score against you, Fred."

"Jock," Fred asked, "I've been meaning to tell you that I've lost my disc.[68] Do you know if I can get another one from the stores?"

"Not for me to say, old son. You'll have to ask the captain. The major's a bit of a stickler when it comes to lost equipment, so you might find yourself on a charge. If you come with me now, I'll see if I can smooth things over for you."

"I'll see you back at the cabin, Fred," said Dexter. "Give me your gun and I'll put it away for you."

"Thanks. I shan't be long."

Fred handed his revolver to Dexter, who left to return to their sleeping quarters. Jock and Fred walked across the airfield to the office. Instead of the recording officer, they found the commander of 'B' flight, Captain James Selby, sitting behind the desk.

Having acknowledged their salutes and standing them at ease, the captain accepted the signed targets and listened to Jock's requests. He scratched his head before replying.

"I'm happy that Johnstone and Dexter take some time to work on their concert so long as they are up to date with the wireless work. With regards to the lost disc, I don't think that presents too much of a problem."

"Why's that, sir?" asked Jock.

"As you know, the dark room Johnnies are very adept at putting together mosaics of the photographs we've taken from the air. Rather than us continuing to use out-of-date army maps, we're going to ask them to produce an aerial photograph for each of the targets and then draw the clock code rings on top of them."

"So we won't need to use discs any more?"

"It'll make your work in the air easier and more accurate."

"What a good idea, sir."

"I'm afraid it was Lieutenant Rowland's idea, not mine, Sergeant.

But if the trial of the new scheme works, we'll need even more men in the photographic section."

"I'm sure it will be worth it though, sir."

"Quite so," replied the captain, who turned to Fred. "Listen Johnstone, if you need a new disc in the short term, I can lend you mine."

"Thank you, sir, but I don't think that will be necessary. As it was, I rarely used the old one."

"Let's leave it at that, then. I'll pass these scores on to the recording officer when he gets back."

Dismissed by the captain, Jock and Fred returned to the hangar where Dexter was already hard at work.

"Dexter, the captain's agreed. So when you're ready, we can go to Julia's and have a practice there."

"All right, Fred. Give me five minutes to finish what I'm doing and I'll be with you."

Chapter 12

Dexter has the Last Word

With the German air force concentrating on the fighting in the Somme valley, fewer enemy scouts were operating around Ypres. As a result, the number of casualties sustained by the squadron over the next three months was relatively low, with more men killed in accidents than in actual combat. There was also a change in command when Major Arthur S Barrett took over from Major Reginald P Mills, amidst continued rumours that the squadron would be moving to a new aerodrome. Yet again, the rumours proved to be unfounded. With winter approaching, the weather gradually worsened. On Friday 20th October 1916, the coldest day of the Battle of the Somme, when the daytime temperature only reached forty eight degrees Fahrenheit, the new major passed the order that the night parade was to be abolished forthwith. That weekend was also the time of a squadron changeover at Abeele. The FE8 single seater scouts of the newly formed Number 41 squadron[69] arrived on the Saturday, with Number 29 squadron leaving two days later, flying forty miles south to their new aerodrome at Izel le Hameau.

It was the night of the November full moon and the weather was cold and clear. Number 6 had begun the month well by carrying out a number of successful night bombing raids. With 'C' flight back from its temporary posting at Droglandt, the squadron was once again at full strength.

"What do you think of my new coat, Dexter?"

"You look like a cave man."

Fred had earlier stopped work to go to the stores, where he had been told that goat skins were being issued to anyone who wanted one. He returned to the hangar with a large shaggy goat skin wrapped around his shoulders like an officer's cape.

"I don't care what it looks like, as long as it keeps me warm. There are some left but you'd better be quick. I took the last white one. The rest are brown."

"I bet it smells," said Harold Edge, another of the wireless mechanics in Fred's flight. "They don't call them 'Stinkers' for nothing."

Fred gave him a disapproving look as he stroked the shaggy fur.

"Of course it doesn't smell. If a goat skin was good enough for Hawker, it'll certainly do me."

"Can I try it on?" Dexter asked.

"If you treat me to supper. I've got something to celebrate."

Fred took off the skin and handed it to Dexter.

"Is it waterproof?" asked Harold.

"I'm not sure, but with the weather we've been getting recently, I'll find out soon enough."

"So what's the big news, then?" asked Dexter.

"I arrived in France exactly a year ago today. That's worth supper, don't you think?"

"On any other day I'd agree with you old man, but today is a special day for me also."

"Trying to steal my thunder are you, Dexter. What's so special about your day then?"

"I've got my commission," Dexter announced simply, looking at the ground as he spoke.

Fred looked at him, dumbfounded.

"You must be joking. Come on, tell us the real reason."

"It's true. The captain told me this afternoon. I'm going to be commissioned as a second lieutenant on probation and return to Blighty to train as an equipment officer."

"Well I never," stammered Fred. "After all our joking, you're going to outrank all of us. Should we be calling you 'sir'?"

"Not yet, Fred. Not until after I get back to England."

"That's a relief. I'm not sure I could do that without laughing. It's hard enough with Jock being a sergeant."

"Well, you can rest assured there's little chance I'll be posted back to Number 6."

"Do you realise this could be our last night out together?" said Harold, slapping Dexter on the back.

"That settles it," said Fred. "We must all go to Margueritas for supper. There are no missions scheduled for tonight so we can all take the night off. I'm sure Julia will fit us in somewhere. That all right with you, Dexter?"

"That's fine, Fred. Not my first choice, but I doubt we would get into the Mill at such short notice."

"It's too far to walk to Godewaersvelde in this weather anyway. Listen, I'll go and square it with the lieutenant and organise the others, if you two go and tell Jock. I can't wait to see his face."

"All right, Fred. We'll meet up at the entrance."

"And don't forget what I said about the capes," Fred added as he left to walk off in the direction of the duty office.

Half an hour later, eight men approached the entrance of the aerodrome where they were challenged by the guard.

"Halt. Who goes there?"

"Snow White and the Seven Dwarfs!" Fred shouted out, unable to stop laughing.

He turned around and looked back at his friends, standing together in a huddle a few feet away. They were all wearing dark goatskins over the top of their Royal Flying Corps greatcoats.

"Well, I can recognise you, Fred, but what is this sorry looking bunch of humanity standing behind you?"

"It's the latest look. Don't you like it?"

"Don't know about that. I'd keep well away from any officers if I were you."

Having shown their passes, Fred and the others strolled out of the aerodrome and along the road to Abeele, where they spent an enjoyable evening at Margueritas. Julia provided them with supper and afterwards Fred entertained everybody in the estaminet by playing on the grand piano. The guests made so much noise that they were oblivious to the sound of a single German bomber flying directly overhead on its way to drop bombs on the aerodrome. Fortunately, though several bombs exploded on the ground around the perimeter of the airfield, none caused any damage. The revellers walked unsteadily back to the aerodrome, guided by the light of the full moon and totally unaware of the excitement they had missed whilst they were out celebrating.

Chapter 13

A Brief Respite

Christmas was a quiet time for everyone on the aerodrome. The weather was cold, wet and windy and there was little operational flying scheduled for either squadron. It was also a time of relative peace, when the men were able to catch up on their correspondence, participate in the season's festivities and carry out much needed building maintenance. Contrary to the consensus of opinion at the Toc H meeting held almost a year earlier, the war had not ended and many wondered how many more Christmases they would spend on foreign soil.

The New Year literally began with a bang when a fight broke out in one of the huts in the early hours of the morning. During the course of the melee a revolver was accidentally fired, the bullet punching a hole through the corrugated tin roof. The offenders were quickly seized by the military police and brought in front of the Air Provost Marshall who sentenced each man to seven days 'confined to barracks'.

"Good morning, Sergeant. Fred Johnstone reporting for duty. I've just been transferred from 'A' flight."

"A Happy New Year to you, Johnstone. I'm glad to see you weren't involved in last night's fracas."

"It was in the hut next door, sarg, so I didn't get much sleep anyway."

"I don't think anyone did. Anyway, come and meet the other

wireless boys. You've worked with some of them already, but there are a couple of youngsters I'd like you to put under your wing until they get to know the ropes."

"That's fine by me, sarg."

"Once you've settled in, Captain Selby would like to have a word with you about your duties."

"I know there's a lot for us to do as all of the wavelengths are going to be changed. What's Captain Selby like to work for?"

"Ex Army, but you'll find he'll leave you alone so long as you do your job properly."

"I can't grumble about that, sarg."

"The captain tells me your due for some furlough. Do you have a date?"

"I'm off next week, but I should be able to get things well and truly sorted out before then."

"That's good to hear. Let's go and see what the rest of the gang is doing. I expect there'll be a few sore heads this morning, so don't expect too much from them."

Having been introduced to the men of the flight, Fred spent the rest of the morning with the sergeant discussing the outstanding wireless work and assigning the tasks to the other airmen in his section. In the middle of the afternoon, whilst going through the inventory of wireless spares, Fred suddenly developed a throbbing headache. Conscious of his new responsibilities he carried on working, but after a while he began to shake uncontrollably. Seeing the state that Fred was in, the sergeant ordered him to report to the medical officer, who informed Fred that he had a mild case of influenza. With orders to go to bed immediately, Fred returned to his cabin, undressed and crawled into bed with the blankets pulled up around his neck and his goatskin spread out on top. He fell asleep almost immediately, sleeping right through the night and for most of the next day, oblivious to what was going on around him.

In the afternoon he was awakened by a commotion outside the hut. He crawled out of bed, put his greatcoat on over the top of his pyjamas and walked to the door. Outside, men were rushing around in all directions. A human chain of soldiers stretched right across the front of the hut and into the distance, each man standing an arm's length from the next. The men were passing full buckets of water in one direction and empty ones in the other.

"What's happening?" Fred shouted. "Have we been bombed?"

"It's the major's hut," replied the soldier who was standing nearest to him. "Somehow it got on fire and we're using water from the pond to try and put it out."

"Is there much damage?"

"The adjutant's saved most of the major's things, but a lot of the squadron's records have been lost."

"They won't be able to write a story about us now," Fred replied. "That's one lost for the history books."

With nothing he could do to help, Fred went back inside the hut to get dressed. By the time he came out again, it was almost dark. The only evidence of the earlier disaster was a wet trail on the flattened grass where water had spilled from the fire buckets. He looked over towards the major's hut. Nothing remained of the building save the floor and a few blackened uprights. The furniture that the men had managed to salvage was roughly piled at the edge of the pond and the adjutant was sitting on the ground next to one of the wooden filing cabinets, sorting through a mass of sodden papers.

Remembering that Number 41 squadron had organised an exhibition of pictures in one of its hangars, Fred decided to walk to the northern end of the aerodrome to see what was on display. With no aircraft in the air or waiting to take off, he walked on the grass, straight up the centre of the airfield. As he approached the first of the hangars, he looked beyond the four scouts that were pegged to the ground in front of the main doors and recognised the figure of Charles Hickie. He ran towards the lieutenant who had already reached the open doors, but by the time Fred caught up with him, his headache had returned. Wheezing from the exertion, he called out.

"Hello, sir. Mind if I join you?"

The lights were on inside the hangar but other than the two men, it was empty. The whole of the floor area had been cleared of aircraft and the ground was covered with a miscellany of chairs and benches.

"Certainly, Fred. I was beginning to think I had the whole show to myself. The major's already had his own private viewing."

"I wasn't sure when would be a good time, sir."

"Right before the carol concert I thought would be the quietest. It seems I was right."

"I'd forgotten all about that. The doctor says I have the 'flu. I'm not really up to singing carols but I'd certainly like to see the pictures."

All of the available space on the inside walls of the hangar, up to a height of six feet, was covered with black and white photographs. On the left hand side were hung photographs of the Battle of the Somme and on the right were prints of photographic slides[70] taken during Scott's ill-fated expedition to the South Pole. From the middle of the hangar, where Fred could see the whole exhibition, there was a stark difference between the two sets of photographs. Those taken on the Somme battlefield were dark and sombre whereas the Antarctic photographs were striking contrasts of black and white.

The two men looked at the scenes of the fighting, neither making any comment as they moved from picture to picture. When they had finished looking at the last photograph, Fred turned to Charles Hickie.

"I always knew that things were pretty grim in the trenches, but these scenes are unbelievable. There's no dignity in the deaths portrayed here."

Charles Hickie leaned across and whispered in Fred's ear.

"I suppose you've not heard that one of Number 41's mechanics took his own life today."

"No I hadn't, sir."

"Poor chap, he was only twenty one. And at Christmas time too. I wonder what they'll tell his parents."

"That he died for his country, I expect."

"Don't mention it to anyone, will you. Their major is telling the men it was an accident?"

"That goes without saying, sir."

"On a brighter note, I hear that Flight Sergeant Cardno is listed in today's London Gazette. Apparently he got a mention in General Haig's last despatch."

"I'm surprised he didn't tell me, though his head's certainly big enough already."

"Come. Let's take a look at the ice scenes before anyone else comes along."

Fred followed Charles Hickie to the opposite side of the hangar where they began to look at the Antarctic scenes, once again without exchanging a word. After a few minutes Fred broke the silence.

"I can now appreciate why they chose to exhibit these photographs alongside the battle scenes."

"Why is that?"

"Well sir, see how clean and pristine the ice scenes are compared to the ruined landscapes captured in the battle photographs. Just look at the natural beauty of this photograph taken from inside an ice cave, with Scott's ship in the background."

"I see what you mean. What about this one next to me? The face of the ice has been worn away by the wind and looks just like weathered sandstone."

"You can't beat nature can you, sir?"

"Especially when you compare it with the mighty works of mankind, eh Fred."

"I didn't take you for a cynic, sir."

As they moved along the line of photographs, Fred stopped in front of one that showed a sled being dragged across broken slabs of sea ice. Charles Hickie pointed to the men who were pulling the sled.

"I wonder if Shackleton's rescue mission will be successful."

"You mean for the rest of the Ross Sea party, sir?"

"Yes. I read in the paper yesterday that he's just left New Zealand."

"I'd be very surprised if he finds anyone alive after all this time. It's hard to believe that the original expedition left before the start of the War."

"If there are any survivors[71] they'll find the world a very different place to what they left behind in nineteen fourteen."

"What some men do to evade conscription!" Fred said with a laugh.

As they were looking at the last of the photographs, a group of men strolled into the hangar.

"Are we right for the concert, Lieutenant?" one of the men called out.

"Yes, take a seat wherever you want," Charles Hickie replied. "The carols will be starting in half an hour."

"I'd better be going, sir," said Fred. "I'm still not feeling the best. I hope the concert goes well for you tonight."

"Thanks, Fred. Get a good night's rest and I'll see you in the morning."

Fred saluted and left the hangar to walk back to his cabin. Well aware that he was scheduled for guard duty the next evening, he hoped that an early night would do him good.

Just before dawn on the following day, the weather was pronounced favourable for flying and the first of the artillery observation sorties left on schedule. The aircraft, a new BE2g, was the first that Fred had worked on when he joined 'B' flight. The pilot for the flight was twenty year old 2nd Lieutenant 'Jimmy' Jameson, already the holder of the MC, DCM[72] and the French Medaille Militaire. At the outbreak of war he had joined the British army at the age of seventeen before transferring into the Royal Flying Corps as a 2nd class air mechanic. Rising from the ranks, he eventually gained his commission and was posted to Number 6 squadron as a pilot. His observer for the flight was thirty one year old Lieutenant William Thomson, an experienced officer on attachment from the Princess Patricia's Canadian Light Infantry.

The crew took off into the gloom at half past eight and set course for the assigned battery, located a few miles south of Ypres. Another aircraft from Abeele took off shortly afterwards to fly as escort for the mission and this was piloted by nineteen year old 2nd Lieutenant George Knight.[73] At first, all went according to plan, as the crew ranged the Canadian 3rd Siege howitzers on to several enemy targets, until their aircraft was attacked by a German scout, two miles west of Dickebusch Lake. Lieutenant Knight realised what was happening and dived down to drive off the attacker, but not before Lieutenant Jameson's aircraft had been hit by machine gun fire. In flames, the stricken machine fell from the sky and crashed near the village of Voormezeele, killing both pilot and observer. Within minutes, news of the loss had spread throughout the squadron.

Fred and the other wireless mechanics worked late that night and for most of the following day, making repairs to damaged wireless installations and installing a new set in one of the replacement aircraft. In the evening before he was due to go on leave, Fred visited the hospital and was examined by the doctor, who gave him a clean bill of health and a letter certifying that he was free from vermin and scabies. Then, having obtained an outfit of freshly washed clothes and underwear, he walked to the recording office where he was given a combined leave and railway ticket for third class return travel[74] to Basingstoke.

That night Fred could hardly sleep, excited at the prospect of seeing Ethel for the first time in more than a year, especially as his leave would coincide with her birthday. He crawled out of bed at three thirty, packed his kit bag and made his way in the dark to look for the tender that he had been told would take him to Poperinghe. At the main entrance he found a lorry parked in the roadway with its headlights on and the engine running. He walked up and spoke to the driver before climbing into the back of the truck. In the pitch dark, he felt his way along the inside of the truck to find a space.

"Over here, mate," a man's voice called out.

A light shone in Fred's face and he moved towards its source, finding a vacant seat next to a soldier whose uniform was torn and dishevelled.

"Thanks," he replied, sitting down on the wooden bench. The soldier grunted and shone the lamp on Fred's spotless uniform.

"Just look at you. All dressed up and somewhere to go. Called back to Blighty for a commission I suppose?"

Fred recognised the unmistakable twang of an Australian accent.

"Me an officer? Not likely. It's my first leave and I can't wait to get home and sleep in my own bed. I can't even remember what silence is like."

"You should try sleeping up at the trenches, mate. I'm so used to the shelling I think I'd go mad if it stopped."

The soldier sitting opposite Fred leaned forward and touched him on the arm.

"Take no notice of Les. He's just envious of where you're going. We've had a bad trot lately and we're all a long way from home."

"No offence taken," Fred replied. "I'm sure I'd feel the same if I were in your shoes."

The tender rumbled along the road in the dark and eventually stopped at Poperinghe station, having first dropped off the Australian soldiers in the market square. By that time Fred was the only passenger. He picked up his kit bag and jumped out of the back of the truck, thanking the driver as he walked past the open cabin on his way to the barrier. Having shown his ticket to the stationmaster, he made his way to the platform where a train was already waiting. The station was in total darkness and it was difficult for him to see the carriages, but he could hear the sounds of a stationary steam engine at the far end of the platform. To his surprise, the train was already packed with soldiers and he had to walk to the coach immediately behind the engine before he could find a vacant seat. He sat down, thankful that he had decided not to board the train at Abeele.

For much of the journey west, the train travelled no faster than a horse drawn carriage and it stopped several times along the way to drop off and pick up passengers. It finally reached St Omer at nine thirty, in the early morning light, and Fred left the station to eat a late breakfast at a nearby estaminet. Returning half an hour later, he climbed on board another train, this time bound for Boulogne, one of the busiest ports for passenger travel between France and England. The second train travelled more quickly than the first and made fewer stops along the way, but it was just as full. After three and a half hours the train arrived at its destination. The soldiers were deposited right next to the quay where the RMS Victoria was waiting to carry them on the fifty mile voyage north across the English Channel to Folkestone.

Fred carried his kit bag to the stern gangplank and waited patiently in line with other soldiers who had already started to form a queue. When the ship's captain gave the order, the gangplank gates were opened and the soldiers climbed on board, most choosing to go below deck. Fred left the others and walked to the rearmost lifeboat, finding a sheltered spot on the quarterdeck that was out of the wind. Remembering the previous Channel crossing when he had suffered from sea sickness, he had already decided it would be preferable to put up with the freezing winter temperature on deck and be able to keep sight of the horizon rather than seek the warmth of a below-deck lounge. He was relieved that the vessel was twice the size of the one he had sailed on for the outward voyage and he prayed that the crossing would be smooth.

The ship left the quay just after high tide at two thirty in the afternoon, black smoke belching out of its forward funnel as it made its way slowly out of the harbour and into the English Channel. It was evident that many of the other soldiers on board felt the same way as

Fred, as there were several groups of men scattered around the deck, huddled together for warmth. They reminded Fred of king penguins, sheltering from an Antarctic storm. Once clear of the dock, the ferry gathered speed and the men standing behind the funnels were enveloped in smoke as the engines went to 'full ahead both'.

The crossing was uneventful and the ship arrived at Folkestone at five o'clock in the evening. Fred made sure he was first in line when the gangplanks were rolled out from the dockside and placed over the side of the ship. When the order was finally given to disembark, the returning servicemen filed across the narrow gangplanks and up on to the exposed quay. The evening was dark and wet, not what Fred had imagined when lying in his bunk back at the aerodrome, and he felt anything but elated. Many soldiers were met by family and friends and quickly left the jetty. Others like Fred, who still had a long way to travel, made their way along the curved railway platform in the pouring rain to look for a seat in one of the carriages of the waiting train. Reaching the covered section of platform that offered some protection from the penetrating rain, Fred left the others behind and ran to the furthest carriage, level with the rear entrance to the harbour master's house. Opening the door, he climbed up into the compartment and was surprised to find that it was already half full. One of the soldiers already on board removed his kit bag from the seat and threw it up on to the overhead rack, offering the space to Fred. Fred thanked him and sat down, squeezed between the window and the soldier, with his kit bag at his feet.

After what seemed like an age, the last of the men climbed on board and Fred heard the whistle blow. The whole train juddered for a few seconds as the driving wheels of the steam locomotive fought to get a purchase on the slippery rails. Gradually the train moved along the jetty, inch by inch at first and then gathering speed as it gained momentum. The carriages rumbled across the revolving harbour bridge and along the arched brick viaduct that jutted out at right angles to the shore, separating the port's inner and outer harbours. Rain streamed down the windows and the smell of damp uniforms permeated the carriage. Looking out of the window, Fred caught a fleeting glimpse of the fishing boats that were moored across the inner harbour. At the end of the pier the track veered to the right and the train lost some of its speed as it passed through the town of Folkestone and ascended the steep incline to the main railway junction at the top of the hill.

Beyond Folkestone Junction the track levelled out and the train quickly picked up speed again. Fred leant back on the seat and tried to sleep without success. By the time the train reached the outskirts of London it was half empty and Fred was able to place his bag on the rack and spread out across the seat. When he finally stepped out, cold and depressed, on to the platform at Victoria Station, he regretted that he had asked Ethel to wait for him at his parents' house rather than meet him in London.

He took out his new pocket watch and looked at the time. It was eight o'clock. He walked through the barrier and over to the main departure board. Looking to find the next train that would pass through Clapham Junction, he saw one that was about to leave from a nearby platform. He walked briskly to the barrier, showed his travel pass to the ticket collector and ran to the nearest third class carriage. Almost before he had time to close the carriage door behind him, the guard blew his whistle and the train drew away from the platform.

Looking about him, Fred found that he was the only serviceman in the carriage and, for the first time in more than a year, he felt self-conscious at wearing his uniform. Within minutes, the train reached the busy junction and once more he picked up his kit bag and got out of the carriage. Finding a ticket inspector, Fred asked which platform he needed for Basingstoke. With twenty minutes before the train was due, he bought a cup of tea and a stale fruit bun at the cafeteria and sat by the fire in the platform waiting room.

The train arrived on time and Fred climbed up into an almost empty carriage. Choosing a rear facing corner seat next to the window, he threw his bag up on to the rack and started to undo the buttons of his greatcoat so that he could make himself more comfortable. Without warning the train lurched forward, throwing Fred off balance, and he ended up sprawled across the seat on the other side of the compartment. Without the energy to move back to the seat he had first taken, he stayed where he was, leaning back with his head resting against the window and his unbuttoned coat draped open at the waist. The train quickly reached full speed and the constant drumming of the wheels against the tracks made him feel drowsy. Anxious not to fall asleep and miss his stop, he forced himself back into an upright position and for the first time since boarding the train he looked around the carriage. The only passengers sharing the compartment with him were a teenage girl and a young boy, and both were staring at his uniform. The boy was the first to speak.

"You in the Army, mister?" the boy asked, playing with the peak of his cloth cap.

"No son, the Royal Flying Corps."

A look of disdain passed across the boy's face.

"Never heard of it," he replied. "What's there to fly and why have you got bandages on your legs?"

"We have all sorts of flying machines and we use them to spy on the enemy. You've played Spies haven't you?" Fred replied, adjusting the top of his breeches. "And these aren't bandages, they're puttees."

"What are they for then, if they're not bandages?"

"If you wear slacks around aeroplanes it's easy to get your trouser bottoms caught up in the works, so to speak. Breeches with puttees are much tidier, though they can make your legs swell if you put them on too tight."

"Sorry about my brother," interrupted the girl. "Jimmy doesn't mean to be rude but he's never seen a uniform like yours. I think it's very smart. Are you an officer?"

"Not me, I'm afraid. Our officers normally wear a jacket with a Sam Browne belt. Rather like those worn in the army."

"I think your uniform looks nicer."

"I'm glad you like it. Where are you youngsters going?"

"Basingstoke," Jimmy replied. "Me nan lives there and we're going to stay with her 'cos me mum's in hospital and me dad's away in the war."

"Is anyone going to meet you at the station?"

"I don't think so," replied the girl. "But I know where we're going. Our nan lives in Penrith Road."

"That's close to where I live," said Fred. "I can walk you there on my way home if you like."

"Thank you, sir. That would be nice."

"And you can wear my coat if you'd like to, Jimmy my lad."

"Cor, thanks mister."

"My name's Bethany Thomas, by the way," the girl added. "What's yours?"

"Frederick Johnstone. Fred to you. A pleasure to make your acquaintance, Bethany." Fred leant across and shook Bethany's gloved hand. She smiled and blushed.

"The same I'm sure, Fred."

"I've not been home for a while and I must say this all feels very strange. I keep expecting to hear the sound of guns."

"That's exactly what Dad said when he came home on leave."

"Why don't you two come over here and sit next to me. You can tell me all about where you come from and I'll tell you a little bit about Basingstoke. I must say it's a pleasant change to talk about something other than the war."

"Thanks, Fred. It would stop Jimmy getting bored, too. You know what boys are like."

Fred laughed.

"I've not had much to do with children, but I think I know what you mean."

The train continued south, stopping at every station along the way. To help pass the time, Fred drew Jimmy a picture of an aeroplane on one of the pages of his notebook so that the boy could take it home and give it to his grandmother. From time to time they caught sight of distant lights through the carriage windows, whenever the train passed close to a village.

After a while Jimmy fell asleep, clutching the picture of the aeroplane to his chest. Fred talked to Bethany about his childhood days in the village of Basingstoke and the allotment he used to tend in the fields behind his parent's house. In return, Bethany told him about her home in Bermondsey, a small flat above a fish and chip shop.

In talking with the two children, Fred lost count of the number of stations they had passed through. As the train slowed down for the next station he stood up and pulled down the carriage door window.

"Basingstoke station. Anyone for Basingstoke?" he heard a voice call out as the train drew to a halt.

"That's us!" he shouted, jumping to his feet. "Wake up Jimmy, this is our station!"

Jimmy awoke with a start and rubbed his eyes. Fred picked up the drawing from where it had fallen on the seat and put it in the boy's jacket pocket.

"Open the door for me would you, old chap? We don't want the train leaving before I've had time to get my things out."

Jimmy opened the carriage door and jumped out, holding the door wide open whilst Bethany helped Fred pull his kit bag down from the rack and throw it out on to the platform. Fred joined Jimmy on the platform and grasped his hand tightly as Bethany darted back inside the carriage to retrieve her suitcase from under the seat. She passed the valise to Fred before stepping down and swinging the carriage door shut.

"Is that all you have?"

"Yes, that's it. I wasn't sure how much we could bring so I only packed spare underwear and Jimmy's teddy bear."

"Let's hope your grandmother has something your size. If not, I might be able to lend you some of my little sister's old clothes."

They were the only people to get off the train and the platform was all but deserted. The guard blew his whistle, before walking away to change the destination indicator for the next train. A blast of steam erupted from the engine as the train slowly pulled out of the station, shrouding the platform in a swirling cloud of dense white smoke. Having completed his duties, the guard disappeared inside the stationmaster's office, leaving Fred and the two children alone on the platform.

Fred helped Jimmy put on the great coat before picking up his heavy kit bag and slinging it over his shoulder. Taking Bethany by the hand, he led the way through the empty barrier and out of the station. The time on the station clock showed a quarter past nine, almost eighteen hours since he had awoken that morning.

"We might as well walk as it's stopped raining. I can take you right to the door if you like, as it's only half a mile from here."

"Thanks, Fred, I've only been there in the daytime and it all looks very different at night."

Fred tried to grab hold of Jimmy as the boy ran past, his arms outstretched and Fred's coat wide open, flapping around his ankles.

"What do you think of the coat, Jimmy?"

The boy stopped and ran back towards them.

"It fits me perfectly 'cos it's shorter than the ones real soldiers wear. Can I keep it, Fred?"

Fred laughed, playfully punching Jimmy in the chest.

"I don't think my captain would be very pleased. Perhaps one day after the war."

"Is that a promise?"

"Yes, Jimmy, that's a promise."

"Yippee," Jimmy cried, skipping off down the street.

Fred and Bethany followed at a slower pace, walking along the pavement arm in arm. The gas lamps had already been lit but the feeble yellow light emitted by them shone like fuzzy balls in the night mist, barely reaching from one lamp to the next. In the distance, Fred could see a solitary figure standing under the lamp on the next intersection and he idly wondered who would choose to go out on such a dismal evening. As they came closer to the intersection, Fred saw that it was a smartly dressed woman. There was something distinctly familiar in the way she was standing. For some reason he thought of Piccadilly Circus and then he realised why. The woman was Ethel.

With his heart pounding and finding it difficult to breathe, Fred grabbed hold of Bethany's hand as he hastened his stride. They quickly overtook Jimmy as he danced along, wearing Fred's coat.

"I want you to meet my intended," Fred said excitedly, squeezing Bethany's hand. "She's come to meet me and I haven't seen her for fourteen months."

"How romantic," Bethany giggled. "I hope she won't be jealous of me!"

Fred let go of Bethany's hand and ran ahead, calling out when he was certain that his voice would be heard.

"Ethel, it's me. Fred."

The woman looked up and dropped the piece of paper she was holding.

"Fred, but I thought . . . "

Fred reached her before she could finish her sentence and they held each other in a tight embrace whilst the two children stood to one side, laughing. After a while they parted and Fred gestured towards the children.

"Ethel, I'd like you to meet Bethany and Jimmy. They're visiting their grandmother whilst their mother's in hospital. We met on the train and I promised to walk them home. Bethany, Jimmy, this is my very good friend, Miss Pocock."

Bethany pushed Jimmy forward and he shook hands with Ethel with a bashful look on his face. Bethany followed suit, making a half curtsey and briefly taking hold of Ethel's gloved hand.

"I'm delighted to meet you both," Ethel responded, bowing her head slightly. "Let's all walk to your grandmother's shall we?"

Fred bent down to pick up the piece of paper that Ethel had dropped. He stood up and handed it to her.

"A train timetable eh? Were you planning to meet someone?"

"I simply couldn't wait any longer at your parent's house, Fred. I thought I'd surprise you instead."

"You definitely did that, my love."

Ethel put the timetable back in her purse and put her arm around Fred's waist.

"Which street are we looking for?"

"This one," Fred replied. "What's the number, Bethany?"

"Number eighteen, Fred. Just along from here."

They crossed the empty intersection and carried on walking along the pavement, stopping outside a small detached house. Jimmy ran up the path ahead of the others and knocked on the door. Light shone from behind the curtains and Fred reached the door just as it opened.

"Nan, it's me, Jimmy," the boy shouted excitedly, pushing past Fred and disappearing inside. The door opened wider and a large middle-aged woman appeared in the gap.

"Is there anyone out there?" the woman called out in a nervous voice.

Fred stepped forward into the light.

"No need to be alarmed, madam. My name is Frederick Johnstone and I've just come down from London on the same train as your grandchildren. I wanted to make sure they got here safely."

Fred's concern that they may have knocked at the wrong house was unfounded as the woman turned around and grabbed Jimmy by the ear, twirling him around as she deftly removed Fred's coat.

"Hello, Jimmy you young rascal. Have you lost your sister already?"

Bethany ran forward, dropping her suitcase so that she could give her grandmother a hug.

"Would you and your lady friend like to come in for a warm drink?" the children's grandmother asked. She looked intently at Fred before handing his coat back to him.

"No, we can't stop, I'm afraid. It's been a long day and I'm on my way home from the front."

"My boy was posted as 'Missing in Action' four weeks ago and we've not heard anything since," the woman continued in a quiet voice. "I'll have to tell the kids soon, but I'm putting it off as his wife, Nancy, is ill."

"I'm sorry to hear that."

"You look a lot like my Bert in that uniform of yours. Are you sure you wouldn't like to come in?"

Fred looked enquiringly at Ethel and she squeezed his hand and nodded.

"Thank you," he replied. "We'd love to, but only for a while. Then I really must get home as my parents will be waiting for me."

So began Fred's week of leave in England. Ethel had already arranged to take holidays so that she could be with Fred and on her birthday they took a train to Weymouth where they spent two nights at a 'Bed and Breakfast' cottage, close to the beach. There they relaxed, taking time in getting to know one another again, with long walks on the beach and several visits to local tea rooms. Being the middle of winter, they were rarely disturbed by other people and those they did meet kept a respectful distance, realising that the couple wanted to be left alone. Not once did they talk of marriage, though they did discuss what life would be like in an England with so many young men never to return.

All too soon Fred's time in England came to an end. He found it difficult to say goodbye to his parents and was relieved when he and Ethel left for the station a little before dawn on his last day of leave. They travelled together on the train as far as London where they parted company, Fred to take another train to Folkestone and Ethel to return to Rochester. After a brief farewell on the platform, Ethel left, walking quickly through the barrier and never once looking back. Fred watched her until she disappeared from view, not knowing if he would ever see her again.

The trip back to Abeele was slow and difficult. Fred had to wait for most of the day in a rest camp at Folkestone before he was able to board the ship for the night-time crossing. With rough seas in the Channel, it took almost three hours for the small ferry to reach Boulogne. The men, tired and seasick from their arduous journey, were disembarked on to the quay at three o'clock in the morning before being marched to a nearby rest camp where they spent the remainder of the night. Fred was assigned to a tent with eight other soldiers and only managed to sleep fitfully. With snow all around, it reminded him of his first night in France.

At daylight, after a hurried breakfast and with time only to splash his face, he caught a train to St Omer where he waited on the freezing platform for the connecting train to Poperinghe. When the train arrived, he managed to find a seat and fell asleep with his head resting on his kit bag. By the time Fred got off the train at Abeele, daylight was fading fast and he walked to the aerodrome feeling down at heart and almost regretting that he had ever gone on leave. Pausing at the entrance to show his papers, he could hear laughter coming from one of the huts.

"What's going on?" he asked the guard.

"Both squadrons have lost men over the last couple of days."

"So why the celebrations?"

"Well, the news isn't all bad. Sergeant Slingsby managed to bring his machine back, after his pilot was killed. They were in one of the new BEs that has a spare control stick, so he thought he'd have a go at landing."

"Well, that's one for the sergeants."

"That's not all. Number 41 had its first victory today. They're having a quiet celebration in honour of the men who died, Lieutenant Cody and Sergeant Tooms."

"That doesn't make sense. I thought you said they had a victory."

"They did. Toomsy was the one who shot down the Hun, just hours before he too was killed."

"No time for him to celebrate then. I don't think I ever met the other pilot."

"Didn't you? Frank Cody was the youngest son of Samuel Cody."[75]

"Looks like a lot's happened since I left."

"Not really. The weather's been shocking and we've had quite a few dud days. We were inspected by Trenchard last Monday and we all had to stand around in the freezing snow."

"The weather wasn't much better back in Blighty."

Fred picked up his kit bag and slung it over his shoulder.

"Anyway, it's time I went and checked in with the sergeant."

"He's expecting you, Fred. The usual place."

"I haven't forgotten," Fred replied. Then, in a voice tinged with regret and sarcasm, he added, "My, it's great to be back."

Chapter 14

The RE8s Arrive

THE WINTER PASSED *slowly for the squadron. Prolonged cold weather, coupled with a chronic food shortage, made life miserable for the men. On several occasions the only official rations were biscuits and they had to buy whatever they could find in the village. The first two weeks of spring were little better, with the whole squadron confined to camp for several days over a missing engine[76] part. Tempers were already starting to fray when, on a single day, four airmen were killed and the order was received to carry out a practice move.*

Having been stationed at Abeele for almost two years, everyone in the squadron was well aware that a move was long overdue, especially as five other squadrons had shared the airfield during that time. The complicated procedure for the practice move required the men of 'A' flight to load their equipment, stores and spare parts on to the squadron's heavy lorries and drive them to the nearby aerodrome of Poperinghe. Once there, the trucks were turned around and driven back to Abeele, where the whole drill was reversed. At the completion of the exercise, the commander of 'B' flight was put on notice that within the next few days, he too would be required to follow suit.

Recently transferred to a newly formed wireless flight, Fred was relieved that he would not be involved in this operation and he sat in his cabin wondering if the latest order was a portent or would turn out to be yet another false alarm. Dragging his bag of watchmaking tools out from under the bed, Fred left the cabin to organise the day's activities with the men of his section. The first person he came across was senior wireless mechanic Harold Edge, who was working by himself in the wireless lorry.

"Harold, we need to take the wireless sets out of three BE2s this morning."

"Why, what's wrong with them?"

"Apparently, the first batch of RE8s should be arriving some time today. Three of them have already been wired up at the depot but the sets weren't fitted."

"Right, Fred, I'll get Hessie to help me. Which machines do you want us to work on?"

"The oldest we have in the flight. The last two 'C's and one of the 'D's. I've already had them moved into the hangar next door as 'A' flight won't be using it today. "

"I saw them there this morning and wondered what was up."

"Be careful how you take them out as we don't have any complete sets for spares."

"Right you are, Fred."

"Let's make a start then. You go and find Hessie and I'll see you in the hangar after I've had a word with Mr Hickie."

Fred climbed out of the lorry and walked to the hangar next door. Inside, Charles Hickie was giving orders to one of the fitters.

"Corporal Jenkins, I want you to put enough petrol in these three to get them back to St Omer. Four tins in each to be on the safe side."

"Right you are, sir, I'll get on to it now. We're low on petrol in the stores but a lorry is due in later on today."

The corporal scratched his head.

"We're even running out of ammunition. Do you think this time the rumours of a move are true?"

"You might be right, but it's anyone's guess. I'm not even sure the major knows any more than we do."

"If any of our machines get shot up in the next couple of days, sir, we're going to be hard put to fix them. We're almost out of fabric and wood, too."

"That's not your concern, Corporal. Just do the best you can."

"Yes, sir."

"You'd better wait until the sets have been taken out of these three before you start pouring any petrol. One spark in the wrong place and the commander of 'A' flight will be expecting me to build him a new hangar."

"Don't worry, sir, we'll be careful. I'll have the full tins stacked outside until we need them."

The fitter left to organise the petrol and Charles Hickie walked over to join Fred, who was standing next to one of the aircraft.

"Hello, Johnstone. Here to say goodbye to the old faithfuls?"

"No, sir. I wanted to ask you about the spares situation. We're going to have to use the Sterlings from these old machines as there are no new sets left in the stores."

"That sounds like a good decision."

"I'm not happy doing it, sir. If for any reason the sets don't work, the RE8s will have to be grounded."

"You're not the first to raise the issue of spares, Fred. I'd better go and have a talk with the major. Even if we are on the move, we must keep the wireless flight operational."

"Thank you, sir. I knew you'd understand."

"Walk with me to the stores. We can find out what's on order and tell them what we need. You can help me fill in the details for the major."

They left the hangar and walked towards the other side of the aerodrome where the wireless spares were normally stored. With no-one close enough to eavesdrop on their conversation, Charles Hickie turned to Fred.

"How are things at home, Fred? Any progress on the marriage front?"

"I'm afraid not, sir."

"Be patient. I'm sure she'll come around."

"It's my parents' wedding anniversary today, sir. That's two years in a row I've missed seeing them on the day."

"Perhaps you should consider applying for a commission. You know you'd get my support. That way you'd get to go home more often."

"That would be one for the books. I can just imagine . . ."

Before Fred could finish his sentence, the noise of aircraft flying overhead interrupted him. He looked up, shielding his eyes from the glare of the sun.

"Look sir, the RE8s have arrived. They sound very different don't they?"

"So they should, they've got a much bigger engine[77] than the old BE2."

The aircraft flew over the aerodrome, low enough for Fred to see the faces of the ferry pilots who were sitting at the controls in the forward cockpits. Flying in two groups of three, the machines headed east towards the village of Abeele before sweeping around in a wide arc and landing into the wind.

"All very impressive, but certainly not pretty," Charles Hickie said, when the last of the aircraft had landed.

"I see what you mean, sir. The way those ugly noses stick up in the air looks like they've had a heavy landing and broken their backs. The BE2 may be 'old hat' but it certainly looks prettier."

The aircraft came to a rest in front of the hangars where, with the assistance of a dozen eager men, they were quickly turned around and manoeuvred into a line facing out on to the airfield.

"I'd better go and find out which ones are ours. I'll send over one of the ferry pilots and you can work out with him what needs to be done."

"How long do we have, sir?"

"They'll probably want to fly back to St Omer this afternoon, so you'd better get a move on."

"Very well, Mr Hickie, I'll go and give the boys a hand to speed things up."

Fred returned to the hangar and set to work with the other two wireless mechanics. By the time the senior ferry pilot arrived, the wireless sets had been removed from the three aircraft and moved to one side of the hangar. The pilot walked up to Fred, who was busy loading spare electrical cable into a wheel barrow.

"Don't worry about tidying up the observer's cockpit, Corporal, as no-one will be sitting there again. We will need some ballast in them, though."

"I can arrange that, sir. What will happen to the old machines?"

"We'll take what spares we can and probably destroy what's left. I don't think any of them are good enough to be reassigned to other squadrons."

"What about the guns?"

"If I were you I'd take them off and keep them. They could come in handy and it would save us a job."

"Lieutenant Hickie will have to make that decision, sir. We've already removed what we can use again for wireless spares, so I'll get the boys to tidy up the ends of the cables and leave it at that."

"That's fine, Corporal. I've already mentioned it to your lieutenant but I'll go back and confirm it with him presently"

"By the way, sir, is Lieutenant Cochrane-Patrick still your commanding officer? He took me up for my first flight last year."

"Not any more, though many wish he was. He was posted to Number 70 squadron more than six months ago."

"Has he had any success, sir?"

"My word he has. He's already a tally of three."

"Where's 70 squadron based these days?"

"Fienvillers, but it's rumoured around the depot that the lieutenant's on the move again. Flight commander in 23 squadron, when they get re-equipped with Spads." [78]

"Are they any closer to here?"

"Number 23 is stationed at Baizieux, down in the Somme valley, so you probably won't bump into the lieutenant unless your squadron moves south too."

Fred looked thoughtful for a moment before replying.

"There's a rumour we may be moving to Arras."

"Well, you'd know better than I, Corporal. I've been with the Pilots' Pool for almost a month and I've no idea when or where I'll be sent. Mind you, I'm not complaining. I've been getting in plenty of flying practice."

Whilst they were talking, Charles Hickie walked into the hangar and approached the pilot.

"Lieutenant, I've had a look at the three machines earmarked for the wireless flight and they have a different gun set up to what we're used to."

"We've fitted them with 'Huntley and Palmers', if that's what you mean," the chief ferry pilot replied.

"What are they when they're at home?" interrupted Fred.

"It's the slang we use for two Lewis's mounted side by side, as they go together like Mr Huntley and Mr Palmers."

"I used to have rooms that weren't far from their factory. I could smell the freshly baked biscuits when they came out of the ovens. Who would have thought their name would one day be associated with machine guns!"

"Strange things happen in times of war," replied the pilot.

"Talking of guns," Charles Hickie interrupted, "I've decided to keep the old ones, if that's all right with you."

"I was just suggesting the same thing to your man here," the pilot replied. "Between you and me, it would save us time and paperwork if you did."

"How long before you have to leave, Lieutenant?"

"I've yet to give your pilots a briefing on the new type, so you can have another couple of hours if you like. Push the machines out on the 'drome when you've finished. We'll come back later this afternoon and take them off your hands."

"What's the time now, sir?" asked Fred, tapping the glass of his watch. "My watch has stopped."

Charles Hickie reached into his tunic and took out his own pocket watch.

"A little after noon."

Fred corrected the time on his watch and wound it up.

"Don't forget that all clocks have to be advanced by one hour next Sunday," Charles Hickie added.

"That won't make any difference to us, sir. We get up in the dark anyway."

"At least we'll then be on the same time as the Huns."

The ferry pilot laughed.

"That's about the only thing we'll ever have in common with the Boche."

"All right, Lieutenant. Give us until three this afternoon and we'll have the old girls ready for you."

Chapter 15
A Matter of Fate

*F*LYING THE NEW *aircraft proved more difficult than was initially expected. There were numerous landing accidents during the first week, four in the space of a single day, but only one of the pilots was injured. Though similar in purpose, the RE8 was heavier than the BE2 it replaced, with the cockpits of the pilot and observer reversed. Its nose-high attitude whilst on the ground made forward visibility virtually impossible and forced pilots to weave from side to side whilst taxying. Even when airborne, the pilots were often obliged to sideslip in order to see what lay directly ahead, as the heavy engine cowling and exhaust stacks blocked their forward view. The new machine also proved to be less than forgiving to any mistakes made by a pilot. The torque of the large propeller made the aircraft swing heavily to the right during take-off and landing. To make matters worse, the flying characteristics at low speeds could make an unwary pilot inadvertently put the aircraft into a stall or a spin; a potentially fatal manoeuvre at low altitudes. As a result, the re-equipping of the squadron took considerably longer than originally anticipated and it was the end of April before the last of the BE2s was replaced and the squadron had eighteen RE8s on charge.*

The practice moves carried out by Number 6 proved to be an unnecessary exercise when the major announced to his officers that instead of moving south to Arras,[79] the squadron would continue to operate out of Abeele. The next few weeks were chaotic and would later be referred to as 'Bloody April', a time on the Western Front when allied air losses far exceeded those suffered by the German air force. On the positive side though, it was also the month in which the United States of America declared war on Germany.

Fred saw less and less of Jock as they were both busy with their own duties; Fred supervising the wireless operations and Jock flying as an observer. Whilst other squadrons were suffering heavy casualties, for some inexplicable reason Number 6 squadron was to experience a month where no-one was killed. Just as surprisingly, this was a period during which both Fred and Jock both achieved individual success.

Having become accustomed to flying the new aircraft, the crews of the wireless flight broke the squadron record in carrying out one hundred missions in a single week. This placed a huge load on Fred and his fellow mechanics. In his spare time, Fred also achieved a personal triumph, being asked to perform in front of the Queen of Belgium at a Belgian Red Cross concert, held in Reninghelst. Jock, by now a fully qualified observer, was also doing well, even managing to shoot down an enemy Albatros scout, for which he was personally congratulated by Major General Trenchard.

The weather for the start of May was hot and hazy and the aeroplanes of Number 6 continued to spend most of their time supporting the artillery. On the day[80] before Fred's twenty fifth birthday, Jock flew on a patrol and sustained burns to his hands when the aeroplane in which he was flying caught fire. The pilot managed to land successfully on the allied side of the lines and a tender was sent out from the aerodrome to pick them up. Jock was taken to the camp hospital to have his wounds dressed but was ordered to stay in bed because of the risk of infection.

Fred visited Jock as soon as he heard news of the accident.

"So these are the lengths you go to in order to get out of buying me a birthday drink!"

Jock lay in bed, propped up by several pillows with both hands heavily wrapped in bandages. He smiled sheepishly as he raised his right arm towards his mouth.

"It's the first time I've been unable to hold my drink. And to make matters worse, I can't even wipe my own arse. I suppose you wouldn't care to assist, my old pal?"

Fred ignored his friend's request and gave Jock a disapproving look.

"How long will they keep you in here?"

"A couple of days, I expect. It's only my hands after all. The left one's pretty good as I had my glove on."

"Did they put anything on your burns?"

"Picric acid would you believe?[81] Quite funny really. On the one hand it's used to blow up people and on the other it cures burns."

"I thought I was supposed to be the comedian," Fred scoffed.

"I've got nothing else to do, stuck in here."

"That's why I'm here Jock. Are you well enough to come out with us tomorrow night? The lads are taking me to a little place near Godewaersvelde station and I thought we could celebrate my birthday and your survival. I'm sure we could get one of the waitresses to hold the glass for you."

"Sounds like a good excuse to me. Count me in, but don't let on to anyone in here that I'm coming."

"With congratulations from old 'Boom' himself, I'm sure you'd get away with murder at the moment, Jock. I'll come for you after the orderly's made his last round and get you back here before morning."

"Who's on guard duty?"

"Don't you worry, I'll sort that out."

"All right, Fred. I'll be ready and waiting."

Fred got up from his chair and left the hospital hut, returning just before dusk the following day with five other wireless mechanics. Wrapping a greatcoat around Jock's shoulders, they smuggled him out of the hospital and into a waiting tender. As they rode down the narrow road that led to Godewaersvelde, little did they know that they were about to embark on four weeks of the most concentrated flying ever carried out by the squadron. Shortly after the revellers returned from their evening out and had tucked Jock safely back in his hospital bed, the duty sergeant came around to the cabins and ordered everyone out of bed. It was three thirty in the morning, more than an hour before dawn, and the order was given for the first aircraft to be airborne within thirty minutes.

With the Battle of Arras more or less at an end, the latest initiative of the Allies was to be a concentrated advance around Ypres, making extensive use of the artillery. Number 6 squadron was an intrinsic part of this operation and over a period of two weeks it achieved a flying record in the Royal Flying Corps; four aircraft in the air all day and every day between the hours of four thirty in the morning and ten thirty at night. Each patrol required the crews to spend close to four hours in the air. As a result, ground crews worked up to seventeen hours each day without relief. Small luxuries like letter writing and evening meals out in the village were put on hold. In addition to maintaining the aircraft, they had to keep a constant lookout for aircraft returning after dark as they had to make sure that landing flares were on hand to guide the pilots safely back to the aerodrome.

Twelve days into the new routine of early morning wake up calls and working late into the night, Fred crawled out of his bunk and dressed in the dark. He met Jock inside the hangar next to the wireless lorry and under the glare of a single electric light they planned the wireless activities for the day. He was grateful that Jock had been permitted to return to the wireless flight, albeit temporarily, whilst the last of the burns to his hands healed.

"I can't wait to get back into the air," said Jock, shaking his left hand in frustration. "It's only my trigger finger now, but the MO won't sign me off as fit to fly. He reckons the cold temperatures will give me problems."

"It makes sense, Jock. The new skin must be very thin and you'd probably get chilblains. You don't want your skin to crack and get infected. Have you tried changing a drum since your accident?"

"I had a go on the firing range and it seemed to work all right wearing thin gloves. I used my left hand to pull back the cocking handle."

"What's a few more days anyway? You'll be back up there soon enough."

"Not soon enough for me though, Fred."

"Anyway, you're a great help here. With Number 41 leaving tomorrow, some of my lads have been giving them a hand getting their machines ready. They've even got them working as riggers, so they must be short-handed."

Fred finished writing the names of every available wireless mechanic on a chart nailed to the wall. Satisfied that the list was complete, he sat down at the work table, lit a cigarette and leaned back on the stool with his head resting against the hangar wall. Jock joined him at the table and the two men looked at the list of outstanding work.

"We're going to be a bit tight for space over the next couple of days. Do you know if another squadron's coming here straight away? We could make use of the empty hangars if they're not."

"I'm not sure when, Fred, but I did hear in the sergeants' mess that Number 4 squadron is coming here. It has RE8s like us and is a Corps squadron to boot."

"So we'll only have a single type of machine on the aerodrome. That's a pity. I've always liked the variety we had here."

"It makes a lot of sense, though. We can share spares and it'll be easier for the mechanics."

"Talking of spares, Jock, who's flying with Lieutenant Brodie until you're better? He took off a couple of hours ago, but I couldn't see who was in the back."

"Alex McKimmie's with him today. Lieutenant Brodie asked me this morning if I was better and I was sorely tempted to say yes. Maybe I'll go tomorrow."

"I wish you wouldn't, Jock."

"Working with wireless is interesting but it doesn't compare with being up there," Jock replied, pointing his bandaged hand towards the roof of the hangar.

Their conversation was interrupted by the arrival of Charles Hickie. As the lieutenant approached the table, they stood up and saluted.

"At ease," said Charles Hickie, a look of surprise on his face. "I'm the bearer of bad news I'm afraid."

"Have we lost a machine, Lieutenant?" Jock asked.

"Worse than that I'm afraid. There was an accident over the lines. When the battery telephoned the major with the details we at once thought you'd been involved, Sergeant."

"Has anything happened to Lieutenant Brodie?"

It was Jock's turn to look startled.

"They were ranging for a howitzer battery when their machine collided[82] with another one of ours. The gunners were watching from the ground but there was nothing they could do to warn them."

"How bad is it, sir? Did anyone survive?"

"Both aircraft broke up in mid-air and all four men were killed when they hit the ground. We've sent out an ambulance and a tender but I doubt they'll be able to salvage anything."

"Whose was the other machine?" Fred asked.

"Captain Clarke's. He was up there with young Diment."

"So we've lost our flight commander and two aircraft in one accident!" It was Fred's turn to look startled.

"Not to mention three other officers," Charles Hickie added.

"Jock, that could have been you!" Fred gasped. "Harry Diment was only eighteen!"

"I thought it was you, Jock. That's why I looked at you rather oddly when I came into the hangar. Though I'm truly sorry about Alex McKimmie, I'm pleased you're still with us, Sergeant."

"Thank you, sir. So am I."

Jock looked out of the hangar door with a blank expression on his face. Charles Hickie touched Fred on the shoulder.

"Johnstone, I'm afraid I must talk business as goodness knows we're already short of wireless spares. See if you can cobble up something for the replacement machines and I'll find out how soon we can expect more from the depot. Just in case we can't get any new Sterlings, I've thought of an alternative."

"What's that, sir?"

"The new squadron should be arriving here in a couple of days. Would you make yourself known to your opposite number as soon as you can and see if they will lend us a couple of sets. If all else fails, I'll ask our major to talk to theirs and see if we can borrow one of their aeroplanes for a few days."

"Right you are, sir. I'll find out what we've got here first, if that's all right with you. With Sergeant Cardno's assistance, I'll have a go at building two serviceable sets out of the bits we have around the place."

"Thank you, Fred. I'll drop by later on today to see how you're progressing."

When Charles Hickie had left the hangar, Fred sat down next to Jock and looked him straight in the eye.

"Wireless mechanics might not be as exciting as flying, but it's certainly safer. Are you sure you want to risk it all and go back up there?"

"Yes, Fred. If I'm meant to die, I will, no matter what job I'm doing. And if I can make even a small difference, then it'll be worth it."

"Just be careful, won't you. You're my oldest friend out here."

"I'm always careful, but with what's been going on recently, I've a feeling that this won't be the last of our losses."

Jock was right about the losses, both in the squadron and back at home in England. Though the newspapers suppressed the news until the following week, two days later on the Whitsun bank holiday Monday, a German daylight raid was launched against the English coastal town of Folkestone. It was the worst day of bombing so far in the war and scores of people were killed or injured. Sixty were killed in a single explosion. For almost a week after hearing the news, Fred feared for Ethel's safety. The newspaper reports only mentioned that the bombs fell on the south east of England and he knew that Ethel was staying with her parents in Rochester. It was only when he received a letter from her that she wrote the day after the raid that he knew she was safe and well.

With the concentration of flying operations continuing unabated, everyone in the squadron was certain that a new allied offensive was in the offing. Early morning wake-up calls had become part of the squadron's daily routine. The birthdays of the Queen and King of England were celebrated within a week of each other, with Number 4 squadron arriving at Abeele midway between the two events. Two days after the King's birthday, Fred was ordered to check the time signals broadcast by various transmitting stations across Europe so that he could synchronise all of the watches in the squadron. It wasn't until late that night that he completed the task, by which time rumours were rife that the waiting was almost over.

The ground crews were ordered out of bed even earlier than usual on the morning of the 7th June 1917 and by two thirty they were hard at work preparing their aircraft for battle. The dull but insistent pounding of the allied artillery, twelve miles to the east of Abeele, could be heard all around the airfield, the noise of the explosions noticeably louder than in previous weeks.

The first group of machines was scheduled to take off at three o'clock. The pilots stood around in front of the hangars with their observers, waiting for their aircraft to be brought out. At ten minutes to three, the allied bombardment suddenly stopped and the noise of the guns was replaced by an eerie silence. Realising that this was but the calm before the storm, the crews clambered aboard their machines and waited for the signal to leave, well aware that this would be no ordinary day. Right on time, the first of the RE8s from Number 6 squadron left Abeele, bound for the front lines to the west of the town of Messines. Flying in the dark was not a new experience for the pilots and had recently been made less hazardous by the installation of rudimentary instrument lighting in all of the cockpits.

With at least two hours before their machines were due to return, Fred and the other mechanics of the wireless flight tidied up the hangars and walked over to the canteen. They planned to take advantage of the lull in the bombardment so that they could enjoy a peaceful and undisturbed breakfast. The silence was short lived when at ten minutes past three, a huge shockwave shook the ground beneath them and Fred realised that the offensive had started. Seconds later he heard the boom of a single huge explosion, closely followed by a series of lesser explosions. Rushing outside, he looked to the east. The skyline glowed bright orange. Fred wasn't to know that nineteen mines, planted in mine shafts under the enemy lines along the Messines ridge over a period of eighteen months, had been simultaneously detonated by the Allies; almost a million pounds in weight of high explosives. The sound of the explosion was so loud that it was heard by the British Prime Minister, Lloyd George in his office in Downing Street. Even before the allied infantry began to advance, ten thousand German soldiers had been killed. The biggest of the craters, at Hill 60, measured two hundred and sixty feet in diameter. By the time the dust had settled, most of the Messines ridge had been levelled.[83]

Number 6 squadron was one of several that took part in the attack, carrying out artillery observation, firing upon enemy positions and taking photographs. Its aircraft also conducted contact patrols for the soldiers of X Corps, involving the dropping of information bags to the Division and Corps report centres, with regularly updated positions of the advancing allied infantry. The pilots were forced to fly only a few hundred feet above the ground so that they could identify the troops and see the flares that the soldiers had set off to mark their positions. As a result, many of the aircrews were wounded by ground fire. By the end of the first day, the number of casualties was the highest so far sustained by the squadron on any single day of the war, with three men wounded, four men killed and one man taken prisoner.

On the following day the Germans launched a counter attack but this was repulsed by the Allies who succeeded in gaining even more ground. By the 14th June the whole of the salient was in the hands of the Allies and the Battle of Messines drew to a close. As a result of the successes achieved by the squadron, the wireless flight in particular, the men were congratulated by the major and Fred was recommended for promotion to corporal.

The end of the battle brought with it a lull in the fighting as the Allies prepared for the next offensive; [84] a bid to secure the strategic ridge around the village of Passchendaele, dominating the eastern side of Ypres. The men of number 6 squadron continued to work long hours each day supporting the artillery, though the risk of attack from the air was greater due to the presence of large numbers of enemy scouts, now flying in groups rather than singly. At about this time, just before the first of the American troops arrived in France, Major Archibald James took over command of the squadron from Major Arthur Barratt.[85] Major James was no stranger to Abeele, having been a lieutenant at Number 5 squadron two years previously.

The Monday that marked the changing over of commanding officers was also a day on which one of the crews of Number 6 squadron achieved an unusual victory. Three RE8s, one on a photographic patrol and the other two flying as escort, were attacked by six brightly coloured Albatros scouts. Though one of the British pilots was injured in the engagement, Lieutenant George Lees, observer in one of the escorting aircraft, fired a whole drum of ammunition into an enemy scout as it attacked from behind. His pilot, Lieutenant Maurice Ballard, fired into the enemy aeroplane with his forward firing machine gun as the German scout passed beneath them. The wings of the Albatros crumpled and the aircraft fell to the ground, crashing near Zandvoorde. It was only when the three aircraft returned to Abeele that the airmen were informed they had been attacked by aircraft of Jasta 11,[86] better known as the 'Circus' or 'Flying Circus' and led by Baron Manfred von Richthofen. That night, the pilots celebrated in the officers' mess, pleased that the much maligned RE8 could defeat one of the elite enemy scouts in combat and on equal terms.

Chapter 16

The Summer of Seventeen

WASTING NO TIME, the squadron began to prepare for the next allied offensive. The date of the attack had yet to be set, as it was dependent upon the successful positioning of the British guns along the new front line, the Germans having unexpectedly withdrawn from a large section of their trenches. At short notice, the men were informed that a third squadron would be visiting Abeele for a few days and that space had to be made for its men and equipment. To make matters worse, they were told that all three squadrons were to be inspected by His Majesty the King and the Prince of Wales.

Number 32 squadron was the third squadron in the Royal Flying Corps to be equipped with DH2 scouts, but by the time it moved to Le Hameau in May 1916 to take part in the Battle of Arras, the DH2 was no longer a match for the latest enemy scouts. Even so, it was a year before the squadron was re-equiped with a more modern fighter. On the 1st July 1917, the last DH2 in service on the Western Front was flown from Number 32 squadron to the depot at St Omer, two days before the squadron flew with its full complement of de Havilland DH5 scouts to Abeele.

"I thought this place was overcrowded last week." Fred whispered to Harold Edge, trying not to move a muscle as he spoke. "Now it looks more like a fairground than an aerodrome!"

Fred and Harold were the last two men in one of the three rows of Number 6 airmen. Standing to attention in full Flying Corps uniform, they could see the men of the other two squadrons standing directly opposite. Behind them in the distance was a cluster of white tents, erected the day before on the western side of the airfield as emergency sleeping quarters for Number 32 squadron.

"Not to mention the sixty odd machines we now have around the place," Harold replied. "If the Hun decides to bomb us now, he would have a field day."

"Sshh, here comes the King with the Prince of Wales. Something to tell your grandchildren when you're old and grey!"

The two men stood in silence as the royal party walked past the lines of men, with Major James and the other two commanding officers in close attendance. The King spoke a few words which they could not hear from where they were standing before moving away to inspect the other two squadrons.

When he felt that the sergeant major was not looking, Harold whispered quietly out of the side of his mouth.

"What do you think of the new major, Fred?"

"I think he should be good for the squadron. I got to know him a little when he was at Number 5, before you came here. He struck me then as being a reasonable sort of chap."

"I wonder if he'll do anything about all these false alarms. Half a dozen times now we've been told we're going to move and then the brass hats change their minds. They must think that we're a bunch of nincompoops."

"I've only ever heard good reports about us," Fred replied. "Just because our troops haven't made any big advances around Ypres doesn't make our work any less important."

"I suppose you're right. Anything we can do to draw the Hun's forces here will help our boys in other places."

"As long as it's not today, Harold."

"Watch out, Fred, they're coming this way again."

With the inspection over, the members of the Royal family and their entourage returned to the motor cars that had brought them to Abeele. After a brief farewell ceremony, the vehicles left with their important occupants. Within minutes, the convoy disappeared from view and the men of the three squadrons were dismissed so that they could return to their normal duties.

On the way back to the wireless lorry, Fred stopped at the sergeants' mess. He knocked on the door, which was opened almost immediately by Sergeant Trotter.

"Hello, Fred. I suppose you've come to practice for tonight's concert?"

"Not exactly, sarg. I'm half way through fixing Lieutenant Wilson's wireless torpedo, but I wanted to have a quick chat with Sergeant Cardno. Is he in the mess?"

"Yes he is, but he's tied up at the moment. We've got a new sergeant pilot. Jock's showing him the ropes as he's not allowed in the officers' mess like the other pilots."

"He'd have very little in common with any of the other sergeants. How's he supposed to plan his sorties with his observer?"

"With difficulty, I expect, though I doubt they'll change the rules for him."

"It's about time they did," Fred replied, returning to the door. "Take what's happened to McCudden. He came to the Corps as a lowly mechanic and is now a flight commander. I'm sure nobody complains when he walks into the officers' mess!"

"That's different and you know it, Fred. Be off now or I'll put you on a charge for insubordination."

Fred raised his hands in mock surrender.

"All right, sarg, I'll go quietly. Tell Jock I was looking for him would you?"

"Sure thing, son. By the way, there's an eclipse of the moon tonight. It should be worth watching if the sky's clear."

"Thanks, sarg, I'll keep an eye out for it."

Major James returned to his office having said goodbye to the Royal visitors. Conscious at how close Abeele was to the front line, he sat down at his desk and started to plan how the security of the aerodrome could be improved. After a few minutes in thought, he called for his adjutant and asked him to summon the three flight commanders.

When the captains had assembled around the table, the major stood up and addressed them.

"Gentlemen, as soon as Number 32 leaves us, I would like us to work on making the aerodrome a safer place." He paused for a moment before continuing. "Being close to the village and with many huts that are hard to disguise, it seems to me that we are very vulnerable to a bombing attack. I'm the new boy here, so I'm open to suggestions as to what we could do to improve the situation."

Captain George Knight, recently promoted to commander of the wireless flight, raised his hand.

"May I speak, sir?" he asked diffidently.

"That's why I invited you here, Knight."

"Well sir, we could dig trenches in front of the huts. They wouldn't save us from a direct hit but they'd certainly give us protection from shrapnel bombs. The Huns have dropped them on us before, but so far we've been fortunate."

"Top notch idea. Where would we find the necessary tools, though?"

"The sappers camped to the north of us would have plenty of picks and shovels. I'm sure we could borrow as many as we need and get the men to dig their own trenches."

"If we start with the Nissens, how many trenches would you suggest?"

"One per hut should be sufficient, sir."

"I agree, and I think it would be good for morale if all of the men could be involved. What else would we need?"

Captain Sydney Smith, the commander of 'B' flight, raised his hand to speak.

"We've got several sheets of corrugated iron sheeting left over from building the Nissens, sir. We could use them to revet the sides of the trenches."

"Very well, gentlemen, I think we have a plan. I'll organise the equipment if you Smith will procure the timber and collect all of the spare sheeting. Let me know if we need more supplies. Let's aim to start the digging directly after the morning service on Sunday. That will give me sufficient time to work out the fine details. Any questions?"

"What about the officers' quarters, sir?"

"Let's see how this exercise goes first, Knight. It will be good for the men to see that we are thinking of them before ourselves."

Four days after the royal visit, the tents were taken down and the aircraft of Number 32 squadron were fuelled up and flown the short distance to the squadron's new base at Droglandt, six miles north-west of Abeele. The departure of the aeroplanes was preceded by more than twenty tenders and lorries, each laden with men or spare parts. In the shelter of an empty hangar, the men of Number 6 who had chosen to attend the morning church service were forced to compete with the noise of the departing aircraft.

After the service and when the men of Number 4 squadron had returned to their quarters, those remaining behind were ordered to wait inside the hangar whilst the other men of Number 6 were summoned. Fred stayed seated at the piano, waiting for the other men to arrive. When everyone was present, Major James climbed up on to a table that had been placed in the centre of the hangar. Raising his arm in the air, he waited for the noise to die down.

"At ease, men. I've asked you here today because I'd like you all to participate in a useful exercise."

Several of the men groaned out loud, annoyed that their rest period had been interrupted. The major cleared his throat before continuing.

"However, first I'd like to tell you some good news. The more seasoned of you will remember that Number 20 squadron took our FE2 fighters, back in the days when I was a lieutenant. Well, two days ago they put up rather a splendid show when six of their machines were attacked by the 'Circus', as many as forty scouts I'm told. To cut a long story short, they destroyed four Albatros scouts. A fifth, painted red, was seen to go down out of control. Though it's yet to be confirmed, we believe it to be the machine of von Richthofen.[87] I'll give you more details as they come to hand."

A loud cheer broke out and the major held up his hand for silence.

"The second piece of news is about Captain Cochrane-Patrick, who most of you know was the OC Pilots' Pool for quite some time and often visited here. I'm pleased to inform you that he claimed his 20th Hun yesterday, with four victories in just two days. I have it on authority that he is now the most successful[88] British flyer alive."

Fred turned to Harold, who was standing at one side of the piano.

"Captain Patrick gave me my first flight, back in fifteen. It made a big impression on me."

"Fancy that," Harold replied. "Mind you, he's got a long way to go to catch up with the Red Baron. They say he's already shot down fifty seven of our chaps. Let's pray it was him in that red machine."

Major James raised his hand again.

"And now to the matter for which I've called you all here. As you all know, we've recently been receiving unwanted callers in the middle of the night and I've decided we should do something to make it safer on the aerodrome. Today we'll be digging slit trenches, one in front of each of the Nissen huts."

There were loud groans from the men at the back of the hangar.

"Quiet now," the major ordered. "The occupants of each hut will be assigned an equal allocation of the other men here and we will make a competition to see which hut can complete its trench in the shortest time. The prize to the winning team will be a night out in Abeele, paid for out of the officers' mess funds."

The men cheered this time and pressed closer to the table, anxious not to miss any of the details.

"If you look towards the rear of the hangar, you'll see several piles of tools, one for each hut. When I give the order, all those who normally sleep in one of the Nissens go and stand by your allotted pile. Sergeant Trotter will randomly select from the remaining men those who will be assigned to each of the digging teams. Captain Smith will be in charge of supplies and the senior man from each hut will go to him and receive the hut's trench plan and allocation of materials. Captain Smith will also be the adjudicator as to which is the winning hut. Any questions?"

There were a few murmurs but no-one asked a question.

"All right then. Good luck, gentlemen, and may the best team win."

The major stepped down from the table and made his way through the throng of men and out of the hangar, leaving behind him a flurry of activity as the men tried to secure a place in what they hoped would prove to be the winning team.

"This won't do my playing fingers any good," Fred said to Harold.

The two men were standing at the back of the hangar, waiting for the other men to be assigned to their team.

"I think I'll choose a shovel as it'll less likely give me blisters. The men with the picks will have the hardest job, especially in this clay."

"I'd rather use a pick meself any day," Harold replied. "We should work as a team though, you and I. I'll dig it up, you shovel it out."

By the time Sergeant Trotter had finished picking the teams, there were more than twenty men assigned to each hut. Upon his command, the competition began and the men rushed off to the huts, the team foremen lining up in front of Captain Smith so that they could receive their instructions. Within half an hour, all of the available men of Number 6 were hard at work digging, much to the amusement of the men of Number 4 squadron.

The men's initial enthusiasm waned somewhat after the surface soil had been removed and the lower levels of heavy clay exposed. Nevertheless they doggedly continued to dig as, inch by inch, the clay was extracted and used to form the sides of the trenches. By late afternoon, one of the teams had succeeded in completing its trench and had begun to lay sheets of corrugated iron along both sides, fastening the revetment by means of wooden stakes. The team for Fred's hut was running a close second. A little after five o'clock, Captain Smith raised his hand and blew on his whistle to indicate that there was a winner of the competition. All of the men stopped work and cheered the men of the winning hut, who then graciously joined in with the others to finish the job.

The major was true to his word and the members of the winning team were awarded an evening out at Margueritas. Fred arranged the booking with Julia, who was delighted to hear that he and Arnold would be accompanying the winners to provide the musical entertainment. It had been weeks since Fred had last visited Julia and she told him she was looking forward to hearing all of his news.

After a long and noisy evening, the men of the winning team trudged wearily back to the aerodrome under the light of an almost full moon.

"Now watch how you go," one of the corporals shouted when they reached the main entrance. "We don't want anyone falling into one of the new trenches!"

"Or you pissing in one of them, corp."

The other men laughed as they walked past the guard and made their way back to their huts. All of the other men in the squadron had long since retired for the night and the returning airmen made sure that they walked quietly past the major's hut.

Three weeks later, on the 31st July, after fifteen days of preliminary bombardment, the Allied launched an attack at Passchendaele.[89] Given charge of the squadron's wireless operations for the commencement, Fred was awakened early and was ready for work before 4:00 am. As he reached the hangar, he could see that two of the wireless aircraft were already being checked out by the ground crews. Dozens of empty petrol tins were roughly stacked against one of the walls of the hangar. With confirmation yet to be received as to when the first flight would leave, Fred felt anxious, as it had been raining heavily for most of the night and the cloud base was only a hundred feet above the ground.

With dawn still half an hour away, Fred called out to the mechanic who had just climbed out of the cockpit of one of the aircraft.

"The weather's not looking too promising, Hugh. Not a good start for Zero day."

The mechanic jumped to the ground. In one hand he held a petrol tin and in the other a chamois leather that he had used to filter petrol into the aircraft's main fuel tank.

"Hello, Fred. You missed the sarg by barely a minute. Apparently the push has started on the ground, but we're still waiting for the order to fly."

"I'm not surprised they're holding off. If the clouds are this low over Ypres, there's not much we could do anyway."

As they were talking, one of the observers in Fred's flight, twenty year old 2nd Lieutenant Geoffrey Smith, walked up to the aircraft. Both mechanics stood to attention and saluted the officer.

"Good morning, Jessop. I've been ordered to go out and have a recce. Would you be so good as to push my machine outside and warm it up for me whilst I go and look for my pilot?"

"Yes sir," Hugh Jessop replied. "Give me five minutes and I'll have her ready for you."

"Good show. I'll be back shortly."

The observer walked off towards the wireless flight's officers' mess. Fred made his way to the back of the hangar where Harold Edge was talking to one of the riggers.

"Harold, would you come and give me a hand with the other machines? I'd like to keep well ahead of schedule as you never know what might happen, especially in this weather."

"Sure thing, Fred, I'm on my way. See you later, Gordon. You can help Hugh move this machine out when it's ready."

Fred led the way out of the rear hangar door and into the hangar next door. At the back of the shed, well out of reach of the driving rain, were two RE8s. The two men climbed up on to the wing of the nearest aircraft and Harold stepped over the side of the fuselage into the rear cockpit.

"You check this one out while I go and test the other wireless set," Fred ordered, once he had passed Harold the tools he would need. "Let me know if you strike a problem."

"Will do, Fred," Harold replied, his voice muffled as he crouched down in the wicker seat.

Fred jumped down from the wing and walked over to the second machine. Just as he was picking up his tools, he heard the sound of a taxying aircraft and realised that it was the first contact patrol of the day. He stopped what he was doing and ran outside. The aircraft had already taken off and it came into view briefly as the pilot made a climbing turn and passed right in front of the hangar where Fred was standing. Within a matter of seconds the aeroplane disappeared into low cloud.

"Best of luck to them, that's all I can say."

Harold had walked up behind Fred and was peering out into the early morning gloom.

"I bet they'll be back before you can say Jack Robinson," he added. "I hope they kept the lamps burning."

The sound of the receding aircraft was soon drowned out by the noise of the rain striking the hangar roof. Fred and Harold returned to their machines to continue checking the wireless installations. After a while, Captain George Knight entered the hangar, having walked over from the officers' mess. He shouted for all of the mechanics to gather around.

"Listen men, we've just had a call from one of the batteries. They'd been watching our machine flying low over the trenches and were keeping an eye on it in case it got into trouble. All of a sudden they saw it drop out of the sky and land heavily at one of the forward landing areas."

"Are they all right, sir?" asked Fred.

"From what I've been told, Johnstone, the pilot's fine but his observer was badly injured."[90]

"What about the aircraft? Can it be repaired?"

"I'll have to come back to you on that one, Johnstone."

"Does that mean no more flying until the weather clears, sir?" Harold Edge asked.

"The major wants us to proceed, no matter what. The boys on the ground need our help if they're going to succeed. Is Lieutenant Barraclough's machine ready to fly?"

"As far as I know it is, sir," Fred replied. "We've finished the wireless work for all of the machines in the flight but I'd need to check with the chief just to make sure. They were fuelling the machines in the hangar next door half an hour ago, so it should only need starting up."

"Go and organise that would you, Johnstone? I'll go back to the mess and inform the lieutenant that they can come over as soon as they're ready."

"Very good, sir."

As George Knight strode off, Fred ran in the rain across to the next hangar so that he could talk with the fitter in charge of the RE8s. Within minutes, the second aircraft of the wireless flight was pushed out on to the airfield and the engine warmed up. When all was ready, the crew clambered on board and took off, heading directly for the lines. Though daylight had arrived, visibility had not improved and rain was still falling heavily on the aerodrome.

With time on his hands, Fred helped Harold clean the floor of the empty hangar whilst two of the other mechanics re-stacked the empty petrol tins into a neat pile at the side of the hangar. He was about to invite Harold to join him for breakfast in the canteen when the noise of a distant klaxon echoed inside the hangar. Looking outside, Fred caught sight of an ambulance bouncing along over the rough surface of the airfield towards the main landing area.

"Here we go again," he said to Harold in a quiet voice.

"It might only be a drill," Harold suggested hopefully. "Let's go and have a look."

Abandoning the idea of breakfast, the two men ran out of the hangar and followed the sound of the ambulance's horn. Rounding the corner of one of the hangars, Fred could see an aircraft resting on its wings at the far side of the aerodrome. He stopped and waited for Harold to catch up. The ambulance was parked to one side of the crashed aircraft and a step ladder had already been placed against the side of the fuselage. Fred strained his eyes to read the number on the tail of the machine as one of the squadron's mechanics climbed up the ladder to pull the heavily clad observer over the top of the Lewis gun and out of the cockpit. With many eager hands assisting the mechanic once the observer was within reach of the men standing on the wings, the officer was carefully placed on a stretcher and carried to the back of the ambulance. The whole procedure was watched over by the pilot, who had waited by the side of the cockpit whilst his observer was extricated from the machine.

"One of ours by the white stripes," Fred said to Harold. "I can't see which one from this distance, but from the large holes in the fabric I'd say he was lucky to bring her back in one piece."

"It would have to be a wireless machine, Fred. I don't think the other flights have sent anyone up yet."

Fred took out his watch and looked at the time.

"It's only five fifteen. They didn't last much longer than the first one. At this rate we'll be forced to shut up shop before we've even had time for breakfast."

"At least Lieutenant Snowden[91] must be alive. The ambulance wouldn't be going that slowly if he were dead, would it?"

They watched as the ambulance moved across the airfield in the direction of the hospital. When it disappeared from view behind the officers' huts, Fred and Harold returned to the hangar.

"And the next, if you please," said Fred, mimicking the sergeant major.

"Who will it be from our flight?"

"The new pilot, Lieutenant Wadham."

"What a day to pick for his first 'op'!" exclaimed Harold. "I bet he's only ever been on balloon crawls this side of the lines."

"He's got a good observer, which should help."

"Who's that?"

"Your namesake, Harry Quigley,[92] that's who."

"What are the odds they'll return unscathed?"

"I wouldn't bet any money on it. I've told the boys next door to make sure the rest of the machines are ready to fly, just in case."

"Do you think Number 4 is having similar problems?"

"I'd say so, Harold. Today's one for the riggers. We're going to be hard pressed to put six aircraft up tomorrow, even if we can get the spare machines into an airworthy state."

"Well, we've done all we can. Let's go and grab breakfast whilst there's still some for the taking."

Twenty minutes later, the third aeroplane of the wireless flight left the aerodrome. For the inexperienced pilot, the take-off went without incident, but he suffered a near catastrophe soon after arriving over the trenches. As had happened with the previous two flights, the low cloud forced the Nicholas Wadham to fly at a height of three hundred feet, not only within range of small arms fire but also dangerously close to the guns of the allied artillery. It was the latter that was almost his undoing.

Having waited for his observer to transmit the first set of coordinates for the infantry positions, Nicholas turned again towards the allied lines. As the machine came on to a westerly heading it was struck by a shell that had just been fired from a British eighteen pound field gun. The rising shell passed through the spinning propeller without touching any of the blades and then neatly drilled a circular hole through the peaked engine cowling before streaking past the front of the upper wing on its way to the target, just as if nothing had got in its way. The force of the shell punching its way through the cowling, coupled with the air turbulence caused by its wake, pushed the nose of the aircraft upwards so that it almost stalled.

The young pilot managed to regain control of the machine and looked around anxiously, checking for damage.

"Quigley, I'm sure the engine took a hit but it still sounds O.K. to me. Can you see anything from where you're sitting?"

The observer raised a gloved hand over the rim of the rear cockpit and pointed it towards the front of the aircraft. Though his face was hidden by a large pair of goggles, by the way he was shaking he was obviously laughing.

"The Gods have been kind to us!" Harry Quigley shouted back. "We've just been hit by a shell, if I'm not mistaken, and the only damage I can see is a four inch hole in the engine cowling. A definite improvement to the old girl's looks I'd say!" The observer swung the Lewis gun around to face the front, aiming it directly over the top of Nicholas' head. "And if I'm careful, I could use the new hole as a gun sight!"

Nicholas instinctively shrank down in his seat, fearful that Harry Quigley might attempt to prove his theory.

"You're mad, Quigley! We're in enough trouble already without any of your little jokes!"

"You take it all too seriously, young Nicholas. You're not in the army now. What say you we press on and finish the job?"

"All right, but no more jokes."

"No more jokes."

"At least we know that could never happen to us again."[93]

The two men continued with their mission and in less than three hours they were back at Abeele in the officers' mess, laughing about their close encounter with a shell.

Chapter 17

Invitation to a Picnic

The next month proved to be the wettest August for a generation, with double the normal rainfall and rain falling on almost every day. In spite of this, Number 6 squadron endeavoured to keep six aircraft on patrol for each of the daylight hours. In addition to their normal duties, the crews had to regularly photograph the length of front over which they were operating to a depth of three and a half miles. This extra imposition was made necessary by the recent heavy shelling that had obliterated almost all of the local landmarks, rendering any map virtually useless. On the night of the 16th August,[94] the aerodrome at Abeele was bombed by German aircraft. Fortunately, little damage was caused and no-one was injured. As if working long hours were not enough for the men, they also had to endure a further five nights of aerial bombing. By the end of August, the strain was beginning to show and the pilots took any opportunity they could to relax and get away from the war.

The sound of a klaxon caught Fred by surprise and he looked around. The major's staff car was approaching with John Worstenholm at the wheel. Fred could see that the lieutenant was laughing. The horn sounded again as the car skidded to a halt in front of the hangar, only inches from where Fred was standing.

"I must be crazy!" John Worstenholm shouted over the windscreen.

"I can fly an aeroplane but I can't get the hang of this! What is wrong with the brakes on this confounded contraption?"

"You're probably accelerating when you mean to slow down, sir. The major's car has the brake and accelerator pedals round the other way."

John Worstenholm pulled on the external hand brake.

"That would explain it. I used this lever to slow down but all it did was make the car slide."

"Not surprising, sir. That brake only works on the rear wheels. It takes a lot to stop a two ton car."

"As you know so much about it, how about joining me for a picnic this lovely autumn afternoon and being my driver?"

"I'm not sure I'd be allowed, sir."

"I've already talked with your boss and he's agreeable, provided he too is invited."

"Anyone else coming, sir?"

"James Stanton and the new observer, Frank McCreary. Five of us altogether. What do you say?"

"If Mr Hickie says it's all right, how can I refuse? After the wireless lorry, the open tourer should be easy."

"Does your lorry have strange pedals like this one?"

"Yes, they're both Crossley's."

"Right then. Get your things and you can drive me back to the mess. We can pick up Hicks along the way."

"What about the food, sir?"

"Already arranged. The mess steward's putting together a hamper for us and I've got three hours before I'm due back in the office." [95]

Fred walked to the hangar to collect his jacket and cap. Returning to the car, he handed his coat to the lieutenant who had already climbed over into the back seat.

"Eric, give the handle a turn, would you?"

Eric Hanson, an eighteen year old wireless mechanic who had recently arrived from England, came out from the hangar, wiping his greasy hands with a dirty rag. He scowled when he saw Fred sitting at the wheel of the major's car.

"It's all right for some," he grumbled. "No-one ever gives me a break."

"Stop complaining, would you? Just do what I ask."

"All right then, corp, let's be having you."

Fred switched on the magneto as the young mechanic bent down, grabbed hold of the starting handle and gave it a hefty swing. The engine immediately roared into life and Fred selected reverse gear. Looking over his shoulder, he carefully reversed the long car between the two hangars and out into the open area. With a parting wave to the young mechanic, Fred headed towards the officers' mess, sounding the klaxon horn as a warning to a nearby group of officers. Recognising one of them as Charles Hickie, he stopped the car.

"Morning, sir. Ready for the picnic?"

"I had a feeling you might agree to this outing, Fred."

Charles Hickie opened the passenger's door and climbed into the front seat, nodding at John Worstenholm who was lounging across the full width of the rear seat.

"Well hello, John, this is a pleasant surprise. I haven't been on a picnic for ages."

John Worstenholm pushed at the peak of his cap which had slipped down over his eyes.

"You're welcome, Hicks. I'm afraid the fare's rather plain as it's hard to get things these days, but the mess steward's done his best."

Having picked up Charles Hickie, Fred drove to the wireless flight's officers' mess. Outside the main entrance, two lieutenants were sitting side by side on a large wicker hamper. Fred recognised one of them as being Frank Stanton but did not know the other man. He stopped the car and the two men climbed into the back, placing the hamper in front of their feet.

"Listen, everyone," John Worstenholm called out from the back seat. "Whilst we're on the picnic, first names only please and no mention of the war."

"What war?" Charles Hickie replied with a laugh.

"That all right with you, Fred? After all, it wasn't that long ago I was a private in the London Regiment."

"I think I can manage that, John."

"Good man. Let's make a start then."

Having been cleared by the guard on duty at the main entrance, Fred started off in the direction of St Omer. When he had reached the Godewaersvelde crossroads he felt a tap on his shoulder.

"I'd better tell you where we're going, Fred. It's a perfect spot, just a few miles from here but away from the sound of the guns."

Fred could not reply straight away as he suddenly came across two Leyland trucks that were bogged in the mud by the side of the road.

"Is it easy to find?" he shouted over his shoulder, once he had steered the car around the obstacles.

"Fairly easy. Drive through Steenvoorde and keep heading west. Go over the first small hill and bear left at the bottom when you see the start of the cobbled road that winds up the hill into Cassel."

"I know it well. It's very slippery in the rain, especially on the corners."

"Well, don't take that one. Look for a track on the left, just past the bottom of the hill."

"I think I've got it, but you might need to guide me when we get closer."

"Will do, Fred."

With the hood of the car rolled back, Fred drove at speed through the French countryside, slowing only to give way to military traffic travelling in the opposite direction and for the occasional band of soldiers marching on their way to the front. Within half an hour they had passed through the village of Steenvoorde and had reached the start of the first hill. Half way up the incline, the car's engine began to labour. Fred tried to change down into second gear but found it hard to match the engine speed with the gears. On his third attempt and with a grating of cogs, he succeeded in selecting the lower gear. The car lurched forward under full acceleration, causing Fred and his passengers to be thrown back in their seats.

"That was pretty painful, Fred. Would you rather I had a go?"

"I should be all right now thanks, Charles. I'm used to driving the lorry and that's a lot slower than this."

The heavily laden car struggled up the hill, its speed reduced to a crawl by the time it reached the summit. From there they could see the outskirts of Cassel, its buildings lining the ridge of the hill opposite. Apart from the two hills, the surrounding countryside was flat as far as the eye could see. To the east in the direction of Ypres, some fourteen miles away, two observation balloons were clearly visible just above the skyline. Tethered in the air they looked close together, but in reality they were several miles apart.

"I'm the observer today," John Worstenholm shouted from the back seat. "Drive down the other side of this hill but take it slowly around the bend at the bottom. You should be looking for a gravel track on the left, but it's easy to miss if you're going too fast."

"That won't be a problem in this bus!"

"Don't hurt the feelings of the major's personal transport, Frank!" James Stanton shouted to the squadron's most recent newcomer.

Once over the crest of the hill the car gathered speed quickly. Unsure of the road, Fred resisted the temptation to change into top gear and remained in third, gently applying the brakes on and off all the way down the hill.

"I'm not taking any chances!" he shouted. "I could get into a real pickle if this bus runs away with me!"

"Make sure you chaps in the back keep a firm hold of the hamper." Charles Hickie instructed.

At the bottom of the hill, just before entering the corner, Fred pressed his foot on the brake pedal as hard as he dared. The car responded sluggishly on the damp surface, but held to the road. Having rounded the corner he suddenly spotted the entrance to a narrow track, only yards ahead. Braking with both feet, Fred wrenched the steering wheel to the left without waiting for the car to slow down. The double wheels at the rear lost their grip on the road and the car slewed around, by good fortune ending up on the centre of the track as Fred corrected the slide and brought it to a halt.

"I thought you were going to give me directions, John!" he shouted angrily. "What happened?"

"Sorry, Fred, my mind was elsewhere. Nicely done anyway."

"I'm glad for all our sakes you're a pilot and not an observer."

"*Mea culpa*. What more can I say?"

"All right you two," Charles Hickie interrupted. "We're supposed to be having fun."

"Sorry about that, everyone. It was just a bit of a shock. Where do I go from here?"

John Worstenholm leaned over from the back seat so that Fred could hear what he was saying.

"Keep going around the back of the hill and look out for a small copse of trees on the left. There's a patch of grass in front of the trees where we can stop."

Fred drove slowly over the rough surface, on several occasions dropping the front wheels into deep potholes where there was no room on the narrow track for him to avoid them.

"Slow down, Fred, it's just over there."

Fred steered the car through a gap in the stone wall and into the field beyond. He stopped in front of a copse of stunted deciduous trees, whose leaves had already turned to the colour of rust. He switched off the engine and all was silent.

"Everyone out," he ordered.

The three passengers in the rear seat climbed out and lifted the heavy hamper out of the car and on to the ground. Fred scrambled out over the side of the car and checked the wheels for damage.

"I'm glad I don't have to explain to the major how his car got dirty," he said, looking back along the length of the car. "Just look at the wheels. The covers look like they've been used as potters' wheels!"

"You could always ask young Hanson to wash it when we get back. That would really make his day."

"Don't listen to him, Fred," Charles Hickie interrupted. "He's the one who organised this party, so he's the one who can sort it out."

Charles, the only man dressed in breeches, took off his jacket and laid it carefully on the folded canvas roof of the car.

"Very casual for a man of your advanced age. You'll be taking your tie and braces off next."

"Well, we are on a picnic after all, John."

"Would someone give me a hand?" James Stanton called from the car. "This hamper's too heavy for me. And did anyone bring any water? All I could find in the back was a tin of petrol."

"I think you'll find it's water," Frank McCreary answered. "I'll come over and have a look. It may smell a bit like petroleum, but it should still be drinkable once it's boiled."

Taking the tin from James Stanton, Frank unscrewed the cap and poured some of the liquid into his cupped hand. Bringing his hand up to his nose, he took a sniff.

"Sorry, my mistake. That's 'eau de Shell'. Vintage nineteen seventeen if I'm not mistaken."

"Sorry to interrupt, but there's clean water in the hamper if you're interested," John Worstenholm called out. "It's in the open wine bottle."

"Now you tell me!" Frank spluttered.

"You'd better watch where you sit, Fred," Charles Hickie warned. "The ground's a bit soft where you are."

"I'm only in my working clothes so an extra damp patch won't notice."

"I think I'll stay here on the running board if you don't mind."

"Up to you Charles, I'll pass the food up to you."

"What do we have here?" John Worstenholm asked, picking up a bottle of red wine from the opened hamper. "I don't recognise the label, but I'm sure none of us will mind if it's not vintage." Reaching over, he took out a corkscrew from the hamper. "I'll open the bottle if one of you will cut the bread and cheese. There's also some tinned sausage somewhere, if you can find it."

Having divided the food into equal portions, the men settled down to their picnic, eating off tin plates with their service utensils and drinking the red wine out of china tea cups. The first bottle of wine was emptied within a matter of minutes and was quickly replaced by a second. For a while they ate without talking, each man appreciating the peacefulness of the picnic site. Charles Hickie was the first to break the silence.

"One thing I've always meant to ask you, Fred, if it's not too impertinent a question. With a man of your background and education, why didn't you apply for a commission?"

"Pretty simple really, Charles. I'm a church going man and the idea of taking another man's life goes against all that I believe in."

"I can understand that."

"Like many people, I thought the war wouldn't last and I held back in making any decision. When it became obvious it would be a long drawn out affair I had to think of a way I could serve my country. Being an officer wouldn't have worked would it?"

"You could have become an equipment officer like me. The closest I've been to the action is when I visit the batteries."

"At least I'm using the skills I developed before the war."

"It is a conundrum, I have to admit" Charles Hickie continued. "Should patriotism come before God and do we have the right to incarcerate conscientious objectors? I'd be the last to condemn anyone."

"We each have to do what we think is best."

"Talking of rank, I'm being gazetted as a full lieutenant shortly. If I'm not mistaken, you may find that your promotion to corporal may be short-lived."

"What have I done wrong?"

"Nothing at all, Fred. With Sergeant Barnes back in Blighty, I'd like you to gradually take on his duties with a view to getting your third stripe. You're already an ace at bobbing and that was always the sergeant's domain."

"Me to be 'Johnny Bob' and a sergeant to boot. Fancy that."

"You'd get a good pay increase too."

"That would certainly come in handy." Fred laughed at the prospect of earning more money. "I've often said that one day the wireless watchmakers would have to take over."

"Can we change the subject," John Worstenholn interjected. "What's next on the entertainment front, Fred? Anything happening on the aerodrome?"

"We've been practicing for a new show that Julia will be presenting this Saturday evening at Margueritas, but as far as I know there's nothing on at the aerodrome in the near future. We've all been a bit busy since Barnsie and a couple of the others have left. Gone are the days of the weekly concerts I'm afraid."

"Put me down for two anyway would you, Fred, when next you see Julia?"

"Usual table I suppose?" Fred replied.

"Enough of this idle chatter you two. Who's going to make the tea?"

"All right, James. I'll be 'mother' if you serve the cake and apples."

Fred stood up, took a bottle of methylated spirits from the hamper and walked over to the Primus stove which had been placed out of the wind, next to the car's running board. After checking that there was enough paraffin in the tank, he opened the air screw and poured a small quantity of methylated spirits into the cup. This he lit with a match. When the last of the flames had died down, he closed the air screw and pressurised the tank with a few strokes of the pump. Within seconds there was a roaring sound of burning paraffin and Fred placed the kettle on top of the stove. Whilst waiting for the water to boil, he rejoined the others and washed the dirty cups as the cake and apples were passed around.

"Most impressive, Fred. We used to have a servant to do that. Those days are gone for good, I'm afraid."

"That surprises me, John," Charles Hickie interrupted. "With your strong Yorkshire accent and the fact that you can't even drive a car, I'd never have guessed you had a privileged childhood."

"My father was a newspaper editor. He'd no need for a car."

"Do you think you'll follow in his footsteps?"

"I really don't know, Charles. Ask me after the War."

With the water boiling, Fred placed six spoonfuls of tea into the pot and walked over to the stove so that he could fill the pot with hot water. After waiting a few minutes for the tea to draw he rejoined the others, filling each of their cups.

"I must record this moment for posterity," said James Stanton, jumping up and taking an old box camera from the hamper. "We can get the lab boys to print copies and then smuggle them home so that our beloveds can see exactly how we are contributing to the war effort."

They all paused in what they were doing whilst James got ready to take the photograph.

"I suppose it would be too much to ask you all to smile."

With the photograph taken, John Worstenholm took out a bottle of brandy from the hamper whilst the other men lit cigarettes.

"Anyone for a snifter? I'm afraid I can't offer you cigars. Next time perhaps."

John reached over and poured a slug of brandy into each of the empty cups.

"A toast, gentlemen. Here's to a speedy victory."

They raised their cups and shouted in unison, "A speedy victory" before downing their drinks in a single gulp.

"Let's make a pact," said Charles Hickie. "What say we meet up exactly two years from now at the Trocadero. That's a good central meeting place. It will be rather jolly to find out what we're all doing. Everyone agreed?"

The other four men nodded.

"That settles it then. Afternoon tea on the fifth of September, nineteen nineteen."

"I'll come in a car," added John Worstenholm. "I should have mastered the controls by then and I can drive you all home afterwards!"

The afternoon sun was fading fast and the temperature had already started to drop. Finishing what was left of the brandy, they packed everything back into the car and prepared themselves for a cold ride back to the aerodrome. Working as a team, they raised the hood and fastened it to the windscreen.

James Stanton walked around to the front of the car whilst the others climbed back on board.

"Magneto off!" he shouted, as if calling the order to start an aeroplane.

"Magneto off!" Fred called back from behind the steering wheel, joining in the fun.

James gave the starting handle a couple of turns before shouting again.

"Magneto on!"

'Magneto on!" Fred replied and he switched the ignition switch to the 'On' position. James swung the starting handle again, this time with more effort. The engine burst into life and he climbed back into the front passenger's seat, everyone in the car laughing at his antics.

"That was a good afternoon," said Fred as he drove back along the road towards Abeele. "Thanks for inviting me, John."

"You're welcome, Fred. We must do it again."

"Home, James," the front passenger cried. "And don't spare the horses."

"Certainly, James," replied Fred and they all laughed.

Chapter 18
Unexpected Departures

*I*F THE MEN *of Number 6 were looking for an omen as to what fortunes the next month would bring to the squadron, they did not have to wait for long. On the first day of September an aircraft was shot down by a red Fokker Triplane,*[96] *with the observer killed and the pilot taken prisoner by the Germans. It later transpired that the pilot of the Fokker was the 'Red Baron', Reitmeister Manfred von Richthofen. Two days later, another RE8 was shot down, with both pilot and observer seized as prisoners of war. September 1917 would prove to be the worst month of the War for the squadron, with seven men killed, three taken prisoner and three injured. Even more upsetting was the fact that two of the airmen had died as a result of their machine being struck in mid-air by an allied shell. Number 4 squadron, also based at Abeele, fared somewhat better, with five men killed and four injured over the same period. The two squadrons were not alone in their misfortune; the casualty rate for all of the Army Corps squadrons on the Western Front had risen to such a level that on almost every mission at least one of the crew was a novice airman.*

In line with other squadrons, Number 6 was brought up to an operating strength of twenty four aircraft, each flight comprising eight machines. There was very little room to manoeuvre on the aerodrome, nor in the air over the lines. Every day, the squadron's aeroplanes worked with the army X Corps on a narrow front two miles wide and three miles deep; an area taking only two minutes for an aircraft to cross. Due to advances in wireless technology, several aircraft were now able to operate in the same area at the same time, presenting yet another hazard to the aircrew.

Fred played the piano at the squadron's morning service on the fourth Sunday of the month, having earlier arranged to take the afternoon off. After the service he lunched in the corporals' mess, a partitioned section of the general canteen, before getting ready to take the short walk to Margueritas. As he was leaving the mess, Fred bumped into John Worstenholm.

"I've been looking for you everywhere, Corporal."

"Hello, sir. I've not been in the hangar today. It's my afternoon off and I'm on my way to Abeele."

"I was hoping to do the same, but I have to stick around just in case the weather improves."

"I've not seen any machines in the air today," Fred added. "Is the visibility bad over the lines?"

"Visibility's not the problem. A forty mile an hour westerly was reported along the front earlier today. That forced us to suspend all flying operations. Imagine how difficult it would be to get home if we were attacked over Hun territory."

"It must be frustrating for you, sir, especially with the big push on at the Menin Road."

"Even one day lost makes a difference to the men on the ground."

The lieutenant scratched his head as if pondering what to say next.

"Fred," he asked quietly, looking at the ground as he removed a sealed envelope from his jacket pocket. "Would you give this to Evelyn so that she can pass it on to Caroline when next she sees her? In return, I'll take you up for a flip in my new machine, if you like."

Fred reached out for the envelope, recognising as he took hold of it the flowing handwriting of the lieutenant.

"Of course I'll do that, sir, and I'd certainly like to go for a flight. I've not much on at the moment."

"I need to check her out properly and you can test the Lewis for me. Firing a gun always relieves tension, don't you think? If anyone questions what you're doing, you can always say that you're carrying out a wireless check."

"I'm no expert, sir, but I'll have a go."

"That's good. We have a deal then."

"Evelyn tells me that Caroline is moving back to Belgium and is looking for somewhere to live in Abeele. Anything to do with you, sir?"

Fred tried unsuccessfully to stop himself from smiling.

"Most certainly not. She's far too mature for me."

John Worstenholm laughed quickly and was quiet for a moment.

"Anyway, go get your trusty helmet and I'll find you some flying clothes. It's bound to be cold up there."

"I'll meet you in the hangar, sir."

Fred walked back to his hut to fetch the balaclava that Lieutenant Cochran-Patrick had given him two years previously. Taking it out from the top drawer of his bedside table, he pulled it over his head before running to the hangar where the RE8 was being made ready for flight. John Worstenholm was already sitting in the cockpit, warming up the engine. One of the lieutenant's ground crew handed Fred a heavy leather jacket and a pair of fur-lined boots. Having put them on, Fred waited until the engine was brought back to an idle before clambering up on to the wing and squeezing himself into the rear cockpit. In doing so, he had to swing the machine gun out of the way, as the opening for the observer was only as big as the gun's circular mount. He sat down on the rotating capstan seat with only his head sticking out of the cockpit, wondering how he would be able to fire the machine gun in such a confined space.

"Ready to go, Fred?"

Fred swivelled around on the stool and tried to grab hold of the gun's handle.

"Almost," he called back. "I now see why you don't need a safety belt in here. I don't think I could fall out if I wanted to."

"Don't worry about the gun just yet. You'll probably find it easier to stand up when you want to fire it. You can also raise the stool if you need to."

"All right, sir, I'm ready now."

John Worstenholm waved to the ground crew who pulled the chocks away from the wheels. He gradually opened the throttle and almost immediately the aircraft started to move. With the landing area clear of aircraft, he wasted no time and applied full power, aiming the machine directly towards the western perimeter hedge. Against a steady headwind the aircraft was airborne in less than two hundred yards. With only a light load of petrol on board, he climbed quickly to four thousand feet, reaching the lines in less than twelve minutes.

Levelling out, John throttled back to ninety miles per hour and trimmed the tail of the aircraft before twisting around in his seat. He reached out and patted Fred on the back of the head to attract his attention and Fred rotated the Lewis gun slightly to one side so that they could communicate more easily.

"Pretty good for a two seater, eh!" he shouted.

Fred, whose head was only two feet away from the lieutenant's, nodded his head and shouted in reply, though his voice was barely audible above the noise of the engine and the whistling of the wind through the bracing wires.

"It certainly knocks the BE into a cocked hat, sir!"

"We're not allowed to fly a 'Harry Tate' upside down in case the wings fall off, but I can still show you a thing or two. Is everything secured back there?"

"Yes, it is," Fred shouted back. "You can start whenever you're ready."

"All right. Make sure you keep a tight grip on the Lewis."

For the next hour, John Worstenholm treated Fred to a display of aerobatics over the city of Ypres, inside allied territory and at a safe height from small arms fire. When it was time to return to Abeele, John brought the machine on to a westerly heading and adjusted the elevator trim wheel for a gradual descent. Unbuckling his lap belt, he turned around to talk to Fred.

"Fire off a few rounds would you, Fred? I'll keep an eye on you in case you get into trouble. I suggest you fire standing up with your back against the front of the cockpit."

With the aircraft descending steadily and requiring no input on the controls, John waited as Fred stood up and leaned over the side of the cockpit to remove a drum of ammunition from its holder. In only a few seconds, Fred had snapped the drum into place on top of the Lewis gun and had swung the gun around to one side of the tailplane. Fred fired a single three second burst of twenty seven rounds. The aircraft shook from the vibration but did not deviate from its course. By the way the gun's muzzle jerked unevenly on its mount, John Worstenholm could tell that this was a new experience for Fred.

"Not a bad effort, but you must keep a firm hold of the handle with your other hand when you squeeze the trigger."

"Let me have another go," Fred shouted back. "I'll get it right next time!"

"Fire a few short bursts instead of one long one. That's a better way to check for jams."

"Will do."

This time, Fred fired several half second bursts as he moved the gun smoothly through a ninety degree arc.

"That's the ticket. You can be my gunner any time."

"Thank you, sir."

"That should do us for today. Before you finish, would you remove the drum and fire the cartridge left in the breech?"

"Right you are, sir."

After Fred had fired the final shot, John Worstenholm set a course for Abeele, landing twenty minutes later without incident. He taxied up to the hangar and brought the machine to a halt right in front of the open doors.

Over the noise of the idling engine, he gave a final order to Fred.

"Leave everything where it is, Fred. The armourer can take care of it when he reloads the aircraft."

"Right you are, sir. Thanks again for the ride."

"You're most welcome. Say hello to Evelyn for me when you see her."

"I will, sir."

Fred remained seated, waiting for the propeller to stop spinning. When all was quiet, he climbed out on to the wing and jumped to the ground. Hampered by the heavy boots lent to him by the lieutenant, he shuffled across the gravel forecourt and into the hangar, where he changed back into his own clothes. He left the coat and boots with one of the ground crew and walked away towards the office, waving one last time to John Worstenholm, who was still sitting in the cockpit.

Within minutes of landing, Fred had picked up his pass and was walking down the lane towards Abeele. The wind had died down and he could hear the sound of many aircraft engines being warmed up on the aerodrome behind him. He walked along with a light step, looking forward to playing the piano and spending a while in conversation with Julia.

The following Tuesday marked the final day in the Battle of Menin Road[97] and John Worstenholm was scheduled to fly at 8:45 am. His crew for the flight was Frank McCreary, an observer still on probation but a man who had already displayed great promise on earlier sorties. The purpose of the latest mission was to gather accurate details of the positions of allied troops on the Gheluvelt plateau, two miles south of Polygon Wood.

Half an hour before they were due to leave, John Worstenholm sat fully dressed in his cold weather flying clothes in the 'C' flight officers' mess, double-checking the expected position of the troops on an army trench map.[98] His orders were to patrol an area represented by squares twenty one and twenty two of zone 'J', some fourteen miles due east of Abeele. As an extra aid for the mission, the squadron's photographic section had provided him with a recent aerial photograph of the area, marked with the same grid lines as were used on the map. Satisfied with his preparations, he said goodbye to the other officers in the mess and walked over to the hangar where he found his observer already sitting in the rear cockpit, checking the operation of the machine gun.

The RE8 in front of him was not his usual machine. The aircraft he had flown with Fred on the previous Sunday had developed a serious oil leak and was at the back of the hangar being repaired, so one of the flight's spare aircraft had been made airworthy at short notice. Climbing up on to the lower wing, John looked into the front cockpit to check the height of the seat.

"Good morning, Frank. Ready for some action?" Reaching down into the cockpit, he removed one of the cushions that had been left by the last pilot and threw it down to a mechanic who was standing near the aircraft. Then, remembering that Frank McCreary had been injured on his last mission with his pilot killed, he called out again in a softer voice.

"I trust you're fully recovered."

"Good morning to you, John," the observer replied with a grin. "Yes, I'm fighting fit and ready to go. We'll need to keep an eye out for shells this morning at the height we'll be flying."

"I know. With the extra artillery positions, we've now got twice the fire power concentrated over half the distance."

"And that's not allowing for what the Huns will throw at us."

"Not much we can do about that, but I'll do my best to bring you back safely."

"I'm sure you will, John."

"All right, let's be on our way."

The departure went smoothly and John Worstenholm steered the aircraft towards the east, setting it in a gentle climb. With orders to pinpoint the positions of troops who were struggling to hold on to fifteen hundred yards of newly gained ground, he knew he would be obliged to fly close to the ground for his observer to be able to spot the soldiers' signals. Breaking with the customary procedure of climbing to a safe height before crossing the lines, he aimed straight towards Zillebeke Lake and in less than ten minutes had reached the assigned patrol area.

As soon as they passed into enemy territory, the German anti-aircraft guns opened fire. Immediately John put the aircraft into a sideslip so that its nose pointed a few degrees away from the direction in which they were travelling, the purpose being to spoil the gunners' aim as they tried to anticipate the aircraft's path across the sky. With patchy low cloud and mist preventing him from flying higher, he flew at a height of two thousand feet as far as Polygon Wood before turning to fly back over Gheluvelt, losing height rapidly as he spotted the first of the allied infantry positions. Comparing the terrain below with the photograph clipped to his cockpit dashboard, John commenced a low-level run over the top of the allied troops. Each time he spotted a group of soldiers he slapped the side of the cockpit with his gloved hand, hoping that his observer had also seen them and was making a note of the map coordinates.

As John flew towards the second infantry position, a wall of thick ground haze forced him to climb to three thousand feet before he could see the extent of its coverage. One mile inside enemy territory, the German anti-aircraft guns started to fire once more. The aircraft was buffeted by the shell blasts as the gunners improved their aim. Once again he turned towards the British lines and had just begun to make a descent towards where he hoped the infantry would be, when the anti-aircraft guns stopped firing. Unsure of the reason, John was about to shout a warning to his observer when the whole aircraft started to shake and his ears were deafened by the sound of the Lewis gun. Instinctively, he applied full power and pulled the aircraft up into a steep climbing turn, hoping that whatever was attacking them would pass by harmlessly underneath. After a few seconds he brought the machine back on to an even keel so that he could take stock of the situation, but as far as he could tell the aircraft had sustained no damage. He twisted around in his seat and saw that Frank McCreary had spun around and was aiming the Lewis gun in his direction but up over the top of the wings.

"What's happening, Frank?" he shouted.

"It's an Albatros DV! I can't see him because he's right behind those clouds off the starboard side, but I know he's there!"

"If I can reach the clouds before he comes at us again, we can hide there for a while and then head back to the lines!"

"That's fine by me. I've already made a note of the first set of coordinates and we can't do much more because of the mist."

"Hold on tight, then. I'm taking her up!"

John Worstenholm opened the throttle to its maximum setting as he pulled the control stick back into his stomach. With no other aircraft in sight, he aimed directly towards a thin strip of cloud. It was only four hundred feet above them and extended for more than a mile.

Without warning, the aircraft was subjected to a hail of bullets. The enemy machine had turned around and was now attacking from below and in front, hidden from view by the lower wings of the RE8. Several of the shots passed right through the dashboard and into John Worstenholm, the force of the bullets almost lifting him out of the cockpit. One of the bullets severed the linkage to the emergency control stick in the observer's compartment before striking Frank McCreary in the hand and exiting through the side of the fuselage. The ascending enemy scout flashed past in the opposite direction, missing the RE8 by a matter of yards as John Worstenholm slumped to one side of the cockpit, one arm still wrapped around the control stick. Almost immediately, the wings tipped over and the aircraft entered into a gentle spiral dive.

Frank McCreary cried out in pain, involuntarily letting go of the machine gun. From where he was sitting he could not see his friend's face, but from the way the pilot's head was wedged between the rim of the cockpit and the cabane strut of the upper wing, he knew that John Worstenholm was badly injured. Unable to move any closer because his leather coat was caught on something down by his feet, Frank reached down inside the cramped cockpit. Feeling around his ankles, he came across the shattered remains of the emergency control stick. The metal rod that normally connected it to the pilot's controls had sliced through the hem of his coat, pinning it to the floor of the fuselage. With no feeling in his left arm, he grabbed the coat with his other hand and pulled until it came free. Looking down at his injured arm, he noticed blood oozing from a large tear in the leather gauntlet.

"Damnation!" he cried out in frustration.

Without thinking, he stood up in the full force of the slipstream, holding on to the rim of the cockpit with his right hand in order to steady himself. Reaching forward with his other hand, he vainly tried to dislodge the pilot's body. Unable to bend his fingers, all he could succeed in doing was to prod his friend in the back.

"John, can you hear me?"

There was no reply. Forcing the image of the spinning horizon from his mind, he reached forward into the front cockpit with both hands, bracing his feet against the inside framework of the fuselage to prevent him from falling out of the aircraft. Though he still could not move the pilot, he was able to dislodge the arm that was wrapped around the control stick and push it to one side. Immediately the machine responded. The wings levelled out and the aircraft gradually came out of the spin, though the rate of descent remained unchanged.

Frank looked across at the inert body of the pilot. By the blank look of surprise on the man's face, he realised that John Worstenholm was dead. He also knew that there was only a matter of seconds in which he could take action before the aircraft smashed into the ground. Though he had never actually flown an aircraft, the principles of flight taught him during his observer training in England remained fresh in his memory. With the emergency controls broken and no time to crawl into the pilot's cockpit, he reached forward once again and grabbed hold of the control stick.

Instinctively, Frank pulled back on the controls and held on tight. Looking ahead through the spinning propeller, all he could see at first was the ground where normally the sky would be, but after a few seconds the sky came into view as the aircraft came out of its dive. With the engine roaring at full power, he was afraid that he would pass out as the machine zoomed up into the sky, its nose almost vertical.

In spite of his predicament, the thought came into his mind that the enemy scout might still be in pursuit. He let go of the stick and slid back into his cockpit. Grasping hold of the Lewis gun that had been swinging freely on its mount, he looked up and saw the Albatros. It was two hundred yards away but closing fast. He tried to fix his sights on to the attacker, with his injured hand thrust inside the spade grip to steady the Lewis gun. Before he had time to take aim, he felt the impact of a stream of bullets as they penetrated the fuselage behind him, just missing the gun and shredding a large area of fabric on the fuselage and lower wing. With no-one at the controls, the nose of the RE8 dropped slightly, but the aircraft continued to climb. For an instant, the enemy scout came into view again as it passed below the tailplane. Frank seized the opportunity and fired a two second burst in the general direction of his opponent and, though he could not be certain, he was fairly confident that he had scored hits on the enemy aircraft as it roared past less than fifty feet away.

Not waiting to see if he had damaged the Albatros, Frank once again let go of the gun and crawled out over the top of the fuselage so that he could lean inside the pilot's cockpit. This time, with the aircraft in a steady climb, he had to wedge his feet against the Lewis gun's ring mounting in order to reach over the body of the pilot and grab hold of the controls. Once he was confident that he would not fall over the side, Frank looked around to see if the enemy scout was still in the area. With no aircraft in sight he had time to plan his next move. The aircraft's engine was running smoothly but the instrument panel and wireless equipment had been severely damaged by the enemy scout's bullets. Looking up at the dashboard, he noticed with relief that the compass and aneroid were undamaged and that the aircraft was heading in a westerly direction. He glanced down over the side and recognised the shape of Dickebusch lake in the distance, proof that he was only a few miles from the allied lines.

The aircraft had by this time climbed to a height of six thousand feet, and though he had no idea how to adjust the elevator trim wheel or reduce the throttle, Frank knew that he would have to do something to make the aircraft descend. Gently pushing the control stick away from him, he was filled with relief when the horizon came into view. Once again he braced himself against the inside of the fuselage and remained precariously balanced between the two cockpits until the town of Poperinghe came into view. By relaxing the forward pressure on the stick he aimed the aircraft straight towards the spire of the St Bernardinus church, located on the southern side of the market square. The speed increased as the machine descended but with the air speed gauge smashed, he had no idea how fast he was going. The faster the aircraft went, the more it vibrated. Not knowing what else to do, Frank held on tight and continued to point the aircraft towards Poperinghe, though the lower it dived, the more it swung away from the city.

After a few minutes, just as the last of the buildings of Poperinghe had passed by on the right hand side of the aircraft, Frank heard a loud bang and guessed that something had broken inside the engine. Smoke poured out from beneath the engine cowling and though the propeller was still turning, the engine was making an unusual noise and producing very little power. He relaxed his grip on the control stick and the juddering decreased, as did the speed. With the aircraft now in a gentle descent rather than a rapid dive, he found he was able to take time to look around. In the distance he could see the spire of Abeele church, standing out from the other buildings in the village. Pulling back on the control stick to try and keep the church in sight, the steeple slowly drifted to the left of the cockpit as the aircraft was caught in a cross wind. Unable to reach the rudder bar so that he could correct the yaw, he gave up on the idea of reaching the aerodrome. He would simply have to aim the machine towards the ground in the hope that he would find an open field in which to crash. He glanced at the aneroid but was unable to read the height, as his goggles had become smeared with his own blood. Painfully, he ripped the goggles from his head and looked at the gauge. It showed a height of one thousand feet.

Looking out over the starboard side, Frank could see the white tents of an army encampment swing slowly into the path of the aircraft. He was close enough to be able to see the colour of the soldiers' uniforms. A chill went through his body when he realised that he would probably crash in the middle of the encampment. Remembering that the aircraft's rudder cable ran along the inside of the observer's cockpit where it was wrapped in a leather grip so that it could be operated by the observer in an emergency, he inched his way out of the pilot's cockpit and back into his own. Unable to see anything in the confined space, he felt along the inside of the fuselage until he came across the wire. Finding the grip he pulled on the cable as hard as he could, praying that this action would swing the tail of the machine around and steer it away from the tents.

Already close to stalling speed, the extra drag induced by the turning rudder caused the aircraft to shudder. Without warning it faltered and fell back in the air, the right wing dropping as it entered into a slow spin.[99] Frank lost his balance but managed to grab hold of the gun ring with his good hand just as he was about to slide over the side of the fuselage. Pulling himself back into the cockpit, he watched helplessly as images of sky and earth spun around in front of him, reminding him of the merry-go-round rides he had taken as a child. With the aircraft out of control and close to the ground, there was nothing he could do but brace himself and wait for the impact.

The crash came quicker than he expected. Instead of plunging straight into the ground, the aircraft careered by chance into the canopy of a copse of young fir trees. The wheels were torn off in the initial impact and the machine cut a path through the branches and out of the wood. It came to rest upside down on the open ground beyond the trees, only a mile from the aerodrome and directly in front of an encampment of Australian soldiers. The trees had cushioned Frank from the impact and he was thrown clear, uninjured except for scratches and the bullet wound to his hand.

Frank lay on the ground stunned, unable to move or take a breath. His hand hurt viciously and his head throbbed with pain. With his eyes closed, he was aware only of a strong smell of pine resin and the crackling sound of burning wood.

"Are you all right, cobber?" a voice spoke as if from afar.

He made an attempt to move but succeeded only in raising one arm.

"Quick, bring a stretcher over here before this chap is barbecued. I'll see if I can get the pilot out before the flames get too big. He's still strapped upside down in the front cockpit, poor blighter."

Frank was placed on a stretcher and carried to the camp whilst the body of John Worstenholm was removed from the burning wreckage and laid on the ground a safe distance from the crash site. The captain who was the first on the scene sent one of his privates across the fields to the aerodrome to inform the authorities of the crash and to arrange for a recovery tender to be sent out.

Within half an hour, the commanding officer of Number 6 squadron arrived in his staff car to find Frank sitting up in a chair drinking a cup of tea, with one arm heavily bandaged.

"How are you holding up, Lieutenant?"

"Not bad considering, sir. Lieutenant Worstenholm was killed by the Hun and I'm afraid I made rather a botch of the landing. I do still have my notes though. I put them inside my coat when we were attacked."

"Splendid, young man. If you're up to it, I'll take you to X Corps HQ on the way to the hospital and you can make your report directly to General Cameron."

"I can manage that all right, sir. I've been well looked after by the Australians. They told me I put on quite a good show for them."

News of John Worstenholm's death spread quickly and an air of despondency hang over the squadron. He had been a popular officer, liked by his peers and the men who worked for him. With five days of the month remaining, September had already become the squadron's worst month for casualties. The white frieze around the walls of 'C' flight's officers' mess, upon which were mounted black and white silhouette profiles of every pilot and observer who had joined the flight, was running out of space, the majority of pictures being for men who were now dead, missing or known to have been taken as prisoners of war.

When Fred heard of John Worstenholm's death, he wanted to break the news to Caroline, but was not able to leave the aerodrome until the following Sunday. By that time Frank McCreary had become a hero within the squadron, especially when it was announced that he had been recommended for the Military Cross as a result of his actions.

"I hope we don't get bombed again tonight. I hardly got a wink of sleep last night."

"Nor I, Fred," replied Harold. "And it wasn't the bombs that kept me awake. It was your snoring! You shouldn't drink so much on a Saturday night."

"Very amusing, I don't think," retorted Fred. "Anyway, I'm off to Abeele for a couple of hours. I've finished everything I had to do today. Anything you need while I'm there?"

"Fresh bread, if you're serious. The stuff we have here you could use to build walls."

"I'll see what I can do."

Fred left Harold and walked off to look for Charles Hickie. He found the lieutenant in one of the hangars, filling out a requisition form for wireless spares.

"Hello, sir. Is it all right for me to pop into Abeele this afternoon? I'm up to date with everything here and I'd like to visit my old billet. The owner was good to me when I didn't know anyone in town and I like to keep in touch."

"That's fine, Fred, I'll see you in the morning. Remind me then to talk to you about your new duties."

"New duties?"

"I'm due for some leave, so you could be very busy in the near future looking after the wireless boys. Now that you're a corporal and likely to make sergeant, we can expect a lot more from you, can't we?"

"I was afraid you might say that, sir."

"Quite the reluctant leader. Don't worry, I'm sure you'll make an excellent job of it."

"Thank you, sir. I'd better go before you give me something else to do."

Fred left the aerodrome and set out on the short walk to the village. The road was busy but the ground was firm and he had no difficulty in avoiding the muddy patches. He reached the estaminet before he had worked out what to say to Caroline and he walked up the garden path hoping deep down that she would not be there.

To Fred's surprise, there was no-one sitting at any of the outside tables and the front door was locked. He took the key from its hiding place above the door and let himself in. The dining room was empty but he could hear the sound of voices coming from the kitchen. Without announcing his arrival, he crossed the dining room floor and entered the kitchen.

"Hello, Evelyn. How are you this fine afternoon?"

"Allo, Fredrik, what a pleasant surprise. Would you like a cup of tea?"

"Yes please. I'm by myself today. Harold sends his regards and wonders if you could spare him some bread."

"That man only thinks of his stomach. I baked some bread this morning so you can take one and share it with your large friend. Please to come and sit with me," she added, pointing to a chair on the opposite side of the table.

Fred took off his coat and sat down, feeling the warmth of the burning stove. The two friends talked for a while about their families and what they planned to do after the War.

"And what about your lady friend?" Evalina asked after a short pause. "How is she?"

"Ethel is well, thank you. I keep asking her if we can make our engagement official, but she always comes up with a reason why we shouldn't."

"I'm sure she will change her mind one day."

"Mr Hickie keeps telling me that, but I'm not convinced. Do you think you'll ever marry again, Evelyn?"

"Who me?" Evalina replied, raising her eyebrows. "No, I don't think so, my young Englishman. Now if you ask my sister, perhaps you get a different answer."

Fred steeled himself to raise the matter of John Worstenholm's death.

"That reminds me, Evelyn, I need to talk to Caroline on a private matter. Is she with you today?"

"Yes, I'm here, Fred. What a pleasure it is to see you after such a long time."

Caroline had walked into the kitchen just as Fred mentioned her name and she was standing right behind him, leaning against the doorway.

Fred turned around and looked at Caroline. He was amazed at how well she looked. Everyone else he had come to know had aged visibly over the past two years, but Caroline looked more radiant than ever and her eyes sparkled.

"Come and join us for the English afternoon tea," Evalina said to her sister. "We're talking about love, but there is not much for me to say."

Caroline blushed but hid her embarrassment by walking to the sink and washing out a dirty mug. She brought the mug back to the table and Evalina filled it with tea as Fred pulled out a chair for her. Caroline sat down and picked up the mug, clasping it in her hands and feeling the warmth of the hot tea.

"One day you and your countrymen will leave," she said, looking out of the window with a wistful expression on her face. "And then we will have to start again with nothing."

"I'm sure the British government will help you financially when the war is over," Fred replied.

Wondering how he could broach the matter of Lieutenant Worstenholm's death, Fred was silent for a moment. Bracing himself, he decided there was no easy way of telling her.

"Caroline, I'm afraid I have some very bad news."

"What is it, Fred? Have you lost a friend?"

Caroline put down the mug of tea and placed her hands over his.

"Yes, Caroline, but it's worse than that. He was your friend too and I wanted to be the first to tell you."

Caroline's face turned grey and a wild look appeared in her eyes.

"Tell me what?" she shrieked.

"It's John Worstenholm. The machine he was flying was shot down four days ago. His observer survived the crash but the lieutenant was hit by machine gun fire and died instantly."

Fred paused before continuing.

"He wouldn't have felt a thing, I'm sure. I'm so sorry, Caroline."

Caroline gasped. Letting go of Fred's hands she jumped up from the table and ran out of the room without saying a word, slamming the kitchen door behind her.

"This is terrible news, Fredrik," said Evalina.

"Yes it is. I couldn't get word to you before now as we've been too busy on the airfield. Only the officers have been allowed off the aerodrome."

"This news she will take badly, I know. She does not say, but I think he is the reason she moves to Abeele."

"I thought that might be the case, though the lieutenant told me nothing."

Fred rose from the table and picked up one of the freshly baked loaves of bread that were airing on top of the stove.

"I have to get back to the squadron before dark, so I'd better leave, Evelyn. Please tell Caroline again how sorry I am about what's happened. This war's changed all of our lives, no matter what we may do to try and prevent it."

"Thank you for coming, Fredrik," said Evalina, getting up from the table. "I see you out. Come back and visit us soon won't you?"

"I will, Evelyn. I miss your company and the excellent food. It's not the same living in the barracks."

Evalina let Fred out by the front door and he walked back to the aerodrome in the evening twilight. The full moon had already risen above the horizon and he could tell from the colour of the sky that it was going to remain a clear night.

"*I wonder if the German bombers will be out again tonight?*"

When he reached the aerodrome, Fred went straight to the workshop lorry and made sure that there was no repair work for him to do before morning. The aircraft had already returned from the last flight of the day and none of the wireless installations had been damaged. Satisfied that all was in order, he walked to the corporals' mess and ordered a double brandy. He needed a drink. He then ate a sandwich made from the fresh loaf before taking out his pocket diary and making a brief entry for the day's events:

Aerodrome bombed last night with no damage. Played at morning service. Walked to Abeele to tell Caroline the sad news.

With no-one else in the mess, Fed put away his diary and buttoned up his jacket.

"Goodnight, Gordon," he called out to the steward. "I'll be in the hut if anyone wants me tonight. Make sure that Harold gets half of that loaf won't you?"

"Right you are, Corporal, I'll give it to him in the morning."

Fred walked from the mess to the first of the Nissen huts. Opening the door and stepping inside the brightly lit room, he gagged at the smell of stale cigarette smoke and rank body odour. He stamped his feet on the door mat to remove the loose earth from his boots.

"You lot are a health and fire hazard. Having to sleep in here is more deadly than fighting the Huns!"

"Get away with you, corp," one of the men complained. "At least we keep each other warm at night."

Fred walked across to the far side of the hut, sat down on his bunk and took off his boots. Pushing them under the bed, he unwound his puttees and rolled them up into tight bandages before placing them in the bottom drawer of his bedside cabinet. As soon as his eyes became accustomed to the harsh light of the naked overhead bulb, he took out a sheet of paper from the top drawer and sat back down on his bunk to write a letter to Ethel.

Since arriving in Belgium almost two years previously, Fred had received at least two letters from Ethel each week and had made a point of writing almost as many back to her. They had both agreed that the best way to maintain their relationship was to write about even the most trivial of matters that affected their daily lives. Fred decided to mention the leave that was promised him at the end of the year, twelve months after his last furlough. Though he was well aware that anything could happen to him in the intervening months, it was one event they could both look forward to.

One by one the men in the hut fell asleep and the noise diminished to the occasional outburst of laughter from those who were still awake. Fred finished writing letters; one to Ethel and one to his father. Still upset at the death of John Worstenholm, he was frustrated that he was unable to mention the matter in either of the letters. Deciding to visit the latrines before he went to sleep, Fred put on his boots, tucked his shirt back in his breeches and walked outside with his braces dangling around his ankles. As he stepped off the verandah, he took great care to avoid the slit trench that ran right across the front of the hut.

The full moon shone above the aerodrome, casting stark shadows around the base of the buildings. The light was bright enough for Fred to see where he was going, though by now he was used to walking around the aerodrome at night, guided only by the chinks of light that shone from around the doors of the closed hangars. Looking up at the moon, he saw that the sky was clear except for the occasional wisp of cloud.

Several aeroplanes were parked out in the open. Fred noticed that the door of the hangar next to the wireless lorry, some fifty yards away, was wide open. He could hear voices and could see men working on one of the wireless flight's machines.

"Something must have come up that required urgent repairs," he muttered under his breath. "I wonder why they didn't send for me."

To make sure that everything was in order, Fred decided to find out what was going on. As he got closer to the hangar he recognised Charles Hickie by his uniform, though Fred was too far away to discern his features. The equipment officer had just finished talking to one of the men and was making his way out of the hangar. Fred was about to call out to the lieutenant when he became aware of a droning noise, coming from the east. From recent bombings of the aerodrome he quickly realised that it was the sound of an aircraft engine. Knowing that it was unlikely to be a friendly machine, he started to run towards the brightly lit hangar, shouting as he ran.

"Enemy aircraft, Mr Hickie! Get back and close the doors so they don't spot us!"

Charles Hickie must have heard Fred's cry, as he looked up and raised his hand in acknowledgment before turning around and running back to the hangar entrance.

The first bomb exploded mid way between the two men, the force of the blast flinging them both into the air but in opposite directions. Fred fell against the soft canvas wall of an adjacent hangar and slid to the ground, ending up on his back. Charles Hickie was less fortunate, striking the propeller of one of the RE8s as he fell to the floor of the hangar and ending up in a sitting position with his arms wrapped around his knees and his body wedged against the wheels of the aircraft.

The air was filled with flying debris and Fred found it difficult to breathe. He heard but could not see the blasts of three more bombs. By the strength and direction of the sound, he could tell that the bombs had fallen in a line across the front of the open hangar. After a pause of what seemed like minutes but was probably only seconds, he heard the sound of six more explosions, each one further away than the one before.

When the dust finally settled on the airfield, all was quiet except for the sound of running men. Having dropped its bombs, the attacking bomber had quickly retreated, the pilot happy in the knowledge that he would reach the safety of Germany before any allied scout could be sent up to intercept him.

"Medical orderly, over here!" a man shouted.

Fred became aware that several men were standing over him but he was unable to open his eyes. There was a loud ringing noise in his ears and his mouth and eyes were full of dirt. With difficulty, he rolled on to his stomach and spat the contents of his mouth on to the ground.

"I'm all right," Fred croaked. "Don't worry about me. Go and see how the lieutenant is."

The orderly picked up the stretcher that was intended for Fred and ran with it towards the hangar, on the way skirting the deep crater that had been created by the first of the bombs. Once inside the hangar, he quickly reached the body of Charles Hickie and knelt down to see if the lieutenant was still alive.

"Help here!" the orderly shouted, looking around to see if anyone else was nearby. "He's still breathing but he's losing a lot of blood!"

Several men quickly arrived on the scene, all in various states of undress. Charles Hickie was carefully placed on the stretcher and carried to the hospital hut where the medical officer was already in the process of setting up a makeshift operating table. With little room for movement, all but the medical orderlies were ordered to wait outside.

A number of small fires were burning on the airfield as a result of the bombing and these were quickly put out before the men began the task of assessing the damage.

George Knight, who had been sleeping in his quarters at the nearby farm, supervised the men in checking the damage. Most of the bombs had exploded in the open, requiring only the craters to be filled with earth. Apart from the injuries to Charles Hickie, no-one had been hurt, though eight of the squadron's machines had been damaged. By a miracle, Number 4 squadron had escaped without any damage to its aircraft or injuries to its men. Standing at the entrance to one of the hangars, George Knight called out to the men who had gathered around him.

"The first priority is to get our machines fixed, as they're needed first thing in the morning."

"We'll do our best, sir," one of the mechanics called out. "How many were damaged?"

"The four in here need repairing and also those in the hangar next door, though their damage is only minor. It's unlucky we had the door open at exactly the time the Hun flew over, or we might have got away with it."

"Sir, do we have to do this all by ourselves?" asked one of the riggers. "There's a lot of patching to be done."

"Townsend, if you can get the men started, I'll go and talk to the other flight commanders to see if we can rustle up a few volunteers. I'll also ask the major if we can open the canteen and provide you chaps with food and drink throughout the night."

"Thank you, sir."

"Leave the craters. They're not going anywhere. The men of the other flights can deal with them. I might even have a chat with the CO of Number 4 to see if he can spare some of his men."

Fred's ears were still ringing from the blast as he walked stiffly to the wireless lorry, parked to one side of the hangar least damaged by the bombs. Noticing several holes in the canvas covering, he climbed up to investigate. Arnold Makepiece was already inside with one of the riggers, sewing a fabric patch over a hole in the roof. As Fred approached to offer his assistance, Arnold looked up and laughed.

"Just look what the cat brought in. Don't let the major catch you looking like that."

"It's all right for you. I feel like I've just fought ten rounds with Jack Johnson."

"Where were you when the bombs went off, Fred?"

"Right in front of the first one, but I was lucky," Fred replied, brushing earth off his shirt and pulling up his braces. "Mr Hickie was hit by the same blast, but he was closer to the explosion than I was."

"How is he? Have you heard?"

"If you've got things under control here, I'll pop over to the hospital hut and find out. You know the lieutenant, nothing gets him down."

"Except you when he can't find you!" Arnold added with a laugh.

Fred climbed out of the lorry and walked over to the hospital hut. Though only half an hour had passed since the bombing, the operation of the aerodrome was already back to normal. Spare earth from the latrines had been used to roughly fill the craters left by the explosions and repairs were already underway on the hangar walls. Fred joined the small crowd of men standing outside the hut, all waiting for news of the lieutenant.

After a few minutes, the door opened and the medical officer came out. In the dim light of the doorway he raised his hands in the air for silence. With dismay, Fred saw that in one hand he was holding a red identity tag.

"Listen men, I managed to dress all of the lieutenant's wounds but I regret to say he died on the operating table. The blast must have ruptured some of his internal organs and there was nothing I could do. I'm sorry."

The doctor turned and walked back inside the hut, leaving the men outside in the dark. For the second time in less than a week, Fred was stunned by the death of someone he liked and respected. He ran from the hospital with his hands clasped over his mouth. When he reached the corner of the nearest hangar, he fell to his knees and vomited.

"God, why did you take these two good men?" he cried out in despair. "What is your purpose?"

Chapter 19

Return to Abeele

THE RELATIVELY DRY *September was followed by a month of bad weather, with only five days free from rain and low cloud. Less than a week after the death of Charles Hickie, Fred fell sick with dysentery and was confined to the camp hospital for a week. He returned to full duties on the 12th October 1917, the day upon which the New Zealand army was called upon to lead the attack in the first Battle of Passchendaele.*[100] *Both squadrons based at Abeele took part in the short-lived offensive, though poor weather conditions forced the pilots to fly at dangerously low altitudes. Three of their aircraft were shot down and forced to land in enemy territory, with one airman killed in action and five taken prisoner, one of them later dying of his wounds. With no improvement in the weather, the Allies decided to put the advance on hold until conditions improved.*

As had happened with many of the squadrons in the Royal Flying Corps, and at a time when the service was rapidly expanding, flying duties in Number 6 squadron became less and less the domain of commissioned officers.[101] *Aircrew who were NCO's or came from the 'other ranks' were required to carry out the same duties and take the same risks as their commissioned counterparts, but they were not afforded the same benefits and were refused entry to the officers' messes. As a result, they had little in* common with men of their own status and were treated as outsiders. Theirs was often a lonely life.

Flight Sergeant George Edwards walked out of the mess and headed across the road towards the hangar where his aircraft was being repaired. The ground underfoot was soggy and the driving rain was all the more penetrating due to a strong westerly wind. Pulling his cap down hard on his head he turned up the collar of his coat. When he reached the hangar, he looked inside to see if anyone was working on his aircraft.

"Hello. Anyone in there?"

"Just me," Arnold Makepiece replied.

The mechanic stood up in the cockpit to see who had called out.

"Makepiece, have you fixed my wireless yet?"

"Not yet, Flight Sergeant," said Arnold, jumping down from the wing. "Corporal Johnstone's fetching some spares from the stores as we can't get the old set to work."

"I'll wait 'till he gets back, then. I'm up again today if the weather clears and I want to be sure that it'll be in my own machine and not someone else's."

"He won't be long, sarg. We've brewed some tea at the back if you want some."

"Thank you, no. I noticed a wreck on the other side of the airfield as I came over and it doesn't look like one of ours. Do you know anything about it?"

"It's what's left of a Biff. [102] It came over early yesterday morning in the pouring rain, sounding really rough. The controls must have been damaged 'cos it was lurching up and down like a bloody porpoise. Lucky to bring it down in one piece, he was."

"What happened to the crew?"

"Some of the men from Number 4 got them out before the fire took hold. The pilot was pretty badly shot up but they say they'll both recover. I'm not sure if the machine's worth salvaging though."

"Getting trapped inside a cockpit has always been my biggest fear."

"Especially being right behind the engine, like you are. Anyway, here's Corporal Johnstone. He can tell you the latest."

Fred stopped in front of the RE8, water dripping from the edges of the canvas cape that covered the upper part of his body. Clutched to his chest, and protected by the cape, was a large cardboard box.

"Help me off with this would you, Arnold? I don't want these parts to get wet."

"That didn't take you long, Fred. Did they have everything you needed?"

"Enough to make the old set work, I hope."

Arnold lifted the waterproof cape over the top of Fred's head. Shaking it to remove the excess water, he hung the cape on a peg at the back of the hangar. Fred carried the box over to a card table that had been pushed next to the wing of the aircraft.

"Corporal, will I be able to use my machine again today?"

"I'd say so, Flight Sergeant. It'll take us a couple of hours at the most if all the parts work."

"If that's the case, I'll go back to the mess and wait there. Would you let me know when it's ready?

"I'm afraid it won't be me, as I have to go to Godewaersvelde. I'll have Makepiece come and find you."

"Thank you, Corporal. I'll leave you to it then."

The sergeant buttoned up his jacket and walked briskly out of the hangar.

"Sorry to drop you in it, Arnold. The captain asked me to check up on Cecil Jones. Apparently they had to take him to one of the clearing stations at Gerties."[103]

"Sure thing, boss," Arnold replied. "Nothing I haven't done before. I'll get Harold to help me test it once I've fixed the old set."

"Thanks. I'll only be a couple of hours."

"Give Cecil our best when you see him."

The rain had almost stopped and Fred seized the opportunity to dash across to the tender that was waiting in the laneway. It was only a short drive to Godewaersvelde, a bustling village three miles south west of the aerodrome. On any other day he would have walked, as the road followed the railway line right into the centre of village, well above the level of the surrounding waterlogged fields. However, the recent heavy rains had made the road impassable to all but heavy vehicles.

It only took ten minutes for the tender to reach the hospital, set up in a large field on the outskirts of the village. Fred climbed down and instructed the driver to wait for him, before walking over to the administration tent to report to the senior medical officer.

"Good morning, sir. I've come from Number 6 squadron to enquire after air mechanic Jones. He was brought here yesterday with severe burns."

"Well, Corporal, we're very busy at the moment and many patients have been moved around today. Tell you what, go to the end hut and ask the nurse in charge there. She should be able to help you."

"Thank you, sir."

Fred saluted and left the tent, unsure in which direction to walk. Looking through a gap between the tents, he noticed a group of wooden huts in the distance and decided to walk towards them. When he reached the last of the huts, he knocked on the door and entered. A nurse was sitting at a desk just inside the door. Behind her were two rows of beds, twelve beds in all.

"Hello, nurse. Can you tell me where air mechanic Cecil Jones is?"

"When was he brought in, Corporal?"

"Yesterday. He had burns to his upper body."

The nurse reached into the top drawer of the desk, took out a clipboard and scanned the names that were typed on a single sheet of paper. She was about to reply when the sound of a low flying aircraft reverberated through the building.

"Someone's lost, I'd say!" Fred shouted. "He's probably looking for somewhere he recognises. I wouldn't want to be up there in these conditions!"

"At least this weather will mean fewer casualties, Corporal."

From the constant drone of the engine, Fred guessed that the aeroplane was circling the hospital.

"I think he needs help, whoever he is. We could lay sheets on the ground in the shape of an arrow to show him the way to the aerodrome. If he doesn't get down soon, we could lose a machine as well as a pilot."

"That's a good idea, Corporal. Come with me to the laundry. They'll be dirty sheets I'm afraid, but that won't matter will it?"

"Not once they're laid out in the mud, it won't!"

The nurse opened the door and Fred followed her outside. The sound of the engine grew louder as he stood on the steps of the hut, knowing where the sound came from but unable to see anything because of the low clouds. Suddenly the ghostly form of an aeroplane became visible, just above the base of the cloud, and Fred could clearly see a large black cross on the side of the fuselage. Grabbing hold of the nurse, he pulled her away from the building.

"Quick nurse, run as fast as you can. It's a Hun. Maybe he thinks this is the aerodrome and not a hospital."

Fred looked up again and saw what he thought to be several small black objects separate from the aircraft and plummet towards the ground. He took hold of the nurse by the hand and ran with her towards the edge of the field, making sure he kept the wooden huts between them and the rest of the hospital so as to provide a barrier against any explosion. When they were well clear of the buildings, Fred pulled the nurse roughly to the ground and lay on top of her, waiting with dread for the all too familiar shock wave to hit them.

Seconds later, four bombs hit the ground, exploding in quick succession fifteen yards apart and in a straight line. Three exploded in a small field to one side of the hospital, creating shallow craters in the ground and spraying the surrounding area with earth and flying shrapnel. The fourth bomb fell through the roof of one of the huts before exploding, the blast destroying the end of the hut and shredding the canvas walls of the adjacent tents.

Unhurt, as they were far enough away to avoid being hit by flying shrapnel, Fred got up and helped the nurse to her feet.

"I'm sorry I was rough with you, but I've been close to exploding bombs before and you don't have much time to get out of the way. These were probably anti personnel types. They're designed to go off at knee height to cause maximum injury."

"Thank you, Corporal. I wouldn't have been quick enough if it weren't for you."

The nurse, unsteady on her feet, leant against Fred as she brushed the front of her uniform with her hands.

"I think you'll have to change your clothes," Fred added with a laugh. "It looks like you're wearing a khaki coloured apron instead of a white one."

The nurse laughed nervously before replying.

"I think I'd change clothes too, if I were you."

The air slowly cleared of smoke and descending debris and they watched as members of the medical staff ran to where the last bomb had exploded. No sound came from the damaged hut but they could hear men screaming in the neighbouring tents.

"I think I was right about the type of bomb. I'd say that there wouldn't be anyone left alive in that cabin and the patients in the nearby tents will have been hit by shrapnel. You'll have your work cut out for you this afternoon, nurse."

"It certainly looks bad but it could have been far worse," the nurse replied. "We only had four seriously wounded patients in that cabin, but there were two nurses there half an hour ago. I'd better go and see if I can help."

"While you do that, I'll go and telephone my major and see if he can order a machine up. We might be able to intercept the Hun on his way home."

The nurse adjusted her cap and held out her hand.

"Goodbye, Corporal. Thank you once again."

Fred shook her hand and was about to leave when he remembered the reason for his visit.

"I almost forgot, nurse. You didn't tell me how Cecil is."

"I didn't get much of a chance, Corporal. Mr Jones wasn't as badly burned as we first thought. Unless he was injured again today, we should be able to send him back to you in a couple of days."

"Would you tell him I'll come back and visit him tomorrow, when things have settled down?"

"Certainly. Now I really must go."

The nurse ran off in the direction of the destroyed cabin, leaving Fred standing alone in the middle of the field. He quickly got his bearings and walked back to the administration tent, finding it empty except for the telephone operator. He was soon connected with the aerodrome and explained the situation to the adjutant before handing the receiver back to the operator. Wondering if the invader would be stopped before he reached the safety of the German lines, Fred walked back to the road where his driver was waiting anxiously in the open cab of the tender.

"Cor blimey, that was a close shave," said the driver. "I could see every explosion from where I was sitting. Funny bombs those. They make a lot of noise but don't make big holes."

"Don't let that fool you," Fred replied. "Those bombs have long prongs on the end and they explode when the prongs hit the ground. If we get bombed at the aerodrome again, make sure you head for one of the slit trenches and lay as low as you can. If you're lucky, the shrapnel will fly past right over your head."

"That explains why the new major made us dig them."

"Let's get back to the 'drome," said Fred. "There's nothing we can do to help here."

Twenty minutes later they arrived back at Abeele and Fred walked up to the only aircraft inside the hangar. Seeing no-one in sight, he called out.

"Are you there, Arnold?"

Arnold's head appeared above the rim of the front cockpit. As soon as he saw Fred, he burst out laughing.

"That's the second time in three weeks you've dirtied your new stripes. Don't you like being a corporal?"

"The hospital was bombed and I was very lucky not to be injured. I'd have been a lot dirtier if I hadn't fallen on a nurse."

"Don't you mean fallen for a nurse?" Arnold replied, laughing loudly. "Seriously, Fred, you've really got to be more careful. The Hun's getting braver with his bombing. It wasn't long ago that we rarely saw them on our side of the lines."

"Well, today he wasn't much higher than tree height. The only reason there weren't more injuries was because the low clouds spoiled his aim."

Fred attempted to brush the mud from his uniform with little success.

"Do I really look that bad?"

"Listen corp, I can finish up here. Under the circumstances you could ask the sergeant to organise a hot bath for you and get that uniform tidied up."

"Yes, I might do that. Thanks Arnold."

"I'm planning on going into Pops with Harold and Billy Power a little later on. Do you want to come along?"

"Where are you going?"

"There's a film of the Battle of Arras showing at one of the cinemas. Afterwards we thought we'd go to dinner at your favourite café in the Rue de la Dunkirk."

"In that case you can count me in, Arnold. Come and find me when you're about to leave. I'll be in the corporals' mess."

A few days later, in spite of continued bad weather, a second attempt was made by the Allies to seize the Passchendaele ridge. Apart from having to cope with persistent heavy rain, aircraft operations out of Abeele were hampered by mist, thick haze and low clouds. Realising the plight of the soldiers fighting on the ground, the major gave the order that the squadron's patrols be attempted at any cost. During the initial attack, one of the squadron's aircraft was hit by a shell and crashed in flames behind enemy territory. Both the pilot and observer were killed and the wreckage shelled by the German guns. Another aircraft was damaged by anti-aircraft fire but the pilot managed to return to Abeele and land safely. The weather on the third morning started out clear but the officers' mess was empty apart from two heavily dressed airmen.

"So what's new, sonny?" asked Lieutenant George Cato, a twenty one year old New Zealander.

"Our op hasn't changed since last night's briefing," his observer replied. "I've just been to get the latest photographs of the targets. Here, take a look Cato."

The observer took out four reconnaissance photographs from a large envelope and laid them out on the table, next to the opened map of the target area. The clock code circles for each of the targets had already been drawn on the photographs.

Lieutenant Thomas Rogers, new to Number 6, was a twenty year old war veteran who had lied about his age when he enlisted in the Royal Engineers four days after Britain declared war on Germany. After three years of service, he applied for a transfer to the Royal Flying Corps and was sent to England for observer training. Within a month he was back on the Western Front and two weeks later he earned the coveted 'feathered O' observer's wing.

"The captain must have confidence in your navigation skills now, Tom."

"Why would that be, Cato?"

"By giving you the dubious privilege of flying early in the morning. Into the sun, where we can't see the Hun."

"Very poetic. My problem's been getting the Morse signals right, not with navigating. My old flight commander told me the battery commanders used to complain that they couldn't understand my signals."

"Everything comes with practice, Tom."

The two men bent down to examine the map so that they could locate the first target. It was identified on the back of the matching photograph with the handwritten coordinates **J28c 65.90** and also drawn as the bullseye for the clock code circles on the photograph. Tom Rogers pointed a finger at the target on the map.

"I've been told it's an enemy supply dump half a mile south of the Gheluvelt crossroads, just off the Zandvoorde road. It looks to me like it's in the middle of a farm."

George Cato folded his map neatly so that it was no larger than a foot square.

"That should be easy to find. I've flown around there dozens of times."

"Isn't that map too small to be of any use to you?"

"Not a bit of it. I can see all of the squares[104] we need today. Small enough for me to clip to my instrument panel and not get in the way."

Tom Rogers raised his eyebrows and checked the map to confirm that the other three targets were also visible.

"Sorry to doubt you, Cato. It does cover all of them."

"Apology accepted. Anyway, we'd better get going."

The two airmen left the mess and walked to the hangar where the engine of their RE8 was being tested by one of the mechanics. The ground crew had worked through the night making sure that the bullet holes from the previous flight had been patched over and that the engine and all of the controls were in perfect working order.

Visibility was good all around the aerodrome. Within minutes they were airborne and climbing towards the lines. Tom Rogers took this time in preparing for the shoot by checking his map and photographs, letting out the aerial and switching on the wireless set. When he had finished, he swung around on his seat and prepared the Lewis gun for action, making sure that the spare drums of ammunition were correctly stowed in the racks. Satisfied that everything was ready, he looked over the side to re-check their position.

Shortly after leaving Abeele, Tom had noticed a dense white ground mist covering all of the land to the east, as far as he could see. Even from a height of three thousand feet, he could still not tell how deep the mist was, though in places the tops of hills and tall trees rose above it. Not knowing what the visibility would be like at the front, he decided to transmit the aircraft's code so at least the battery would know the identity of the approaching aircraft, even if it couldn't actually see it. After only a month on the Western Front, Tom already felt confident in what he had to do. He looked down at the battery call signal that was written on the photograph, took hold of the transmission key and tapped out the complete code. [105]

•--- •---- •---- •- •-• ••--- -••• -••• -•••

He repeated the signal a few times as the aircraft approached the position of the battery. Looking down at the map strapped to his knee, Tom examined the contour lines and tried to visualise the shape of the high ground close to the battery's coordinates - **I17c 75.20**. With an image of the terrain fixed in his mind, he peered into the distance over the top of the spinning propeller and recognised the summit of Hill 62, the highest land in the vicinity though only two hundred feet above sea level.

According to the map, the battery was located half a mile north east of the village of Zillebeke. Tom swung around on his stool and peered over the side of the cockpit, trying to locate the large lake to the west of the village. Covered in mist, the lake was indistinguishable from the surrounding flat land. The hill to the north of Zillebeke was visible and he used that to estimate the position of the battery. Once he was confident of the location, he thumped hard on the front of his cockpit to catch the attention of the pilot.

"See that small hill on the left, about a thousand yards away! The battery's on this side of it and should be out of the mist!" he shouted. "Drop down, would you, so that we can see what signal they're showing?"

"Right you are, Tom," George Cato replied. "Hold tight!"

The pilot made a skilful but almost vertical turn to the left, losing height as he swung the aircraft around until it faced the north. His timing was perfect and they passed right over the battery at two thousand feet and the signal which had been set up on the ground next to the outside gun was clearly visible. However, instead of the expected letter '**A**', indicating that the battery had received their signals and was ready to fire, the white cloth strips clearly spelt out the letter '**T**'. This meant that the battery was unable to fire and was requesting them to return to base without attempting their mission.

"Looks like it's a dud!" George Cato shouted. "I'll turn around again and you can send him the '**CI**'. Then when you've wound in the jolly old aerial I'll get us out of here!"

"All right, Cato, I'll let you know when I've finished."

Tom Rogers swivelled around to face the front of the cockpit so that he could use the Morse key again. When the aircraft was pointing towards the battery, he tapped their identifying signal followed by the 'going home' code.[106]

•--- •---- •---- •- •-• ••--- -••• -•-• •• -•-• ••

To ensure that the signal would be received by the battery, Tom waited for a few seconds and then repeated the whole message sequence. Satisfied that he had done all that he could in the circumstances, he pulled the plug out of the wireless set and reeled in the aerial.

"All finished!" he shouted, thumping once again on the dashboard.

Tom was pressed hard against the side of the cockpit as the aircraft was put into another steep turn. They flew over the battery one more time and he waved to the men below, not knowing if they could see him and feeling frustrated that he had been unable to carry out the shoot.

The pilot throttled back to reduce speed.

"Fancy a spot of aerobatics? It would be a shame to waste such a golden opportunity. I can show you that the old 'Harry Tate' is a lot better than its reputation would suggest."

"All right, Cato. Give me a moment to secure everything back here. Then you can do your damndest."

George Cato nodded and turned around again to face the front. He opened up the throttle again and set the aircraft in a climb, trimming the tail by adjusting the large wheel fastened to the right hand side of the cockpit. After five minutes of climbing, he levelled out once more.

"Are you ready yet, Tom?"

"Almost. Just let me check that everything is stowed."

Tom Rogers felt around inside the cockpit and made sure that nothing was loose. He did not want to have to explain the loss of his maps to the recording officer when they got back to the aerodrome.

"Ready when you are!" he shouted.

Almost immediately, Tom sensed the nose of the aircraft drop and the sound of the engine increase to a roar. He felt light-headed for a moment as the machine plummeted towards the ground. Before he had time to grab hold of his seat, his body was forced back against the mounting ring of the machine gun as the aircraft rotated and the horizon came into view above his head briefly before disappearing from sight below the wings. With its nose pointing straight up and the huge propeller grabbing at the air like an exhausted swimmer, the aircraft gradually slowed in its ascent and then stopped altogether. Hanging motionless in the air for a moment, the machine began to slip backwards. Before Tom had time to catch his breath, the nose of the aircraft flipped forward. The horizon reappeared, this time from below, stopping right above his head with the aircraft now plunging straight towards the ground. The force of three times that of normal gravity pushed him down on to his seat as the machine came out of its dive and zoomed once more into the sky. This time it did not climb vertically but continued to rotate as if prescribing a loop in the sky. The sensation of immense heaviness ceased as quickly as it had started when he found himself hanging upside side down in the cockpit, with only the gun mounting preventing him from falling out of the aircraft.

Tom braced himself with his legs pressed against the sides of the cockpit and his hands grasping the gun. Forcing himself to open his eyes, he looked up and found that what had previously been a view of a cloudy sky had been replaced by a panorama of mist-covered ground. He was about to shout out a warning of the dangers of looping, when the scene changed again as the aircraft rolled one hundred and eighty degrees so that the ground was once more directly below. Exhilarated, he thumped on the dashboard and shouted to the pilot.

"What was that, Cato? I've never experienced anything like that!"

The pilot eased back on the throttle and turned around in his seat, a broad grin visible beneath the peak of his balaclava.

"A good old fashioned tail slide followed by an Immelman turn. She doesn't behave too badly, does she? Do you want some more or did that make you feel sick?"

"More please, but no more zooming! It felt like I was being sat on by an elephant!"

"We're close to home now, so I'll just do one more stunt. I'll put her into a spin and give the PBI[107] below a surprise. The mist is clearing now so they'll get a good show. Just when they think we're in trouble, I'll swoop up in front of them!"

"Any risk of me falling out, Cato?"

"No. Just keep your eyes open and try and breathe normally, as spinning could make you feel a bit sick. We can't have you making a mess of your new uniform, can we?"

Tom Rogers took a deep breath and looked around the inside of the cockpit. Nothing had moved during the earlier stunts and he prepared himself for the final manoeuvre.

Sitting in the front cockpit, George Cato cut the throttle and pulled back gently on the control stick to keep the aircraft level. With the forward speed reducing by the second, he waited until the aircraft started to judder before pushing hard on the left rudder bar, at the same time pulling the stick back as far as it would go. The nose rose momentarily before the wings stalled and the left wing dropped, causing the machine to roll over and over in an anticlockwise spiral as it fluttered down like a falling leaf.

Looking ahead over the spinning propeller, all that George could see was a kaleidoscope of colour as the sky and ground spun around in circles. He gazed intently at the constantly changing patterns, trying to discern the land features so that he did not leave it until too late to initiate the recovery. As soon as he could clearly see the soldiers on the road below, he brought the aircraft out of the spin by applying full right rudder and centralising the stick. He then neutralised the rudder and pushed the stick forward to gain airspeed. Having brought the aircraft out of the spiral dive, he pulled back on the control stick and opened up the throttle, clearing the ground by less than fifty feet as the machine zoomed up into the sky.

Leaning over the side of the cockpit, George waved to a group of soldiers who had been marching along the Ypres road to the east of Poperinghe. They had stopped in their tracks and were staring up at what they thought was a stricken aircraft facing imminent disaster. As the machine climbed quickly away from the ground, George looked back and caught a glimpse of the soldiers cheering and throwing their hats in the air. By the time he levelled out at fifteen hundred feet, he could see the aerodrome in the distance, with rays of sunshine filtering through the clouds and reflecting off the roofs of the buildings.

"At least we didn't waste our time in the air, Tom!" he shouted over his shoulder. "See, the mist is clearing. The next machine should have better luck."

One month after the death of Charles Hickie, it was again the night of a full moon. The men of the two squadrons retired for the night fearful that they might once again be subjected to a bombing raid. The sky was relatively clear and the moon cast long shadows around the buildings on the aerodrome, causing them to stand out starkly from the surrounding farmland.

A few hours before dawn, the sound of an aircraft approaching from the north was heard by one of the perimeter guards. He quickly raised the alarm and everyone on the airfield jumped out of bed and ran for cover. The men of Number 6 squadron who had been sleeping in the Nissen huts rushed outside and lay down in the slit trenches. Those officers whose quarters were on the aerodrome had less protection, as their wooden huts had roofs made of canvas. The best they could do was to roll out of bed and lie flat on the floor, hoping that any flying shrapnel would pass over their heads.

The solitary twin-engine German aircraft dropped a stick of twenty pound bombs, similar to those that fell on the hospital at Godewaersvelde ten days earlier. Two bombs scored direct hits on two of the Nissen huts and the other two exploded on the ground, firing fragments of steel in all directions. After the sound of the aeroplane had died away, the men stood up and assessed the damage. Apart from the two Nissen huts which were completely destroyed, several other buildings were damaged. As far as casualties were concerned, four men had been killed with three men injured. By morning, the Nissen huts were still smouldering and the homeless airmen continued to sift through the charred timber and corrugated iron, looking for personal belongings that had not been destroyed in the attack.

"Sarg, do you think it would be all right if I slept off the aerodrome for a few days? I can stay at my old billet in Abeele. It won't cost the squadron anything."

Fred was standing inside the hangar next to the wireless workshop lorry, with all of his personal belongings laid out in front of him, ready to be packed into his kit bag.

"I don't see why not," Sergeant Trotter replied. "Let me check with the adjutant. It'll probably suit him as there may be a delay in rebuilding the huts."

Fred raised his eyebrows.

"Don't say it was me who told you, but the squadron may be on the move."

"Pardon me for not believing you, sarg."

"I know we've had false alarms in the past, but I've been ordered to run down what we have in the stores and tidy up everything around the place."

"We've managed to outlast any of the other squadrons that have been stationed here. I can't see that ever changing."

"I could do with a change of scenery myself."

"I like it here," Fred replied. "It's become like home to me. I know more people in Belgium than I do back in Blighty. I'd be sorry to have to say goodbye to them all."

"Did you lose anything in the attack last night?"

"I was lucky, sarg. Most of my personal belongings were in the lorry, so I've only lost clothing. I could do with a new uniform anyway. It's had a bit of a battering over the past few weeks."

"I'd agree with that assessment."

Sergeant Trotter glanced down at the clipboard he was carrying.

"Look, Fred, I'd better get moving and see what else we need to replace. I'll see you later."

"Right you are, sarg."

The sergeant walked off in the direction of the major's hut and Fred started to pack his belongings into the kit bag. The air around the huts was thick with the smell of old bonfires and Fred was excited at the prospect of once more being billeted in the village.

Half an hour later, with his kit bag slung over his shoulder, Fred left the aerodrome and walked towards the village, pausing along the way to talk to a group of passing soldiers. Gone were the days when people made fun of his Flying Corps uniform and he walked down the muddy road with a jaunty swing to his stride. He soon reached the village, turned into the familiar cul-de-sac and followed the path by the stream. As it was when he first arrived in Belgium, the estaminet looked deserted. The grass was uncut and the tables and chairs were stacked against the side wall of the house.

He walked up the path to the front door. Out of habit, he reached above the door lintel for the spare key that Evalina always kept hidden in the ivy. Remembering the last time he visited the estaminet, he changed his mind and knocked on the door. After a few moments, the door opened and Evalina's anxious face peered around the opening. Her sad expression turned to one of delight when she recognised Fred.

"Fredrik, my good friend, so nice to see. Please to come in and put your bag down."

"Hello Evelyn, I wasn't sure that I should come as I didn't know if Caroline would be here."

"My sister, she is in France. I have not seen her since the bad news you gave. I think it will be a long time for her to be happy again. Come into the kitchen and I will make you tea. I have fresh bread and jam."

"Thanks, that would be lovely."

He stepped inside the familiar hallway and placed his kit bag at the foot of the stairs. Evalina led him into the kitchen and gestured towards one of the chairs.

"Sit down and tell me your news. There is no-one else here to disturb us. I will boil some water, yes?"

Fred did as he was bidden and soon the old friends were deep in conversation, eating bread and jam and drinking hot black tea. After a while he raised the matter of the recent bombing raid and asked Evalina if she had a spare bed that he could sleep in for a few nights.

"Of course you can stay, Fredrik. You can have the same room as before. I keep it empty for Caroline, if she comes again."

"That's very kind of you, Evelyn. It won't be for long as the squadron might be leaving Abeele in the near future."

"We will be sorry to see you go. The people of the village have known you well since you arrive. Give me warning and I will arrange you a party."

"I'd like that, though I'm not one for saying goodbyes. Perhaps we could have a musical evening where anyone who wants to can play or sing. I know Stan and Arnold would like to come."

"Leave it to me, Fredrik. I will talk to people just in the case."

Fred laughed at her use of words.

"Just in case," he corrected her. "I'm not sure why, but that is what we say."

Evelyn blushed. "Your language has many funny words that mean nothing. I keep trying anyway."

Fred looked up at the clock on the wall and put down his empty mug.

"I'd better get back to the aerodrome, Evelyn. There's still a lot of clearing up to do. I'll leave my things in the bedroom if you don't mind."

Evalina got up from the table and walked through to the hall, Fred following close behind. She opened the door of the spare room and walked over to the fireplace.

"I'm afraid it is very cold here," she said. "I light a fire this afternoon for you to be warm tonight."

Fred brought his bag in from the hall and walked over to the window. Looking out on the wintry scene reminded him of his first day in Abeele and the moonlight that had shone through the window as he wrote his first letter to Ethel. He turned to face Evalina.

"You know, Evelyn, it's funny how often there's been a full moon when things have happened to me"

"What do you mean, Fredrik?"

"There was one when I said goodbye to my Ethel, one on my first night here, one when I was promoted to corporal, one when Lieutenant Hickie died and one last night when we were bombed. There are probably more than that but I can't think of them offhand."

"I hope you are not as you say, superstitious."

"No, but it's very interesting isn't it?"

Chapter 20

Squadron on the Move

The anteroom of 'C' flight mess overflowed with crews waiting for the order to fly. Many of the officers had positioned their easy chairs in a semi circle around the hot stove and were reading magazines, whilst others listened to music on the gramophone or played chess. It was early afternoon but the sky had already begun to darken. The day had so far been a washout, with rain and low clouds effectively closing the aerodrome. To make matters worse, the squadron had already been informed by the batteries that there was zero visibility over the lines.

Lieutenant Robert Richardson put down the newspaper he was reading and got up to place another log in the stove.

"I'm off on leave tomorrow," he said, to no-one in particular.

Tom Rogers was sitting in a chair on the other side of the room. He looked up in interest.

"Lucky you, Robert," he replied. "I'm not due any for ages."

The two men had similar backgrounds, both having served in the Army on the Western Front before transferring into the Royal Flying Corps and being trained as observers. Both also hoped that one day they would earn their pilot's brevets. Compared to their fellow officers in the squadron, many of whom had only recently left school, they felt like old men and had little in common with their peers. Tom was five years younger than Robert and, despite his extensive war experience, had yet to celebrate his twenty first birthday.

"By the time I get back, our new captain should have settled in. It must be hard for him, taking over from 'Jimmy' Riddle."

"How old do you think he is?"

"Even younger than you, Tom! I'd be surprised if he was much more than eighteen."

Before they could discuss the matter further, the door burst open and the duty officer entered the wooden hut. Striding across the room to the roaring stove, he brushed the rain from his coat.

"Anything doing?" one of the pilots asked casually.

The expression on the pilot's face suggested that he had little interest in whatever the captain might say in response to his question.

"The order's just been issued for 'zero machines up'.[108] One machine from each flight."

The pilot swore under his breath.

"Who's on first crawl today?" the duty officer continued.

"Me and Cato, I'm afraid," Robert Richardson replied, frowning at the prospect of leaving the warm mess. "Why are they bothering to send us up when there's little chance we'll actually see anything?"

"Don't ask me, I'm only the duty officer. They haven't put the yellow flag up yet so it looks like there won't be any photographic sorties today. You'll have to make do with the photographs you already have. You're on a contact patrol aren't you?"

"Yes we are. I've already picked up the latest photographs, just in case there was going to be a show."

"That's good then. Now if you'll excuse me, I'd better go and let the other flights know what's happening. Good luck."

The duty officer left the mess, closing the door behind him. Robert Richardson walked over to Tom Rogers and bent down to whisper in his ear.

"Be a bean and swap with me would you, Tom? You're down as fourth up so there's no chance you'll be flying today."

"Who's your pilot, Robert? I wasn't really listening to your earlier conversation."

"Cato."

"I went up with him the other week. He's an ace pilot. We had a washout and he treated me to some stunts instead."

"Stunts in a Harry Tate?"

"He put the RE8 through manoeuvres I'm sure aren't in the book."

"I've no complaints with Cato either, except that he's a bloody Colonial!"

"Well, I'm happy to swap with you if our new commander agrees. It wouldn't have been a problem with Jimmie but I don't know about Captain Finch."

"He's in the dining room. Let's go and ask him."

The two men walked through the anteroom to the main dining room, where they found their flight commander talking to the mess steward.

"Excuse me, Captain," Robert Richardson interrupted. "We've just received orders to fly."

"That's good news, Lieutenant. Thank you for bringing it to my attention."

"Sir, would you mind if Lieutenant Rogers swapped with me for the first show. He's flown with Lieutenant Cato before, so there shouldn't be a problem from that angle."

"Are you not well?"

"I'm off on leave tomorrow, sir, and I'd rather not chance it this afternoon if I don't have to."

"That would be highly irregular," replied the young captain. "If I gave you permission, other crews would be asking for the same thing once they got to hear of it and then there'd be no point in setting up rosters, would there?"

"I don't mind doing it, sir," Tom Rogers interrupted. "And my Morse has improved a lot if that's a concern."

"I'm sorry, but that's my decision. With the weather the way it is I doubt very much you'll see any other machines, friendly or otherwise. You'd better hurry along now, or you'll be late."

"Thank you sir," Robert Richardson replied, a look of disappointment on his face.

The captain turned away to resume his conversation with the mess steward and the two observers walked back to the anteroom.

"I'm sorry I couldn't help you, Robert."

"That's all right, Tom. Thanks for offering anyway. Keep my seat warm and we can laugh about it over dinner."

Robert glanced over towards the stove where George Cato had just finished buttoning up his heavy leather jacket and was in the process of pulling on a balaclava.

"Are you ready to go, Cato?"

"Most certainly, my boy," George Cato replied.

"All right old man, just because you've been with the squadron two months longer than I. Show a little respect for your elders would you."

"Only joking, Sir Robert. I'm not sure why we're bothering at all today as I doubt we'll see much over the trenches. That's even if we get that far."

Having pulled on their flying boots, the two men trudged out of the mess, slamming the door behind them. Those left behind huddled closer to the fire as a cold draught swept through the room.

Tom Rogers reached towards a small table and picked up an old Punch magazine. He scanned the pages for cartoons he had not already seen and was attracted to one depicting two off-duty soldiers dressed in threadbare uniforms, standing barefoot outside a tent in a blizzard. He leaned over to one of the other officers and showed him the cartoon.

"Have you seen this one? It would be funny if it weren't so true. Having served in the army, I know just how bad it can be in the trenches."

The other officer grunted but said nothing, so Tom sat back in his seat and browsed through the rest of the magazine. After twenty minutes, he got up and walked through to the inner room.

"Steward, could you rustle up a special cake for dessert tonight? Lieutenant Richardson's going on leave tomorrow and I'd like to give him a proper send-off."

"I'm afraid our stores are a bit on the low side, sir. What if I make some artificial icing and decorate a piece of Madeira cake?"

"That would do nicely. You've got a couple of hours before they come back."

"That's plenty of time, sir. I promise it will look like the real McKay."

Happy with the outcome, Tom Rogers was about to return to the anteroom when the door swung open and the duty officer walked in.

"Don't tell me the major has decided to send up another machine!" Tom said, a look of incredulity on his face.

"Not with what's just happened, Tom. We've had a call from the battery to tell us that their wireless operator's been wounded."

"Is he all right?"

"I think so, but they've put a hold on any more sorties for the moment."

"That's a relief. The conditions really aren't good enough for putting machines into the air."

"That's not all, I'm afraid," continued the duty officer. "They were keeping an eye on an RE8 that was flying nearby, when it suddenly broke up in mid air and plunged into Dickebusch Lake. By the time they got to the scene both men had drowned. We don't know yet if they were shot down or if there was a fault with the machine."

"Was the RE8 one of ours?" Tom asked, a feeling of dread surging through his body.

"Cato's, I'm afraid. There's no doubt about it, the battery commander wrote down the aircraft's number. I'm truly sorry, Tom. I know Rob was a good friend of yours."

"But they were both sitting here by the fire only half an hour ago!" Tom cried out in disbelief.

"You never get used to it do you? Here one minute, gone the next and another two empty seats at the dinner table."

Tom struggled to reply but was unable to form the words. He brushed past the duty officer and returned to the anteroom where he slumped into the nearest empty chair. As he sat staring into the distance, his gaze was involuntarily drawn to the frieze of air crew silhouettes, pasted on the walls. Finding the profiles of Cato and Richardson amongst the more than forty airmen on display, he wondered how many more of the faces would join the ranks of those 'never to return'.

After the church service on the following Sunday, the major called together the whole of the squadron. With the men assembled in front of him, he confirmed the rumour that a move was imminent and that the aircraft of 'B' flight would be flying out the next day, with the rest of the squadron following towards the end of the week. He added that the squadron would no longer be under the command of the 2nd Wing and had been ordered south to Bertangles, away from the fighting at Ypres. This did not come as a surprise to anyone, as rumours had been rife for almost a week and some of the squadron's heavy tenders had already been loaded with equipment from 'B' flight stores. The news that the move was official both excited and saddened Fred, as he was not looking forward to saying goodbye to all of his friends in Abeele and Godewaersvelde.

With all flights cancelled due to bad weather and no outstanding repairs to be carried out, Fred sought permission to be excused for the rest of the day so that he could take a trip into the village. Armed with a pass for the afternoon, he found out from the adjutant when the next tender was going to Poperinghe and then arranged with its driver to be dropped off at Abeele. With no other passengers on the trip, Fred sat in the front of the lorry. Sitting as close as he could to the middle of the cabin, he managed to avoid the stream of rain water that ran off the canopy and down the inside of the door, collecting in a puddle at his feet.

For the first time that he could remember, the road to Abeele was deserted and they saw no other traffic on the short drive into the village. Instead of asking to be dropped off at Café Evalina and risk getting soaked in the laneway that was too narrow for the tender to negotiate, Fred asked the driver to stop on the main road right outside Margueritas. Thanking the driver, he climbed down out of the tender and ran around the back of the lorry on to the pavement. As he ran up the path to the house in the pouring rain, he could see that lights were on in the dining room. Shaking the water from his greatcoat, Fred opened the door and stepped inside. He took off his coat and cap and handed them to the girl at the cloak counter before walking into the dining room. It was half empty. Those who had braved the elements were mostly men in uniform but there were a few local civilians. He smiled at the girl before walking down the hall and entering the kitchen by the side door. Julia was standing in the middle of the room with her back towards him, giving orders to two uniformed waitresses. Hearing his footsteps, she turned around.

"Hello, Fred. I'm surprised to see you on such a horrible afternoon."

She waved her hand to dismiss the two girls, who returned to the dining room to wait on customers.

"Hello, Julia. I came because this might be the only opportunity I'll get to say goodbye. We heard this morning that the move is on and we could be packed up and out of here by the end of the week."

"I suppose I've been expecting this, but I'm very sad you're leaving. With most of the men in the village fighting at the front, I've come to rely a lot on you and your friends. Who am I going to talk to when you've gone and who will play the piano for me?"

Julia took Fred's hand and held it to her cheek.

"I'll miss you too, Julia. You've been a good friend to me also." He paused. "I wouldn't worry too much about being deserted as I'm sure we'll be replaced by another squadron. And they're bound to have at least one good piano player!"

"Play for me one last time, would you?" Julia implored. "There are only a few people in there having afternoon tea and I'm sure they won't object to a little free entertainment. Afterwards, you can join me in the parlour for a private tea."

"Certainly, I'd be delighted. As this is to be the last time, I'll play my favourite piece. That should get everyone's attention."

"Very well, Fred, I'll make the announcement."

Julia walked into the dining room and clapped her hands. When the talking had died down she addressed the audience in English.

"Excuse me, ladies and gentlemen. If you come here regularly, the man standing next to me will be no stranger to you." She waited for silence before continuing. "Well, this afternoon will be the last time he will play here for a while and he has chosen to play the Prelude by Rachmaninoff. Some of our Canadian friends may also know it by the name of 'The Bells of Moscow'. Please would you welcome Frederick Johnstone."

The diners applauded Fred politely as he walked to the dais and sat down at the piano. Fred watched as Julia moved to the back of the room and stood next to the window, looking back at him with a sad expression on her face. At first he felt awkward at the prospect of playing to an audience whilst dressed in his simple corporal's uniform, especially as there were several high ranking army officers in the room. But, after striking the three opening chords, he forgot about the audience and immersed himself in the music. Though not a particularly complex piano composition, the piece demanded to be played with feeling and Fred found that he was able to vent some of the pent-up emotion that was buried deep inside him. Five minutes later, when he played the final two soft chords, he lifted his hands from the keyboard and sat back on the piano seat, feeling that an important part of his life had come to an end.

Many people in the audience cried out as Fred was given a standing ovation. He stood up and bowed, feeling slightly embarrassed at the unexpected praise. Holding his hand briefly in the air as a sign of appreciation, he placed the cover over the keyboard and quietly left the stage.

"Well, that's one for the piano players," he muttered under his breath.

By the time he reached the parlour, Julia was already laying out the plates on a tablecloth made from Ypres lace.

"You know, Julia," Fred said, once he had sat down at the table, "I feel that an important chapter in my life has closed and that there's no going back."

"I know what you mean, Fred," Julia replied sadly. "I felt that way last week when the village held a concert for you and your friends. Do you think you'll ever visit Belgium with your young lady after the War? There are many people who would very much like to meet her."

"Much as I'd like to think we would, I doubt we'll be able to travel abroad in the foreseeable future," Fred added. "I'm not even sure that I'll get my old job back. One thing I will promise you, Julia, is that I will write to you."

"Please forgive me if I don't write back," she replied. "I don't think your young lady would understand. I can't see me moving away from Abeele so you'll always know where to find me. Anyway, enough of this sad talk. Let us enjoy one last afternoon tea together."

The following morning, most of the men of 'B' flight left Abeele, travelling by lorry to their new aerodrome at Bertangles. They were joined later in the day by the aircraft of the flight, which were flown the short distance by their regular crews. For the men of the other two flights, operations proceeded as normal in spite of the poor weather and the squadron claimed its last victory whilst flying from Abeele, when one of its pilots succeeded in shooting down a German scout.

By mid afternoon, after a morning overcast with heavy cloud and mist, the sky had already begun to darken as the ground crew of 'C' flight waited for the last of their aircraft to return. The machine was thirty minutes overdue and the men were concerned that it might have run into trouble, though the squadron's recording officer had received no news to that effect. The men had plenty to keep them busy, as another aircraft had been damaged that morning and was up on trestles at the back of the hangar. The pilot had flown the crippled aircraft all the way back from Ypres before crash landing on the airfield. With the machine extensively damaged, the fitters and riggers of the other aircraft in the flight had all offered their assistance.

"What a bunch of busy beavers. Can anyone join in?" Fred asked.

"Hello, corp," replied one of the riggers, looking up from his work. "Are you swinging the lead again or are you here on business?"

The rigger put down the large curved needle he had been using to sew a circular patch of fabric over a hole in the side of the fuselage.

"The former. I've not much on at the moment."

"I think we can manage here all right, thanks, but I for one could murder a drink if you're offering."

Echoes of agreement came from the other men and Fred held up his hands in mock surrender.

"All right, all right. I give in. I'll pop down to the mess and grab a bite to eat and then I'll see what I can bring back for you all."

"Keep an eye out for our missing machine," added the rigger who had first spoken. "It's just possible that they'll still make it back tonight, though there's less than an hour of light. All of 'A' flight's machines have been put away so we're not waiting for anyone else."

"Not much chance of me being caught by surprise, then." Fred said. "Not even with my history."

Fred laughed as he turned to walk out of the hangar. The afternoon had turned cold and he pulled his old flying helmet out from his coat pocket. Taking off his cap he replaced it with the leather balaclava.

"That's better," he muttered to himself.

Buttoning up his coat, Fred strode out of the hangar and walked across the aerodrome. Stopping at the main entrance, he looked up and down the road for his old friend Arnold Makepiece, who he knew was on guard duty. Realising that Arnold might be on the far side of the aerodrome, Fred gave up on the idea and crossed the road, heading for the corporals' mess. Once inside, he found that the anteroom was empty, so he took off his helmet and sat down by the fire. After a few minutes the mess steward entered via the rear door.

"Can I help you, corp?"

"A beer if you don't mind, Alfie. And something to eat. What do you have on the menu tonight?"

"I'm sorry, we're all out of beer but I can offer you egg and Pom Fritz; as good as any you'll get in town. If you ask nicely at the sergeants' mess they might oblige you with a beer, especially with the move and all."

"Thanks. I'll go and try the other mess then. Cheerio."

"Good night, corp."

Fred left the hut and walked over to the sergeants' mess. He knocked at the door and it was opened almost immediately.

"Hello, Fred. What brings you here tonight? Come to play for us?"

"Hello, sarg, I've come to scrounge some beer for 'C' flight. They've a long night ahead of them and we're out of beer in the corporals' mess."

Sergeant Trotter gestured for Fred to enter.

"Come in out of the cold, Fred, and I'll see what we can do. Tell you what, how about playing us a few tunes while you're waiting and I might throw in a bite to eat as well."

"Thanks, sarg, you're most kind."

"Nobody's ever accused me of that before. We've missed your tinkling of the ivories over the past few days and I'm sure that Jock would like to bore you with his latest exploits before he leaves."

Chapter 21

A Change of Plans

Four days later, on the day of the big move,[109] the aerodrome was buzzing with activity. In pouring rain, a convoy of fifteen lorries left at midday, crammed with men and equipment. Later in the day when the weather had cleared, the pilots made ready their machines for the one hour flight to their new home. With eight aircraft for each flight as well as two spare machines, the men who had volunteered to stay behind were kept busy fuelling the aircraft and manoeuvring them on to the airfield.

One by one the pilots took off and headed south for Amiens. As they cleared the aerodrome perimeter for the last time, they waggled the wings of their machines in a parting gesture. With Number 6 now officially pulled out of the line, the mechanics loaded what was left of the equipment on to the remaining lorries before jumping on board the last tender. The vehicles travelled the short distance to the border check point before merging with the traffic on the main road south. As a result of recent rains, the roads from Hazebrouck leading south to Bethune were so full of potholes that it was not until nightfall that the trucks finally arrived at Bertangles.

The men spent the next few days getting used to their new surroundings whilst anxiously waiting to hear what the squadron's new role would be. Number 6 was the only squadron on the airfield so there was no shortage of room, and with the ancient city of Amiens only a few miles south of the aerodrome, there was plenty to do and much to see.

On the Monday after the move, the major informed his flight commanders that a surprise attack[110] was planned to take place on the following day, near the important German railhead town of Cambrai, and that Number 6 squadron would be called to take part in the action. He also told the three captains that the move to Bertangles was part of a plan to disguise the strength of the allied air support from the enemy, and that the squadron would shortly be moving to Bapaume, an aerodrome closer to Cambrai. In the meantime, for reasons of security, everyone would be confined to camp.

Just after dawn on the following day, the major once again summoned his flight commanders and announced that the attack had commenced along a six mile front. Led by the entire British Tank Corps,[111] the plan was for them to clear a way through the fortifications of the Hindenburg Line, so that the cavalry could break through, encircle the town from the south and join forces with the infantry troops advancing at Bourlon Wood. The major confirmed that two divisions of cavalry would be involved in the early stages of the battle and that Number 6 would be called upon to assist them once they had broken through the German lines. It was only a matter of time.

It was starting to get light when the briefing ended. Once outside, Captain George Knight gathered the men of his flight inside one of the empty hangars. Asking for an empty ammunition box to be brought to him, he climbed on top of it so that they could all hear him.

"Right men, listen to me. Ours will be the first machines in the squadron to be used in this action and we'll be working closely with the cavalry of second division. It'll be dangerous work as we'll be forced to fly close to the ground, well within the range of small arms fire and beneath the trajectory of some of our guns."

"So what's new, sir?" shouted Arnold, who was standing at the back of the group.

"To answer your question, Corporal Makepiece, we'll be operating in a new area and flying from an unfamiliar aerodrome. Added to that, there's bad weather forecast for the next few days. If the Hun doesn't get us, we'll be lucky to find our way home."

"Is this to be our home, sir?" asked one of the pilots.

"Now that the attack has begun, I can tell you," the captain replied. "Our new base will be at Bapaume. I can't tell you much about it as I've yet to go there myself, but it is closer to the new battle front."

"Not another move," groaned Arnold. "I've only just unpacked."

The captain held up his hand for silence.

"Listen chaps. Our weather experts have told us to expect strong westerly winds over the next few days, maybe even some snow. This will make it all the more difficult on the return journey."[112]

There were a few murmurs and the captain raised his hand again.

"Look, I'm not trying to alarm you. I just want you all to be especially careful over the next few days. I should also warn you that a record number of squadrons will be taking part in this offensive, so there'll be literally dozens of our machines[113] flying around in a small area."

"What will the targets be, sir?" asked one of the observers.

"I can't be specific at the moment, but for those of you who don't already know, the Hindenburg Line is one of the best constructed and best defended enemy positions on the Western Front. The machine guns are hidden in concrete fortifications and will be difficult to spot from the air. They were shelled and bombed earlier this morning, but we don't yet know how effective that was."

The captain paused to take breath and waited for his words to sink in.

"That's all I need to say at this point, men. I'll talk to you again after I receive the next progress report from the major. In the meantime, I suggest that you inspect your machines and make sure they're ready to fly at a moment's notice. Any other questions?"

There was silence for a few seconds before the men started to talk amongst themselves. One of the officers raised his hand to catch the captain's attention.

"What will we be carrying, sir, and will the whole flight be flying at the same time?"

"We'll leave here with full tanks and a normal supply of ammunition for the Lewis and Vickers guns. No bombs to be loaded here. Corporal Makepiece will be responsible for the wireless installations until Corporal Johnstone is fit enough to rejoin us. Be very careful when you take off, as none of us has taken off from here with a full load. I don't want any of you ending up in the wood."

The captain noticed that some of the more seasoned pilots smiled wryly at his last comment and he remembered past summer months at Abeele when they had been forced to take off in still, hot air; the worst combination when trying to coax a heavy aircraft off the ground in the shortest possible distance.

"The short answer to your second question, Lieutenant McCreary, is 'Yes'. When we receive the call, I will lead the whole flight, including the spare machine, on the short hop to Bapaume. Six of you will land there, top up with petrol and the armourers there will arm you with Hales bombs. I'll fly on with the other two machines to the battlefront south of Cambrai. The plan is that we'll patrol our allotted section for two hours to see what the form is before being relieved by the next group of three machines just this side of the lines. We'll then return to Bapaume after three hours in the air, or earlier if any of us runs into difficulty."

The noise of an aircraft taking off directly opposite the open hangar forced the captain to pause yet again.

"If we do it this way, we can keep three aircraft over the battle area in rotation for the whole of the day. The same goes for the other flights when they're called. Initially, you'll be flying a maximum of two sorties each day, as we'll only be wanted during daylight hours."

"Will the crews be allotted the same time every day, sir, or will we be rotated like we were at Abeele, sir?"

"That's a good question, McCreary. I haven't decided that yet, but I'll be talking to each of you before I put together a flying roster. One thing I can confirm though is that observers will be taken as we're not planning to use any heavy bombs."

"That's a relief, sir," Frank McCreary added. "I thought we might have been put out of a job."

"Obviously any schedule will depend upon our casualty rate," the captain continued. "But it will be fair to everyone. There's not much more I can tell you at this point. Just don't get too comfortable where you are as things will be very different at Bapaume. That's all for now."

George Knight touched his cap with his cane before stepping down from the box. He strode out of the hangar in the direction of the officers' mess, leaving the men of his flight to return to the task of readying the aircraft for battle.

Much to the surprise of everyone, Number 6 squadron was not called into action that day. Nor was it called the following day, when bad weather put a stop to almost all of the flying in the region. The men became more and more restless as they were still confined to camp. On the Friday morning, Major James ordered the whole squadron to convene inside an unused hangar.

"Good morning, men, I wanted to speak to you all at the same time as I have some important news that will affect us all."

The major waited whilst the men at the back moved closer.

"As you know, the Allies launched a surprise attack three days ago with an unprecedented level of involvement by the Royal Flying Corps. Our forces have already made significant inroads into enemy territory and it was planned for us to support the cavalry, once they too had broken through the enemy lines."

He paused once again for the men to fully absorb what he was saying.

"Though I'm not at liberty to provide you with any details at the moment, I can tell you that the cavalry has so far been unable to capitalise on the advances made by the tanks and infantry. As a result, there will be a slight delay in our involvement."

"How long will that be, sir?" asked one of the pilots.

"I am in constant communication with the GOC Cavalry Corps and until such time as we are called into action, we shall remain here on standby. Effective immediately, you will no longer be confined to camp."

A cheer broke out from a group of mechanics who were standing at the back of the crowd.

"Mind you, it goes without saying that I expect you all to behave in a responsible manner and be ready to move to Bapaume at short notice and with a minimum of fuss. Thank you for your attention."

The major turned to his three flight commanders who had been standing by his side whilst he addressed the men.

"Come with me to my office. There have been further developments which I'd like to discuss with you in private."

After the meeting, with no flights scheduled for the rest of the day, George Knight sought permission from the major to drive back to Abeele. He wanted to look for wireless equipment that had been mislaid during the squadron's move, but he also knew the trip would provide him with an opportunity to visit the injured wireless mechanic of his flight.

After a meagre lunch in an almost empty officers' mess, George went to find the major's car. Having checked that it was full of petrol, he climbed into the driver's seat. Leaning across, he placed a parcel on the floor, right under the dashboard. With the assistance of one of the drivers from the pool, he started the car and drove out of the aerodrome, heading north in the direction of St Omer.

Four hours later, when he reached Abeele, George was at first surprised to find that there was no room on the service road for him to park the car. Then, remembering that another squadron had already taken the place of Number 6, he turned the car around. Finding a space in the entrance to the farmhouse where once he had quarters, he parked the car under the trees between two tenders and walked down to the main entrance of the aerodrome. George chatted briefly with the soldier on duty before making his way to the major's office. Knocking on the outer door, he opened it and stepped inside. The adjutant of Number 10 squadron was sitting behind the desk, talking to a lieutenant whom George thought he recognised.

"Excuse me, sir," George interrupted, addressing the adjutant, "I'm Captain Knight from Number 6. I'm here to visit a patient in the hospital, as I mentioned on the telephone this morning."

"Ah yes, Captain. We've been expecting you. Everything is ready."

The adjutant reached up and took down a small wooden object from the shelf behind his desk.

"Thank you, sir. It's still hard to believe, isn't it?"

"I've not heard of a similar occurrence in all my time in the service. He's certainly a lucky man in my book."

"I'll go and see him now, if that's all right with you, sir. Would you pass on my thanks to the men who were responsible for this?"

"Certainly. Come back when you've finished and I'll organise a bed for you. It's far too late for you to be driving back to Amiens tonight."

"You're most kind. Now, if you'll excuse me, sir."

George Knight saluted the adjutant and walked to the door.

"Do you mind if I come along, sir?"

"By all means, Lieutenant. Lead on. You'd remember the way, I'm sure?"

"Yes, Captain."

The two officers left the building. When they reached the hospital, George Knight went ahead and walked down the aisle between the rows of empty beds. The familiar creaking of the floorboards reminded him of the many times he had been there, talking to wounded aircrew and giving special words of encouragement to those who were unlikely to recover from their injuries. He had also been there as a patient on more than one occasion.

Only the bed furthest from the door was occupied and George could see that the heavily bandaged patient was sitting up with the aid of several pillows. A medical orderly was sitting on a chair next to the bed, attempting to feed the man by dipping pieces of bread into a bowl of broth and placing them in his mouth.

"I'll be over by the fire if you need me, sir."

"Thanks, Lieutenant. I won't be long."

The orderly looked up at the sound of their footsteps and stopped what he was doing. Placing the bowl on the floor he rose to his feet and saluted.

"Sorry, sir. I didn't see you coming. This is the first real food Corporal Johnstone's had since the accident eleven days ago and he's still very weak. Be careful that you don't tire him, if you don't mind me saying, sir."

"That's fine, Corporal. I'll take it gently. I've brought him something from the squadron and also a parcel that arrived for him at Bertangles yesterday. I thought it might buck his spirits up if I came here in person."

"In that case, sir, I'll leave you to it. Just make sure that you talk slowly. His eyesight and hearing are not quite right yet."

"Thanks, Corporal, I understand. I'll come and find you on my way out."

Fred became aware of voices as he tried to swallow a piece of bread. With his ears still ringing since the accident, he was unable to make out any of the words of the conversation. He narrowed his eyes to try and get a clearer image of the person who was talking with the orderly at the end of his bed, but in the dim light of the hospital ward, anything further than a yard away appeared blurred. All he could be certain of was that the man was an officer. Fred wondered if it was the Medical Officer, whom he had not seen since the previous day when his dressings were changed.

"I'm afraid your face is still very swollen," the doctor had told him. "That's mostly from the broken nose. The swelling will reduce in a couple of days but it'll look colourful until the bruising fades."

"Will I have any permanent scars?" Fred had asked.

"Only from the gash on the back of your head, but your hair will grow over the top of that. You'll have temporary scarring from the cuts on your face but that will fade also. Let me clean them up a bit and then I'll change the dressing on the back of your head. Hold still, this might sting."

The memory of the pain made Fred wince involuntarily. He closed his eyes and lay back on the pillow. As with every time he had tried to concentrate since first waking up after the accident, his head began to throb. He was about to drift off when his thoughts were interrupted by a clear voice.

"Good afternoon, Corporal."

Fred heard the words as if they were uttered from afar.

"And how are you, today? From all accounts I'd say that God has been watching over you."

Fred struggled to raise his head from the pillow so that he could look in the direction of the voice. After straining his eyes, he recognised the face of his flight commander and he raised a hand in greeting.

"Hello, sir. It's good to see someone from the squadron. I was beginning to think that I'd been forgotten."

"Not at all, Johnstone, we wanted to let you get some rest before we bombarded you with information. How are you feeling today?"

"All right, as long as I don't think or move, sir. My vision's a bit blurry and I still can't hear properly, but the MO reckons I'll make a full recovery."

"That's splendid. I don't want to tire you but I've brought you a parcel from home as well as news from the squadron. Do you think you're up to it?"

"Yes sir, I can manage. Just don't ask me too many questions as thinking gives me a headache."

"In that case I'll do most of the talking. I only have a few minutes as I have other business to attend to."

"Thanks for taking the time to visit me sir. If you don't mind, I'll open the parcel after you've told me the news."

George Knight sat down on the visitor's chair and placed the parcel at the foot of the bed.

"First things first," he said, leaning forward so that Fred could see what he was holding. "I have a rather unusual award that I would like to present to you. You may not recognise it at first but it's something that has already made a deep impression on you."

The captain held back a smile.

"Corporal Johnstone, in recognition of your services to the squadron and for your determination in the face of a descending aircraft, with the authority vested in me by Major Archibald William Henry James, commanding officer of Number 6 squadron, Royal Flying Corps, I would like to present you with the Order of the Propeller."

Fred put his hand out to take hold of the smooth wooden object. It was about twelve inches high, made out of laminated mahogany and mounted on a wooden base. He ran a finger along the edge of the polished timber, immediately recognising it as the tip of a propeller.

"Is this the one that hit me?"

"Yes, I have it on authority that it is the very one. There wasn't much left of the RE8 that could be salvaged, but a couple of the boys in 'C' flight thought it would make a fitting memento for you to take home to Blighty. They left it behind when we moved so that it could be presented to you when you were well enough."

"Thank you very much, sir, I really appreciate the gesture. It will look good on top of my piano."

Fred's thinking was still rather hazy and he had not yet realised the implication of the words 'take home to Blighty'.

"The MO has told me I should be able to travel in a week or so. Would you organise the transport for me sir?"

George Knight leant forward and placed his hand on Fred's shoulder.

"That won't be necessary. You probably won't be aware that our move to Bertangles was for us to take part in a new offensive. Well, a lot has happened since then and the situation has changed. I won't bore you with the details, though no doubt someone here can fill you in when you're feeling better."

"I wondered why everything seemed to be 'hush hush' whenever I tried to ask questions."

"To cut a long story short, the major announced this morning that the future of the squadron is under scrutiny. There's even been some talk about us becoming an instructional squadron."

"Oh my Lord," was the best that Fred could manage.

"This is strictly between you and me," the captain continued. "I'd say that what I've just told you will in fact happen. And if it does, it'll come into effect before Christmas. It will be quite a change from what we're used to doing."

"Will anyone be sent to another squadron?"

"I'm afraid so. We'll be obliged to reduce the number of aircraft and send the observers away."

Fred frowned when he heard the news about the observers, wondering what impact it would have on Jock. His expression changed to one of alarm when he considered his own future.

"How will this affect me, sir?" Fred's head was buzzing as he tried to think. "Will they still need me to work on the wireless sets?"

"Easy, Johnstone, no cause for alarm. I've talked to the major and he's recommended you be shipped back to England to recuperate. Once you're fully recovered, you'll be transferred out of the squadron to a new Wireless School at South Farnborough.[114] Your operational experience will be invaluable in the training of new wireless operators. I doubt you'll ever make sergeant, I'm afraid, but it'll mean you'll be going home to Blighty for good. What do you say to that, eh?"

Fred was stunned by the news and it took him a few moments to reply.

"Thank you, sir. I've been feeling pretty glum lately but this has certainly cheered me up. I can't wait to write home with the news."

"It could well be the last letter you write from here, Corporal.

Anyway, I'm glad it's all worked out well for you. On behalf of the squadron, I'd like to wish you luck and thank you for all that you've done, both on and off the aerodrome. You've been a good champion for the Corps in all your dealings with the Belgians. That's probably why the major's taken the trouble to arrange this new appointment for you."

George Knight stood up, bent forward and shook Fred's hand.

"And now I must leave. I have a war to fight as they say."

The captain picked up his stick and touched the peak of his cap with it in a final salute. He strode out of the hospital, nodding briefly to the lieutenant who was still standing by the fire.

The meeting with his flight commander had left Fred exhausted. All he wanted to do was close his eyes and sleep, but he was intrigued to find out what Ethel had sent him. He looked again at the wooden trophy before putting it down and reaching forward to pull the small parcel up from the end of the bed, unable to imagine what it contained. Was it chocolate, Woodbines or something warm to wear? Food and clothing had been in very short supply over the past few months and most of his letters to Ethel contained requests for such basic necessities. Just as he was about to tear off the brown paper covering, Fred heard a noise and looked up. The lieutenant who had been warming himself at the stove had approached unbeknown to him and was now standing at the foot of his bed.

"Didn't they teach you to stand to attention when in the presence of an officer?"

The voice sounded vaguely familiar and the uniform reminded Fred of Charles Hickie. He wondered if he was imagining things.

"Sorry, sir, I didn't notice you standing there. I've had a bit of an accident and my vision is not that good at the moment."

"Feeble excuse, Corporal Johnstone. Or may I call you Fred."

A smile appeared on Fred's face.

"Dexter, you old rascal. What are you doing here?"

"Hello, Fred, old man. I was passing by on my way to St Omer and thought I'd drop in on the old squadron. It never crossed my mind that Number 6 would ever leave Abeele."

"It all happened very quickly and I've missed out on all the gossip. How did you know I was in hospital?"

"I bumped into Captain Knight by chance. He came into the adjutant's office just as I was finding out what had happened to the squadron. He told me all about the accident on the way over here. You're quite famous you know."

"I've been stuck here for days with no-one to talk to. I've no idea what's going on."

"Well, you won't recognise the place when you're up and about. Number 10's filled our hangars with 'Big Acks'."

"What are they when they're at home?"

"Armstrong Whitworths, the FK8. Similar to the RE8, but much larger.[115]

"I thought the machines sounded different, but I put that down to the problem I've been having with my hearing."

"I'm glad to see you're still yourself, Fred. When they told me what had happened, I wasn't sure what to expect."

"The MO reckons I'll be as right as rain in a few days and that I won't have any permanent visible scarring."

Fred reached forward and picked up the parcel that Ethel had sent him.

"I might need a hand, Dexter. Be a chum would you and undo the knots? I can't see too well close up."

Fred passed the parcel to Dexter, who carefully removed the string before handing the package back to him. With his head still aching from the earlier conversation, Fred tore off the brown paper and examined the contents; a single page letter wrapped around a pair of hand knitted socks. In removing the letter he thought he felt a lump inside one of the socks, but he put them to one side, anxious to see what Ethel had written. Though he could not read the words, he recognised the handwriting as that of the woman he had met when he was only eighteen, but had known at their first meeting he would one day marry.

"I'm sorry to ask you to do this, Dexter, but would you read it for me? You can stop if you come across anything too personal."

"Anything for you, my old watchmaking friend. I'll even take the socks if you don't want them!"

Fred passed the letter across to Dexter, who moved closer before starting to read.

"Dearest Fred," Dexter read in a clear slow voice, in an attempt to hide his embarrassment. He stopped for a moment, cleared his throat and started again.

Dearest Fred,

I have been thinking about our situation since receiving your last letter and have come to a decision. I know you have tried to understand my reticence to us being engaged, especially as the war shows no sign of ending and you are about to move to another aerodrome - with more unknown dangers. Who knows when I will be able to see you again? I have to admit that the difference in our ages has troubled me more than I have intimated in the past and I suppose it is something I will just have to put behind me. The other day I took out one of your old letters. Though I know you could not be specific (the censors would not have let it through had you been) it is evident that your squadron has had a difficult time of it recently and I feel I have been rather selfish over the whole matter. I would like to make amends by accepting your proposal of marriage, if that is agreeable with you. As a token of my love I am sending you something which I hope you will carry always and one day wear, God willing. You will see that it is inscribed with the letters GEE to remind you of your responsibilities and priorities in life – God, England and Ethel. Remember what you told me in the Lyons Corner House? Though I cannot foretell the future, I look forward with all my heart to being married and maybe starting a family when these troubled times are behind us.

As Ever,
Your loving Starlight.

With a look of relief, Dexter handed the letter back to Fred.
"Why 'Starlight'?"
"It goes back to the night Ethel and I said goodbye in London."
It was Fred's turn to look embarrassed.
"We were standing in the street looking up at the stars and I stupidly told her that she was my starlight. The nickname stuck, though it's only between us of course."

"I think I would have kept quiet about it too, Fred. Not the sort of thing you'd mention to the lads is it?"

"Don't you dare tell anyone, either. Anyway, let's have a look at what Ethel sent me. Apart from the colourful socks, that is."

When Fred picked up the socks, a small jewellery box fell out of one of them. He opened the box and removed the gold ring that was inside. Holding the ring up to the light and squinting, he could just make out the letters 'G', 'E' and 'E', engraved on the inside surface of the band.

"For God, England and Ethel," he murmured. "Fancy that."

He tried the ring on. It fitted perfectly.

"Just look at this, Dexter," Fred said, holding up his hand so that his friend could see the ring. "I get to hear that I'm going home for good and Ethel agrees to marry me, all on the same day."

"That's really good news, Fred. And did you know that Jock's been called back to Blighty for pilot training?"

"No, the captain told me that the observers were being sent away, but I've had other things on my mind."

"Like an aeroplane?"

Fred grimaced in pain.

"Oh, don't make me laugh!"

"Sorry Fred, I forgot about the bandages."

"Being an officer hasn't changed you one bit, Dexter, has it?"

"Did you expect it to?"

"I suppose not. Anyway, good for Jock, I say."

"It looks like we've each got what we wanted. But your news is the most unexpected."

"It certainly is," Fred replied. "One for the wireless watchmakers, I'd say."

Epilogue

FRED, MY GRANDFATHER, fully recovered from his injuries and married his sweetheart Ethel in January 1918. As promised, he was transferred out of the squadron and returned to England to work at the No 1 (T) Wireless School, where he remained until he was demobbed in January 1919.

Ernie Dexter, as a qualified wireless equipment officer, left the Western Front in mid 1918 and spent some months in Canada, where he was involved in the training of technical officers in the fledgling Canadian Air Force. The two old friends met unexpectedly later that year when Dexter returned to England to attend a wireless refresher course.

Jock's dream was realised when he was ordered back to England in January 1918 to undertake pilot training, eventually adding the pilot's brevets to his observer's wing. He returned to the Western Front as a sergeant pilot for Number 29 squadron, at that time based at St Omer and flying SE5a scouts. Sadly, within a matter of weeks, Jock was shot down over enemy territory during an aerial combat and reported as 'Missing in Action', presumed dead. His body was never recovered.

Number 6 squadron returned to action on the Western Front in March 1918 and remained there until the end of the Great War, still flying the RE8. From its formation in January 1914, the squadron was in continuous service until it was disbanded on 31st May 2007, a record unequalled by any other air force squadron in the world. In the ninety three years of unbroken service, Number 6 squadron operated from ninety one bases, with more time spent overseas than in the United

Kingdom. It is planned that the squadron will reform in 2010, flying Typhoons.

After leaving the Royal Air Force[116], Fred returned to his old job at Botley and Lewis, qualifying in time as a master jeweller and specialising in antique silverware. He never returned to Belgium and worked at the same company for more than forty years, holding the position of manager until his retirement. Ethel gave birth to their only child Denise (my mother) in June 1919. True to the inscription on his wedding ring, Fred never missed going to church with his family and he played the organ until he died in 1969 at the age of seventy seven. Ethel, though twelve years his senior, outlived Fred by four years, dying in 1973 at the grand old age of ninety two. Denise married in 1941 and gave birth to two girls and a boy (myself) over the next four years, all of whom grew up in England before marrying and raising their own families. With three of Fred's great grandchildren also marrying and producing offspring, his descendants now have links to five continents.

Steve Johnson, Hunter Valley, Australia
February 2009

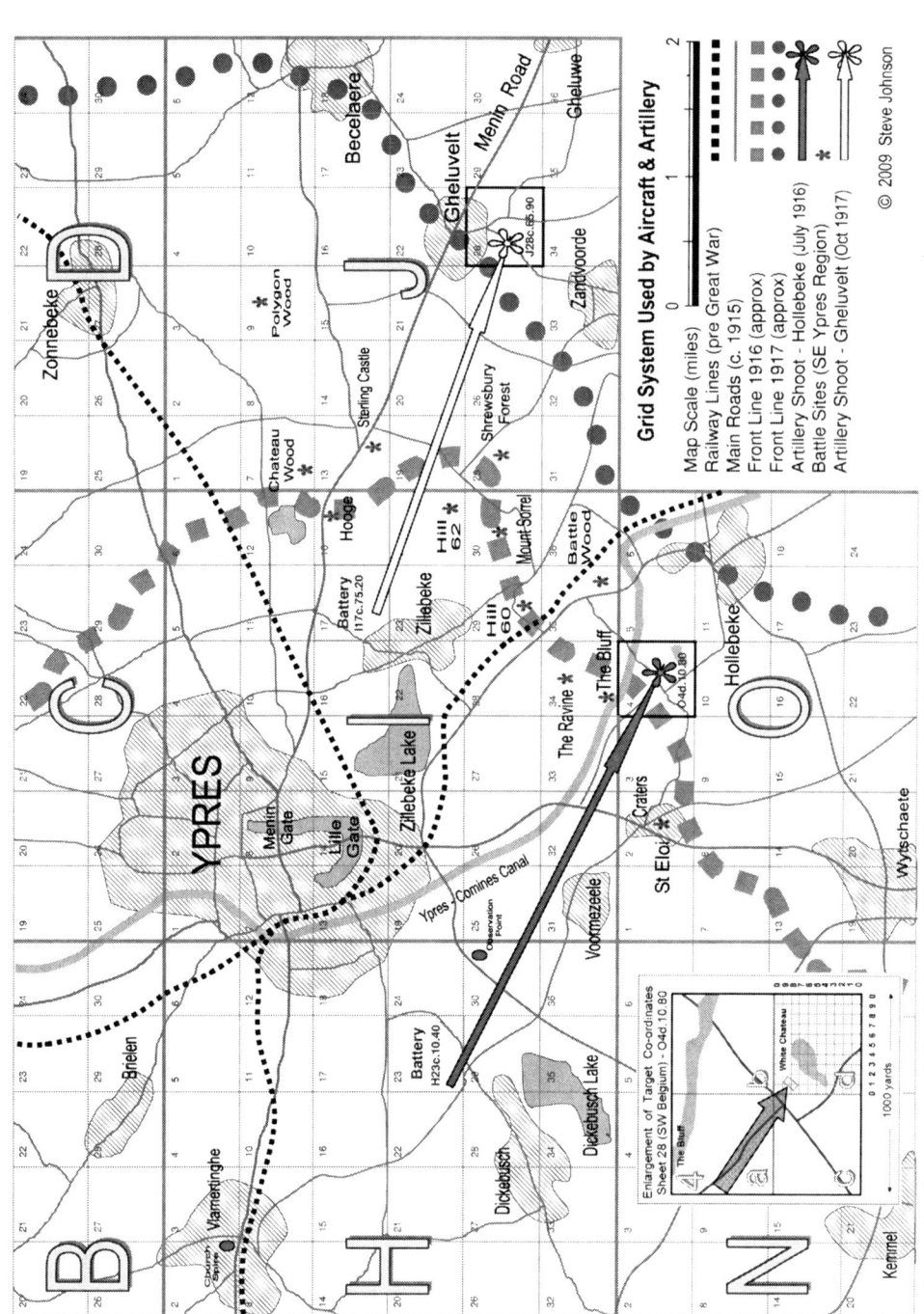

Endnotes

1   'Harry Tate' was a rhyming slang nickname for the RE8 two seater reconnaissance aircraft, built by the Royal Aircraft Factory as a replacement for the ageing BE2 aircraft (also designed and manufactured by the Royal Aircraft Factory). Harry Tate was a contemporary music hall performer of WW1, who is acknowledged as being the creator of the expressions "How's your father" and ". . . , I <u>don't</u> think."

2   Casualty Clearing Station. These were set up within easy reach of the front line for the speedy treatment of casualties. Each Casualty Clearing Station had full hospital operating facilities, something not often available at a front-line aerodrome.

3   The complex at Farnborough incorporated what was at the time (October 1915) the only large RFC training school and aircraft repair centre. The Royal Aircraft Factory was a large factory where military aircraft and aircraft engines had been designed, built and tested since 1908, when the establishment was founded by the Ministry of Defence as the HM Balloon Factory. As soon as aircraft were ready to be sent to the Western Front, they were flown by ferry pilots to St Omer in France. On one side of the aerodrome was an Aircraft Park whose main purpose was to repair damaged aircraft and carry out aircraft maintenance.

4   At the time, Fred was not to know that if he had waited another month before enlisting he would have received extensive training at the newly formed 1st School of Wireless, set up in a building on the Brooklands aerodrome. Following that period of training, he would have been posted to one of the Reserve Aeroplane squadrons in England and it would have been several months before he would have been posted to a front-line squadron in France. As it was, he was sent to France less than a month after enlisting in the Royal Flying Corps.

5   These included his apprenticeship papers from Akroyds the Jewellers in Basingstoke and a Diploma from the Goldsmiths College in London, now part of London University.

6   The Regent Street Polytechnic also organised the opening and closing ceremonies for the 1908 Olympic Games as well as the marathon race, the latter causing widespread controversy at the time when the distance of the race was increased by just over a mile so that the English Royal Family could watch the start in comfort from Windsor Castle.

7   By late 1915 many of the horse-drawn Omnibuses were motorised as the demand for horses increased on the Western Front. However, in spite of the increased production of motorised buses, there was still a shortage of buses in London as many were sent to France to be used for transporting troops to and from the front.

8   One of the main operators of London buses at the time of the Great War was the **L**ondon **G**eneral **O**mnibus **C**ompany and their buses were given the nickname of 'Generals'.

9   Piccadilly Circus was created in 1819 to connect Regent's Park with Carlton House at the junction of Piccadilly and the (then) newly constructed Regent Street.

10   The Shaftesbury Monument was erected in 1893 as a memorial to the philanthropist Anthony Ashley Cooper, the seventh Earl of Shaftesbury. It is commonly referred to these days as the statue of Eros (also the Angel of Christian Charity).

11   The construction of Shaftesbury Avenue was completed in 1886 and the road ran from Piccadilly Circus to New Oxford Street.

12   Gladys was the nickname for a J Lyons & Co waitress at the time of WW1. Later, in 1926, they became known as Nippies.

13   'A Little Bit of Fluff' turned out to be hugely successful, with a total of 1,241 performances in London alone, before the production moved to America in 1916. It was even made into a film in 1919.

14   At the time Fred was being trained, Aircraft Repair Depots had yet to be established in France and it was the policy of the Royal Flying Corps to repair aircraft 'in the field' wherever possible. This meant that in 1915, the inclusion of at least one workshop lorry was an operational necessity for every squadron.

15   St Omer aerodrome was in 1915 the largest British airfield on the Western Front. It had been established one year earlier at the start of the war and had expanded quickly since that time, though none of the buildings were permanent erections. By the time Fred arrived in November 1915, not only was St Omer the home to the squadron of the Royal Flying Corps headquarters, it also had an Aircraft Park where almost everything used by the Royal Flying Corps that couldn't be repaired at the aerodromes was mended before being sent back to the squadron. The stores section alone held a huge inventory, from the smallest of aerodrome tools to complete aircraft. Attached to the Aircraft Park was the Pilots Pool. This acted as a temporary base for

pilots who were awaiting a posting to a squadron. It also provided a permanent pool of regular pilots who were employed to carry out flight tests, occasional training as well as the ferrying of new and repaired aircraft to the various allied aerodromes on the Western Front. It was to St Omer that the majority of newly formed squadrons were flown and from there they were sent to their operational aerodromes in Belgium and France. Though by the end of 1915 the turnaround of squadrons was high, St Omer nevertheless always managed to maintain at least one operational squadron on its airfield.

16   Major William John Charles Kennedy Cochran-Patrick MC with Bar and DSO, finished the war as the commanding officer of Number 60 squadron. He was the highest scoring ace in Number 23 squadron as well as the highest scoring ace in any air force flying Spads, finishing with a total of twenty one victories. He died in a flying accident in South Africa in 1933 at the age of thirty seven.

17   The top speed of 72 mph was achievable in level flight at 6,500 feet.

18   The Strange Mount was so named after Lt Col Louis Strange, DSO, OBE, MC, DFC who, as a lieutenant in Number 5 squadron as far back as 1914, devised various ways in which guns could be strategically mounted on to aircraft, the most commonly used device being a pole mount. Incidentally, Lieutenant Strange was promoted to captain and posted to Number 6 squadron as a flight commander in May 1915.

19   The Royal Aircraft Factory FE2 (Farman Experimental No 2), or 'Fee' as it was more commonly referred to by its crews, was a two seater 'pusher' engine fighter biplane. Though designed before the war, it was not introduced into service until the latter part of 1915 when five aircraft were delivered to Number 6 squadron in Abeele. The FE2 proved more than a match for the Fokker Eindecker and it was used to protect reconnaissance aircraft like the BE2 from being attacked by enemy scouts. It could carry three Lewis machine guns which were able to be fired in any direction except directly to the rear of the aircraft, where the engine and propeller were mounted. It was most successful when fighting with other FE2s in a circular formation, each one protecting the aircraft in front.

20   Though totally destroyed as a result of German shelling, Cloth Hall was rebuilt after the Great War, using the original plans to ensure that the new building was an exact replica of the old one. The original building took 100 years to complete and the reconstruction lasted from 1933 to 1967.

21   Several of the bell tents (used for officer accommodation) were erected on what is now the Abeele War Cemetery. To the left of the pathway that leads from the road to the cemetery, back in 1915 there stood three aeroplane hangars. Most of the field boundaries and landmarks that were present in 1915 are still discernable from the air, though the large pond has all but disappeared and the farm has grown in the number of its buildings. Obviously, the pathways and entrances used by the Royal

Flying Corps during the Great War are no longer there and there are no permanent reminders of any of the aerodrome structures.

22   Captain Lanoe Hawker (later promoted to major when he was given the command of Number 24 squadron, flying DH2 scouts) left Number 6 squadron in September 1915, having already been credited with seven victories whilst flying his Bristol Scout and a FE2a. He was the first British pilot to achieve 'Ace' status and was killed in a dogfight with Manfred von Richthofen on 23rd November 1916, the Red Baron's 11th victim.

23   It wasn't until the Allies withdrew from Gallipoli at the end of December 1915 that soldiers of the AIF (Australian Imperial Force) started to appear on the Western Front, the first troops arriving in March 1916.

24   Initially, only five aircraft (comprising three Maurice Farman and two Caudron machines) made up the Australian Half-Flight of the Australian Flying Corps, going to war on the 20th April 1915 in Mesopotamia (now Iraq). The first complete squadron to be formed was Number 1 squadron in early 1916. It flew BE2c two-seater aircraft and was also employed in the Middle East. There were three squadrons formed by the Australian Flying Corps to take part in the action on the Western Front. Number 3 squadron was formed in September 1917 and flew the two-seater RE8. Number 2 squadron was formed two weeks later and flew the DH5 fighter until December 1917 when it was re-equipped with SE5a fighters. Number 4 squadron was formed in December 1917 and was equipped with Sopwith Camel fighters, later changing to Sopwith Snipe fighters.

25   The Vickers FB5 (Fighter Biplane No 5), or 'Gunbus' as it was more commonly referred to by its crews, was a two-seater 'pusher' engine biplane armed with a single Lewis machine gun that was mounted in the front cockpit. The aircraft entered service in February 1915 with Number 5 squadron and was the first British aeroplane designed specifically for air to air combat. However, in less than a year, its performance was overtaken by the newer tractor-engine scout aircraft and it was eventually relegated to reconnaissance duties.

26   When Geoffrey de Havilland formed his own company in 1920 all of his earlier designs that were manufactured by AMC (the Aircraft Manufacturing Company) were retrospectively given the prefix of 'Airco' – e.g Airco DH2.

27   The DH2 prototype first flew in June 1915 and was sent to Number 5 squadron the following month for evaluation. Within three weeks however it was shot down and captured by the Germans and the momentum was lost in the development of this type of aircraft. The FE8 first flew in October 1915 and though a successful design, it was initially plagued with production problems.

28   The Blip switch, fastened to the top of the control stick (more commonly known these days as a joy stick), was a means by which a pilot could reduce the revolutions of the engine, and hence the thrust produced by the propeller. By pressing down on

the spring-loaded switch, the ignition would be momentarily cut off, preventing the engine from firing until the switch was released.

29   The order for 'No combat flying' was given as the original prototype of the DH2, sent to Number 5 squadron six months earlier in July 1915 for evaluation purposes, was flown by Captain Maxwell Pike on several operations. The aircraft was brought down and captured intact by the Germans on the 9th August 1915, with Captain Pike injured, later dying of his wounds. The loss of the prototype DH2 delayed the roll-out of the aircraft into the RFC squadrons.

30   Captain 'Freddie' Powell MC left Number 5 squadron in March 1916 as arguably its best fighter pilot, to join Major Robert Loraine (his former flight commander at Number 5) in the newly-formed Number 40 squadron in the role of senior flight commander, flying FE8 scouts. During his stay at Number 5 squadron, Captain Powell scored six confirmed victories (four whilst flying 'his' FE8) and nine unconfirmed victories. He served as chief fighting instructor with Northern Groups in 1917 before being promoted to major and commanding Number 41 squadron, flying SE5a scouts. He was shot down in early 1918 and held by the Germans as prisoner of war until December 1918. He died in 1987 at the age of ninety one.

31   Major Robert Loraine MC was a prominent stage actor (both before and after the Great War) and pre-war aviator. In 1910 he became the first man to fly across the Irish Sea and also in the same year was the first pilot to transmit a wireless signal for a distance greater than one mile. He left Number 5 squadron in February 1916 and was sent back to England to train on the FE8, returning to the Western Front six months later as the commanding officer of Number 40, a squadron flying FE8 scouts.

32   2nd Lieutenant Archibald William Henry James MC left Number 5 squadron in March 1916 but returned to Abeele in June 1917 as major in command of Number 6 squadron. He continued to serve with the RAF until 1926, rising to the rank of Wing Commander and later receiving a knighthood. He became a Member of Parliament at his second attempt in 1931 and held his seat until 1945. During his time in Parliament he also held several governmental positions. He died in 1980 at the age of eighty seven.

33   Every effort was made to repair damaged aircraft on the aerodrome itself, where a large number of spares were stored and the mechanics were skilled in all aspects of aircraft maintenance. If the damage was deemed to be too great however, the pieces would be transported by lorry to the Number 1 Aircraft Depot at St Omer where the aircraft would be rebuilt or struck off charge.

34   Talbot House (or 'Toc H' as it became more commonly known using signalling phonetics) was established in December 1915 by the Reverend Thomas Clayton as a place where soldiers of any rank could take time out from the war and seek fellowship with others or find a few moments of sanctuary. It is from there that the

Toc H movement grew after the Great War, with hundreds of Talbot Centres later being opened in England and several other countries. The original Talbot House in Poperinghe is now a museum that also provides accommodation.

35   The tracks in the forest were even given London road names on the maps at the time of the Great War.

36   'A la Poupée' or 'The Doll' was a famous café during the Great War, providing music and food to thousands of officers ('other ranks' were not permitted to enter). Towards the end of WW1 it became more commonly known as 'Ginger's', after the name of the owner's youngest daughter who was renowned for her beauty. It was also one of the few places in Poperinghe where liquor was obtainable. It remained popular until the mid nineteen thirties but today the building is occupied by a baker / confectionery shop under the name of 'De Ranke'. On a personal note, I can thoroughly recommend the coffee and the liquor chocolates.

37   'Petit Paris' was the red light area of Poperinghe. All prostitutes were required to undergo regular medical examination to ensure that they were free from venereal disease.

38   Since the Great War, most of the French street names in Poperinghe have been changed to Belgian names. For example, 'Rue de l'Hopital' is now called 'Gasthuisstraat'.

39   The Air Military Mark V was a pocket watch commonly carried by pilots when they flew on missions, having a black face with white numerals. It has been suggested that the pilots in the Royal Flying Corps started the trend for men to wear wrist watches, which up until the time of the Great War was a practice only adopted by women.

40   Many watchmaking companies of the time of the Great War considered that the additional two jewels on the centre wheel were unnecessary as the centre wheel moved very slowly compared to other wheels in the watch's mechanism and was therefore less subject to wear.

41   The top floor of Talbot House had been used for drying hops prior to the start of the Great War.

42   The earliest airborne wireless transmitters were so bulky and heavy that they took up most of the space in the observer's cockpit and the pilot was required to both fly the aircraft and transmit wireless messages. However, from the latter part of 1915, the lighter Stirling wireless sets which had superseded the Rouzet sets made it possible to install wireless equipment in the observer's cockpit yet still provide enough room and lifting capacity for both an observer and a Lewis machine gun. Resulting from this development, new observers were required to undergo training in the use of wireless and the sending and receiving of Morse code. However, the role of sending

wireless messages was not always the realm of the observer and varied from squadron to squadron.

43   In the early months of 1916 the codes used by the various Corps squadrons varied from squadron to squadron and were constantly being developed and fine-tuned. The codes listed below were those used by Number 6 squadron at that time.

A	Stand by	KQ	Are you ready to fire?	QM	Mostly left
AR	Air	L	Lyddite	R	Right
B	Are you receiving signals?	M	Mostly	RD	Ground signals seen
BF	Battery fire	MQ	Stop firing - Wait	RUF	Are you firing?
CI	Going Home	N	Guns in position at	S	Short
F	Far	NF	Guns firing at	SW	Switch
G	Fire	NT	Guns not firing at	T	General answer
GF	Fire for effect	O	Over	VO	Salvo
GO	Continue firing in own time	OK	Target range	W	Wash out
GZ	Graze	P	Percussion	X	Change to
J	Just	Q	Left	Z	Time shrapnel

44   A wavelength of 180 metres represents a frequency of approximately 4,760 Hz.

45   As well as fine-tuning the wavelength, the wireless operator on the ground would decrease the aerial coupling to the lowest acceptable level for hearing the aircraft's signals whilst at the same time reducing the background radio interference to a minimum. This procedure, known as 'netting', was carried to ensure that the operator picked up the transmissions from the correct aeroplane. When several wireless aircraft flew in the same area at the same time, it was very easy for messages to get scrambled due to the close proximity of simultaneous transmissions.

46   The whole manoeuvre for guiding artillery on to a target required the pilot to fly in repeated patterns of a flattened 'figure of eight', as viewed with the battery to the left and the target to the right. This enabled the observer to transmit whilst pointing directly towards the battery – providing the strongest signal for the operator on the ground – and also minimised the risk of the aircraft being struck by a friendly artillery shell. The disadvantage in this was that the German anti-aircraft gunners could easily predict the path the aircraft would take.

47   As well as being able to report the direction (or angle) of the shell impact from the intended target by means of sending the appropriate clock hour number (viz. 1 to 12), the distance from the target was also transmitted, as determined by a code representing one of eight concentric circles: Y – 0 to 10 yards, Z – 11 to 25 yards, A – 26 to 50 yards, B – 51 to 100 yards, C – 101 to 200 yards, D – 201 to 300 yards, E – 301 to 400 yards or F – 401 to 500 yards.

48   CI – 'Going Home'

49   The average life of a WW1 pilot in 1916 was less than three weeks, though some died on their first mission whilst others managed to survive the war. It was a similar situation with aircraft. One particular BE2c was built in 1912 and flew with two squadrons before it was sent to Number 6 squadron. Though it had to be rebuilt twice over time, it remained in operation until September 1915 when it was damaged beyond repair, sent back to England and placed in a museum.

50   The allied plan was to straighten the German salient that encroached into the British lines by blowing up mines buried beneath the ground of the artificial mound and attacking with infantry whilst the Germans were caught off guard. The surprise attack began at 4:15 am on Monday 27th March 1916 when six huge mines were detonated, some 30,000 tons of explosives. Four mines were planted beneath the German trenches and two in 'no man's land' to give protection to the advancing infantry. A barrage of allied artillery shells rained down on the German positions one minute before the infantry left the safety of their trenches. The blasts were deafening and were felt by the airmen as they flew towards the battlefield. They were also felt by those on the aerodrome at Abeele, ten miles to the west of St Eloi, and were heard as far away as Folkestone.

51   Number 29 was the second of three squadrons operating on the Western Front to be equipped with the DH2 scout. Number 24 was the first squadron in the Royal Flying Corps to be established with a single type aircraft and also the first to be equipped with DH2s, with twelve aircraft flying out to France on 7th February 1916 under the command of Major Lanoe Hawker, one time flight commander of Number 6 squadron. The third squadron to be equipped with DH2s was Number 32, which arrived in France on 28th May 1916 after losing five aircraft en route from England. It was intended that Number 29 squadron would take part in the St Eloi bombing but on the 25th March, just two days before the attack, misfortune struck the squadron on the flight out from England. Ten aircraft flew into a snow storm and were forced to land, with four machines destroyed. Another aircraft was forced to ditch in the Channel and yet another crashed whilst landing at St Omer. Over the next three weeks in the course of building the squadron up to its full complement, a further fourteen machines were destroyed or seriously damaged and only ten aircraft set out for Abeele aerodrome on the morning of 15th April 1916.

52   The new 'Zone Call' system meant that an aircraft could transmit the location of an enemy position in the form of an open signal which could be picked up and responded to by any of the Allied gun batteries that were in the nominated zone and thus capable of striking the target. This meant that a single aircraft was able to support many batteries at the same time and not just a single battery as had previously been the case on artillery registration missions.

53   'Rag Picker' was a popular song of the day, written by the then 'up and coming' songwriter Irving Berlin.

54   Nineteen year old Lieutenant Henry Segrave attacked a German Aviatik scout on the 1st May 1916, forcing it to land near Gheluvelt. Within weeks he was promoted to captain and flight commander when the squadron was expanded to three flights. He eventually rose to the rank of major and was later knighted in England in 1929 after he became the first person to simultaneously hold the land and water speed records.

55   In the first week of the battle at Mount Sorrel, news came through that the British Secretary of State for War, Lord Kitchener, had died when the armoured cruiser on which he was travelling to Russia on a diplomatic mission had been sunk by a German U-Boat in the North Sea.

56   As a lieutenant in January 1915 Reginald Mills shot down a German aircraft with a hand-held rifle whilst flying his BE2c.

57   Saturday July 1st 1916 was the first day of the Battle of the Somme. The battle would continue for twenty weeks, ending on Saturday November 18th 1916.

58   Over the preceding ten days the final changes had been made to the squadron's line-up. The Bristol Scout, the only fighter left in the squadron, was sent to another squadron and the ageing fleet of BE2c aircraft was augmented with six of the newer BE2d machines.

59   The Wireless and Observers' School was established at Brooklands in the autumn of 1916.

60   Three BE2c aircraft of Number 6 squadron took part in the attack on Cambrai, along with nine BE2s from other squadrons that were based near Amiens. The distance from Abeele to Cambrai was so great that the aircraft had to stop off on the way at Vert Gallant aerodrome in order to take on more fuel and group with the other aircraft. The engine of the BE2c consumed about 5 pints of oil each hour and when flown on long-distance missions it was standard practice for it to be overfilled by as much as 5 pints (total of 30 pints for the RAF type 1a engine). With each of the aircraft carrying two 110 lb bombs they were not able to carry observers on the mission. The station at Cambrai was hit by seven bombs and a train was blown up. Lieutenant Coxe's aircraft was forced down and he died in a German dressing station.

61   The 26 cwt howitzer fired six inch shells and in July 1916 the shells most commonly used each weighed 100 pounds. Using a maximum charge a shell this size could travel up to 11,400 yards.

62   Major Edmund Graves Meredith Cape DSO was mentioned twice in Sir Douglas Haig's despatches and awarded the DSO for the role he played in the Battle of Vimy Ridge in April 1917. By the end of the Great War he held the rank of lieutenant colonel and returned to Canada where he founded the engineering and general contracting company E G M Cape & Co. His company grew from strength

to strength, constructing a wide variety of structures over the next eighty years, including the marble arch for the National War Memorial in Ottawa, the seventeen floor library building at Toronto University and the Artillery Station at Botwood, Newfoundland in 1939, built to protect the harbour and equipped with two 4.7 inch guns that each fired shells weighing 149 pounds.

63 A number 2 charge in six inch howitzer shell yielded a muzzle velocity of nine hundred and fifty feet per second.

64 For a graphical representation of the map gridding system used by the allied armies as well as the 'shoots' referred to in this book, refer to the diagram in this book - **Grid System Used by Aircraft & Artillery**.

65 A total of thirty six BE2 bombers took part in the bombing of the station yards at Courtrai on the evening of 29th July 1916, escorted by ten FE2b fighter/bombers and twelve DH2 scouts. As an indication of the importance of the operation, the number of aircraft that took part represented fourteen percent of the entire Royal Flying Corps at that time.

66 The heavier BE2d took thirty six minutes to reach six and a half thousand feet, twice the time that a fully loaded BE2c would normally take.

67 James Thomas Byford McCudden transferred from the Royal Engineers to the Royal Flying Corps as an air mechanic. He rose through the ranks, eventually reaching the rank of major just before his death in a flying accident in July 1918. He was the most highly decorated pilot (in the British Empire) of the Great War, being awarded the VC, DSO and Bar, MC and Bar, MM and Croix de Guerre. With 57 confirmed victories he was also one of the highest scoring allied aces.

68 The clear celluloid disc was used by observers to gauge the accuracy of a shell's explosion with respect to the coordinates of the intended target. Each disc was marked with a bullseye in the centre, eight concentric rings spreading out from the bullseye and radial lines marking the twelve hours of the clock. The disc was placed on top of a map with the bullseye over the target and the "12 o'clock" line facing due North.

69 The irony of the arrival of Number 41 was that by the time the British had succeeded in getting the FE8 into full production, the Germans had introduced new aircraft which had superior performance.

70 The photographs were taken by the renowned photographer Herbert Ponting, who accompanied Scott on Scott's final expedition.

71 Amazingly, 7 of the 10 men of the Ross Sea Party, who had been stranded on Ross Island since 7th May 1915 when the other 18 men of Shackleton's support expedition were swept out to sea on the Aurora, were found alive by Shackleton when he returned in the Aurora on on 10th January 1917.

72   The Distinguished Conduct Medal (DCM) was awarded to 'Other Ranks' in recognition of gallantry in action, the second highest award next to the Victoria Cross. In the Great War the equivalent medal for commissioned officers was the Distinguished Service Order (DSO)

73   Five months after this action, Lieutenant George Knight MC was promoted to captain and given command of 'C' flight in Number 6 squadron.

74   For some reason the mode of transport was restricted to above ground railway only, as the ticket had printed on it in red wording, 'NOT available on the London Tube Railways'.

75   Samuel Franklin Cody was a pioneer of manned flight and was the first man to fly in the British Isles in October 1908

76   A seemingly trivial incident where the loss of a magneto, belonging to an engine taken from a captured German aeroplane and in transit from the crash site to Abeele, developed into a major incident for Number 6 squadron.

77   Though several engines were used in the Royal Aircraft Factory RE8, the one most commonly installed was the air-cooled Royal Aircraft Factory V-12 engine that produced 150 hp. This was significantly more than the 70 hp air-cooled Renault V-8 engine or the later 90 hp Royal Aircraft Factory engine (based upon the Renault design) that were both used in the BE2.

78   The seventh version of the French single seater biplane scout made by SPAD (original company formed in 1910 but taken over by the aviation pioneer Louis Bleriot in 1914) went into service in many French squadrons during 1916. It could fly at close to 22,000 feet and reach speeds of almost 120 mph. The 'powers that be' in England initially considered the aircraft unreliable and unsafe and it was not until 1917 that this type was introduced into the Royal Flying Corps squadrons. More than 5,500 SPAD VII aircraft were built.

79   It was planned that Number 6 squadron would take part in the British offensive at Arras, following the Germans unexpected withdrawal to the Hindenburg Line.

80   10th May 1917, three days after British ace Albert Ball was killed near Douai.

81   In WW1 Picric Acid was commonly used as an explosive (in shells).

82   Lieutenant C G Brodie with Lieutenant A McKimmie as his observer was flying his RE8 at six thousand feet, directing the six inch howitzers of the 179th Siege on the 23rd May 1917, when he collided with the RE8 of Captain W L Clarke and 2nd Lieutenant H S Diment.

83   In the words of the British commander, General Plumer, at the final briefing to his commanders the night before the attack at Messines: 'Gentlemen, we may not make history tomorrow, but we shall certainly change the geography'.

84   The Third Battle of Ypres, more often referred to as Passchendaele, began on the 31st July 1917 and continued until 10th November 1917 when, due to bad weather, the Allies called off the offensive after the village of Passchendaele was finally taken.

85   Majors Arthur Barrett and Archibald James both transferred to the Royal Flying Corps from the British Army early in the war and both were destined to receive a knighthood, Barratt remaining in the Royal Air Force and eventually reaching the rank of Air Chief Marshall in 1946.

86   At the time of this engagement, Jasta 11 was the highest scoring unit on the Western Front and would within days join Jastas 4, 6 and 10 to form a mobile fighter group called Jagdgeschwader 1, under the leadership of Manfred von Richthofen.

87   The fifth aircraft mentioned by the major as being forced down on the 6th July was indeed that of the 'Red Baron'. In attacking one of the defensive circle of FE2d machines head-on, Manfred von Richthofen was struck in the head by a bullet and forced to crash land. At the time of the crash he had already claimed 57 victories. Though he recovered sufficiently to return to the air a month later and continue to lead Jagdgeschwader 1, he never fully recovered from his head wound. He died in April 1918 when shot by a single bullet and crashing in his Fokker Triplane. At the time of his death he was credited with 80 victories, a feat not bettered by any other pilot in the Great War.

88   As at 8th July 1917, the date at which Major James addressed the men of his squadron, the most successful British pilot in the Great War was Captain Albert Ball who, at the date of his death on 6th May 1917 had already claimed 44 victories. Captains Fred Thayre (pilot) and Francis Cubbon (observer) had claimed 20 and 21 victories respectively, most scored whilst flying together, before both men were killed in action by an anti-aircraft shell whilst flying a FE2d for Number 20 squadron on the 9th June 1917. Also by the 8th July, Canadian pilot Captain Willy Bishop had claimed 31 of his eventual 72 victories, his compatriot Lieutenant Raymond Collishaw 31 of his eventual 60 victories (six enemy aircraft being downed by him on a single day) and Australian pilot Lieutenant Robert Little 27 of his eventual 47 victories. Other British pilots flying at the time who were to later become WW1 aces were Lieutenant Edward McMannock who had already claimed 2 of his eventual 61 victories and Captain James McCudden, who with 5 claimed victories flying as a flight sergeant had recently been promoted to flight commander and would eventually claim 57 victories. Of all these men, only Lieutenant Colonels 'Billy' Bishop and 'Collie' Collishaw and Major William John Charles Kennedy Cochran-Patrick would survive the Great War.

89   This was to be the start of what was later called the Third Battle of Ypres, or simply, Passchendaele.

90   Twenty year old observer 2nd Lieutenant Geoffrey Cholerton Smith died of his wounds on 31st July 1917. Though he had been with Number 6 squadron for less than three months he was already the holder of the Military Cross

91   Twenty year old 2nd Lieutenant Henry Jackson Snowden was severely wounded in the legs and later died in England of his injuries on the 11th August 1917.

92   2nd Lieutenant Harold Quigley transferred to the Royal Flying Corps from the Canadian Rifle Brigade. By the time of the beginning of the Third Battle of Ypres he was an experienced observer, having already been awarded the MM and MO with Bar.

93   In what may have been unique for a pilot serving on the Western Front, on the 9th October 1917 Lieutenant Nicholas Wyndham Wadham was to again experience the misfortune of being struck by a British shell whilst flying on a reconnaissance mission for Number 6 squadron over Hooge. This time he sustained injuries and the damage to his RE8 forced him to crash land. Luckily his observer Lieutenant Tyler was unhurt.

94   The 16th August 1917 was also the day upon which the 'Red Baron' returned to operational flying (after suffering a head injury on the 6th July) and scored his 58th victory against Number 29 squadron whilst flying an Albatros DV single seater scout.

95   The cockpit of an aircraft was often referred to by both pilots and observers as 'the office'.

96   The RE8 of Lieutenants J Madge and W Kember was the 60th victim of the Red Baron, the first aircraft he had shot down whilst flying his new Fokker Triplane Dr1. Incidentally, this particular RE8 was the only one of the Red Baron's claimed victories that operated out of Abeele.

97   The Battle of the Menin Road was the third in eight allied offensives that formed the Third Battle of Ypres, or 'Passchendaele' and lasted six days, from the 20th September to 25th September 1917.

98   The most commonly used British Army trench maps in WW1 had a scale of 1 : 40000 and were used by both pilots and observers as they were small enough to fold and clip on to the cockpit dashboard while still providing sufficient detail for accurate spotting. The maps of Belgium and France were divided into rectangular Sheets, each Sheet being given a number (e.g. Sheet 28 – Ypres) and representing a width of 36,000 yards. Every Sheet was then divided into 24 smaller rectangles or zones, 6,000 yards wide and either 5,000 or 6,000 yards deep (depending upon the particular Sheet) and identified by a letter of the alphabet (A to X). These rectangles were further divided into squares, each of 1,000 yards and numbered 1 to 30 or 1 to 36 depending upon the size of the larger rectangle. Each square was then divided into four quarters, labelled 'a', 'b', 'c', 'd', which in turn could be further divided into 100 squares, the side of each square representing 50 yards. By estimating a position within one of the small squares (ie. number of tenths) it was possible to report a coordinate to an accuracy of 5 yards (e.g. **Sheet 28 J22c.54.67**). For a graphical

example of mapping coordinates refer to the diagram in this book - **Grid System Used by Aircraft & Artillery**.

99   With the engine idling and the aircraft gliding, the RE8 rapidly lost speed below 65 mph, with stalling occurring at just less than 50 mph. Any additional drag, such as that generated by movement of the rudder or even by the observer standing up in his cockpit, could be enough to induce a stall with little or no warning.

100   Friday the 12th October 1917 later became known as 'Black Friday' due to the heavy losses sustained by the allied infantry on the first day of the battle (1st Battle of Passchendaele, being the seventh of eight offensives that formed the 3rd Battle of Ypres or 'Passchendaele').

101   In October 1917, Number 6 squadron had two pilots who were sergeants, one observer who was a private whose former duty was that of a driver and another two observers who were ex air mechanics.

102   The Bristol Fighter (F2b) of Number 20 squadron was attempting to return to its aerodrome at St Marie Cappel, thirteen miles further west, but was forced to crash land at Abeele. The pilot had been wounded in an engagement with the enemy and the engine and controls were damaged.

103   The village of Godewaersvelde had a name that was hard to pronounce and was given the nickname of 'Gertie wears velvet' by the allied troops.

104   The map was folded such that squares C, D, I and J and a bit of O and P were visible. Refer also to the diagram in this book - **Grid System Used by Aircraft & Artillery**.

105   The morse signal for **J11AR2BBB** represented '**J**' for Number 6 squadron, '**11**' for Thomas Rogers' personal identifier, '**AR2**' for the battery call signal and '**BBB**' representing 'Are you receiving signals?'

106   This particular morse signal translates as **J11AR2CICI**.

107   PBI – 'Poor Bloody Infantry'

108   'Zero Machines Up' was the term used for ordering the first aircraft into the air on any particular day.

109   On Friday 16th November 1917, four days after 'B' flight had flown to their new base at Bertangles, the aircraft of 'A' and 'C' flights left Abeele to join them.

110   This was the first time in the Great War that an allied advance was made without first carrying out a preliminary allied bombardment, thus giving the enemy no warning of the impending attack.

111 The Tank Corps on the date of the attack comprised a total of four hundred and seventy six machines, including three hundred and fifty armed tanks.

112 Westerly winds posed a real problem for allied pilots. With most aerial combats taking place over enemy held territory, German pilots could simply glide back to their bases in the event of an engine failure or fuel shortage whereas their British counterparts were often unable to return to their aerodromes or even reach the safety of the allied lines, thus running the risk of being shot or taken prisoner.

113 A total of two hundred and eighty nine aircraft from fifteen RFC squadrons took part in the Battle of Cambrai, flying over an area less than ten miles wide and eight miles deep.

114 In September 1918 the No 1 (T) Wireless School moved to Flowerdown, outside Winchester. At the same time, a new airfield was also established at nearby Worthy Down so that whatever was taught in the classroom could be put into practice immediately.

115 The Armstrong Whitworth FK8 used a Beardmore engine and was four feet longer than the RE8. The wings were so long that it was possible to stand twenty men side by side between the wingtips.

116 The Royal Flying Corps remained in existence until the Royal Air Force was formed in April 1918.

Lightning Source UK Ltd.
Milton Keynes UK
UKOW021222061211

183293UK00011B/103/P